Book
BKM
New

ROMANCE

WITHDRAWN

P9-CRC-821

Large Print Gow
Gower, Iris.
When night closes in

MAR   2001

STACKS

NEWARK PUBLIC LIBRARY
NEWARK, OHIO

GAYLORD M

WHEN NIGHT CLOSES IN

WHEN NIGHT CLOSES IN

Iris Gower

Thorndike Press • **Chivers Press**
Thorndike, Maine USA   Bath, England

This Large Print edition is published by Thorndike Press, USA
and by Chivers Press, England.

Published in 2001 in the U.S. by arrangement with
Caroline Sheldon Literary Agency.

Published in 2001 in the U.K. by arrangement with
Transworld Publishers Ltd.

U.S. Hardcover 0-7862-3203-X (Romance Series Edition)
U.K. Hardcover 0-7540-1579-3 (Windsor Large Print)
U.K. Softcover 0-7540-2441-5 (Paragon Large Print)

Copyright © Iris Gower 2000

All rights reserved.

The right of Iris Gower to be identified as the author of this
work has been asserted in accordance with sections 77 and 78
of the Copyright Designs and Patents Act 1988.

All of the characters in this book are fictitious, and any
resemblance to actual persons, living or dead, is purely
coincidental.

The text of this Large Print edition is unabridged.
Other aspects of the book may vary from the original edition.

Set in 16 pt. Plantin by Minnie B. Raven.

Printed in the United States on permanent paper.

British Library Cataloguing-in-Publication Data available

Library of Congress Cataloging-in-Publication Data

Gower, Iris.
    When night closes in / Iris Gower.
      p. cm.
    ISBN 0-7862-3203-X (lg. print : hc : alk. paper)
    1. Missing persons — Fiction. 2. Large type books.
I. Title.
PR6057.O845 W48   2001
  823′.914—dc21
                                                 00-066628

To my dear friend Joan Barratt,
with love and thanks
for always being there.

NEWARK PUBLIC LIBRARY
NEWARK, OHIO 43055-5087

Large Print Gow
Gower, Iris.
When night closes in

634 4195

Acknowledgements

Anita Pugh and John Lahane,
computer buffs.

1

Lowri Richards was aware of the heat, of the sensuous feel of the sun on her near-naked body, and as she settled herself more comfortably in the padded recliner her silk robe fell open, allowing the sunshine to bathe her legs. It was completely private on the balcony of the Swan Hotel and Lowri turned up the sound on her Walkman. Below her, the tide washed in against the shore from the Bristol Channel, a soft soothing sound that heightened the state of euphoria that came with the afterglow of love-making. She slept.

She woke to the chill of the late August night. The sun had long since disappeared and the balcony was in deep shadow. Below her the sea was invisible, except for the strip of phosphorescent light at the shoreline. The nightmare had come to plague her again; why now, when she was so happy?

She tried to rise. Her limbs felt leaden, her mouth was dry, unnaturally dry. Surely she had not drunk that much whisky? She felt again the sense of impending doom that always came after the nightmare and shivered.

Usually she could shake it off almost on waking, but now it hung over her like a black cloud.

Lowri stretched her arms above her head, breathing in the night air, trying to focus her mind. She smiled as she thought of Jon, who was probably asleep in the room behind her. Or was he waiting until she woke, ready to snatch her into his arms and make passionate love to her again?

She realized she was shivering, and as she fumbled with the sliding doors of the balcony she felt the cold of the stone floor beneath her feet. It suddenly struck her as strange that Jon should leave her to sleep out on the balcony for so long.

The door slid open and Lowri stepped into the warmth of the bedroom. The mirror on the old-fashioned dressing-table reflected a little light but once the balcony curtains closed behind her, the room was plunged into darkness. Lowri edged forward, her bare foot coming in contact with her overnight bag.

She almost fell as she cannoned into the bedside table and the water jug rattled against a glass. Lowri smelled whisky, strong and pungent, and immediately remembered lying in Jon's arms as he poured the amber liquid onto her breasts, licking it off eagerly

8

as he took her nipple into his mouth.

Everything was strangely quiet and she hesitated, trying to see into the darkness.

'Jon?' The room felt empty and yet Lowri had the eerie feeling that she was being watched.

'Jon, where are you, darling?' There was no answer and the silence was unnerving. She tried again. 'Jon!' Her tone was sharper now. Something was wrong, the lights should be on, Jon should be showering, pouring another drink, anything. She felt the bed with her knees; as she touched it, she knew it was empty.

She reached up to find the switch and light flooded the room. No sign of him. Lowri tried to breathe deeply. It was silly to panic; Jon had obviously slipped out for some reason and would be back soon. Then why was she so apprehensive?

She looked round the room: it appeared soulless, unoccupied. The bed was neatly made. Frowning, Lowri opened the wardrobe door where Jon had hung his jacket. It was gone. So was his overnight bag. She had seen him stow his belongings away only hours ago, resisting the urge to tell him that his jacket was crooked on the hanger.

'Where is he?' Her voice sounded strangely loud in the emptiness of the room.

She hurried towards the bathroom; it was as pristine as the bedroom. No sign of Jon's shaving-tackle, no toothbrush, nothing.

'He's gone!' she said in disbelief. 'He has really gone.'

She sat on the bed and shivered. 'Jon, why are you doing this to me?' Her voice was a wail of despair. She looked down at her fingers: she was still wearing the beautiful ring Jon had given her earlier in the day. She believed the ring was a symbol of his love, so why on earth would he walk out on her?

Something must have happened to him. Jon would never walk away from her without a word; it was just not in his nature. She reached for the phone and dialled reception. 'Miss Richards here, has anyone checked out of the hotel in the last few hours?'

The voice was smooth, masculine. 'No-one has checked out, not officially, madam.'

'What do you mean, officially?'

'I mean no bill has been settled.'

Lowri panicked — something was badly wrong. 'All right, did you see anyone leaving the hotel carrying a bag? His name is Jon Brandon. A tall man with dark hair, very good-looking, you couldn't miss him.'

'I don't really concern myself with the guests' comings and goings, madam. So long as the bill is paid before all parties vacate the room I mind my own business.'

'Get me the manager.' Lowri was trembling with fear and frustration. 'I want to speak to the manager right now.'

'You are speaking to the manager, madam. I'm Mr Peters.'

Lowri gritted her teeth and stared at the phone as though she hated it. 'Well then, Mr Peters, perhaps you will answer my questions and stop being such a tight arse!'

She heard a sniff at the other end of the line. And then a click and the line went dead. She immediately redialled. 'If you don't get up here right now, I'm calling the police!' she shouted.

'No need for that, madam. In any case, you would need to obtain an outside line. Now, keep calm and I will be with you as soon as I can.'

Lowri slammed down the phone and got to her feet and walked restlessly around the room. Her mind was racing with questions, questions that seemed to have no answer. In a few minutes that seemed to drag on for hours, there was a discreet tapping at the door.

The manager was steely-eyed behind his glasses. 'I don't know what I can do for you, madam.' He inclined his head. 'I understand your . . . your companion has left?'

'Don't patronize me!' Lowri said. 'You must know if a man has checked out tonight or not. Is it too much to ask that you confirm that for me?'

'As I told you on the phone, no-one has checked out and if this man has gone, he didn't think to appraise me of his departure.' His eyes narrowed. 'I do hope this is not a ploy to avoid paying your bill.'

'Of course it isn't!' Lowri said, attempting a conciliatory tone. She would get nowhere if she continued to antagonize Mr Peters. 'I'm just worried, Jon would never walk out on me like that, something is wrong.'

She saw the manager glance around the room, at the freshly made bed, at the table holding a whisky bottle, a jug of water and . . . there was only one glass. Lowri frowned. What was happening, was she going mad?

'I think I should ask you to settle your bill at once, madam,' the manager was saying. 'I would be obliged if you would . . .' he hesitated, 'get some clothes on and come to reception and settle up.'

He looked at her skimpy wrap with a grimace of distaste. He had summed her up and found her wanting. His next words came as a blow.

'It might be better if you left at once.' Mr Peters looked down at her overnight bag. 'I see you have not unpacked. That's all to the good. I shall expect you in reception in ten minutes. I will have your bill ready.'

Lowri began to panic. She had left her credit cards at home. After all, Jon had said he was paying.

The manager read her expression. 'No money.' He sighed.

Lowri felt fear tingle along her spine. 'I don't care what you say, Jon would not just vanish. I want the police brought in, in fact I insist on it!'

'There's no need for that, I assure you!' the manager said quickly. 'If you don't have enough cash with you, just give me proof of identification and your address and you can put a cheque in the post as soon as you get home.'

'Look, Jon is missing, something has happened to him, you must get the police. If you don't phone them, I will.'

'Just be calm, madam, I'm sure it will all sort itself out in due course.'

'I want the police!' Lowri was aware she sounded like a spoiled child but she no longer cared. Panic was racing through her. Jon must be ill, must have suffered a brainstorm or met with an accident.

Reluctantly, Mr Peters picked up the phone and Lowri could hear him instructing someone on reception to call the police.

She sank onto the bed. She would have to report Jon missing, he could not have vanished into thin air, but where on earth was he? Only a few hours ago she had been warm in his arms and now she was alone with the manager, who was staring at her as if she was a crazy woman. She shivered suddenly. The room in which she and Jon were to spend a happy weekend together had begun to feel like a prison.

'This man you say you were with, what's his name again?' The manager was looking down his pinched nose at her.

'Jon, Jon Brandon, you must know it, he made the booking.'

'I don't think so, miss. You signed in yourself, at least you did if your name is Lowri Richards.'

He was right, she had signed in while Jon fetched the bags from the boot of the car. The car — it must be still at the entrance to the hotel.

'His car must still be outside,' she said. Mr Peters shrugged.

'If the gentleman has left, he's probably taken his car with him.' He smiled a little maliciously. 'We are quite remote here, as you no doubt realize.'

'He couldn't ditch me here without transport, it's just not like him,' she protested. But then perhaps it was exactly like him. Just how well did she know Jon? Questions ran round in her head until she felt she was going mad.

It seemed an eternity before the police arrived. Meanwhile, the manager stood in the doorway, arms folded across his thin chest, as though afraid she would make a run for it.

The uniformed officer who finally stepped into the room seemed weary, as if he had been on his feet all day. 'What's happened here?' He glanced towards Lowri.

'Miss Richards says her companion, Mr Jon Brandon, has left. He hasn't paid the bill.' Mr Peters got in first.

The police officer threw the man a glance. 'I would like Miss Richards to answer the question herself, sir, if it's all right by you.'

'Look, officer, I came here with my fiancé, now Jon has vanished and I'm worried sick about him.'

Mr Peters coughed. 'I would be obliged if you would take Miss Richards somewhere, officer, away from my hotel.' He shrugged. 'Business is bad enough without me looking for complications.'

Lowri ignored him. 'Please,' she spoke calmly, 'can't you search the place or some-

15

thing? Jon could be ill, or he might have received an emergency call while I was asleep and had to dash off. There just has to be a logical explanation.'

The young constable looked doubtfully around the room. He checked the bathroom and then shook his head. 'There is no evidence of anyone but you ever having been here, miss,' he said slowly. 'Perhaps you'd better just pay up and go home?'

Lowri sighed. 'I don't think I've got enough money on me, but I work for a solicitor, a Mr Watson of Watson Jones and Fry. Why don't you ring him, he'll vouch for me.' She paused. 'And I think you should make a note of the fact that I've reported a man missing. It might be as well to speak to a senior officer in case Jon is in some kind of trouble.'

'I don't know about that, madam, the senior officers only attend serious cases.'

'I'm telling you this is a serious case. Now are you willing to take the risk or not?'

The young policeman shook his head again and Lowri saw him click into his radio. She heard it crackle a response. She stared at her hands, unable to think clearly. She shivered, feeling cold suddenly.

'Better put something on, miss.' The constable sounded sympathetic. He avoided looking directly at her and Lowri felt an insane desire to laugh. Something awful might have happened to Jon and this fresh-faced young man was worrying about her modesty.

Lowri opened the door to the wardrobe and took out the skirt and blouse she had arrived in. Suddenly she felt sick and leaned against the wall for support.

'Do you feel all right, miss?' the policeman said.

'I'm wonderful!' she said, her voice rising. 'Jon has vanished, there's this man insisting I pay up, and I've got no money to speak of. Of course I don't feel all right.'

The officer moved away and Lowri heard him speaking quietly to the manager. He mentioned tea and, suddenly, her throat was so dry it felt as if it was closing up. She began to cry. Silent tears ran down her face and trickled saltily into her mouth. She wiped them away with the back of her hand. This was a nightmare, a real one. The one that haunted her sleep was nothing like this. She sank onto the bed, clutching her clothes against her.

The tea was brought and Lowri sipped it, comforted by the warmth. She pushed aside the balcony curtain, longing for daylight. Outside, darkness filled the balcony; the sea rushed in towards the shore. But now it did not have a soothing sound — it was menacing, cold.

'Please!' She appealed to the constable again. 'Won't you go and look for Jon — he could be lying hurt somewhere?' She heard the hysteria in her voice and hastily drank some more tea.

The constable hesitated, and looked up with an expression of relief as another man came into the room.

'Ah, sir, thanks for coming.'

'There was no-one else, Constable.'

Lowri studied the new arrival. He was wearing a suit, too dark and heavy for the summer weather, but he was older than the constable and presumably more experienced, and his presence was reassuring.

'Detective Inspector Lainey,' he said. He stared down at her for a long time.

'There seems to be a problem.'

Lowri looked up at him hopefully. 'That's right.'

'I'll have to ask you some questions, do you understand?' he asked.

She nodded. But she did not understand any of it. All she wanted was to go home.

'Can I be excused for a minute?' She was surprised at the humble tone in her voice. She was acting as though she was guilty of something; it was absurd. The detective agreed, after making a note of her name. With a sigh of relief Lowri went into the bathroom and closed the door, leaning her head against the cool tiles. At least she had a few minutes to herself to think.

Her knickers and bra, discarded in her haste to get into bed with Jon, lay in a crumpled heap on the floor. Absently, she picked them up, remembering how eagerly she had run naked into the bedroom. They had made crazy, passionate love, not once but several times, and yet the bed had been remade while she slept. Why? She wondered if the sheets had been changed. If not, surely there would be something to prove that Jon had been there with her? For some reason she needed to convince the police and herself that she had not imagined the whole thing.

She splashed her face with cold water and dressed quickly before returning to the bedroom. The detective inspector's next remark threw her.

'You haven't unpacked yet, Miss Richards. Perhaps you were in a hurry to leave?'

'No, I wasn't in a hurry to leave, why should I be?' she said, exasperation clear in her voice. 'I didn't unpack because my fiancé and I had a sudden urge to make love until we dropped, any objections?' She took a deep breath and moderated her tone.

'Look,' she said, 'Jon drove us here in his car, it should still be outside.'

'I'll check, shall I, sir?' The uniformed officer seemed eager to leave the problem in his superior's hands. DI Lainey nodded.

'Perhaps the manager here could assist you.' He glanced at Mr Peters. 'Between the two of you it should be easy to establish if the cars outside are accounted for.'

Lowri gave the two men details of Jon's car, and they went out. The detective looked at her. 'Why is the bed so neat and tidy if, as you explained so graphically, you were overcome with passion?'

'I don't know!' Lowri dragged back the bedspread. The sheets were pristine, the pillowcases showing no signs of the whisky that had run between her breasts. She flushed hotly at the memory. There was an uncomfortable silence.

'We can go down to the lounge, if you like,' the detective suggested, 'we can talk just as well down there.' He picked up her overnight bag and handed it to her.

As she left the room Lowri saw faces staring at her from half open doorways. The other guests, curious about the comings and goings at her door, were clearly wondering if she was a thief or worse. She wanted to scream out that she had done nothing wrong. She had fallen asleep on the balcony a happy woman and had woken up to a nightmare .

In the dimness of the lounge, the constable was waiting. 'I've searched around, miss, but there's no sign of anyone lying hurt out there. No sign of the car either.' He peered at his notebook. 'Perhaps you could confirm your friend's name and address, miss?' he asked.

'His name is Jon Brandon, he lives in a rented cottage in Plunch Lane, number 4.'

The constable looked questioningly at the detective. Lainey nodded.

'I know it. Got a phone number we can try?'

Lowri shook her head. 'As I said, the cottage is only a holiday place. Jon doesn't have a phone. I think he's only there until he finds something more permanent.'

The detective frowned. 'How do you normally contact him, then?'

'He has a mobile,' Lowri said. 'I haven't got the number with me. It's so long I can't remember it offhand.'

She rubbed her eyes. 'Please, I want to go there, to see if he's home. Something has to be wrong for him to go off like that. Why don't you try to find him? Can't you see this is no ordinary situation? Jon and I haven't quarrelled; he could be in all sorts of trouble for all we know.'

Mr Peters loomed up at Lowri's shoulder. 'I would like proof of identity, madam, before you leave.'

Lowri rummaged in her bag and took out some cash. 'Is this enough to pay the bill?' she asked, her tone icy.

The manager took it. 'Not enough, no, there's the bottle of whisky you ordered from room service.'

Lowri took out her driving licence. 'I've said I'll pay your bill and I will.'

'Ah but . . .'

Lainey intervened. 'Look, sir, if I understand you correctly you don't want any trouble.' He smiled, a strangely innocent smile that Lowri was beginning to realize concealed a quick mind. 'But if you want to make a formal complaint that's fine by me.'

'That won't be necessary.' The manager spoke hastily.

'Perhaps you will trust the young lady to send you the balance, then.' Lainey turned to Lowri. 'Could I check your means of identification, Miss Richards?'

She handed him her driving licence. 'Will this do, or do you think I'm a master forger on top of everything else?'

'I'm sure it will be enough to satisfy Mr Peters that you are not going to run off with the few extra pounds you owe.' His sarcasm was lost on the man, who glanced at her licence and industriously wrote down her address.

'If we learn anything we'll be in touch.' The detective looked at her sympathetically. 'Better get off home now, don't you think?'

Lowri walked through the foyer of the hotel in a daze and found herself standing in the chilly dawn, her overnight bag in her hand. Her tiny semi was almost eleven miles away in Jersey Marine Village. She had no idea how she was going to get there at this time of the morning.

She began to walk; there was nothing else she could do. The street lamps were paling in the dawn light. Early dew shimmered on the pavements. She felt her throat constrict; now she was alone the full import of what had happened seemed to swamp her. Lowri was angry and fearful in turn; she and Jon had been going out together for only a few months, but she had thought they had something special.

They did have something special! What if he had gone for a drive and had met with an accident? But then why had he taken all his clothes? Nothing made sense.

She suddenly felt faint. She leaned against the wall of a house, trying to breathe deeply. She felt alone and frightened.

'Are you all right?' A car drew up beside her and DI Lainey looked up at her from the driving seat. 'Daft question. Hop in, I'll take you home.' He climbed out of the car and took her bag, and Lowri allowed him to help her into the back.

He slid the car into gear and she sank back gratefully, struggling against waves of nausea and darkness.

'Try putting your head on your knees,' Lainey said, pulling smoothly away from the kerb. She obeyed and after a few moments, she felt the darkness recede. She sat up, gulping in air from the partly opened window, and as she looked at the big shoulders of the man in front of her she wondered why he was being so kind.

'Aren't you afraid I'll bring out a knife and attack you or something?' she said shakily. 'Mr Peters obviously thinks I'm barking mad and perhaps you agree with him?'

'No,' he said. 'I don't think you're mad, just confused perhaps. Or simply stood up?'

'Jon would not do that!'

'I believe you,' Lainey said. 'There must

be some other explanation for your friend's vanishing trick.'

'Will you help me to find out what's happened to him?' Lowri asked. 'Please?'

Lainey sighed. 'The truth is that folk go missing all the time, especially men who might be married and are, if you'll pardon the expression, having a bit on the side.'

Was that the answer: was she Jon's bit on the side? How could she really know? If there was one bright spot in all this, it was that this stranger, this policeman believed in her and was concerned about her.

She leaned forward and touched his shoulder. 'Thank you, Mr Lainey.'

He moved abruptly. 'Don't thank me, not yet, sometimes problems of this sort have no solution.' He paused. 'All I can promise is that I will do my best to trace this man for you.' He glanced at her. 'Will that do?'

She closed her eyes wearily; it would have to do. 'Thank you,' she said again, then feeling she sounded ungracious, she added, 'Thank you very much, Mr Lainey.'

All she wanted now was to get home, to shower and change and sleep the day away. Perhaps, when she woke, an explanation would present itself though, somehow, she doubted it.

2

She was running in the darkness, her feet sinking into the sand. The small waves lapping the beach were silvered with moonlight. Lowri wanted to scream but no sound would come from her throat. Footsteps pounded behind her, drawing nearer. Then she was caught in a cruel grip and forced down onto the sand. She could feel it in her hair, gritty with sharp shells. He was above her, his face masked, eyes black with venom peering through slits. He was dragging her towards the sea, drawing her deeper and deeper into the water. Just as the water covered her face, she reached out to grasp his mask.

The scream woke her, her own scream. She sat up in bed, panting with fear. She was bathed in sweat. It had come again, the nightmare that had haunted her since childhood. Lowri slid out of bed and padded downstairs to the kitchen. Her fingers were shaking as she switched on the kettle.

She took her coffee into the sun-filled living-room; she could hear the bells of St Mary's summoning the faithful to morning prayer. It was Sunday and she should have been spending it with Jon.

The nightmare receded, to be replaced with reality, and Lowri felt the overpowering weight of loss and pain edged with fear. 'Oh Jon, where are you?' She moved towards the window and looked out at the small village street. Across the road, the hills, riotous with summer greenery, towered above the houses.

She usually loved Sunday mornings; they were lazy times when she could sit around, have a luxurious bath and get ready to spend the rest of the day with Jon, if she hadn't been staying overnight at his cottage in Plunch Lane. Later they would walk on the beach by moonlight, hand in hand. She shuddered, remembering the nightmare.

She would dress, go out and take a walk in the fresh air — perhaps it would clear her head. But what if Jon phoned, or the police rang with news of him? No, she had better stay in.

When she was dressed she scrambled an egg and sat picking at it with little appetite. The phone remained stubbornly silent. Lowri wondered if DI Lainey would be on duty on Sundays — if so she would be able to contact him at the police station. But even as she reached for the phone, she thought better of it. She would only confirm the impression he must have received last night that she was an hysterical female.

The day seemed to drag on endlessly, and when evening came at last she felt weary and swamped with despair. No-one was going to ring her, not Lainey, not the young constable and not Jon.

She was in the bath when the ringing of the phone shattered the silence of the house. Grabbing a towel, she ran downstairs into the sitting-room, leaving wet footsteps behind on the carpet.

'Hi, Lowri, it's me.' A feeling of such disappointment filled her that for a moment she could not speak. It was Sally from the office.

'Lowri, are you there?'

'Yes, Sal, can't speak now, see you first thing in the morning.' She replaced the receiver and heard the phone click. What if someone else had tried to get through when Sally was on the phone? Lowri dialled her BT answering service and an impersonal recording told her she had no messages.

That night she slept on the sofa, hoping to ward off the nightmare. She woke unrefreshed and as she drank her coffee, she waited for the sound of the postman. When the post did arrive, it contained nothing but circulars. Lowri dropped them in the bin with a grimace of disgust. She would be glad to go to work; at least there she would have to concentrate on something other than Jon's inexplicable behaviour.

It was hot in the office — the air-conditioning had broken down yet again. Lowri leafed through several pages of Mr Watson's barely decipherable notes. Somehow, she would have to translate them and put them on the computer.

Sally, as usual, was late. 'Morning, Lowri.' She sank into the chair at her desk and examined her brightly varnished fingernails. Today they were puce. The phone rang. Sally picked it up and began to switch the caller through to one of the solicitors. Everything appeared so normal.

Lowri swallowed hard; she was still living in a nightmare world where nothing would ever be normal again. She looked around her, seeing the office through fresh eyes, everything familiar and yet changed. What was she doing there, working as though her life had not been shattered into little pieces?

'Right,' Sally said. 'Now perhaps you'll find time to help me with some notes I've got to type up?' She shuffled the mail and then looked across at Lowri. 'What's wrong? You've got a funny look in your eyes. Jon not fulfil expectations in the bedroom department?'

'You know we went to an hotel for the weekend. Well, he disappeared, Sal. We made love a couple of times, I fell asleep and he just vanished. All his clothes were gone, his shaving stuff, everything.'

Sally for once seemed lost for words. She shook back her hair and put on her glasses in order to see Lowri's face more clearly.

'I keep going over everything again and again, trying to work out what happened, trying to make some sense of it all,' Lowri said.

Sally found her voice. 'Want a coffee?'

Lowri smiled and nodded. Sally's way of dealing with any problem was to serve coffee. If an awkward client wanted reassuring for the umpteenth time that the searches on his house were progressing as quickly as possible, Sally would smile sweetly and offer coffee.

Lowri dropped Mr Watson's notes and they spread out in a fan on the desk. She was not able to give the job her full attention. She felt as though she was outside her life looking in — it was difficult to explain even to herself.

'Why not go over to his place to look for him?' Sally suggested. 'You've been there millions of times.' She had a gift for exaggeration. 'He probably hasn't disappeared at all, perhaps he was called away or something. He could just be home by now, couldn't he?' She put a cup of steaming coffee on top of the pristine sheaf of legal documents on Lowri's desk and Lowri picked the cup up hastily.

'No, he would have phoned.'

'Could it be that he's married, do you think?'

Lowri felt a pain, as if Sally had stabbed her. 'I don't think so. If he *is* married then he can't see a great deal of his wife, can he?'

'No, but how do you know he hasn't got a family somewhere?'

Lowri shook her head; she loved Jon. How could she think of him as a married man with children?

'As you pointed out, he might have been called away suddenly, perhaps so suddenly that he had no time to leave a message,' she said.

'You've tried phoning him, I take it?'

Lowri felt momentarily surprised. 'No, I haven't phoned him. Perhaps I'm afraid of what I might find,' she added truthfully. She bit her lip, fighting the tears.

The office phone rang, stridently shattering the sudden silence, and both girls jumped. 'I'll answer it.' Sally picked up the receiver. 'Watson Jones and Fry,' she said. 'Oh right, Mr Lainey, I'll see if Miss Richards is free.'

Lowri practically snatched the phone from Sally's hand. The inspector's voice sounded warm, as if he was in the room with her, but what he said sent a chill down her spine. After a few moments, she put the phone down and looked at Sally.

'The police, they went to his place in Plunch Lane.'

'And?' Sally sounded impatient.

'And it doesn't belong to Jon, he was simply renting it for the summer. Apparently his lease ran out on Saturday.'

'What the hell is going on?' Sally said.

Lowri shook her head. 'I don't know, Sally, what does it mean? Was he just having me on a string, was I just a diversion for the summer?'

'If so, why not enjoy the entire weekend with you instead of going missing Saturday night?' Sally said reasonably. 'Look, why not go over to Plunch Lane and see for yourself what's happened? Jon might have left a letter or something.'

'I couldn't ask for time off though,' Lowri said uncertainly.

'Of course you could! Mr Watson thinks

the world of you. He'd give you all the time off you wanted, you know that.'

Lowri did know that. 'I think I'm scared but you're right, I will go over to the cottage and have a look for myself.'

'Good for you! You're entitled to do some digging; after all, you've been going out with Jon for nearly six months now, haven't you? He could be dead of course,' she added darkly. 'Fallen over those cliffs near the Swan.'

Lowri rubbed her forehead tiredly. Sally was not the soul of tact. 'Taking all his clothes and his shaving tackle with him? Don't be dramatic, Sally.'

'Only trying to help.' Sally moved to the filing cabinet and searched through the documents, her brow furrowed. Lowri drank her coffee — it was hot and sweet, just as she liked it. Sally was a good girl, a little bit of an airhead but she meant well.

'Talking of old Watson . . .' Sally mumbled, 'ah, yes here it is.' She drew out a buff folder and leafed through it. 'I thought I was right, our firm does hold the lease to those properties. Here's Jon's name and that copper's right, the lease expired Saturday.'

Lowri put down her coffee. 'Anyone else taken the place?'

'Maybe, I haven't dealt with the mail yet.

You do know the whole row of cottages on Plunch Lane are actually owned by Mr Watson.' She almost bit one of her nails but remembered in time that she was growing them. 'Cor, old Watson's rich!' Sally added. 'Got no kids, has he? Play your cards right, girl, and he could leave the lot to you.' She shook back her silky blonde hair. 'There's not much in the file but you could just go in and ask old Watson himself about Jon, about references, that sort of thing.'

Lowri picked up her handbag. 'No, I couldn't. It would just be a waste of time. I'm going round there, now. I just have to see for myself that he's really gone, taken all his stuff and that.'

'I'll come with you, shall I?' Sally sounded hesitant. Lowri shook her head.

'You'd better stay here. We can't both leave the office.'

Having gained Mr Watson's smiling assent to her departure, Lowri went out to her car. It had been standing in the sun and the first thing she did was to open all the windows. Plunch Lane was a few miles away: a holiday site near the sea. She had enjoyed the weekends she and Jon spent there, but when he had suggested they stay at the Swan in luxury Lowri had been delighted. Now she saw that staying at the hotel was not

34

some generous gesture on Jon's part, but necessity, if the lease was up on number 4 Plunch Lane.

The drive took a little over fifteen minutes, the narrow road curving and bending, the hedgerows bright with flowers. It was a route that Lowri had taken many times before.

Those sun-filled days had been wonderful, so romantic. Jon would lay on a meal, cool some wine and play classical music for her. The evenings had, invariably, turned into passionate nights. She swallowed the sudden constriction in her throat. What had happened to him — was he dead or alive?

She parked on the grass verge opposite the cottage and slipped out of the driving seat, grateful for the cooling breeze drifting in from the sea. It all looked so familiar, so sane, so normal. She took a deep breath and swung open the gate; it creaked in the way it always did and she half expected to see Jon open the door to her. But when Lowri rang the old bell, it was a stranger who appeared: a woman who stood staring at her through large spectacles that almost covered her face.

'Can I help you?' She was young, not much older than Lowri herself, a beautiful woman in spite of the severely tied-back hair and the imposing glasses.

'I'm looking for Mr Jon Brandon,' Lowri said. 'I believe he rents this place from my firm Watson Jones and Fry?'

'So?' The woman sounded cagey. She had a cultured voice, a well-educated voice. 'As of today, I'm renting the cottage.'

'I do apologize,' Lowri said quickly. 'We usually have to check the premises before a new tenant takes over to look for breakages, that sort of thing.'

'You'd better come in.' The new tenant left the door open and walked through the hall into the lounge. She did not introduce herself but stood impatiently as Lowri looked around the tiny living-room.

Nothing had changed since Lowri had been there last. The curtains were the same dull green, the lampshades matching them perfectly. The carpet was rose pink, as were the cushions set against the green uphol-stery of the sofa.

Lowri could hear the soft strains of music, her and Jon's music, and the memories came flooding back. Memories of them lying on the rug in front of the fire, making love, drinking wine, talking endlessly.

'Do you mind if I sit down?' she asked.

'Yes, please do. Come to think of it, you might be able to help me.' The woman rubbed her wrists as if she was cold, even though the sun was blazing down outside. 'My husband should be here. I've tried his mobile but it seems to be switched off. He hasn't contacted your office by any chance?'

Lowri felt her stomach lurch. 'What is your husband's name?' She was aware that her question was abrupt but she could hardly speak.

'Jon Brandon.' The woman frowned. 'Sorry, I thought you would have realized. I'm Mrs Sarah Brandon.'

Lowri felt as though the breath had been snatched from her body. She opened her mouth but no sound came out.

'I haven't seen him for over a week now,' Mrs Brandon was saying, 'but that's nothing unusual, he's often away on business.' She smiled a little icily. 'He's away from me more than he's with me but he does usually keep in touch.'

'The lease expired Saturday,' Lowri said through stiff lips. 'Has your . . . Mr Brandon extended it, then?' She was unaware that her hands were clasped tightly together. Mrs Brandon paused as though uncertain how much she should say, and yet it was clearly a relief for her to talk to someone.

'No, I told you, I renewed the lease. Jon probably forgot.'

'But you are still together, you aren't separated or anything?'

'Good heavens no, nothing like that.'

Lowri cursed Sally's incompetence, she
should have updated the files at once. She
looked around in desperation, searching for
some answers. She began to notice that Mrs
Brandon had made small changes in the
room, there was a different picture hanging
over the fireplace, a good painting of a
mountain scene. Lowri caught sight of a
photograph on the piano. The frame was
silver, very ornate, and in the picture a
couple stood together, arms entwined.

She was not aware of walking over to the
piano, of her hand reaching out to pick up
the photograph. All she could see was Jon's
face looking out at her, smiling into the
camera in a way that was so familiar, his eyes
crinkling at the corners.

'That's my husband,' Mrs Brandon said.
'You might have met him sometime?'

Lowri nodded, unable to speak. Her lips
felt frozen but her mind was racing as she
tried to digest the fact that Jon was a married man. How had he managed to keep it
from her all these months? But then it
seemed his wife had given him every opportunity to cheat on her. She said she scarcely
saw him. Lowri bit her lip as she replaced

the picture and looked up to see Mrs Brandon watching her.

'You seem to recognize him.'

'Maybe,' Lowri said, 'it's very possible, seeing as we handled the leasing of the property.'

'Yes of course,' Mrs Brandon said. 'When Jon decided to take a lease here for a few months, I was delighted.' She paused. 'At first I thought he had simply forgotten to renew it but as you see, there's no sign of him. What a fool I am to go on believing in him.'

Now she had begun to talk Mrs Brandon seemed unable to stop. 'We were going to make this our hideaway, an escape from the pressures of business. Make a fresh start.' She looked at Lowri, her eyes filled with tears. 'I see now that coming here was simply an opportunity for him to find another mistress.'

Lowri was silent. The pain was so deep, the sense of humiliation so sharp that she felt like crying. Jon was a cheat and a liar and she had been fool enough to believe he loved her.

She picked up the photograph again; she had to assure herself that it really was Jon they were discussing, the same Jon who had caressed her, who made love to her with such tenderness. There was no mistake. Suddenly she wanted to smash the picture into tiny pieces.

'Take it away!' Mrs Brandon said flatly. 'Drop it in the nearest bin. If my husband is not here now then he won't be coming.' She crossed to the door, making it obvious she wanted Lowri to leave. Lowri followed her, the picture clasped tightly in her hand.

As she stepped through the front door the soft perfume of the roses drifted towards her, a poignant reminder of the times she had been here with Jon.

'Are you married?' Mrs Brandon asked abruptly.

Lowri shook her head. 'No.'

'Well, take my advice and don't bother! Live with them and leave them, don't put your faith in any of them.'

As the door closed behind her, Lowri stood for a moment, staring unseeingly up at the gathering clouds. He was married, he did not love her, did not even love his wife. He was the worst sort of man, a weakling and a liar. Why then was she clutching the photograph to her as though it would bring him closer?

As she drove back along the lanes, Lowri glanced at her watch. She had been out for much longer than she had expected, she had better be getting back.

She drove as though the hounds of hell were after her, negotiating the familiar lanes at a speed that made every corner a hazard. She was angry and hurt, and her foot pressed against the accelerator was a reflection of those feelings.

When she arrived outside the office, she jammed on the brakes and parked defiantly on double yellow lines. 'Sod it!' she said, flinging her bag over her shoulder. 'Sod everything.'

There were clients waiting: the small reception area seemed full of people. Mr Watson's door was open and he looked at her over his glasses, a smile on his face.

'Just in time to help me out, Miss Richards. Mr Jones and Mr Fry finished work earlier so I need all the help I can get. Can you get me the files on the last two or three properties we're handling?'

He was a tall man, little more than fifty years old. He might have been striking once but now he wore tired suits and old-fashioned shoes. Lowri felt an affection for him — she had worked for Mr Watson ever since she left home.

For almost an hour, Lowri was busy dealing with paperwork for impatient clients who thought that the business of buying a house could be completed in a few days instead of taking weeks.

It was almost four when Sally kicked off her shoes and put her feet up on the desk. Mr Watson had just left. 'Thank goodness the boring old fart's gone home!' she chuckled. 'Now, come on, give.'

Lowri sat on the chair in front of the computer, clicked the instructions until the screen was blank and switched it off. After a moment's hesitation, she reached in her bag for the photograph and put it on the desk.

'Sally, meet Jon Brandon and his wife.'

Sally stared at the photograph, her eyes wide. 'No!' She was galvanized into action, swinging her feet to the floor and leaning forward to look more closely at the happy smiling couple. 'So he *is* married?'

Lowri, too, stared at the photograph, saw the man she loved with his arm around his wife and wanted to cry. It seemed that once, on that summer day, he had been happy to be with his wife, or was that also an empty sham?

'Bloody hell!' Sally leaned back in her chair, her bare feet beating a tattoo on the floor. 'Who would have thought it?'

She pointed at the photograph. 'So that's why I never got to see this lover of yours, he was keeping his head down, the crafty devil!'

42

Lover. Lowri played with the word in her mind and decided it was too mild for the relationship that had been built between her and Jon over the past months. But now she could see it had all been an illusion, shifting sands, a snatched leg-over when he was away from his wife. Sally was right, he was a devil.

'God I hate him!' She slammed her fist on the desk and the photograph shuddered before falling onto the floor. The glass smashed, the photograph slid from the frame and with it, a piece of folded paper.

'Look, a clue!' Sally said.

'You can be so childish at times,' Lowri said but, nevertheless, she picked up the paper and unfolded it.

'Well, come on, what does it say?' Sally took it from Lowri's hand. 'Oh, it's just a phone number. Whose, I wonder?'

'Probably one of his other women,' Lowri said bitterly.

Sally began to pick up the pieces of glass. She swept them into a neat pile with her shoe and scooped them up onto the photograph.

'Why did you bring the photograph here with you?' she asked, suddenly serious. She tipped the glass into the bin and the shards sparkled like diamonds in the sunlight.

'I don't really know.' Lowri rubbed her forehead. 'I suppose to convince myself I wasn't imagining the whole thing.'

'Look, go on home,' Sally said, 'there's only a half-hour or so left, no-one will know.'

'Perhaps I will,' Lowri said gratefully. 'My head is splitting, I still can't believe what's happened these last few days.'

'It's the shock,' Sally said. 'I mean you go off for a dirty weekend and your bloke goes missing. If that's not enough, you find out he's married.'

Lowri picked up her bag and slipped the photograph and the frame inside. 'Oh, where's the piece of paper?'

Sally looked puzzled. 'Perhaps I threw it in the bin with the glass, did I?'

'I'll look.' Lowri saw the paper at once and rescued it. 'I'll maybe pluck up courage to phone the number and see who replies,' she said. 'Then again, maybe I will just burn the damn thing.'

Outside, the sun was still bright and the long main street was thronged with holiday-makers. 'Blast!' Lowri said. There behind the windscreen wiper was, unmistakably, a parking ticket. A perfect ending to a perfect day.

Once in the cool sanctuary of her house, Lowri kicked off her shoes and tucked her feet under her. Then she took out the photograph and stared at his face, Jon's face, so familiar, so dear. 'You lying cheating bastard!' she breathed.

She picked up the phone and dialled the number from the piece of paper — it was stamped indelibly on her mind. She was poised, ready to slam down the receiver if a woman answered. It was a man.

'Hello, I'm sorry to trouble you . . .' she began. The line crackled.

'Miss Richards?' The voice was familiar.

Lowri felt a shiver of surprise run along her spine. 'Who is this?' she demanded.

'It's DI Lainey, you've rung the police station, my direct line. Can I help you?'

'No, I'm sorry, wrong number.' Lowri slammed the receiver back in place, her mind spinning. Why on earth would the police-station number be hidden behind a photograph of Jon Brandon? Suddenly she was trembling; she put her head in her hands, trying to stop the tide of fear that swept over her. Something was very wrong and she would find out what was happening if it killed her. 'And it might well, my girl.' Her voice echoed around the empty room and, suddenly, she was afraid.

3

'What the hell's that you're reading, now?' Charles Richards strode into the large plant-filled conservatory and his wife realized at once he was in a bad mood. Rhian Richards sighed; she did not feel like a row right now.

'And I've asked you a hundred times if I've asked you once to have a drink waiting for me when I come home,' Charles continued.

It was pointless to argue that she never knew exactly when he *would* come home. She rose to her feet. 'I'll get you a drink, Charles.'

'Answer my question first. What's that?'

'Just a letter.'

'I can see it's a letter but who is it from?'

Rhian took a deep breath. 'It's from Lowri.' She tucked the letter in the pocket of her smartly cut trousers and slipped her feet into her leather sandals.

'I might have guessed that by the look on your face. Your precious Lowri means more to you than anyone, doesn't she? You've always favoured that girl.' He sank into one of

46

the easy chairs. 'Go on, fetch that drink, I'm badly in need of one.'

She brought him a whisky and stood near the open doorway, feeling the summer breeze on her face. 'I don't favour Lowri,' she said reasonably. 'I treat both our children in exactly the same way.' It was a mistake.

'Like hell you do!' Charles said. 'We all know that your bastard child comes first.'

A wave of anger and guilt brought a flush to Rhian's face. Would Charles never stop taunting her about the past? As for their son, she had not seen him for years; he had left home at sixteen and settled in Canada. Charles conveniently forgot that.

'Well, what has she got to say for herself?' Charles demanded.

'Not a lot.' Rhian spoke softly.

'A whole letter of "not a lot"! How literate she must be. All that university education wasted on a girl, I said it would do no good.'

Rhian struggled against the tightening of her shoulders. 'It seems she's parted company with Jon Brandon,' she volunteered. But it was not as simple as that. It seemed the man had disappeared into the blue. Lowri was clearly troubled and unhappy but the last place she would come was home. She had been only too glad to leave at the first opportunity that presented itself.

'Blast the girl!' Charles sounded angry and Rhian looked at him, puzzled.

'Why blast the girl?' she asked, anger building inside her. 'Lowri has the right to go out with anyone she chooses.'

'There, you see?' Charles stared at her. 'I try to take an interest in her and you bite my head off. She's not asking for money, is she?'

'Now when has Lowri ever asked for money?' Rhian did not point out that, in any case, the money in the bank was hers; Rhian had inherited the estate when her father died. It was courtesy of his wife that Charles lived such a comfortable life. He worked, of course he did, he was a businessman, but whatever money he had, he kept to himself.

'In any case,' he was like a dog with a bone; once he started on the subject of Lowri, he was difficult to stop, 'she's only a girl, she should marry someone with a fortune and let him keep her.'

'Like you did?' As soon as the words were spoken Rhian regretted them. She pushed her hands in her pockets and kept her back turned to her husband. She could just picture his face red with anger, his eyes bright with hate. Rhian sometimes thought Charles would like to put his hands around her throat and slowly strangle her.

'You bitch!' he said and his voice was filled with venom. 'I took you in when you were pregnant with another man's child, I gave you respectability, my name.'

She spun round. 'So you keep telling me and I am supposed to be eternally grateful, am I? Well think of it, Charles, if it wasn't for me you would be living in a semi somewhere, not in an eleven-bedroomed house with eleven acres of land round it.'

Charles stood up. 'I can always trust you to rub my nose in it, can't I? You think that you'll emasculate me with that evil tongue of yours — well, it won't work, do you understand?'

'You mean you're still a ram in the bedroom?' She spoke coolly now. 'Well I wouldn't know, would I? What energy you have you save for that trollop of a mistress of yours.'

He strode towards her, his hand raised, and Rhian did not move.

'Just once, Charles, just once and it's all over. I'll do what I should have done years ago and leave you.'

She walked to the door leading into the large sitting-room. 'Just in case you think you'll get rid of me permanently, think again.' She half smiled. 'I've got all eventualities covered.'

She left him fuming in the conservatory and walked easily up the wide staircase. Oh yes, she had all eventualities covered all right. Her last will and testament was in safe hands. With it was a letter pointing a finger at Charles in the event of Rhian's untimely death. Let him try to get the better of her if he liked, but he would not win. Neither would he deprive Lowri of her inheritance, however much he wished to leave her penniless.

In her room, Rhian took out the letter and read it again and then sank onto the bed, her hands over her eyes. She wished that Lowri were here so that she could hold her and comfort her. Perhaps it was time she took a trip to Jersey Marine Village. Charles would not like it, but it was many years since Rhian had cared what her husband liked.

She kicked off her sandals and stretched out on the bed. Through the open window she could hear the lazy drone of the bees in the honeysuckle.

It was a soothing sound and after a while, Rhian slept.

It was Sunday, a hot dreaming summer day. A day very much like the one when Lowri and Jon set out for the Swan Hotel two weeks ago. Lowri sat in the sitting-room drinking coffee and trying not to feel alone in the world. She should shake herself free of her memories of Jon. He had vanished from her life; he had lied to her about everything. She was better off forgetting him. But it did not feel that way.

Her loneliness was edged with a feeling of guilt. However unknowingly, she had been having an affair with a married man. She could still see Sarah Brandon's troubled face, the eyes behind the large glasses filled with tears.

It might help if she could simply be angry with Jon, find a way to hate him, but Lowri's emotions were mixed; one minute she wanted to kill him with her bare hands and the next she was praying he was alive and well. The dreadful feeling of unfinished business only added to her confusion.

She pressed her fingertips to her temples. What had happened in that room that night? How could she have slept through it, whatever it was? She went over it all again for the hundredth time. They had arrived at the hotel; she had signed the register while Jon fetched the overnight bags from the car.

Hand in hand, they had climbed the ornate staircase to their room, and once there they had made love with an urgency that, at the time, Lowri did not question. She had showered, put on her robe and left him in the bathroom while she settled herself on the balcony to listen to music on her Walkman.

As usual, she had the volume turned up quite high to get the full benefit of the sweeping sounds of the music. Eventually, she must have fallen asleep. What happened then? Had Jon left the hotel as soon as her back was turned? Her mind went round like a rat in a trap, trying to make sense of the nonsensical. Oh Jon, what's happened to you?

Lowri made fresh coffee; her head had begun to ache and she knew she would drive herself mad if she kept speculating about what might have happened. She had no choice but to admit she had been fooled by a married man. How stupid he must have thought her. Even as he made love to her, pleasuring her, he had probably been laughing at her. The thought hurt.

Lowri looked around her for something to do. She was restless and needed to occupy herself with something other than her tortured thoughts. But the house was spotless, the carpet in the small sitting-room hoovered, the furniture dusted, and for once, all the dishes were washed and put away. There was nothing else for her to do.

'Oh God help me!' She pushed away her cup and put her head on her hands, feeling the softness of the tablecloth between her fingers. She wanted to cry but what good were tears?

The doorbell rang, shattering the silence. Lowri sat up, her heart beating rapidly. Who would be calling on her on a Sunday? The bell shrilled out with a harshly repeated insistence.

Could it be Jon? She was fooling herself, she knew it and yet her heart was beating rapidly as she moved towards the small hallway. Through the glass, she could see the shape of a man standing outside. 'Who is it?' she called, trying to sound calm and in control of the situation and failing miserably. The figure moved very slightly.

'It's DI Luiney, can I talk to you, Miss Richards?'

She hesitated and then opened the door. 'What do you want?'

'Just a word, if I may.'

'You'd better come in.' She led the way into the sitting-room and stared at him. He was at least some sort of link with Jon and perhaps he had some news. 'Would you like a coffee?'

'Thank you. Black, no sugar.' He seemed to fill the room. Strange she had failed to notice his height and the broadness of his shoulders when she first saw him at the Swan.

She gave him the coffee and picked up her own cup, sitting as far away from him as possible, apprehensive and hopeful at the same time. 'Why are you here?' She paused. 'Have you found out anything?'

He looked uncomfortable. 'I thought it a good idea to talk to Mrs Brandon.' He took a drink as though to give them both time to think. 'Unfortunately, she doesn't seem to know her husband very well. I thought she might help by telling me about his work, if his passport was up to date, that sort of thing.' He shrugged. 'She seems to think he's left here for good.'

'If his . . . his wife can't help you what makes you think I can?' Lowri looked up at him; his eyes met hers and she was the first to look away. 'I didn't even know the bastard was married.'

He almost smiled. 'That's the spirit!'

'Why are you so interested? Jon is just another person gone missing, it happens all the time.'

'I said I'd try to help. In any case I don't like unsolved puzzles,' Lainey said. 'Did you hear anything that night, the sound of raised voices perhaps?'

She shook her head. 'I didn't hear anything but my music. I suppose I drifted off to sleep then. I expected him to be there when I woke.' She stopped speaking abruptly. She felt such a fool, such a bimbo for allowing Jon to take her in so easily.

'Look, don't be too hard on yourself.' DI Lainey spoke softly. 'We have reason to believe that Brandon was a first-class con man.'

'What do you mean?'

He shrugged. 'At the moment I just have a gut feeling about this. But I can tell you that we want to find Mr Brandon so that he can help us with our inquiries.'

'And you think that I might have aided and abetted him in whatever he was doing? It all sounds a bit melodramatic to me.'

He shook his head but did not comment. They sat in silence for what seemed a long time and then he put his coffee-cup on the table. 'I understand you went to see Mrs Brandon?'

'That's right. Is there a law against it, then?'

He held up his hand. 'I'm trying to help you, bear with me, will you?' He smiled and she realized how attractive he was. His teeth were white, even. His hair was thick and shining with red highlights in the sunshine pouring in through the window. Perhaps she could trust him. It would be good to trust someone.

'Tell me, Mr Lainey,' she said abruptly, 'why would your phone number be hidden behind a photograph of Jon Brandon and his wife?'

'Was it? Then your guess is as good as mine.'

'So you'd never met Sarah before you went to see her — or Jon?'

'Hey, I'm supposed to be the cop.' He seemed to relax a little. 'And don't be so formal, why not call me Jim? This is an unofficial visit, you know.'

'No, I didn't know. Why should I want to call you Jim?' she asked warily. 'How do I know I can trust you?'

He actually laughed. 'Because I'm an honest cop, of course!'

'It's not funny!'

'I know it's not. Why would an intelligent woman like you get mixed up with a man like that?'

'That's none of your business.' Lowri felt the heat in her cheeks.

'Oh, everything is police business when we suspect a crime has been committed.' He sighed and looked at his watch. 'Well, I'd better go.' His eyes, blue, clear, met hers.

'That's if you can't think of anything that would help.'

'I don't know anything.' She searched her mind desperately. 'He lied about being unattached.' She laughed shortly. 'He probably lied every time he said he loved me. Come to think of it, when did he ever tell me the truth?'

'And you never suspected anything amiss? You must have spent time at Plunch Lane, didn't you see signs of another woman about the place, things in the bathroom, clothes in the wardrobe?'

'It was a holiday place with a short lease, remember. There were no signs of anyone being there except him.' She hesitated.

'Yes?' he said, moving a little closer to her. 'Have you thought of something? If so tell me.'

She sighed. 'There were things in the spare room, travel bags and a leather briefcase, but then it's not unusual to have stuff like that around when you go on holiday, is it?'

He answered her question with one of his own. 'You are not a suspicious sort of woman then, one who likes to turn a man inside out?'

'Speaking from bitter experience, detective?' She felt a sense of glee: he had a chink in his armour, he was not invulnerable.

'Maybe.'

'Look, sit down,' she said impulsively. 'I'll make more coffee. I've been acting as though you are to blame for everything.'

He sat down readily. 'Another coffee would be wonderful.' He looked so young when he smiled, though she guessed him to be in his mid-thirties. As she made the coffee, she felt her spirits lighten. Jon's disappearance was not the end of the world — she was just another foolish girl who had been taken in by an older man.

They talked for almost an hour about her job, her time at university, her parents, the reason why she had left home. Jim Lainey told her he was divorced, there were no children of the marriage and though he made light of it, Lowri could see that the break-up still had the power to hurt him.

He changed tack so smoothly she hardly noticed. 'Who else from the office met Jon Brandon?' Jim asked. 'I know your Mr Watson spoke to him on at least one occasion. The girl, Sally, had she met him before, did you go out together for evenings or anything?'

Lowri shook her head. 'Jon always said he wanted time to be alone with me.' She glanced up from under her eyelashes. 'It might seem strange to you now but I was actually flattered about that. In any case, Sally enjoys a different sort of night out.'

'When you visited Sarah Brandon, was she suspicious of your motives?'

'I don't know.' She smiled, though she felt more like crying. 'I don't think so. She thought I was simply there on business though she did imply that Jon was never the faithful kind.'

'Well that doesn't surprise me. I think you've had a lucky escape from Mr Brandon.'

'What do you mean?'

He sighed. 'I can't say, not just at the moment.' He looked at his watch.

'You have to go,' she said, rising to her feet.

'Yes, I have to go.' He walked across the room and stopped in the small hallway. 'Perhaps I could come and talk to you again, some time?'

Lowri shrugged, feeling somehow let down. 'It's a free country.'

'I'm not rushing home to an eager girl-friend,' he said, 'there's just some business I have to see to.'

'Nothing to do with me,' Lowri said flatly and closed the door in his face. She returned to the sitting-room and looked down at the two cups standing side by side on the table. Funny, it had never bothered her before, living alone. Being with Jon at the weekends had seemed to be an ideal arrangement. Now, for some reason, she felt lost.

She stood in front of the mirror and studied her appearance. She was fairly tall, her hair a natural dark red, well, almost natural, helped now and again with a rinse. She had unremarkable features though her eyes were quite good, large, long-lashed and a sort of hazel green. She usually made the most of them with the right shadow and mascara. Now they were naked, unadorned. But then she had not been expecting company.

She sank into a chair. That was twice DI Lainey had seen her at a disadvantage and yet, and yet, there had been an unmistakable light of interest in his eyes. Or did he merely want to prise information out of her? Well, if that was the case, he was not going to get very far. It seemed the inspector knew more about Jon Brandon than she ever had.

'Why not come out with me and Timmy tonight?' Sally was swinging her long legs, admiring her slim ankles. It was quiet in the office: the lunch-time flurry of clients had gone back to work. 'It doesn't do any good to sit in brooding, that will get you nowhere.'

'I don't want to be a gooseberry,' Lowri said.

'For heaven's sake!' Sally shook her head. 'You won't be a gooseberry.'

'Where are you going, anyway?'

'Just out, we haven't really decided yet. Maybe just a drink at the Ship Inn. I've heard that a good crowd go there and if we're hungry, we can always have a bar meal. Come on, get your pretties on and do up your eyes and you'll have the men running after you in droves.'

'I doubt that,' Lowri said.

'Snap out of it!' Sally said in a hard voice. 'You know what you're doing, don't you?'

'You're going to tell me, I can see.' Lowri attempted a smile.

'You are letting that bastard pull you down. He's dented your self-esteem or whatever the hell you call it. You need to build up your confidence again.'

Lowri gave in. 'All right, I'll come.' She had been going to have a night in, have a relaxing bath, listen to music or watch some undemanding soap on the television. It was something she had enjoyed from the security of her relationship with Jon. Now the thought of a night alone had lost its appeal.

'That's settled. We'll pick you up at half seven. OK?'

Lowri was saved from replying by the sound of the buzzer signalling the appearance of a client. She looked up and felt a frisson of surprise to see Sarah Brandon standing in the doorway leading through from reception.

She moved into the room, tall, well-groomed, with a look that would freeze the sea. She stared at Lowri without interest and then turned her attention to Sally, who was still sitting on the desk admiring her legs.

'I want to know something.' She dispensed with any niceties. 'You dealt with the lease for the property in Plunch Lane, didn't you?'

'Well, not personally,' Sally said. 'Our Mr Watson holds the lease to all the properties along the coast there.'

'But you knew my husband? You went out with him? There is no way Jon would stay in this dead-and-alive hole unless he had found a woman and you are just his type, blonde, leggy and a little common.'

'Excuse me!' Sally slid from the desk. 'I don't know who you think you are talking to but I don't have to take that from anyone.'

Lowri rose to her feet. 'Mrs Brandon,' she said, 'please, Sally did not even meet Jon — Mr Brandon.'

Sarah ignored her. 'Tell me you didn't sleep with him then?' Her eyes never left Sally's face. 'I smelt your perfume on the pillows and shower gel of the sort I would never use was in the bathroom.'

'What makes you think it was me?' Sally said. 'I don't believe in going out with someone old enough to be my father.'

'Liar!' Sarah spoke harshly. 'He had money, he flattered you, gave you a good time. Don't try to get out of it, I found your name and address and phone number in his suit pocket at home. He knew you before he even came here. You are Sally White, aren't you?'

'Well, yes.' Sally looked trapped. 'But I really don't know why he should have my name and address, I didn't know him from Adam!'

She was lying, even Lowri could see it. But why, what did Sally have to do with Jon? Sally threw an agonized glance in Lowri's direction.

'Look,' Lowri spoke more forcefully, 'we sometimes give out our private number so that clients can contact us. Now if you have a complaint about the property we have leased you, why don't you make an appointment and come back when one of the solicitors is free?'

Lowri felt she was invisible. Sarah Brandon ignored her and looked Sally up and down with insulting deliberation.

'He likes his bits of stuff to have little or no brain, those are the types he can fool easily. Jon likes to play the field, he believes that variety is the spice of life and he boasts about his conquests to me afterwards.' She turned away in disgust. 'Women can be such fools!'

The door clicked shut behind her. Lowri looked at Sally. 'Wow!' She took a deep breath. 'Why did Jon have your name and address, Sally, *were* you involved with him?'

'No!' Sally sat at her desk and rubbed her face with her hands. 'No of course I wasn't. I didn't even meet him, you know that.'

Lowri felt tired. It seemed that Jon led a complicated life. Well, perhaps one of those complications had finally caught up with him in the shape of a jealous husband. Perhaps that was why he ran off so suddenly.

'Let's forget him,' Sally said angrily. 'All he's brought us is trouble. It would have been better if he had never set foot in this place.' She sounded near to tears and Lowri had shed enough tears of her own without trying to deal with those of anyone else.

She opened her appointment book and checked the time she was meeting the next client. 'Another one for Plunch Lane,' she remarked. 'The place is very popular all of a sudden and summer's almost over. Well, I'd better be going.' She picked up her jacket and bag. 'You'll be all right on your own?'

'Yeah. I don't suppose there will be much to do this afternoon.' Sally did not look at her and after a few moments, Lowri left the office.

The sunlight was bright and she blinked as she walked round the back to the small parking area where she kept her car. The little red Mazda would be like an oven — there was no shade at the back of the buildings.

'Can I talk to you?' A hand fell on her arm and she looked up into the face of Sarah Brandon. 'I'm sorry I was so scathing about your colleague but she is just his type,' she said. 'I know you must think me a bitter, twisted woman and you'd be right but I have to know what's happened to my husband.' She was pale in spite of the heat.

'We didn't really get on, you see,' she was babbling, 'we hadn't slept together for years so it's my fault he had other women. I hated him for being unfaithful and yet I loved him too. If only I knew something about those last hours before he vanished . . .' She stopped speaking as Lowri drew her arm away.

'I'm sorry, Mrs Brandon, I really can't help you. Please excuse me, I have to meet a client and I'm already late.'

Lowri slid into the driving seat and started the engine and, as she drew away, she could see Sarah standing there like something carved from stone. She was clearly unstable, an odd woman, and yet Lowri felt deeply sorry for her. 'Jon, you are a first-class shit!' she said. 'And you deserve everything you get.'

The Ship Inn was situated on the cliff top overlooking the bay. Ironically, it was not more than two hundred yards from Plunch Lane. It was a place that Jon Brandon must have frequented on a regular basis but he had never taken Lowri there. Now she knew why: he was afraid his wife might find out.

'Looks a nice place,' she said as she slid out of the back seat of Timmy Perkins's car. Below, on the rocks, Lowri could hear the wash of the sea. How many times had she listened to the sound of the waves when she had been in bed with the man she loved, the man she thought she knew?

'Yeah, it's all right, I suppose,' Sally said. 'We don't come down this way very often, do we, Timmy?'

'Not really, it's a little on the quiet side, mostly old fogies,' Timmy said. Lowri smiled. Timmy was all of nineteen, to him anyone over the age of twenty-five would be an old fogey, herself included.

There was a warm atmosphere inside the small lounge bar. The décor was traditional, with horse-brasses either side of the inglenook fireplace. Ships' lamps hung from the beams. Smoke filled the room and the sound of some bland musical tape made a backdrop to the laughter and the raised voices of people enjoying themselves.

'Evening, folks.' The landlord was tall and swarthy, with thick white hair that seemed to sprout all over his head and face. 'Nice to see you again.' He was looking at Sally. 'What'll you have? Your usual?'

'Please.' Sally shrugged off her jacket and slipped into a corner seat, crossing her slender legs in the shiny black leather boots and making sure her skirt was revealing enough to be interesting.

'Lowri?' Timmy asked.

'A glass of red, please.'

She sat beside Sally and wished she had

not worn trousers. She felt drab and unexciting, part of the older element that Sally and Timmy so scorned. 'Why did you suggest this place, Sally?' she asked conversationally.

Sally looked guarded. 'I just thought it might suit you, that's all.' She lit up a cigarette, more to display her well-shaped, colourfully varnished nails than because she enjoyed a smoke, Lowri thought.

'And you don't come here often, then?' Lowri played with the beer-mat, pretending she was making small talk and fooling no-one.

'Don't go getting suspicious of me now, Lowri!' Sally said. 'No, I haven't been here very often, have I, Tim?' She smiled. 'I suppose the old man noticed me because he thinks I'm pretty.'

Underneath her incredible display of vanity it was clear that Sally had picked up on Lowri's thoughts. The landlord knew what she drank: that suggested that she was more than a casual customer.

Perhaps she was becoming paranoid, Lowri thought, accepting her drink from Timmy with a murmur of thanks.

'But why did Jon have your address and phone number on him?' She only realized she had spoken her thoughts aloud when

Sally sighed in exasperation.

'I told you I don't know! Probably the old bat made it up; she didn't show us the paper, did she? She's just clutching at straws, jealous of anyone younger and prettier than she is.'

'Don't go being over-modest, now, Sal.' Timmy laughed as he sat astride a bar stool facing the women. 'And what's this about someone having your number, eh?'

'Oh, nothing,' Lowri said quickly. 'As Sally says, the woman is disturbed, she's probably making the whole thing up.'

And yet doubts and questions as elusive as a butterfly's wing ran through her mind. Was Sally lying, could she have been involved with Jon, had she slept with him? Lowri rubbed her cheek; she was getting more and more confused. She must pull herself together.

'Wake up! Do you want another drink, Lowri?' Timmy was leaning forward, holding out his hand for her glass. She looked down at it and saw to her surprise that it was empty.

'Yes, why not?'

'For goodness' sake, Lowri!' Sally hissed. 'You're acting like a wet week! Cheer up can't you?'

'Evening, folks, mind if I join you?'

Lowri looked up to see Jim Lainey standing over her. He was wearing a casual open-necked shirt tucked into slim-fitting trousers and he was smiling at her as if liking what he saw.

'Oh hello!' Sally smiled enthusiastically. 'Come and sit here next to me and tell me your name and explain why I've never met such a handsome hunk as you before.'

'A pint, mate?' Timmy was standing beside the table, a tray in his hand, and he was looking pointedly at Jim Lainey.

'That's very good of you,' Lainey said smoothly before turning to face Lowri. 'I'm glad I found you here, I was hoping to see you,' he said and Timmy visibly relaxed. Soon the four of them were sitting together, cramped into the small corner space as the room filled with people. Lowri wondered if DI Lainey was following her. She was very much aware of his thigh, hot against hers. She wished again that she had worn a skirt. Her legs were shapely and long, and they looked good in sheer stockings.

She knew what she was doing, she was trying to bolster her self esteem. Sally was right about that, Lowri's confidence had taken a beating. She drank her wine and allowed her glass to be refilled. Soon, she felt pleasantly relaxed.

She and Lainey became engrossed in conversation and, to Lowri's relief, he did not mention Jon once.

It was a surprise when the ship's bell rang through the room to call time. Lowri glanced at her watch: it was after eleven.

'Can I drive you home?' Lainey asked quietly. Behind his back Sally was making faces, mouthing encouragement.

'Thank you, I'd like that very much.'

It was good to sit beside a man, to feel relaxed, to hear the soft hum of the engine and to know that she was being looked after, if only for a short while. Neither of them spoke but the silence was a comfortable one. All too soon the drive was over, and Lowri waited while Lainey switched off the engine. It was all going to end now, in a minute she would step into her little house and she would be alone again.

'Would you like a coffee?' she asked quickly, afraid that she would lose her nerve. 'I could do with one myself — I feel a little light-headed.'

'I'd love a coffee,' he said.

Lowri was filled with a sense of euphoria as she gave Lainey the key to open her front door. Her life was not over after all — she was young and she had a handsome man at her side. She must forget Jon, forget he ever existed.

Lowri made the coffee and sat beside Lainey on the sofa, close but not too close. Lainey put his head back and closed his eyes.

'It's so peaceful here,' he said.

She closed her eyes too, drinking in the companionable silence. There was no sound except for her own breath and the sound of Lainey breathing evenly at her side. She slept.

She woke and looked at her watch. It was half past three. Lowri stared around her in confusion. Lainey was still asleep.

Lowri watched him for a moment before bringing a blanket from upstairs and putting it over him. Then she switched off the light and went to bed.

Before she went back to sleep, she wondered if Lainey would feel embarrassed in the morning, if the easy closeness between them would vanish with the sunlight. She need not have worried. In the morning, Lainey was gone.

4

Lowri was about to leave for work when she heard an urgent knocking on her door. She opened it, expecting the postman, but it was Jim Lainey standing on her step. Lowri felt a prickle of apprehension run down her spine. Lainey looked so formal, his expression was grave, with no sign that he'd spent most of the night on her sofa. Standing behind him was another, younger officer.

'Detective, come in but I can't stay talking for long, I've got to get to work.' She had a busy morning ahead and her mother had rung last night before she'd gone to the Ship, asking to be met at the station. Clearly she'd rowed with Charles again. Mr Watson was a compassionate boss but he would not let anyone take advantage of his good nature.

'What can I do for you?' she asked when the two men stood in her small sitting-room. Jim gestured towards the other officer. 'This is Sergeant Brown, perhaps you could take a look at the items he's holding.'

The sergeant obligingly held up the

plastic bags and Lowri stared at them, waiting for an explanation.

'We've found some clothes,' Lainey's tone was businesslike. He was now the policeman at work. 'At the foot of the cliffs below the Swan Hotel. I would like you to see if you can identify any of them.'

'I'll have to ring work.' Her mind shied away from the implications of Lainey's question. 'Though it's going to be difficult to explain to my boss that I need time off to help the police with their inquiries, isn't that what you call it?'

It was Sally who answered the phone at the office. 'Morning! Watson Jones and Fry, Sally speaking, can I help you?'

'It's me,' Lowri said. 'I'm going to be late, will you be all right?'

Sally was silent for a moment. 'I don't know what's wrong but you'd better get in here as soon as poss.' She lowered her voice. 'Old Watson's got a lady visitor and he doesn't seem too happy about it.'

'Too bad,' Lowri said. 'The police want to talk to me.' Before Sally could ask any questions Lowri replaced the receiver. Jim looked at her.

'Trouble?'

'No, not really, just Sally panicking as usual.'

'Will you take a good look at these things?' he said. She suddenly felt intimidated by Lainey. He seemed so focused, so serious as he took the plastic bags from the sergeant and held them towards her. Inside, she could see a creased shirt, a pair of buff chinos and a solitary shoe.

'Recognize anything?'

She recognized the shirt all right, it belonged to Jon. A renewed sense of loss swept over her. Whatever Jon had done, he had been her lover, her friend and she missed him like hell.

'I think so,' she said. 'The shirt is the right make. Jon — Jon always wore good shirts, crisp and clean as the day they were bought. That was one of the things I liked about him.' She was not aware of Lainey self-consciously touching his own collar as if to assure himself it was in place.

'And the trousers?'

'Well, I don't know, they all look the same. Jon is size 32-inch, are those the right size?'

Lainey did not answer. He seemed disappointed that she had not been more positive. A thought struck her and she looked at the shirt again. It was white, slightly crumpled but clean.

'That shirt hasn't been worn,' she said.

'It doesn't look like it.' Lainey waited

for her to speak again.

She closed her eyes momentarily. 'What do you think has happened to him?'

'That's what we are trying to find out,' Lainey said. 'Are you all right?' He seemed to move closer to her, his brow furrowed, as if he was genuinely concerned. Lowri wished she did not remember the closeness that had been between them so briefly.

'Yes, I'm all right,' she said, 'just a bit hung-over.' She looked up at him, meeting his eyes for the first time that morning. 'And I'm confused. I don't know if I should be angry at being deceived by the man I thought I loved, or if I should be grieving for him.'

'That's understandable,' Lainey said quietly.

Lowri met his eyes. 'Do you think he's dead?'

'I don't know.' He shook his head. 'Can't you think of anything that would help, Miss Richards? Even the most insignificant detail might prove valuable.'

She moved away from him. 'I'm sorry, there's nothing. He just went out of my life, vanished as if he had never been, that's all I know.'

'Well, never mind. Shall we go, Sergeant?' As he opened the front door and stepped outside, she had the absurd impulse to call after him. She watched him walk away along the road towards where his car was parked. He did not look back.

Lowri sank into a chair. In little over an hour she would be meeting her mother — perhaps it would be a good idea to take the whole day off. There was no way she could concentrate on work, not now.

What did the discarded clothes mean? Had Jon gone for a swim and then drowned? The currents around the coast could be treacherous at times.

She changed out of the smart suit she kept for work and pulled on a thin cotton shirt and a pair of pants. She felt restless, as if she had an itch she could not scratch. Why were there always questions and no answers?

Lowri went into the kitchen. It was filled with sunlight and the yellow and green checked cloth on the pine table looked fresh and clean. Like Jon's shirt. She looked in the fridge: the salad was ready in the bowl, all she needed to do was to boil some potatoes and make a dressing. She closed the door again and wandered aimlessly around the house. 'Damn and blast Jon Brandon!' she said.

The train had arrived early, and Lowri found her mother waiting in the snack bar on the station.

'Mum! It's lovely to see you again.' The two women hugged and Lowri felt some of her tension ease. 'Come on, let's get home.' She slipped her hand in the crook of her mother's arm and together they walked to the car.

'How's Father?' Lowri asked.

'Just as difficult as ever.' Her mother spoke edgily. 'You know Charles, he likes everything cut and dried; his drink in his hand the minute he steps in the door, his every wish obeyed. I had to get away for a few days.' She laughed to soften the words. 'Nothing ever changes. Anyway, how are you? Are you going to tell me more about this strange man you were living with? Why did you split up?'

'I wasn't actually living with him,' Lowri said. 'Though as good as, I'll grant you.' She sighed. 'Turned out he was married and now he's gone missing. Same old story, I suppose.'

Lowri did not care to go into details. 'I've got a nice salad for lunch and then if you like we can spend the afternoon on the recliners in the garden, catch the sun.'

'No fear!' her mother said. 'After we've eaten you and I are going on a shopping spree up at the enterprise zone.'

'I know what that means, Mum, you are

78

going to spend your money on me. Well, I don't need it, honestly. I'm a big girl now, I can look after myself.'

'Don't take one of my few small pleasures in life away from me, Lowri.' There was an edge of sadness in her mother's tone and Lowri nodded.

'All right, I give in, a spending spree it is.'

That evening, to Lowri's surprise, Sally called. 'God, you look awful!' Sally said with her usual tact. 'Heavy night with the lovely detective, was it?'

'Come in,' Lowri said, 'meet my mother.'

Sally put her hand over her mouth. 'Oops! Sorry, have I put my foot in it?'

Rhian Richards looked up with a smile as Sally came into the room. 'Hello there, Sally,' she said.

'Oh, you were in the office earlier today, weren't you?' Sally said. 'I could hear you and old . . . er Mr Watson arguing.'

'Sally!' Lowri said, 'don't be silly. My mother's only been in town a few hours and we've been shopping since she arrived.'

Sally shrugged. 'There I go again, opening my big mouth and putting my foot in it. What did you buy? Come on show me.'

It was a pleasant evening. Sally kept them amused with her talk about her boyfriend, about some of the clients who came into the

79

office and she even poked gentle fun at the trio of solicitors.

It was about half nine when Rhian rubbed her eyes, put down her glass and rose to her feet.

'Think I'll turn in,' she said. 'I need an early night.' She kissed Lowri and hugged her warmly. 'We can talk more in the morning, darling.'

After she'd gone, Sally leaned forward. 'Come on, tell me, what happened?'

'Between me and Jim? Nothing happened.'

'Come on! You seemed very keen last night, you were positively drooling.'

'Don't rub it in.' Lowri felt uncomfortable. 'I thought Jon was the love of my life, the man I could settle down with.' She looked up at Sally. 'Then I flirt with the first handsome man I see.' She sighed. 'I still can't believe Jon took me in so completely, I must have "easy lay" written across my forehead.'

'You're behind the times, love, everyone does it now, didn't you know? Did you sleep with the detective?'

'Of course I didn't!' Lowri said.

'Why are you blushing then?' Sally pushed back her hair impatiently. 'I mean when you phoned the office you said the police were with you. He wouldn't call round this morning just to pass the time of day.'

'It was business.' Lowri made an effort to change the subject. 'You say my mother was in the office earlier? She didn't mention it.'

'Aye, that's right,' Sally said. 'Anyway,' Sally tucked her legs up under her. 'I won't be sidetracked, what did the police want you for?' She looked like a little girl expecting to be told an exciting adventure story.

'I suppose there's no harm in telling you they'd found some clothes by the cliffs. They wanted to know if I had seen them before.' She shivered. 'A shirt and some stone-coloured chinos.'

'Were they his?' Sally asked. She had put her hand in her drink and was swirling it around. Briefly Lowri thought of offering her a spoon but then she realized it was just a reflex action on Sally's part. Sally put down her cup. 'Were they?'

'I don't think so.' It was a lie. Suddenly, it seemed important to keep her own counsel. 'I've never seen him in anything like that.'

'But he did like wearing chinos.' Sally stopped abruptly. 'At least, that's what I thought you *said* he liked wearing.'

'When?' Lowri asked. 'When did I say that?'

'I don't know!' Sally shook back her hair.

'What on earth has got into you, Lowri? You never let me meet this wonderful man but you talked about him a hell of a lot, remember?'

'I suppose I did.' Lowri felt remorseful. 'And the only reason you didn't meet him was because we mostly got together on the weekends. You were usually doing something with Tim.'

'I know, I'm not blaming you!' Sally's cheeks were pink. 'Perhaps I'd better go.'

'I'm sorry, Sally.' Lowri rubbed her eyes. 'I'm so strung up about all this. First Jon walks out on me, leaving me flat, and then I find he was married all along. I don't know what to think any more.'

'I'm sorry.' Sally's tone softened. 'You've had a hell of a shock and I'm a nosy bitch, aren't I? Come on, it's still early enough for us to get a drink at the pub. A bit of lively company will do you the world of good.'

'Oh, I don't know, my mother . . .'

Sally stood up. 'Get your jacket, we're going to the Plough and Harrow, it's got a nice lounge. And the drink's not bad.'

The last thing Lowri felt like was going out to a pub, but she had offended Sally enough for one evening. She picked up a lightweight jacket and slipped her bag over her shoulder.

'Where's Timmy tonight?' she asked as she closed the door behind her. Sally was already out on the pavement. She shrugged.

'He's studying for his exams, they are something to do with the law part of his course. Well, I'm not staying in for anyone.'

Timothy Perkins was studying Information Technology. He was not Sally's type, he was far too earnest. Sometimes he could be a real bore. Sally took him entirely for granted, of course. Come to think of it, it was a wonder the relationship had lasted for so long.

It was a pleasant night. The air was still warm and the breeze drifted towards them, fragrant with roses, as they walked the short distance to the Plough and Harrow.

Sally saw her as a charity case, Lowri thought ruefully, she was doing her good deed for the day by taking Lowri out of herself. Sally was in casual mode tonight, wearing trainers and jeans. She somehow made Lowri feel a hundred years old.

'Your mum's a classy woman, Lowri,' Sally said as she pushed open the door of the pub. 'I bet your father loves her to pieces. Go and sit down while I get us a drink.'

Lowri chose a corner seat and felt somehow alone in spite of the crowded lounge. She thought about her childhood, about the happy times she enjoyed when Charles was away on business. Those were the times when the large rooms in the Victorian house had been filled with warmth and laughter, which lasted only until Charles came home again.

To an outsider, it might look as though her mother had everything a woman could want. A sunny home, an easy, pampered lifestyle and plenty of money to spend. But Charles seemed able to put a stop to any happiness and laughter the minute he entered a room. Her stepfather was a fairly successful businessman: he enjoyed finding ways to screw his latest competitor, taking an almost unholy pleasure in the power it gave him.

When Lowri left home, Charles had predicted she would never make anything of herself. She almost felt she hated him then. But perhaps he was right; she had not come very far in the last few years. She could hardly call working in a solicitor's office the peak of ambition.

'You're not sulking, are you?' Sally's voice broke into her thoughts and Lowri forced herself to smile.

'No I'm not sulking, I don't have to talk all the time, do I?'

'Oh excuse me for breathing!' Sally's sarcasm was edged with anger.

'Anyway,' Lowri said, 'let's talk about you. Quarrelled with Timmy, have you?'

Sally made a wry face. 'He needs to grow up!'

'I've got news for you,' Lowri said, 'men don't change, they never grow up.'

'Mind now, mother of the universe,' Sally said, 'anyone would think you were a dried-up spinster.'

'Sometimes that's how I feel.' They sat in silence for a time and Lowri was aware of Sally fidgeting, looking around for someone to enmesh in more animated conversation.

'Another drink?' Sally said and Lowri got to her feet at once.

'My round.' She hated walking up to the bar; it felt strange to her, not quite ladylike somehow. She was probably an anachronism in a world of women who liked to be independent, liked to drink pints as men did, and probably liked using men for sex the way men had always managed to use women. She pulled herself up. She was getting bitter — that would never do.

The door swung open and a crowd of men came into the bar. They stood around Lowri, one of them shouting to the barmaid to get a move on. She glanced over her shoulder and her colour rose as she realized that Jim Lainey was standing behind her.

'Hi.' She spoke as naturally as she could. 'How's everything?'

'Fine!' He smiled down at her. 'You feeling OK?'

'I'm fine, thanks.'

'Look,' Lainey leaned towards her, 'I'm off duty, perhaps I could take you home later?'

'I'm sorry, it's not possible.'

He turned away at once. 'All right, no problem.'

'Wait,' she said quickly, 'my mother's visiting, she's already in bed, I don't want to wake her.'

'As I said, no problem.'

She returned to sit with Sally, wishing miserably that she could leave. She looked down at the ruby wine glinting in the lights from overhead and knew she had blown her chances of even a friendship with Jim Lainey.

'Nice-looking guy, that Lainey,' Sally said. 'Got his phone number?'

'You don't miss a trick, do you?' Lowri said. She got up. 'Excuse me, I've got to powder my nose.'

As she passed them, one of the men at the bar made a remark that Lowri could not hear and a gust of laughter went up from the rest of the crowd. Lowri stared at herself in the long mirror in the ladies' room, wondering what she was doing here, wondering what she was doing with her life, come to that.

She ran the cold water over her wrists. She was becoming impossible to be with, she knew that, but her life had been turned upside down and no-one seemed to realize it.

When she returned to the lounge, Jim had gone. Sally had gone too and Lowri looked round impatiently.

'Blast Sally!' Still, she had asked for it, she could hardly blame Sally for taking offence. She picked up her bag and left the bar, walking briskly towards home.

She was just putting her key in the lock when a figure moved out of the shadows. Lowri stepped back, her heart thumping, her mouth suddenly dry.

'I want a word with you, Miss Richards.' Sarah Brandon was dressed all in black and, in the pale light of the moon, her face seemed devoid of colour. Somehow, Lowri knew that her appearance on the doorstep meant trouble. She glanced behind her but all she could see were the tail-lights of a car disappearing into the distance. The small street was deserted.

'I'm rather tired, Mrs Brandon.'

'This won't take very long and I mean to talk to you if I have to stand outside your door all night.'

There was an edge of hysteria in Sarah's voice that filled Lowri with a sense of foreboding. She knew that what she was about to hear would not be good news. She switched on the light and held the door wide. 'You'd better come inside,' she said.

5

Sarah Brandon looked out of place in the small lounge, her elegantly painted fingernails resting on an expensive leather handbag. Her feet were tucked under the chair, as though there was not enough room to accommodate her long legs.

'It's rather late, please keep your voice down, my mother is in bed,' Lowri said. 'What can I do for you, is it about the lease on Plunch Lane?'

'You could say that.' Sarah's voice sounded strange. 'It's about the time when you were there, in early spring it must have been.' Her large eyes were narrowed. She appeared like a cat about to pounce on an unwary mouse.

Sarah paused as if to examine one of her fingers and Lowri saw the glint of a gold wedding ring. 'I found a photograph, you see.' She paused as though to take a breath. 'You were naked, abandoned. It was quite obvious from the photograph that you had just been making love to my husband.'

Lowri felt as though she had been slapped

in the face. She ran her fingers through her hair, not sure what to say. There was no point in denying it; the photograph was proof enough.

'Where did you find it?' she asked.

'That's not important.' Sarah's tone was icy.

'It is to me,' Lowri said.

'That's just too bad! Now, how long has this affair been going on?'

'Look!' Lowri was aware of the anger in her voice but there was little point in trying to hide how she felt. 'I've been going out with Jon for almost six months. It wasn't just a cheap affair, far from it, I thought he loved me.' She was near to tears. 'So don't you dare come here attacking me in my own home! None of this is my fault. I have done nothing wrong, get that into your head once and for all, Mrs Brandon.'

'Nothing wrong?' Sarah's voice rose. 'You sleep with my husband in my bed and leave your stink on my sheets. You call that nothing wrong? What sort of woman are you?'

Lowri's small rush of anger faded. 'I'm the gullible sort.' She looked across at Sarah. 'I didn't know he was married.'

'Don't lie!' Sarah's eyes were blazing. 'You might say you're gullible but I am not.

You slept with Jon, time and time again. How many times, Miss Richards, or are they too many to count?'

Lowri shook her head, crushed with guilt in the face of Sarah's pain. But Sarah went on relentlessly.

'You spent that last weekend with him at the Swan, didn't you?'

'Yes, I did.'

'And he's never been seen since. What happened, did you have a row, did he walk out on you?'

Lowri rubbed her eyes. 'I don't know what happened.' She felt beaten. 'He just vanished from the hotel. It's as if he never existed.'

'I loved him so much,' Sarah said in a low voice. 'But you are the last straw, I could never live with Jon now, not after this.'

Lowri was silent. How could she defend herself? Why had she been so unquestioning, so trusting? She believed she would marry Jon so why had she learned so little about him?

Sarah rose to her feet and Lowri stood up too. Sarah surveyed her up and down and Lowri was aware that she must look a wreck. Even now, as the injured wife, Sarah managed to appear composed and beautiful.

'What happened to him?' Sarah asked in a

cold voice. 'That night in the hotel, did he tell you it was all over? Did you kill him rather than let him leave you?'

'Don't be absurd!' Lowri shook her head. 'I don't know what happened. I fell asleep on the balcony — I was listening to music. I just don't know anything, I wish to God I did!'

'He'd had sex with you by then, of course,' Sarah's voice was like a lancet, picking away at a wound. 'He was good at that. I know how good, I had the benefit of his libido for some years before he found me too dull, too unadventurous in bed.'

She smiled thinly. 'He must have enjoyed you very much to stick with you so long but remember this, what he really enjoyed was punishing me. He slept with you as a little diversion, you were never important to him, just understand that.'

'I understand,' Lowri said emptily.

'He couldn't be faithful to me so I'm sure he wouldn't be faithful to a trollop like you! You were just one of many.' Sarah paused and peered closely at Lowri.

'Have you asked that girl, that bottle-blonde tart Sally White, if she slept with Jon? Because I would put my last penny on it that she did.' She shook her head. 'If it moved, he'd take it to bed.'

'Please! Leave me alone.' Lowri put her hands to her cheeks — they were burning. 'Look, I'm tired, will you just go, please?'

'So you're tired are you? Poor soul. Well, I'm devastated. I've lost my husband, he's maybe dead or lying somewhere injured and you, you pretend to know nothing about it all. Do you think I'm stupid?'

Sarah gritted her teeth, her face was suffused with colour and Lowri thought for a moment that she might attack her. But Sarah made an effort to regain control.

'You are disgusting, do you know that?'

It was pointless trying to explain that Jon was a convincing liar, that she had really believed that he was free to marry her. What married man out for a fling took his mistress to his home, even if it was a holiday cottage? But perhaps Sarah was right and Jon's main aim in life was to punish his wife, to taunt her with his other women.

'Just go!' she said. Her brain felt scrambled, her emotions fluctuating between anger and despair. 'I can't deal with this, not now.'

Sarah pushed her face closer, her eyes seeming to pierce Lowri's skull. 'You'll have more to deal with before I've finished with you, madam.'

She walked to the door and glanced back,

and the hate in her eyes was frightening. 'You wouldn't have lasted much longer with him. Look at you, skin and bone, bags under your eyes. You were getting too old, my dear.'

She put her hand on the front-door catch. 'I've been watching you, you've found another fool to take you out. You didn't let any grass grow under your feet, did you?' She paused, a thin smile barely touching her lips. 'I saw you, in the pub with him. He just picked you up at the bar, did he? Well, enjoy it while you may but I think you'll find it a slippery road to ruin from here on in, Miss Richards. I am not a woman you would want as an enemy, believe me.'

She walked outside, leaving the door open. As Lowri slammed it shut, her heart was thumping. The woman was deranged; there was no way of reasoning with her. But then would any wronged wife want to listen to excuses made by the other woman, especially when the excuses were so bizarre?

Lowri went into the kitchen and switched on the kettle. Was she going mad — had she imagined the love in Jon's eyes, the tenderness in his touch?

She made tea and her hands trembled as she lifted the cup. She felt tears constrict her throat and swallowed painfully. What was happening to her? She was losing control; she was being swept this way and that. Suddenly, she wished that Jim Lainey, with his kindness, his reassuring presence, was here with her.

Before she went to bed, she took great care locking up; her nerves were on edge, her heart still beating unnaturally fast. She carried her tea into the bedroom and switched on all the lights. She put down the cup; perhaps she should check on her mother. Maybe she had been disturbed by Sarah's angry voice.

Her mother was asleep curled into a ball, half hidden under the bedclothes. Beside her on the table was a bottle of sleeping-pills.

Lowri's face softened. Her mother looked so young in sleep, so vulnerable. She did not deserve the treatment meted out to her by her husband. Lowri picked up the bottle and took out a tablet. She needed to sleep, needed to forget all about Jon Brandon and his crazy wife. Quietly, she closed the door and went into her own room.

Lowri sat at her desk feeling weary, defeated. Her mother had reacted to an irate phone call from Charles and had rushed back home, and even at the last minute

Lowri wondered if she should talk to her about Jon. In the end she said nothing; her mother had enough to cope with.

'I feel my life is disintegrating into one huge mess, Sal.' She closed her eyes, resting her head in her hands.

'I can see you're off colour,' Sally said. 'Time of the month, is it? I'll make you a nice cup of coffee now.'

Lowri rose to her feet, filled with the need to do something, anything. 'No thanks.' She felt suddenly charged with energy. 'I'm going to drive down to the Swan. Perhaps one of the staff might have seen Jon leave.' She smiled grimly. 'At least I can find out if he's been there again with another girl-friend.'

'No, don't go!' Sally said. Lowri looked at her in surprise.

'Why not?'

'Well, what about Mr Watson?' Sally asked. 'He'll get fed up of you taking time off work.'

'No, he won't.' Lowri smiled. 'You've said yourself, he thinks I'm wonderful.'

'Wait, Lowri, do you really think this is a good idea?' Sally seemed agitated. 'I don't want you to throw away your job here, I'd be lost without you.'

'That's very touching, Sal, but it won't

come to that.' She sighed. 'I have to do something, I just can't sit around twiddling my thumbs. Jon must have gone somewhere and someone must have seen him leave. I won't be too long.'

Lowri left the office and walked round to the back of the building to pick up the Mazda. As she slipped into the driving seat, she hesitated: could she face going back to the hotel? She started the car; she was going and that was that.

Even if the police were any nearer to finding out where Jon had gone, they were keeping quiet about it. She would have to try to discover for herself the truth about Jon Brandon and his vanishing act.

The roads were busy and the drive to the hotel took longer than she had anticipated. By the time she got there, Lowri was hot and uncomfortable. Sally was right about one thing: it *was* that time of the month.

She turned into the gravelled courtyard and drew the car to a halt, pulling on the handbrake. She climbed out and looked up at the fine old building, wondering at the secrets hidden behind the many windows. Had Jon met another woman that night? Had a more tempting offer come along? Perhaps she would never know.

She looked up at the hotel again; would

anyone there recognize her? Perhaps it would be just as well to hide her identity for a while. Casual, seemingly innocent enquiries usually caught people off guard. She put on her sunglasses and then moved around to the back of the car and opened the boot.

A scarf decorated with white stars against a sharp blue background lay in a pool of silk and shadow. Lowri picked it up. Sally must have left it there when she and Lowri had gone to see a prospective client a few days ago.

Lowri tied it around her short hair and with the large sunglasses covering most of her face, she would pass, she decided. In any case, she and Jon had only been there once, for one night. It was doubtful anyone would remember her.

The receptionist was busy writing; she glanced up at Lowri without curiosity. 'Be with you in a minute,' she said. Lowri did not recognize her; the girl was young, very pretty. Just the type Jon Brandon would go for, according to his wife.

'Now, madam, how can I help?' The girl looked up and smiled suddenly. 'Oh, hello, I remember you, you've been here before, haven't you?'

Lowri nodded. 'Lowri Richards. I came

here with my boyfriend Jon, Jon Brandon.'

'What I remember, actually, is your scarf, it's so distinctive,' the girl said. 'Of course I only saw you from the back or I would have recognized your face right away. I'm good on faces.'

Lowri swallowed hard. 'Do you remember the man I was with?'

The receptionist smiled. 'I do, he was very dishy as it happens. He turned and winked at me, some looker.'

'That's right, he is dishy isn't he?' Lowri hesitated. 'Could I look round the room, do you think?' She smiled. 'I know the place has probably been cleaned since I was here but I lost an earring. It's just possible I might find it there. Room 101 I think it was.'

'I don't see any harm in that.' The receptionist consulted the register. 'You're in luck, number 101, the one with the balcony and it's free. Here, take my key, but promise you won't pinch the towels!'

'I promise.' Lowri smiled. 'Sometimes my sister borrows my scarf, it might have been Sally you saw.' She sighed. 'I have been wondering if she's got her eye on my fella.'

The receptionist gave her an understanding smile. 'Men eh? I'm sure you've nothing to worry about, though. I don't think your own sister would want to borrow your man as well as your scarf. Your chap is tall, isn't he? Lovely dark hair and so handsome. I could have fallen for him myself.'

Lowri sighed. 'Well, Jon fits that description but then so do many men.' She forced a smile. 'I shouldn't be so suspicious but it's the good-looking ones you have to watch.'

She ignored the lift, it was old and very small and it creaked alarmingly. In any case, room 101 was on the first floor — it was quicker to walk up the stairs. She paused outside the room, her thoughts reeling. Jon and Sally? Surely not. She had allowed Sarah Brandon to plant the seeds of suspicion. No doubt there were other scarves just like the one Lowri was wearing.

She opened the door and stared around her at a scene of normality. The bed was made, the room was fresh and clean, it was a hotel room like any other.

Lowri walked over to the balcony doors, trying to stem the nostalgia that washed over her. She took several deep breaths. The balcony was empty, the plastic chairs neatly turned up on the tabletop.

She moved nearer to the bed: it was as pristine as the rest of the room. It was hard to believe she and Jon had lain there, making love like crazy people. Had he known even then it would be for the last time?

Lowri sank into a chair and rubbed her forehead tiredly. Sarah Brandon seemed to think Sally was Jon's type of woman. If she was, and Jon had fallen for her, why had he disappeared?

Lowri felt she was going mad. She was sitting in the Swan Hotel expecting to find clues to what had happened that last night with Jon. She realized now that she had very little chance of that. Impatiently, she stared down at the brightly patterned scarf, shimmering in a shaft of light from the window.

The room was cold, impersonal. It was as though it had never been inhabited by real people. She would learn nothing here. She picked up the scarf and pushed it into her pocket and then pulled the door shut behind her before going downstairs. As she approached the desk, Lowri stopped abruptly. There was now a man in charge of reception.

She still had the key to 101 clutched in her hand, what should she do with it? She headed towards the lounge, cursing her bad luck.

'Excuse me, Miss Richards?' Startled, Lowri looked round. 'Thank goodness I spotted you.' It was the young receptionist. 'Have you got the key?'

'Here it is and thanks.'

'Did you find your earring?'

Lowri shook her head. 'No, I suppose it was a long shot but I thought it worth a try.'

'What a shame.' The girl hesitated. 'I thought I should tell you that the lady I saw wearing the scarf wasn't you at all. When I saw you coming down the stairs I knew straight away I was mistaken. The other girl had long hair and it wasn't reddish like yours.'

'Was she blonde by any chance and was she wearing lots of nail polish?'

'Yes, that's right! She had her arm around the man's back and I spotted the bright nail polish.' The receptionist's face fell into lines of sympathy. 'Your sister with your chap, do you think?'

'It sounds like it,' Lowri said. 'What name did they register under?'

'I wouldn't know that, I wasn't on duty, you see. As I said, I only saw her from the back and admired the scarf.'

'Thank you anyway,' Lowri said. 'These men, you can't trust any of them, can you?'

'Look on the bright side, as you said, the same description could apply to lots of men.' The girl seemed sympathetic. 'I'm sure it's all just a coincidence.'

'Off duty, now, are you?' Lowri asked.

'I'm on my way home, thank goodness.

What a busy morning it's been!'

'Please,' Lowri said, 'can you spare the time to have a drink with me? I feel lonely on my own.' She smiled wryly. 'Mad too at my boyfriend.'

The receptionist hesitated. 'All right then, I'm not supposed to mingle with the guests but I suppose a few minutes won't matter.' She settled herself into a chair. 'Oh, it's good to relax. Look, don't take too much notice of what I've said, mind, I don't expect your chap would chance bringing your sister to the same hotel, would he?'

'No, I suppose you're right.' Lowri sat beside her. The large comfortable lounge was furnished with huge sofas and chairs. The overhead lighting was subdued, befitting a place where lovers met illicitly. Lowri smiled wryly.

'Have you and your chap quarrelled?' the girl asked, crossing her legs and leaning back against the plump cushions.

'Not exactly. What would you like to drink, Miss . . .'

'Trisha, just call me Trisha. I'll have a gin and tonic please.'

Lowri held up her hand as a young waiter hovered near and ordered the drinks. 'Can I confide in you, Trisha?' She leaned forward in her chair. 'If Sally is going out with Jon she's in for a shock, I've just found out he's married.'

'Oh, dear. No wonder you're mad.' Trisha accepted her drink from the waiter and leaned back in her chair, looking up at him. 'Paul,' she said. 'Do you remember a man and woman who booked in a week or two ago? He was tall, dark and handsome,' Trisha smiled, 'which is why I noticed him, and she was a small blonde girl, with long hair.'

The boy shook his head. 'You must be joking, Trisha! It's summertime, people are booking in all the time.'

'What about room service?' Lowri asked. 'Would you be dealing with that, perhaps?'

'Yes I would. Come to think of it, I did take a tray of drinks up to one of the rooms one night. He grinned. 'I remember that the girl was small and blonde with gorgeous legs. She was wearing really high-heeled shoes, not the sort you see very often these days.' He rubbed the side of his face. 'I remember they had champagne,' he finished hastily.

'And?' Trisha asked.

'And they were on the bed.' Paul laughed nervously. 'Naked as a jaybird she was. Small, as I said, and she was wearing a lot of that eye stuff on her lids and her lipstick was

104

a sort of bright colour like her nails.' He grinned. 'And she still had her shoes on, odd that.'

'What about the man?' Lowri asked.

'Sorry! I didn't pay him much attention.' Paul looked over his shoulder. 'I'd better get back to work or I'll be out on my ear.'

As he walked away, Trisha looked at her watch. 'I'd better get off home too. Was any of that any good?'

'Some, perhaps,' Lowri said. 'Thanks for your help and could you do one more thing for me? Could you look through the bookings to see if the name Brandon or White turns up?'

'Sure, no problem.' Trisha shook her head. 'Men, why do we bother with them? They cause us nothing but trouble!'

When she had gone, Lowri sipped her Scotch slowly. The last time she had drunk it was when she was here with Jon — it seemed a lifetime ago now. Since then her world had turned topsy turvy.

Trisha appeared at her side. 'I've had a quick look at the register but the name Brandon wasn't there, nor White.'

'Oh, well, thanks for looking anyway.'

'Oh, right then,' Trisha said. 'I'm off home now.'

Lowri finished her drink; she had better

be getting back to the office. She walked slowly to the car, slipped into the driving seat and wound down all the windows. It had been a fruitless journey. What exactly had she achieved by going back to the Swan? She had found that a woman who might or might not have been Sally had stayed at the hotel with a man who might or might not have been Jon Brandon.

It was all so tenuous, like trying to grasp at mist. Sally and Jon might have been lovers; the possibility seemed more likely now. But so what? For that small snippet of gossip, she had only added to the questions racing through her mind.

When she got back to the office, she did not say anything to Sally about the scarf or what the receptionist had told her.

'So you didn't find out anything, then?' Sally pulled a face. 'You wouldn't make a good Miss Marple, would you?'

'Have you ever stayed at the Swan, Sally?' Lowri asked casually.

'No never, poor old Timmy wouldn't be able to afford the prices there.'

Sally was lying for some reason of her own. Forget it, she told herself, there was little point accusing Sally of anything.

Lowri was glad when it was time to get in her car and go home. She could not concentrate on work and Sally's bubbly talk was wearing her nerves to shreds. She drew up at the kerb and parked. For once, there was plenty of room. She walked briskly towards the house and had the distinct feeling that something was wrong. It was.

One of the panes in the sitting-room window was shattered and pieces of glass sparkled like diamonds in the pile of the carpet. In among the broken glass was a stone with a note tied around it. It was all too melodramatic for words, but frightening too.

Lowri unwrapped the note. It was unsigned and it read:

'I'm out to get you. From now on, you had better watch your back.'

Lowri picked up the phone to call the police but the line was dead. She dropped the receiver and searched in her bag for her mobile phone.

She got through to the police station. 'I want to report an incident,' she said and then she began to cry.

6

DI Lainey looked at the broken glass on the carpet and then read the brief note. 'Some crank did this,' he said. He looked at Lowri. Her face was white, her eyes had dark circles below them. It was clear she had not been sleeping very well. 'You were out when this happened?' he said. 'Just as well, I'd say.'

'I'm not so sure about that.' She glanced up at him, as if seeking reassurance. 'Earlier, I went to the Swan hoping to find something out about Jon. Perhaps I was followed.'

Lainey thrust his hands into his pockets. He was glad his sergeant was searching the rest of the house.

'Are you sure you've told me everything, Lowri?' he said quietly, looking directly at her. 'Did you have anything here belonging to Jon Brandon? Did he ask you to keep anything safe for him?'

Lowri shook her head. 'No, nothing. Why?'

'Just a thought. Can I call someone for you?' He tried to sound impersonal, resisting the urge to show any sympathy. 'A friend to stay overnight perhaps?'

Lowri shook her head. 'No, I'll be fine, thank you.' She sounded dispirited, as if the broken window was the last straw.

'Look,' he moved closer to her and spoke in a low voice, 'I really think you should get away from here for a few days. A hotel perhaps.'

Lowri looked up at him. 'I don't seem to have much luck in hotels and anyway, they cost money.'

'What about your parents? I could run you home if that's what you want.'

'No thanks. Why are you so concerned? Do you think I'm in danger or something?'

'A stone through the window is hardly a friendly gesture, is it? Well, the offer of a lift is there, take it or leave it,' he said, turning away from her.

'I'll stay here, but thanks anyway. I'll have to go to work tomorrow. I have a living to earn, you know.' He watched as she sank wearily into a chair.

'Look, I'll board up the window for to-night and tomorrow, perhaps you can get it done properly.'

'You won't find out who broke the window, will you?' Lowri asked him, her eyes large. 'Why can't you take fingerprints or something?'

He shook his head. 'I'll see if forensics can

find anything.' He shrugged. 'But this is just a petty crime. Uniform would usually deal with it but it was the connection with Jon Brandon that I was interested in.'

'Why, what has he done?' Lowri asked. 'Other than dumping me, of course.'

'I'm not really sure but I'll find out, eventually.' He walked to the door. 'Lock up after us, I'll speak to you again tomorrow.'

Lainey pulled the front door shut behind him and waited to hear the bolt slip into place and then, with his sergeant at his heels, he walked towards his car.

Mr Watson met Lowri in the hallway. He paused and looked at her over his glasses. His cheeks were pink, his sparse hair like a pale halo around his face. He had grown old before his time Lowri thought.

'You're not looking at all well, my girl,' he said. 'You young girls don't eat enough breakfast.' He walked into his office and stood in the doorway.

'Is everything all right, Lowri? At home I mean. Mother well, is she?'

'Yes, of course, Mr Watson,' she said. 'It's just man trouble, that's all.'

Lowri went into the office she shared with Sally and slumped into her chair, rubbing her eyes wearily.

'What's wrong now?' Sally switched on the coffee-machine. She busied herself with the mugs and did not look up.

'I'm fed up!' Lowri said. 'I am so fed up I could cry.'

Sally made the coffee and then pulled her chair towards Lowri's desk.

'Well don't cry for heaven's sake, you look a right mess as it is.'

'Thanks,' Lowri said dryly. She took the coffee, cupping the mug in her hands, drawing comfort from the warmth. 'I got a stone through my window yesterday,' she said. 'And a note telling me to watch my back.'

'Oh, good heavens!' Sally's eyes were round. 'You must have been frightened to death!'

Lowri shook her head. 'I wasn't there at the time, luckily for me. It happened while I was here, or at the Swan. I found out a few interesting facts while I was there, mind. Seems I wasn't the only woman Jon took to the Swan for a dirty weekend.'

Sally's eyebrows almost met her hairline. She looked as if she would ask more questions but she closed her mouth firmly and returned to her desk. The phone rang, shattering the sudden silence. Sally picked it up and then put her hand over the mouthpiece.

'Mrs Brandon for old Watson,' she said, her eyebrows raised. 'I'll connect you right away, madam,' she said in her best telephone voice. 'What does the old bat want him for?'

'Don't ask me.' Lowri sat and stared through the window into the street. The sunlight splashed on the walls of the building opposite. It was a hot day but then it had been a wonderful summer until that night at the Swan Hotel.

The intercom buzzed and Mr Watson's voice came over the line, requesting some property details.

'Looks like our Mrs Brandon is wishing to terminate her lease at Plunch Lane,' Sally said. 'Don't worry, I'll see to it.' She went out. Lowri allowed herself a smile. Sally was nothing if not curious: she would want to know exactly what Sarah Brandon was up to.

Lowri switched on her computer and waited for it to warm up. It whined and buzzed — it was getting old but the firm of Watson Jones and Fry was resistant to change.

Lowri clicked onto the details of properties and tenants, wondering who had rented the cottage in Plunch Lane before Jon took it over. There was a list of names but none of them meant anything to her.

Perhaps she could do some hard-disk clearing and delete anything unwanted from her files. She ran the cursor down the lists until she came to Jon Brandon's name. His home address was Bellingway House, in a select area of Bristol.

What had brought Jon to the small village on the coast? Was it his job of which he hardly ever spoke, or had there been a more sinister reason behind it? And why had he chosen Watson Jones and Fry to draw up the agreement for his rented holiday home?

A man would have to be a fool to offer his wife a holiday home and then have a liaison with a woman who lived nearby. Perhaps Jon's wife was right and being caught was part of it all, part of the crazy fiasco that had been their love affair.

When precisely had Jon Brandon walked into her life? Was it before he rented the cottage or after, and did he have an ulterior motive in setting up in a small Welsh seaside resort? The details of the rental agreement should be in the filing cabinet which was Sally's province.

Lowri tried the cabinet and found it was locked. She walked slowly over to Sally's desk — the key must be there. She hesitated. She was not normally a snoop but then she was not interested in Sally's personal belongings, just the contents of the file on Jon Brandon.

Impulsively, she opened Sally's drawer and began to search through the untidy pile of papers. There was the usual paraphernalia of a young woman's belongings, a file, a bottle of nail polish and a clutter of pens. Beneath the rubbish was a handwritten note and Sally had pencilled something in the margin.

Lowri turned the sheet around, studying Sally's scrawl. It was just a time and a date, innocuous enough except for the fact that the brief note looked remarkably like Jon's handwriting. It said: 'I need more information, contact me ASAP.'

Lowri rubbed her forehead as if she could wipe the questions from her mind. She was becoming paranoid, suspecting everyone, but suspecting them of what? The phone rang suddenly, shattering the silence. Startled, Lowri stared at the instrument for a long moment, her heart thumping wildly. At last she snatched up the receiver, expecting she knew not what.

'Is that Sally White?' It was a woman's voice.

'I'm sorry, she's in a meeting right now. I'm Miss Richards, can I help?'

'I suppose you will have to do. It's Sarah Brandon; I'm at the cottage in Plunch Lane. I need you to get here fast.'

'Excuse me, Mrs Brandon, but I'm not a taxi service.'

'Just get here.' The line went dead.

Lowri made a face as she replaced the receiver. The woman was impossible — she felt she only had to snap her fingers and people would come running. Still, Lowri was curious: what could Sarah Brandon want? Only minutes earlier she had been on the phone to Mr Watson.

Lowri was undecided — should she just tell Mr Watson that Mrs Brandon had called? Or send Sally on the errand perhaps? But her curiosity got the better of her and she scribbled a note and then left the office.

She stood for a moment in the sunshine of the street, taking stock of her situation. It was high time she changed her life around; became again the strong-minded woman she had been when she left home and the bullying of her stepfather behind her.

She climbed into her car and gunned the engine of the Mazda into life. 'This had better be good,' she said. Out on the road she headed in the direction of Plunch Lane. The wide streets of Jersey Marine quickly narrowed into winding country lanes bounded by thick hedgerows.

Through the open window of the car she could smell the tea roses, the corn, almost ready to cut. It was a lovely day, a day when she should be free of worry, free of her stupid infatuation for a married man.

As she neared the row of cottages she saw the two police cars at the bottom of the lane. Mrs Brandon was standing at the side of the road looking pale and anxious, but she managed to glower at Lowri as she drew the Mazda to a halt.

'What now?' Lowri muttered. She caught sight of DI Lainey — he was in his shirt-sleeves and his hands were thrust into the pockets of his trousers. Lowri could not help noticing that he had a very pert bottom.

'Why are the police here, what's happened, Mrs Brandon?'

'The place has been burgled!' Sarah Brandon looked at Lowri as though she was responsible. 'I went to the call-box and rang your boss to tell him I was terminating my tenancy here. I stopped to buy some groceries from the van that comes round. I must only have been gone about twenty minutes. When I got back the place had been wrecked.'

'I don't know what you expect me to do

about it, Mrs Brandon,' Lowri said. 'The police are here, I'm sure they have the matter in hand.'

'I don't know about that, the detective there has been quizzing me as if I'm a criminal!' She sounded outraged, as if, at any moment, she might burst into tears. 'What I want to know is will I be compensated for the loss of my personal belongings?'

'I wouldn't think Mr Watson is responsible for your possessions, but you didn't get me out here just for that, did you?'

'No, in the mess that was made of the dressing-table drawers I found some underwear that wasn't mine. I also found a credit-card receipt for them, and Sally White's signature was on it. I really would like to know what's been going on here. Has Jon been conducting orgies in my absence?'

Lowri took a deep breath. 'I don't know anything about that, Mrs Brandon.'

'Well, I blame you! If you hadn't been fooling around with my husband none of this would have happened.'

'Hang on, now,' Lowri protested but Sarah Brandon waved her hand impatiently.

'You'll have to take me back to town, I can't stay here, not now.'

'Where's your own car?' Lowri demanded, feeling angrier by the minute.

Sarah Brandon pointed to a low sports car parked near the cottage.

'There it is,' she said. 'With all its tyres slashed.'

'I don't quite see what this has got to do with me,' Lowri began and then looked up as a shadow fell across her face.

'You always turn up at the scene of a crime, don't you, Miss Richards?' Lainey's face was expressionless and Lowri had no idea if he was serious or not. She saw the twinkle in his eyes and guessed he was not.

'I have an alibi this time, Inspector. I was at the office.'

'Well, you are not a suspect, Miss Richards.' Lainey spoke soothingly. He moved a little closer and the scent of his aftershave drifted towards her. It was clean and fresh and very attractive.

'I'm glad to hear it.' She looked up and saw he was staring down at her with a curious expression on his face.

'You're wishing you could read my mind, aren't you?' she said quietly. 'But there's nothing there to help you with all this . . .' She waved her hand, encompassing the cottage. 'I don't know what the hell is going on, I promise you.'

He allowed himself a smile. 'You are half right except that I wasn't thinking of the case.'

'Are you going to give me a lift into town or not?' Sarah Brandon demanded. 'And tell your boss I will expect adequate compensation for all my worry and stress.'

'I'd better go.' Lowri grimaced and caught a half-suppressed smile on Lainey's face.

Sarah climbed into the back seat of the car and Lowri was aware of the heaviness of the woman's perfume.

'Drive carefully, now, I'm a nervous passenger.'

Lowri felt like telling her she would drive any way she chose and if Mrs Brandon did not like it she could walk back to town.

As she negotiated the lanes Lowri felt a sense of pleasant warmth. She was sure Lainey liked her, she could see it in his eyes, hear it in the way he spoke. But then was that his official 'bedside' manner, the one he adopted with everyone? Soon, the roads broadened and Lowri heard Sarah Brandon sigh with relief.

She dropped her at the entrance to a small hotel on the edge of Jersey Marine. Sarah walked into the hotel foyer without so much as a glance at Lowri over her shoulder.

'Thank you too, Mrs Brandon,' Lowri sighed, putting the car into gear. She was just about to drive away when she saw a man go in through the double doors of the hotel. Lowri frowned. From the back the man looked exactly like her stepfather. But what would Charles Richards be doing in Jersey Marine? Lowri shook her head; she must be mistaken. When she returned to the office, Sally was holding the telephone to her ear.

'Excuse me, madam,' she said quickly, 'I'm going to have to get back to you on that one.' She replaced the receiver and looked at Lowri, waiting for an explanation.

'The place in Plunch Lane has been burgled and Sarah Brandon is bleating about compensation.'

'Why would anyone want to burgle a holiday home?' Sally asked.

'Don't ask me.' Lowri sank into her chair, her head resting in her hands. 'I wish to God I had never got involved with Jon Brandon. The man's brought me nothing but trouble and heartache.'

'Oh, you'll get over it,' Sally said brashly. 'Think of it like this, Jon was just another man and men are ten a penny.'

'By the way,' Lowri said casually, 'Sarah Brandon found some of your undies in the bungalow and the receipt that went with them. You do have a Visa card don't you, Sally?'

Sally put her hand to her mouth. 'Oh my

Lord!' she said. 'I must have left my shopping bag at Plunch Lane when I was there a few days ago.'

'You were over there, why?' Lowri asked.

'I had to take a copy of the lease Jon Brandon took out — his wife wanted to see it. There was some question about overlapping rent or something.' She looked at Lowri. 'Ask Mr Watson if you don't believe me.'

Suddenly Lowri was tired of being suspicious of everyone. 'I believe you, Sally. Come on, let's go out for a bite to eat. My treat.'

Sally did not have to be asked twice. She swung her jacket off the hook and slipped her arms into the sleeves.

'About time you cheered up,' she said, 'I was sick of seeing you with a long face. There's plenty more fish in the sea, just remember that.'

'Oh, I will.' Lowri smiled. She was thinking of a very special fish, but that was something she intended to keep to herself. She might feel she had to trust Sally, but she did not trust her that much.

As the two girls stepped out of the building, a fire-engine sped past them with the siren blaring. 'Busy chaps, hunky too!'

Sally stood and waved to one of the men

in the cab and he waved back.

'You are a terrible flirt, Sal,' Lowri said, laughing in spite of herself.

'Well, why not, it's what makes the world go around, isn't it?'

7

It was cold in the hospital corridor and dark after the brightness outside. Lowri, dwarfed by Lainey and his sergeant, felt a sense of unreality as she walked towards a set of double doors leading to the mortuary.

'Had we been able to contact Mrs Brandon, she would have been here and not you.' Lainey glanced sideways at her. 'Did you know the place in Plunch Lane has burned down?'

'No. Right now I don't care. Just let's get this over.' Lowri was surprised at the calmness of her voice. Inside, she was trembling.

'He isn't a pretty sight,' Lainey said, 'the body has been in the water for days.'

Lowri swallowed hard. She felt ill suddenly, as if the walls were closing in on her. She looked at Lainey.

'If it is Jon, what then?'

'It's too early to say. The results of the postmortem will be crucial, of course.'

'All right, let's get it over with.'

If she had thought the corridor cold, then the mortuary was like the grave. Not a happy comparison but already Lowri was shivering, partly with cold but mostly with fear. A white-shrouded figure lay on a slab and Lowri bit her lip. 'I'm sorry,' she said, 'I don't think I can go through with it.'

She stood beside the body with Lainey hovering near, watching her reaction. The young sergeant stood back as if to dissociate himself from the proceedings.

Lowri began to feel panic building up within her; she was dreading the moment when she might look into the dead face of the man she had loved. *Had,* was it really the past tense? Did love die so quickly? 'I'm ready,' she said.

The covering was drawn aside and Lowri stepped back a pace. The smell of death hit her like a blow. The face she saw was bloated; there were no eyes, just empty sockets. The mouth was unrecognizable, the lips eaten away. Lowri wanted to vomit. She forced herself to look at the hair which had settled into clumps like matted yellow wool.

'It's not him.' The bile rose to her throat. She felt darkness pressing in on her and arms caught her as she passed out. She regained consciousness to find herself seated on a chair in the corridor. Lainey was holding a glass to her lips.

'I'm sorry,' he said, 'but it had to be done.'

He watched as she sipped the water. 'How can you be so certain that wasn't Jon Brandon?'

'The hair mainly and the shape of him. The physique was all wrong.' She glanced away. 'After all, I did know him intimately.'

'Anything else? If so, you must tell me now,' Lainey did not look at her. She swallowed some water. She was certain that the corpse was not the man she had laughed with, had lain with, had loved.

Tears blurred her vision. Why had he deceived her? Why had Jon Brandon turned out to be a man leading a double life?

'The hands were wrong, what was left of them,' she said. 'They were too large.' She shook her head. 'I'm certain that man in there is not Jon Brandon. Now, can I go home?'

He drove her to the house himself and waited while she unlocked the door.

'Come in,' she said, 'if you can spare the time, that is.'

Lainey followed her across the hall and went straight through to the kitchen. She heard him switch on the kettle and soon the hum of boiling water and a fragrant aroma told her that he was making coffee. She almost smiled; he was as bad as Sally. Coffee, the panacea for all ills.

He returned to the room with two mugs and handed one to her. She sat in the window alcove and leaned against the wooden panels.

'I'm sorry, Lowri,' he said. 'I had to find out if you were lying to me.'

She shuddered, seeing that man, that corpse, trying not to throw up at the stink, had made her realize that Jon might really be dead. 'You were testing me? How could you, Jim? Didn't you think it might tip me over the edge?'

'I did hope that the shock of seeing the corpse might make you slip up in some way. But I would never wish you to go over the edge. A breakdown is a terrible thing.'

'Speaking from experience?'

'I might be.' He moved towards her and crouched down so that his face was on a level with hers. 'Look, I really think you should get out of this place for a while, and stay somewhere else in the neighbourhood. This has all the wrong memories, you surely must see that?'

'Oh, yes,' she said. 'All the wrong memories.' She sipped the coffee but the sweetness made her feel sick. She put the mug on the floor. 'Perhaps I will go away from here, move out of Jersey Marine for good.'

'I don't think that would be advisable, not

just now.' Lainey's voice was mild. She nodded, grimacing a little.

'If you think Jon is dead then are you saying that I am a suspect?'

'Too early to say anything of the kind.' He rose to his feet and moved to the door; his hand on the latch, he looked back at her. 'For what it's worth I think Jon Brandon is very much alive. I mean to solve this puzzle, to find out exactly what is going on and my first step is to find out where Mrs Brandon has taken herself off to.' He let himself out and, as the door closed, Lowri resisted the urge to run after him.

She got to her feet and went upstairs to the bathroom; she realized she was nervous of being alone. She switched on the light over the mirror and applied some blusher to her cheeks. She would go out, perhaps do a bit of shopping. She could not bear to go back to the office to face questions from Sally.

The weather was cooler now; the sun had disappeared behind the clouds. Soon the leaves would turn red, then fall. Summer was coming to an end. She drove into the High Street and parked the car and began to stroll along the road, pausing now and then to look in the shop windows. She caught sight of her reflection and saw a pale, thin stranger. Perhaps she should grow her hair, find herself a new image. Her life with Jon was over for good and she must just make the best of it.

'Lowri not in?' Mr Watson stood in the doorway and Sally looked up at him, hastily pushing her nail-polish bottle out of sight.

'She had to go somewhere with the police, Mr Watson, they came when you were out.'

Mr Watson grunted. 'I would very much like to know what's going on around here, Sally. Why are the police hounding Lowri?'

'Well sir, you must know that her boyfriend Jon Brandon's gone missing. The police have found a body and they want Lowri to do the identity thing.'

'Damn nerve!' Mr Watson said. 'She should have called me.' He put his finger to his glasses. 'And where in heaven's name is Mrs Brandon? She made enough fuss about being compensated for the break-in at the cottage.' He sighed. 'Goodness knows what she'll try to claim now that the place has burnt down.'

'I don't know,' Sally said. 'Perhaps the cops . . . the police thought it better to take Lowri.'

The phone rang and Sally picked it up, hoping that her freshly applied nail polish would not smudge. 'It's the police.' She mouthed the words at Mr Watson and he pursed his lips in disapproval. After a few minutes, she put down the receiver and sighed heavily.

'What now?' Mr Watson asked.

Sally shrugged. 'They want to see you, Mr Watson, they want you to go to the police station to answer some questions about the Brandons' tenancy.'

'Well ring them back, Sally, and tell them they must come here if they want to see me. I'm not going running at their beck and call, I'm a busy man.'

She made the call and passed on Mr Watson's message. Satisfied, he nodded and returned to his office. As soon as he was gone, Sally dialled Lowri's number but there was no answer. Where could she be, had the police taken her into custody, perhaps? Well, there was nothing she could do about it. Opening her drawer, Sally pulled out the details of the cottages in Plunch Lane. She studied the sheet for some time before scribbling some words in the margin. Then she put the paper away again and sat back in her chair, smiling. Things were working out very well, very well indeed.

Lowri sat in the small waiting-room

staring at the magazines lying on the coffee-table. She could not believe she was in Summer's Dean, in yet another hospital. A nurse hurried past, a covered tray in her hand, and Lowri shuddered. She wanted to ask how her mother was but everyone seemed so busy.

Almost as soon as she had returned from shopping the phone had rung. It was her stepfather. 'You'd better come down here,' he said without preliminaries. 'Your mother has been taken to St Mary's in Summer's Dean.'

'What's wrong, what's happened to her?' Lowri clutched the phone as if she could extract information from it.

'How do I know? I'm not a doctor.' Charles was his usual graceless self. 'Just get here as soon as you can.'

She had thrown some clothes into an overnight bag and driven out of Jersey Marine without stopping to let anyone know. Two hours later she was at St Mary's, no wiser than she had been when she left home.

This was turning out to be some day. First there had been the awful visit to the mortuary and now she was at another hospital, surrounded by the sights and smells of sickness.

A rough-looking man in an anorak heaved

his way into the room and sat down opposite her. She averted her gaze quickly, he had obviously been crying.

'Miss Richards,' a nurse appeared at her side, 'you can go in to see your mother now. Room three, down the corridor on the right.'

Rhian Richards was in a private room, at least Charles had managed that much. She was lying against the pillows, an oxygen mask over her face. Her eyes were open and she was trying her best to smile.

Lowri sat beside the bed. 'How are you feeling, Mother? No, silly question, don't bother to answer it.' She took Rhian's hand, noticing how slender her fingers were. Her mother really needed to take better care of herself.

'The gas fire,' Rhian whispered, 'carbon monoxide poisoning. An accident.' She closed her eyes for a moment. 'Don't blame Charles, he was away. It was my own fault.'

'Mummy!' Lowri said. 'You always make excuses for him. He should have seen to it that the fires were checked.'

Rhian shook her head and Lowri dropped the subject. It was pointless to blame Charles — her mother would always defend him.

'I'll stay at the house for a few days,' she

said. 'I could do with a break from work anyway.' She smiled. 'I'll have to make a few phone calls, let people know where I am, but it won't hurt me to have a rest, will it?'

Her mother struggled to sit up. 'What about your job, Lowri?'

Lowri frowned. 'Don't worry, Mother, there's more here to consider than my job. You are much more important and I want to be with you.'

Rhian patted her hand. The door opened and a nurse bustled in. 'I think Mrs Richards should rest now.'

Lowri nodded and got to her feet. 'I'll come back tomorrow morning,' she said and, with a last glance at her mother, left the room.

When Lowri returned to the Grange she could see that Charles was home. His brand-new Mercedes was parked directly in front of the double doors to the hall, and Lowri scowled as she manoeuvred her way past the gleaming vehicle.

Charles was in the library, drinking his habitual glass of whisky in front of the ornate gas fire. No doubt he had seen to it that all the chimneys were swept and all the appliances checked now that it was almost too late.

'How is she?' His question was casual, as if her mother simply had a cold.

'As well as can be expected after being almost suffocated.' Lowri threw down her jacket. 'Want a cup of tea? I'm going to make one.' She offered more out of politeness than because she expected Charles to accept.

'Wouldn't mind some dinner,' he said. 'Anything in the fridge you can throw together?'

Lowri stared at him. 'It is allowed for men to cook these days, Charles.' The edge of anger she was feeling was in her voice.

Charles put down his glass and pushed himself up from the chair. 'Don't bother!' he said huffily. 'I'll go out and get something.'

The front door slammed and Lowri heard the Mercedes being gunned into life. Charles treated his cars the way he treated his women: he had no respect for either. Lowri made some tea and sat in the kitchen at the scrubbed pine table that had been her grandmother's.

She made a phone call to Sally. She was out, so Lowri left a brief message. She really should call Lainey, but he could enquire at the office if he needed to get in touch.

She sighed, wishing Charles a million

miles away. In Canada perhaps, with her brother. Charles had never been good enough for her mother. When had Lowri begun to hate him? Was it after the hundredth time she had seen her mother crying over his affairs? Or was it when he had first slapped Lowri across the face for what he called her impudence?

She had burst into their bedroom once when they were quarrelling and Charles had been holding her mother by her hair. He did not see her at first.

'Just remember, madam,' he was saying venomously, 'you accuse me of having other women but at least I haven't brought any bastards home to roost.' He looked up then and saw Lowri's shocked face.

'Yes, that's right, girl.' His tone was vicious. 'You are a bastard, do you know what that means? You are illegitimate, a nothing.'

Lowri had run back to her own room and begun packing her clothes. Her mother had followed her and held her close and told her she loved her so much that life would be impossible without her. So Lowri had stayed. Until she went to university in Cardiff.

She had embarked on a law degree intending to become a solicitor or even a barrister. It was Charles who put a stop to her university career. He had come up to Cardiff for a dinner to honour one of the retiring masters. Her mother was ill and had stayed at home.

Lowri lifted her cup to her mouth, remembering the agony of the embarrassment Charles had caused her. He had made a pass at one of the lecturer's wives and had his face soundly slapped for his pains. The evening had ended with a drunken Charles being forcibly ejected from the hall.

The next day Lowri gave up her course and, because she had nowhere else to go, went home to Summer's Dean. Charles, far from being contrite, ranted and raged at her for being a fool. She knew that she could not stay at home, not while he was living there, so once her mother was well, Lowri began to look for work.

It was through a family connection that she got a job with Watson Jones and Fry, and Mr Watson had taken her under his wing. He was a kindly man with a face like a cherub, and Lowri established a rapport with him almost right away.

She looked around her; she might as well go to bed. She would stay in Summer's Dean only long enough to make sure her mother had fully recovered from the accident and then she would go back home.

Home? Did she have a home? She suddenly felt rootless, the nobody that Charles constantly told her she was. Perhaps it was time she began to think like an independent woman. She had relied on Jon, believed in him, thought she would marry him. He had made a fool out of her, no doubt about that. Well, to hell with Jon, and to hell with all men. Lowri would sort out her own life, make her own way in the world.

She got up and looked in the pine-framed mirror on the wall. 'I am the master of my fate: I am the captain of my soul,' she recited and slowly a smile crept around her lips.

'That's better,' she told her reflection. 'Life is for living and it's about time I realized that.'

It was in a cheerful mood that she snuggled down into bed. She fell asleep immediately but woke abruptly, sweating, frightened. The dream had come again. The masked man had held her under the water. She had felt the coldness wrap around her, the dread fill her heart and mind.

Lowri put her hands over her face and began to cry.

8

'So, Jon Brandon's business is booming.' DI
Lainey leaned over the desk and studied the
computer screen. 'Lucky man. Print it out,
Sergeant, I can't "see" it properly until I have
it in black and white.'

Sergeant Brown clicked a few buttons and
the printer began to hum into life before de-
livering several sheets of paper in rapid suc-
cession.

Lainey waited until the last sheet spewed
from the mouth of the printer and then
picked them all up. They felt warm; the machine had been working overtime this
morning. 'Right, I'll take these into my office and have a good look at them.'

He closed his door and threw the sheaf
of papers on his desk. The pristine rows of
figures stood out black and bold. Lainey
sat down, wishing he had thought to ask
for some coffee. Figures gave him a headache; he was not the most numerate of
men.

He studied the pages before him and,
even to the most untutored eye, it was

clear that Jon Brandon was doing very well for himself. Why then would he disappear?

He ran his finger along the columns and saw that the rent for the cottage in Plunch Lane was fully paid up. He checked the figures before him again: Brandon was a suspiciously wealthy man.

It was all extremely odd. He grimaced; he never trusted 'odd'. There had to be a logical explanation for everything. He marked the sums of money deposited in the business in the last few months. They were random and varying in size, but they all added up to quite a substantial amount.

Brandon's business was supposed to be importing and exporting computer software, not the most lucrative of ventures unless you struck it lucky. There was too much competition from the big boys for that. Even customized software for expanding companies abroad would not make anyone a fortune. Unless . . .

'Damn and blast!' Lainey pushed his chair away from the desk and stood up, running his fingers through his hair. 'Why didn't I think of it before?' He picked up his jacket and left the station. His brain was buzzing. The mystery was beginning to unravel — just a little.

'There, Mother, we're home.' Lowri helped her mother from the car and led her up the steps to the Grange. 'I wish you would have come up to stay with me, if only for a few days.'

'No, darling, my place is here in my own home.' Rhian smiled at Lowri. 'And for all Charles pontificates and fusses, this is still *my* home in my name. One day it will be yours, Lowri.'

Lowri did not want the house; she would never live in it. The Grange held too many bad memories for her.

'Thank goodness Charles is in Canada on business. Perhaps he'll even have time to visit Justin.' Rhian Richards's voice was still hoarse. 'Now we're on our own we can have a good old natter.'

Lowri settled her mother in the sitting-room and put one of the throws from the sofa over her legs. Charles had always favoured his son. 'Justin is Charles's two eyes,' she said dryly. 'He always did give him anything he wanted.'

'It's getting cold,' Rhian changed the subject, 'but I think the fires are safe enough now.'

'Yes, Charles made sure that he wouldn't be poisoned,' Lowri said. 'I just don't trust him. Tell you what, I'll cook us something quick, shall I? A few eggs, scrambled or poached perhaps?'

'Lovely.' Rhian looked tired. She was almost fifty but usually looked much younger. But now she had circles under her eyes and her hair was showing some of the grey that she normally took great care to conceal.

Lowri busied herself in the kitchen and soon had a pot of tea, some toast and a dish of scrambled eggs ready on a tray. She padded across the hall to the sitting-room and heard her mother's voice. Rhian was speaking to someone on the phone.

As Lowri pushed open the door with her foot, she caught sight of her mother's face. Rhian looked like a young girl in love. Her cheeks were flushed and her eyes were shining. 'Must go,' she said hastily and replaced the receiver.

'Who was that, you dark horse?' Lowri said teasingly. Her mother smiled.

'Just a friend.'

'All right, if you don't want to tell I won't make you. Now come on, eat some of this, put some flesh back on your bones.'

It was cosy sitting together with the silence of the old house around them. The place had always been peaceful when Charles was not there.

'How are you getting on at work?' Rhian asked, biting into a slice of toast. 'I mean, is it enough for you being a clerk in a solicitor's office when once you hoped to qualify yourself?'

'Mr Watson is very good to me — look how well he's taken my unexpected absence. He hasn't got Sally to ring up and demand I get back to work. He's the kindest boss I'm ever likely to find.'

'So you're happy there?' Rhian asked.

'Yes, I am happy there but I don't know if it's for ever, Mum,' Lowri said. 'I sometimes think I would like to go back to college but then, college costs money these days, a lot of money.'

'Well I have plenty, Lowri, and what good is it doing in the bank?'

Lowri shook her head. 'No, I want to make my own way, just like everyone else.'

'I don't know, young people today, you are so independent. In my day it was accepted that parents helped their children through college.'

'Well, things are different now, Mother, people of my age group don't expect hand-outs, we have to make our own way in the world.'

'Ah well, I suppose that's progress of sorts.' Rhian ate a small piece of toast. 'By

141

the way, Lowri, have you heard any more about that boyfriend of yours?'

Lowri shook her head. 'No, Mum, I haven't. I don't really want to talk about it either.'

Rhian held up her hand. 'All right, that's fine by me. I don't want to pry. Let's talk about something else, shall we?' She smiled. 'Before you go back I am going to insist you take a cheque I've written out for you; get yourself some new clothes or something.'

'OK, if it will make you feel better.' Lowri laughed. 'You see, I do what I'm told, sometimes.'

Rhian grimaced. 'Aye, you're a good girl, I'm lucky to have such a wonderful daughter.'

'And I have an equally wonderful mother, so let's cut the mutual admiration crap and talk about just what sort of clothes I'm going to buy with your money.'

It was several days later when Charles returned home. The peace of the house was shattered as soon as he came in the front door. The way he spoke to her mother set Lowri's teeth on edge and she knew it was high time she went home.

The drive was pleasant enough; she had the motorway virtually to herself. The time passed quite happily with Lowri listening to music and thinking about Lainey.

For once, she was able to park the Mazda outside the door of her house. She felt hot and sticky; she was really looking forward to a cool shower. As she closed the door on the outside world, Lowri rested her head against the wooden panel and sighed with relief.

She kicked off her shoes on the way to the kitchen and filled the kettle. She could murder a cup of coffee. She made herself some, and a sandwich, and sat down in the kitchen, glad to be home.

She must have dozed because the sound of a bell ringing jangled into her sleep and she sat up, aware that her coffee was cold and her sandwich untouched.

'Come in, Jim.' She stood aside for him to enter. He looked at her neat skirt and tanned legs and then at her tousled hair, but he said nothing.

'What can I do for you?' she asked, needing to break the silence. He perched on the edge of the table.

'Answer some questions. Firstly why did you run off without telling me?'

'I did tell you. Well, in a way. I phoned Sally at the office and told her to make my excuses to you all.' She shook her head. 'My mother was in hospital, she needed me down at Summer's Dean, what was I supposed to do?'

'Your message never got through to me. Mother all right now?'

'Yes, she's fine. She should just look after herself, that's all.'

'You look tired, feel up to answering some questions?'

'I'll do my best though I seem incapable of rational thought these days,' she said. 'The more I search my mind the worse everything becomes. But go on, shoot. I'll do my best.'

'What did you know about Jon Brandon's business?' He was wearing a light jacket and his white collar was pristine. He looked very handsome and very remote.

'Not much,' she said. 'He sold parts for computers, something like that.'

Lainey moved from the table to stand in the window, the set of his shoulders revealing that he was not as relaxed as he pretended to be.

'Why, Jim? Is it important?'

He turned to look at her. 'Would you say that he was spending a lot of money on you?'

She blinked rapidly. 'Jon was always generous, I'll give him that. Just before . . . well, before he vanished he bought me a beautiful

144

diamond ring as well as offering to treat me to a weekend at the Swan. I thought that meant we were engaged. What a fool!'

She wondered if it was worth mentioning her suspicions that Jon had been to the hotel with Sally but dismissed the idea, it all sounded most unconvincing.

'What is it?'

She shrugged; he was more perceptive than she had given him credit for. 'When I went back there, to the hotel, the receptionist recognized the scarf I had on.'

He frowned. 'So?'

'So, it wasn't my scarf, I've never worn it before.'

'Whose is it?'

'It belongs to Sally from the office.' Lowri shook her head. 'Look, I may be barking up entirely the wrong tree but Sally had been there, the description of her long blonde hair and the bright nail polish she wears was spot on.'

'And her companion looked like Jon Brandon.' It was not a question.

'How did you know?'

He smiled. 'You wouldn't be so worried if she had been there with her boyfriend, Timmy whatsit.' He stood and moved away, leaning against the wall, looking at her.

'That makes sense,' Lowri said.

'It's elementary, my dear Watson.' Lainey's smile widened. 'Watson, that's the name of your employer, isn't it?'

'You know it is. Why?'

'Nothing. Just checking.'

'Can I make you a cup of coffee?' she asked.

'No thanks. Just one more question. Are you sure Jon Brandon never left anything in your keeping? CDs, perhaps?'

She shook her head. 'No, nothing.'

He nodded. 'Right then. I'll be in touch.'

She watched as he walked away down the street in the sunlight. She wanted to call after him, to ask him to come back; she needed to talk to him. He turned the corner and was out of sight.

It was early next morning when the phone rang, startling Lowri from her sleep. She reached over and picked up the receiver and heard Sally's pleading voice.

'Lowri, are you coming into work today? I really need you.'

'Yes, I'll be there Sally, but it's barely seven thirty!'

'I know but you have to come in as soon as possible.'

'Why? What's wrong?'

'I'll tell you when you get here. Just come, that's all.'

'All right, I'll come at once if it's that desperate.'

Lowri did not bother with breakfast. She swallowed a cup of coffee, showered and then pulled on a dark green blouse, her grey skirt and matching jacket.

Sally was in reception talking on the telephone when Lowri walked in. She quickly replaced the receiver and rose from her chair.

'I'm trying to do two jobs at once here!' she said. 'When are we going to get the new receptionist old Watson promised us?'

'Don't ask me. Now, what's going on?'

'Give me a chance to catch my breath and I'll tell you!' Sally's face was shiny, she appeared harassed. This time it was Lowri who suggested making coffee. Sally nodded eagerly and followed Lowri into the back office, watching as Lowri spooned sugar into the two mugs.

'Tell me,' Lowri said. 'What on earth is the panic?'

The door rattled and swung open, letting in a gust of wind that had a definite touch of autumn chill about it. 'I'll go,' Lowri said but Sally followed her into reception. Sarah Brandon was standing there.

'Mrs Brandon, we've been trying to get in touch with you,' Lowri said.

'That's the panic.' Sally mouthed the words.

'And I have been trying to contact you!' Sarah Brandon's eyes were cold. 'I understand you viewed a corpse that was thought to be that of my dead husband. How dare you!'

Lowri felt as if she had been punched. 'The police wanted to find you.' She heard the defensive note in her voice. 'But they couldn't so I had to go to the mortuary instead of you.'

'That's right, Mrs Brandon, I can vouch for that,' Sally said.

'Be quiet!' Sarah glared at Sally. 'You are as guilty as she is. You slept with him, too. Don't bother to lie, he gave his favours to anything that caught his fancy.'

She stared down at Lowri. 'Well, now are you happy? Now you have got what you wanted out of Jon?'

'I don't know what you mean.' Lowri was confused by the abrupt turn the conversation had taken. 'Have you seen Jon?'

'Of course not but before he vanished Jon gave you a package to look after for him, that's what I mean, and I want it back. The contents are valuable to me.'

'Valuable? Jon never gave me anything that was really valuable, like the truth.'

'Don't play games with me. Where have you hidden it?'

'Hidden what?' Lowri was growing exasperated.

Sarah pulled open a drawer and tipped the contents onto the floor. 'I'll find it, if it kills me!'

'Stop it this minute!' Lowri was surprised at the fierceness of her own voice, 'I would advise you to calm down, Mrs Brandon, before you find yourself in trouble with the police.'

Sarah glared at her. 'I just want what's mine. You've already slept with my husband — you are not having his business too!'

'I don't want anything to do with him or his business. Now please leave.' Lowri picked up the telephone and Sarah held up her hand.

'All right, I'm leaving.' She pushed the papers on Lowri's desk onto the floor. 'But I shall fight you, I shall have what is mine. Eventually.' She left the office, slamming the door behind her. Lowri sank back into her chair.

'What was all that about?' she said.

Sally shrugged. 'Don't ask me!' She shook her head. 'She phoned me at home last night wanting your number, and when I wouldn't give it she threatened all sorts of things. She finally shrieked down the phone that she would be here first thing. But then she's a nutter, isn't she? You can't believe a word she says.'

Lowri picked up her bag and paused, looking directly at Sally. 'Have you ever stayed at the Swan Hotel?'

Sally glanced up. 'You asked me that once before. It's the one that's on the cliffs over-looking the sea, isn't it?'

'That's right.'

'I remember now, I did stay there once.' Sally looked down at her hands, frowning as she saw a tiny chip in the varnish on one of her nails. 'Dash! I'll have to do that one again.'

'Who did you go there with?' Lowri tried to sound casual. Sally's head was bent and it was difficult to see her expression.

'With Timmy.'

That was a lie. The description the recep-tionist had given Lowri was of a man, not a young lad like Timmy.

'Why are you lying?'

Sally's head jerked up. Her eyes were wide, startled, the colour was rising in her cheeks. 'Why should I lie?'

'Look,' Lowri said, 'I know you were there with an older man than Timmy, a man with dark hair. Was it Jon Brandon? Tell me, Sally, I must know.'

'You're mistaken, I've never been there with an older man and definitely not with Jon Brandon.'

'You were seen,' Lowri persisted, 'with a man who fitted Jon's description. Come on, Sally, what's going on, were you sleeping with him too? Sarah seems to think so.'

'No!' Sally said fiercely. 'You're crazy, Lowri. Whoever you talked to, they were wrong. All this is going to your head. Do you think you ought to see someone, a doctor or something?'

It was quite a long speech for Sally. Lowri rubbed her eyes. Perhaps she *was* going mad — it certainly seemed like it at the moment. She picked up her keys.

'Sod it! I'm going home,' she said. 'And I may never come back.' On the way out, she almost collided with Mr Watson.

'Good heavens, Lowri, what's wrong? Not bad news about your mother, I hope?'

'No, nothing like that. I came in to help Sally but I think I've done all I can so I'm going home. Is that all right?'

He touched her cheek. 'Of course it's all right. Off you go with my blessing.'

Lowri climbed into the Mazda, slammed the door behind her and drove as if the furies of hell were at her heels. She would go home and call Lainey, tell him that Sarah

Brandon was back in town and he had better see her before she did anything foolish.

Sergeant Brown answered the phone. 'Detective Inspector Lainey is in a meeting,' he said. 'But I'll tell him you called.'

Lowri put down the phone. Why was it men were never around when you needed them most?

9

Lowri woke late the next morning. Her head ached and she had never felt less like work. She was disappointed that Lainey had not got back to her the previous day and she badly wanted to talk to him, but she was damned if she was going to call him again. She came downstairs yawning sleepily just as the thump of the mail on the mat told her the postman had arrived. Almost immediately the bell rang and, rubbing her eyes, Lowri opened the door.

'One to sign for, love.' The postman held out a pen and she signed her name. 'Here's your letter then, hope it's something nice.'

Probably not, Lowri thought grumpily. Morning was never her best time. She left the envelope in the hall and made herself coffee. Just as she sat down the phone rang.

'No peace for the wicked,' Lowri grumbled to herself. It was Sally. 'She's been here again, accusing you of all sorts.'

'I suppose you mean Sarah Brandon?'

'Of course I mean Sarah Brandon. She's

saying that Jon left you a fortune.'

'How does she make that out?'

'I don't know, do I? But that detective has been here too, he wants to talk to you. I rang to warn you he's on his way now.'

'Shit!' Lowri caught sight of her reflection in the mirror. She looked a sight with her hair, longer now, tousled around her pale morning face. Perhaps she would just have time to shower. The rapping on the door told her she was too late.

'Come in,' she said reluctantly.

Lainey had his sergeant in tow and the two men stood in the hall, blocking out the light from the doorway.

'My neighbours must be having a field day!' Lowri said bitterly. 'Come through into the kitchen and if either of you want a coffee there's the tap and there's the kettle. You must be as at home here now as I am!'

She sat on one of the kitchen chairs and looked up at Lainey. 'You've heard this stupid nonsense about Jon giving me a valuable package, I take it?'

'That's right.' Lainey sounded distant. 'What can you tell us about it?'

'Absolutely nothing. All Jon left me with was egg on my face.'

'Well, Mrs Brandon seemed sure of her facts.'

'Really? I don't think that poor lady is even sure of her own name.' Lowri shrugged. 'But search the place if you like. I have nothing to hide. In any case, I thought you believed Jon was still alive, so why don't you find him and leave me alone?'

'I might have been wrong,' Lainey said. 'Those things on the hall table, today's letters are they?'

'Yes, why?'

'Mind if I take a look?'

'Well, I don't know about that.'

Lainey seemed not to hear her. He went into the hall and she heard him tearing open envelopes. He returned waving the letter she had signed for. 'And here it is.'

He leaned against the sink and read the document through. 'According to this, you are a partner in Brandon's latest business venture, a company called Software International. Have you got a computer here, Miss Richards?'

She shook her head. 'Never heard of the company and no, I don't have a home computer.'

'There must be records of Software International's financial transactions somewhere. Have you got them?'

'No.'

'Come on, I think you know more about

Jon Brandon's disappearance than you are telling us.'

'Rubbish!'

'Do you mind if I sit down?' Lainey did not wait for a reply.

Lowri shrugged her shoulders. 'Make yourself at home.' Her sarcasm was not lost on him. 'You too, Sergeant.'

The sergeant perched on the edge of an upright chair. 'Did Mr Brandon ever talk about business to you, Miss Richards?'

'No Sergeant Brown, he didn't.'

'Why not, if you were so close?' Lainey asked.

'I don't know why not. I suppose it never occurred to me to talk about his bank balance, that's all.'

Lainey leaned forward, his arms resting on his knees. 'Are you sure he never left anything with you, a file perhaps?'

'I've told you. Search the place, go through everything I've got, you won't find anything of Jon's here.'

'Did you ever go abroad with Brandon, on a holiday perhaps?'

'No, I have to work for a living or have you forgotten?' Lowri pushed back her hair. 'Look, I'm sick and tired of this. Are you going to charge me with anything?'

'You are just helping us with our inquiries.' Lainey spoke dryly. 'I thought you wanted to find Jon Brandon as much as we did.'

'I've helped you all I can.' Lowri did not say that she could not care less whether they found Jon or not. He was a married man, he had made a fool of her and the sooner she was allowed to forget he ever existed, the better she would be pleased.

Lainey got to his feet. 'Can we look around or do you want the formality of a search warrant?'

'Feel free. I've told you before, I've got nothing to hide.' She walked to the door. 'Is it all right by you if I take a shower? You can search the bathroom later if you like.'

'We'll look there first,' Lainey said.

She shook her head. 'I don't believe this, not any of it. What on earth could I be hiding that would be of any value to anyone?'

Laincy did not answer and she sat there in the small kitchen, listening to the sounds of opening drawers and banging doors. Suddenly she was angry.

'Mr Lainey!' she called up the stairs. 'As soon as I'm dressed I'm going to see a solicitor. I've had enough of being harassed by the police.'

'That might be the best thing you could do,' he called back, and Lowri bit her lip. It sounded as if she was in serious trouble. Why was Lainey being so arrogant and suspicious suddenly?

The search of the house was completed quite quickly and Lowri slammed the front door the minute Lainey and his sergeant stepped outside. She had thought she could trust the detective to look out for her, and here he was treating her like a criminal.

Later, as she walked into the office, Lowri saw that Sally was sitting at her desk. 'Taking my place already, are you?' Her tone was icy.

'No,' Sally appeared flustered, 'Mr Watson wanted a file and I thought you might have it in your desk.'

It sounded reasonable enough and Lowri was suddenly ashamed. Sally was not the brightest of people but she was very kind.

'Sorry to be a grump.' She sat on the edge of the desk. 'Look, shall we go out tonight? We could go down to the pub or something.'

Sally's face brightened. 'That would be lovely. Don't bring your car, we'll pick you up, Timmy and me. Half seven be OK?'

'It's a date. Will you phone through to Mr Watson, ask him can he spare me a few minutes?'

Sally obliged and Lowri heard her boss agreeing at once to see her.

'I'm sorry, Mr Watson,' she said as she entered his cluttered office, 'I think I am going to need help.'

He lifted his spectacles; without them he looked more like a benign cherub than ever. 'Then you have come to the right place.'

As briefly as possible Lowri outlined what had been happening. 'So the police seem to think that I am an accomplice in whatever it is Jon has done.'

'Well, we can't have that, can we? What is this detective's name?'

Lowri hesitated. 'I don't want to make trouble for him. Up until now he's been very kind.'

'His name?' Mr Watson insisted.

'Lainey, Detective Inspector Lainey.'

He picked up the phone and dialled a number. 'I want to speak to Detective Inspector Lainey and I want to speak to him right now, please.' He nodded.

'Yes, I am Watson from Watson Jones and Fry and this is a police matter,' He winked at Lowri and put his hand over the mouthpiece of the phone. 'The police hate solicitors and what they don't realize is it's mutual. Hello?' He listened for a moment and then spoke again.

'I want all inquiries about Miss Richards to be channelled through me in future. Well, when you have this evidence we'll talk again. Good day to you.'

'There my dear, that settles that. These police will take advantage if you don't know your rights. Now take the day off, you look all in.'

Lowri had a coffee with Sally and then left the office. She took a deep breath of air, wondering what had become of her life. She had believed she was in love with Jon, had imagined foolishly that he was in love with her. It had all been a sham from start to finish.

The crunch of dried leaves beneath her feet and the unmistakable smell of mist in the air brought with it a feeling of what she could only describe as grieving. She had meant to share the autumn days with Jon. They had even discussed moving in together, sitting at the fireside in winter, making toast and tea, all the things normal couples did together. Now she was alone and she wondered if she would always be alone.

She climbed into the Mazda and negotiated her way out of the tiny car park just as Timmy was pulling in. She waved to him and he waved back. Sally was lucky, Lowri thought, Timmy was the sort of person whom you could trust. She ought to grab him with both hands. She pulled out into the main road and headed for home, ignoring the tears of self-pity that were suddenly rolling down her cheeks.

Lainey studied the papers before him, details of Lowri's bank account. Lately, there had been an influx of funds. Fairly large amounts of money had been deposited at irregular intervals. He only hoped she had some sort of explanation. He sighed. He would just have to talk to her again, bearing in mind she would have her solicitor present. That might prove a nuisance.

He glanced at his watch: it was almost five, Watson Jones and Fry would be closing for the day. He stared out of the window for a moment; perhaps he should knock off early and see her on his way home.

He took his jacket from the back of the chair and left the office. The corridor was quiet, which made a change. Usually the place bristled with eager-beaver young constables.

Once outside, he breathed in deeply of the misty autumnal air; he felt alive, his senses heightened as they always were when he was presented with a particularly difficult case. He could swear that Lowri Richards was innocent of any crime. He had never lost his first impression of her, crouched in a chair at the Swan Hotel, her slim body clad only in the tiny scrap of cloth she called a wrap.

She had looked shocked, her face pale beneath the fall of hair hanging over her eyes. If she knew anything at all about the case she must be the most superb of actresses. And yet . . . and yet.

He sighed and climbed into his car. He had begun slowly to unravel a little of the mystery. He had looked into Jon Brandon's business affairs but even while he found one piece of damning evidence against the man, something else had emerged that seemed to implicate Lowri Richards.

When she let him in, he saw that she had been crying. He sat uneasily on the edge of the table in the sitting-room and cursed his inability to comfort her. She was a suspect in a fraud case, perhaps she was even a murderer. It was very strange that there had been no sign of Brandon after that last night at the Swan.

'I need to talk to you,' he said heavily. She nodded. He noticed her hair was longer now, she was letting it grow. It suited her.

'I guessed as much. You do know you should have gone through my solicitor, don't you?'

'Yes, but I wanted to keep this as informal as possible, that's why I've come alone.' He

162

hesitated, looking down at his hands.

'I understand that there have been a few, shall we say unusual, transactions in your bank account.'

'Really? Then you know more than I do.'

'You do get statements, don't you?'

'Yes, but as there's never much coming in or going out I don't check them regularly.'

'But there has been quite a lot coming in, very large amounts actually. How do you explain it, were you keeping money safe for anyone?'

'Who?' She looked directly at him, her eyes wide with surprise. 'Oh I see. Do you think Jon was paying me for something?'

'I didn't mention Jon Brandon. What about his partner?' It was a long shot and he watched her carefully. She did not flicker so much as an eyelash.

'What partner? I didn't know he had one,' Lowri said angrily. 'I don't know anything about his business or about the money. I don't want any of this. I just want my life to get back to normal!'

'Brandon was supposed to be in the import and export business. I have his phone bills as well as his faxes and e-mails. He communicated a great deal with firms in Europe as well as in the Caribbean. Did you know that much?'

163

'I never asked him about his business and he never volunteered anything,' she said more calmly. 'Though I did get a postcard from him when he was abroad once.'

'Where is it?' He watched her walk to the drawer and rummage through the contents. It was weird how much rubbish women kept for sentimental reasons. She drew out a crumpled postcard and handed it to him. He read the brief message.

'He says we are having a good time. Who is the "we"?'

She shook her head. 'I have no idea. Perhaps it was this business partner you mention.' She smiled a little ruefully. 'In light of what I know now it probably meant him and his wife. At the time I thought it was just a slip of the pen.'

'Ah.' He flipped the card over. The picture was of a spectacular sunset over a beach in Jamaica. It told him nothing.

'What was he doing in Jamaica, could he have been trafficking in drugs do you think?' He watched her face carefully. Was he hoping she would give something away or was he hoping she would not?

Lowri shrugged. 'I hardly think that's likely, do you, Inspector?' Her voice was heavy with sarcasm. 'Jon Brandon was a bastard, a womanizer, perhaps a thief and a liar but I don't see him as a drug smuggler.'

'Anything's possible.' And yet he was inclined to agree with her. He had never met Brandon but his gut feeling told him that the drug idea was too obvious, too easy. But the man had been into something illegal, that was for sure.

'Lowri, have you any idea at all why you should be involved in all this? As I said, someone's paid money into your account. Who would that be?'

'I just don't know.' Lowri looked angry. 'My mother perhaps? In any case, how dare you search through my private account? Isn't that illegal?'

Lainey felt a pang of sympathy. 'Look, I can't go easy on you. I might have to take you down to the station for questioning at some time and no-one will go easy on you there.'

He rubbed his chin. 'This is nothing personal, but you must see you are bound to be under suspicion. After all, you were the last one to see Brandon before he vanished, and his wife seems to think you have something of value hidden away. Can't you help me at all, Lowri?'

She bowed her head and he thought she seemed beaten, but when she looked up at him her face was white with anger.

'Can't you see I'm the fall guy in all this? What happens next, Inspector? Do I meet with a fatal accident and then someone collects whatever it is Jon's hiding? This partner that you mentioned, are you hassling him the way you are me? I doubt it!'

She stormed across the room and stood at the window. He could see her shoulders were shaking. 'I have done nothing wrong and here you are harassing me with stupid questions about the money. Oh, sod it!' She burst into tears and, instinctively, Lainey rose and put his hand on her shoulder. She pushed him away.

'Leave me alone!' She glared at him. 'I have no-one I can trust, I suspect everyone, even silly little Sally. I'm going crazy with all this and you lot, our wonderful police force, are no nearer to solving any of it!'

He thrust his hands into his pockets. She was right; in all truth he had not got very far with the investigation and the weeks were slipping by. If a crime was not cleared up in the first few months of discovery there was little chance of this ever happening.

'Coming back to your bank statements,' he said, 'the amounts paid in tally with the withdrawals from Brandon's account. You must have known about it.'

She looked at him. 'Perhaps Jon wanted to

implicate me in some way but I've told you the truth, I don't know anything.'

'Are you sure, Lowri?' His tone was soft.

She shook her head. 'Want a drink? I need one if you don't.'

He nodded, wondering if she was giving herself time to think. She went into the kitchen and he heard the chink of glasses. He stared around him. If Lowri was innocent, if she was as she claimed the fall guy in all this, she must be going mad. There certainly were no signs of any money being spent on the house. Was she too clever for that?

She returned from the kitchen and placed the glasses carefully on cork coasters. Small drops of wine spilt onto the shiny surface of the table. Lowri wiped them away with her sleeve. He felt pity tug at him; she had lost weight even in the short time he had known her.

'Lowri, look at this from my point of view.' He paused; she seemed intent on her drink. 'Most people check their statements, why didn't you?' He had to ask, though somehow he felt he was betraying her. She drank a little of the wine before answering.

'I'm usually overdrawn. I don't earn very much, you know, office-workers don't usually. So I don't bother to check, I'm just grateful when I don't get any irate letters from the bank manager.' She glanced up. 'But I will certainly go over them now!'

He sighed. 'What I need is a crystal ball,' he said. 'The more I search and dig, the more problems I come up with.' He watched her face. 'What did you think of Jon Brandon's wife?'

She was thrown by his sudden change of tack and was silent for a moment. 'I think Sarah is unbalanced,' she said at last. 'But then who wouldn't be unbalanced with a husband like Jon?' She glanced up at him. 'She has a very poor opinion of him, she thinks Jon has slept with Sally and anyone else he could get into bed. Oh! I just don't know what to think any more.'

'I'd better leave.' He was getting precisely nowhere — all he was doing was upsetting Lowri. As if reading his mind, she put down her drink and crossed the room towards him. 'Please, Jim, can't you help me?'

She seemed near to tears again and, without thinking, he took her in his arms. She leaned against him and briefly, he nestled his chin against her sweet-smelling hair, feeling an ache in his heart.

He moved away from her. He was becoming too involved in all this. Lowri Richards could be having him on a string, how

168

could he tell? He had heard enough lies in his career to know they were most difficult to detect when spoken by a lovely, apparently vulnerable woman.

He patted her shoulder awkwardly. 'I'll do my best to sort it out, I promise,' he said, putting some distance between them.

'I am innocent of any crime, Jim, I promise you.'

'I believe you. Look, I'd better get on. Are you sure there is nothing you can tell me? Anything at all, even the smallest detail might lead to some answers.'

She shook her head helplessly and he nodded. 'OK, I'll speak to you again, as soon as there's anything to report, right?'

She followed him to the door and he felt as though he was leaving her in the lurch. 'Look,' he said, 'I'm in no hurry to get home, what if I take you out to dinner somewhere?'

She looked up at him, her eyes appearing too large for her face. 'Thank you but I can't. Sally and Timmy will be here soon.' She smiled wanly. 'We're going to the pub, they think they're cheering me up. I should be grateful to them really.'

As he left the house, he saw curtains twitching along the road and resisted the urge to put up two fingers. He climbed into the car and headed back home. Home to a house that was empty and cold and very, very lonely.

'You see, you're actually laughing!' Sally was jubilant. 'At least you've got over the miseries for now.'

Lowri did feel good. Ever since Lainey's visit her spirits had risen dramatically. In spite of everything, of all the evidence to the contrary, he seemed to believe in her innocence. Somehow, the thought made her feel much better about the whole sorry mess.

'Some nice talent here tonight,' Sally said. 'Look who's over there.'

Lowri glanced up and saw Sergeant Brown standing near the bar, a pint glass in his hand. There was no sign that Lainey was with him. 'Excuse me a minute,' she said and, ignoring Sally's blank look, crossed the room and tapped the sergeant on the shoulder.

'Sergeant?' she said and he turned abruptly.

'Oh, Miss Richards.'

'Tell me, Sergeant, why should anyone put money into my bank account? I mean what would they gain by it?'

Sergeant Brown looked embarrassed; he smelled strongly of beer. 'I'm off duty,' he said, swaying a little.

'That's all right, this is all unofficial. Just talk to me, tell me why the money is suddenly in my account.'

'Search me.' He smiled blearily. 'But if I were you, I'd get the money out and skip the country.' He swallowed some of his beer.

'What would happen if I did take the money and run? If you've thought of that possibility, don't you think a man like Jon would have thought of it too?'

'Perhaps he knew you better than that.' He turned away slightly. 'Or perhaps the plan is that when the rumpus dies down the two of you will run off into the sunset? On the other hand, perhaps the money in your account was just part of a bigger scam.'

'What about his wife? Why not involve her, why not leave her everything?'

'He didn't want her, did he? He's put you firmly in the driving seat. You have the cash in your bank and shares in this software company he's recently set up.'

'What do you know about the software company?'

'Shit! I shouldn't have said that. Look, Lainey thinks you're innocent and that's good enough for me. He can be a bit of a bastard at times, don't pull his punches, but he's a good cop and an honest one. I'd trust him with my life.'

Lowri digested that in silence; she had never thought of Lainey as a bastard. He was thorough, yes, but there was a kindness about him that was endearing. Of course, it could all be an act to get what he wanted.

'By the way,' Brown said. 'Remember Mrs Brandon went missing when the holiday place went up in flames? Well, we've found out where she was.'

'And?'

'And nothing. It was innocent. She went to stay with relatives over Bristol way. We checked it out just in case she set the fire herself.' He smiled. 'Pots of money in that family by the look, she will never be short of a bob or two, so don't you go worrying about her.'

'Really?' Lowri said dryly. 'And there was I feeling sorry for her.'

'Well, she has no motive for getting rid of her old man, does she? She didn't need anything from him, she has enough money to live comfortably for the rest of her days.'

Lowri looked at him steadily. He caught her eye.

'What?' he asked innocently.

'Only a man would come to that conclusion. Some women are greedy and vindictive, especially when the husband plays around. Do you think I had a motive, Sergeant?'

'We're talking hypothetical now, aren't we?'

'Well, excusing your grammar, yes, I suppose we are,' Lowri said.

'In that case, hell yes!'

'What would I have to gain?'

'Money, it's obvious. You are a small-time office-worker and Brandon has acquired, by fair means or foul, pots of dosh. Now he's vanished and you have the pots of dosh.'

'And I am the prime suspect,' Lowri said. 'That wouldn't be very clever of either Jon or me, would it?'

'I suppose no-one has given you credit for being clever. Except perhaps Lainey.'

Lowri sighed. 'Thank you for your time, Sergeant.' She left him standing there and crossed the room to where Sally was sitting.

'I'm going home.' She rested her hand on Sally's shoulder. 'See you tomorrow, thanks for coming out with me.'

'Wait, we'll run you,' Sally said.

'No need, the exercise will do me good.' As she walked out into the cool evening air, Lowri felt suddenly sick and afraid. How could Lainey go on believing in her innocence. A case was building up against her: she was being seen as a gold-digger, perhaps worse. She buttoned up her jacket. Well, she could do nothing about it right now, what she needed was a good night's sleep.

She shivered a little. It was going to be a long walk home and she only had herself and her stupid pride to blame.

10

Lowri could not sleep. It had taken her the best part of an hour to walk home and, as the night closed in, she had become cold and frightened. It had been a relief to let herself into the house and lock the door behind her.

She thumped her pillows and wondered if she should get out of bed and make herself a milky drink but, even as she pushed the duvet away from her, she changed her mind. It was just too much trouble.

She tried to relax, to breathe deeply. She needed to sleep; she was overwrought and angry. She turned onto her stomach and pressed her face into the pillow. Sleep seemed to be closer now and she welcomed it.

Suddenly, Lowri was wide awake. Someone was in her room. She smelt the sweat of a man, felt the weight of him sink into the bed beside her. She tried to sit up but a hand was over her mouth, strong fingers were digging into her cheeks.

'It's all right, don't scream, I'm not going to hurt you.' The sharp tang of aftershave washed over her, bringing with it a wave of fear. The voice was soft, the words lightly spoken close to her ear. What did he want, was he a rapist? The pressure was removed from her face.

'What do you want?' Her voice was tremulous.

'I just want to talk to you. If I let you go, promise you won't scream or try to run away or anything.'

She nodded. What choice did she have?

He shifted away from her and as Lowri sat up, she saw him illuminated by a wash of moonlight. His hair was pure white.

'What do you want?' she demanded.

'I need your help. I know you and Jon were close, he trusted you, didn't he?' He did not wait for a reply. 'So where is it?' He spoke quietly but she sensed that he could be dangerous.

'I don't know what you mean.'

'I don't want to hurt you but I have to know.' He sounded breathless, as though he had been running.

'Tell me what you're looking for!' she said desperately. 'If Jon left something with me, I'll give it to you, believe me.'

She reached over and clicked the light-switch. He looked more menacing when she could see the hardness of his features, and yet he was dressed in a neat suit and a shirt and tie. She wondered what she had expected, a striped jersey and a bag marked swag?

He looked round the bedroom. 'Where have you put it?'

'I don't know what you're talking about. Search the place if you like but the police have beaten you to it.'

'You mean they found it?'

She shrugged. 'I don't know what "it" is.'

She slid out of bed and pulled her warm dressing-gown around her, tying the belt tightly. 'It's cold,' she said. 'Let's go downstairs and I'll light the fire.' He nodded.

She felt more secure in the sitting-room. She turned on the gas and a glow appeared. She rubbed her hands together, wondering why she was so calm. Was she getting used to odd things happening to her?

'Tell me all you know,' he said, staring down at her as if she was a creature from another planet. 'I have a right.'

Lowri attempted to sound confident. 'I don't know what you expect from me. All I can say is that Jon and I went to the Swan for the weekend and suddenly he disappeared. And would you believe no-one saw him, no-one at all. Perhaps I dreamed the whole damned thing!' She was growing angry. 'I wish I'd never met Jon Brandon!'

He listened intently and, all the time, he never took his eyes off her face. It was as though he was trying to see into her skull. His silence was unnerving. She lowered her voice.

'That's it. So you see, I know nothing and yet I'm reduced to a nervous wreck, I suspect everyone I meet. And I am the main suspect into the bargain. I imagine the police think I've done away with him.'

'Shit! I believe you. Got anything to drink?'

Lowri thought it best to humour him. She brought a couple of cans from the fridge. 'Only Sprite, I'm afraid.' She handed him a can and he held it, staring at it as though suspecting she had poisoned it.

Lowri felt more in control of the situation now. 'Can't you tell me what it is you and everyone else are looking for?' she asked. 'What the hell was Jon hiding?'

He shook his head. 'I hoped you might help me out there.' He stared at her. 'I'm getting hassle from some nasty people who think I have it, whatever it is, and I want them off my back.'

They sat in silence for a moment and then the man took out a pack of cigarettes and offered one to her.

'I don't, thanks.'

He shook out a cigarette for himself and lit it. 'Anything unusual happen, like stuff being left at your bank for you to pick up?'

'Nothing like that,' Lowri said honestly. 'I can't understand any of this. Is Jon dead, do you think?'

'He's probably very much alive.' The man spoke evenly. 'He's very clever, the greatest escape artist of all time.' There was an edge of bitterness in his voice that was not lost on Lowri.

'He'd have to be!' she said. 'Anyone who can vanish without trace from an hotel room is a genius in my book.'

'Or he paid big bucks not to be noticed.' The man sucked on his cigarette. Lowri sighed, digesting his words in silence. He could well be right. He was certainly much more streetwise than she was.

'The police trying to pin everything on you, are they?' he said. 'That's typical, that is. Rather than take the trouble to solve anything they nab the most convenient person to carry the can. Look, just forget that I broke in. I don't mean you any harm, I just want to put an end to the harassment. I'm Snowy by the way.' He coughed over his cigarette. 'If you have any sort of theory it might be as well to talk it over with me.'

Lowri stared at him — should she talk to him? But then what did she have to lose? She was getting nowhere alone.

'What about Sarah Brandon?' she said. 'The wronged wife can't be ruled out of any crooked scheme, and you must admit, she is a little, well, strange. She knows Jon had many women before me and she could be the vengeful sort.'

'No, it's nothing to do with Sarah,' he said, 'I've already established that. So I might as well tell you —' He stopped speaking abruptly as the front door burst open with a mighty crash. Lainey led police swarming into the house, wearing flak jackets and brandishing guns. The man was pressed flat against the floor, his hands forced behind his back and secured with handcuffs.

'You all right?' Lainey's hair was dishevelled and he appeared flustered. 'We got a call from a neighbour who saw a man creeping about outside. She said he had a gun.'

'In that case, you took your time getting here!' Lowri said. 'I could have been dead by now if he'd meant me harm. Anyway, he hasn't got a gun.'

'We were led to believe you were in danger,' Lainey said. 'It takes time to get permission to arm the men, you know.'

'So I see.' Lowri watched helplessly as the intruder was dragged towards the door. 'You were premature, Mr Lainey. He was about to tell me something.'

'Well, now he can tell us instead.' Lainey's voice was cool.

'I don't think he'll do that.'

'He'd better, it's an offence to withhold information.'

'He'll tell you he doesn't know anything.' Lowri was suddenly angry. 'Can't you policemen use a little psychology once in a while?'

'No time.' Lainey walked away from her. 'We're too busy trying to protect the public from villains.'

'Wait!' Lowri followed him and pointed to the door, swinging brokenly on its hinges. 'What am I supposed to do about that?'

'I'll send someone round to fix it in the morning.'

'And in the meantime, any Tom, Dick or Harry is free to walk into my home?'

Lainey looked at her steadily. 'Seems they already do. Sergeant, you're a handyman, can you do a temporary repair?'

Brown did as he was told but he was not happy about it. Lowri was glad when the door was safely battened up and she was on her own again. She had not realized how very tired she was until she slid under the duvet. She curled herself into a ball, shivering a little as she realized the danger she could have been in.

She went over the events of the past hours time and time again, trying to sort out some clue from what the intruder had said. At last she abandoned all attempts to think and drifted into a fitful sleep.

Sally stared at Timmy. 'Can't you go home to sleep?' she said.

'What do you think I am, a bloody rent boy!' Timmy was outraged. 'I take your bloody friend out for the evening, then I bring you home and give you a good seeing-to and now you want to get rid of me. Why can't I sleep here?'

'Oh, all right,' Sally said. 'Get in.' She punched her pillow before Timmy had settled himself against her, then flicked off the light.

'So what gives then, why was Lowri talking to that cop at the bar?' he asked.

'What the hell are you talking about now!'

'Your friend. What's up with her, the police are after her for something, aren't they?'

'So what? They don't know anything. The police are not half as smart as Jon Brandon.'

'I thought you didn't ever meet Jon

Brandon,' Timmy said accusingly. 'That's what you told the police, wasn't it?'

'Yes, you lemon, it was. I didn't want to get involved in anything that might be hooky, did I?' Timmy was beginning to bore her.

Sally sat up. 'Oh sod it!' She fumbled for the light-switch and clicked it on. 'Hand me a ciggie, I can't get to sleep with all your nattering.'

Timmy did as he was told — he was good at that. God help him when he went out into the big bad world to earn a living. She leaned against the pillow and stared up at the smoke from her cigarette as it rose towards the already yellowed ceiling.

She turned her attention to her hands, studying her nails with pleasure. They had grown very long now, just the way she liked them. Timmy's back gave testimony to that. He seemed to enjoy a bit of pain but then these posh types often were kinky.

'What I don't understand is why you seem to dislike poor old Lowri.' Sally flicked ash from her cigarette onto the floor.

'She's a fool, isn't she? She's carrying the can for what her boyfriend has done. I chatted with that Sergeant Brown the other night, he was quite informative.'

'Come on then.' Sally was impatient. 'Tell me?'

Timmy smiled. 'I've got you interested now, haven't I?' He sat up and took her cigarette from her, puffing ineptly at it. She liked him when he was like this, playful and yet mysterious. Perhaps that was what she had fancied him for in the beginning, his air of knowing more than she did, than anybody did.

'Perhaps I was going to tell you, then again, perhaps I changed my mind.' He looked dark and dangerous suddenly and Sally felt herself grow warm.

'It seems the police think the Brandons and your precious Lowri are in it together.'

Sally edged closer to him. 'Well? In what, then?'

'I don't think I'll tell you.' He laughed and Sally pouted up at him.

'You are deliberately teasing me,' she said. She took the cigarette from him and held the glowing tip close to his nipple. 'Tell me, or else.'

Timmy's eyes grew dark. 'Put that damned thing out!' He guided her hand beneath the sheets. 'Do you like that?'

'I like it.'

'Do something with it then.'

'After you tell me.'

'No, before.'

'Promise?'

'We'll see.' Timmy rolled on top of her, breathing heavily, 'But I'll tell you this much, there's a great deal of money lying in some foreign bank accounts and it looks as if it's all belonging to your dear friend Lowri Richards, isn't that fun.'

Timmy stopped talking and went into action but Sally hardly noticed; thoughts were whirling around in her head. As Timmy climaxed, too soon, she wrapped her arms around him. He had his uses, even if it wasn't in bed.

As sleep began to overtake her, she wondered briefly about Jon Brandon — now he was a real man and a good lover. In addition, he was well set up, a good-looking guy. He sure knew how to please a girl. What a pity he had not chosen her instead of Lowri, otherwise she might be a very rich woman right now.

Lowri woke to the sunshine and the sound of hammering. It seemed a workman had come to fix the door properly. Brown's repair must have been pretty ropey.

She pulled on her housecoat and a pair of socks, her feet were freezing.

In the hallway, she saw Lainey chatting to the workman. They both looked her way and she saw Lainey frown at her state of undress.

'Excuse me,' she said abruptly, 'I wasn't expecting visitors.'

She showered and dressed hurriedly. Downstairs, she picked up her coat and her car keys.

'No breakfast?' Lainey asked.

'I don't eat breakfast.'

'What about locking up after us?'

'You do it.' She handed him a spare key. 'I trust you, you're a policeman.' She left the house and climbed into the car, gunning the engine into life. She was angry with Lainey, really angry. He took liberties, he treated her like a criminal one minute and a friend the next. She hated men. She had put up with enough from men to last her a lifetime.

Once out on the main road, she put her foot down. Work would be a relief, toiling over searches and making phone calls to the Land Registry was a doddle compared to being a police suspect in the hands of a clever man like DI Lainey.

Suddenly, in spite of herself, she was smiling.

11

Lowri arrived at the office at the same time as Mr Watson. 'Morning, Lowri, you're looking beautiful this morning,' he said, pausing in the small hallway. He removed his hat and his white hair stood up like a halo around his plump face. 'You should leave that car at home and get a brisk walk into work now and again. A young thing like you needs exercise.'

He leaned towards her. 'Any more hassle from that DI Lainey?'

Lowri shook her head. 'No, thank goodness,' she lied.

'Well, make sure he keeps his distance.' He walked towards the reception area. 'By the way, we've got a new receptionist, a Mrs Jenkins.' He smiled. 'And don't say about time too because getting the right person can be the devil of a job. I told her to start a little later than the rest of us. Let her ease her way into the office routine in her own time.' He paused. 'Take it easy now, do you hear?'

Without waiting for a reply, he disappeared into his room. Lowri had been on the point of telling him about the man who'd broken into her house last night, but, on second thoughts, perhaps that was something she should keep to herself. Involving a solicitor, even one as kindly as Mr Watson, sometimes resulted in a worsening of the situation.

She went into the office and shivered. 'Good heavens, who's opened the window?'

'That's down to the new receptionist,' Sally said. 'She was in here first thing this morning complaining about the smell of cigarette smoke. Then she went out again for some unknown reason.'

'Oh? Where did she go?'

Sally shrugged. 'I don't know and I don't care, she seems a bit of a dragon. Can't see her enjoying a knees-up. She looks more like a policewoman than a receptionist.'

'Well, give her a chance,' Lowri said. 'She'll probably settle down. I'm surprised we didn't get a new receptionist before now. We certainly need one.'

'I saw one girl coming for an interview,' Sally said. 'Probably the pay wasn't enough for her. In any case, she looked a bit on the flighty side. Still, anyone would be better than the one we've got stuck with now.'

Lowri closed the window and felt the radiators; the heating had not yet been switched on even though the September weather had taken a decidedly chilly turn.

'You OK?' Sally asked. 'You look a bit down.'

'I'm all right really. Just cold, that's all.' The nightmare had come again after the intruder had been removed, driving away any chance of restful sleep. She huddled in her chair, wrapping her jacket around her, and stared miserably at the pile of mail on her desk.

'I'd better do some work, I suppose.' She began to open the letters, most of which contained the usual paperwork concerning the buying and selling of property. One, however, was addressed to Mr Watson personally, and Lowri studied the postmark with interest.

'Anything wrong?' Sally asked. Lowri shook her head.

'Not really but this letter should have been put in Mr Watson's room, it's marked private and confidential.' She got up from her chair. 'I'll take it to him now.'

She had noticed the postmark was Summer's Dean. A coincidence, or was it?

The new receptionist was now sitting at her desk. She frowned as Lowri crossed the room to Mr Watson's office.

'Can I help you?' Her tone was curt and

Lowri shook her head.

'I don't think so. I've been working here for some time now, I think I can manage.'

'Please yourself.' Mrs Jenkins was a woman in her forties. She had cropped hair and wore thick black tights and flat shoes. Sally had hit the nail on the head when she said Mrs Jenkins looked more like a police-woman than a receptionist.

Was it possible Lainey had put a constable in to watch her? Lowri pressed her lips to-gether in annoyance. If that was the case Lainey could just keep his nose out of her business.

She knocked on the door to Mr Watson's office; there was no reply. The superior voice of the receptionist stopped her as she lifted her hand to knock again.

'Mr Watson has gone to the cloakroom, if you'd asked I would have told you.'

Lowri opened the office door and put the letter on the desk and then with a grim look approached Mrs Jenkins.

'Look here, did you get up on the wrong side of the bed this morning or is this per-sonal?' she said flatly. 'In any case, you seem quite unsuited for the job, so why are you working here?'

The woman looked up at her. 'That's a stupid question. I could ask you why *you* are

190

working here.' She had a strange way of hardly moving her lips when she spoke. 'I presume it's because you like the work and, more importantly, because you need the money.'

'Are you sure no-one has put you up to this?' Lowri said. 'You've hardly got a good bedside manner as it were.'

Mrs Jenkins half smiled. 'Neither am I a raving beauty?'

Lowri was nonplussed. 'Well no, I didn't mean that exactly.'

'I am expert at my job, Miss Richards. That is why I'm here.' The woman returned to her work, clicking the mouse, moving speedily from one command to the next on the computer.

'I've always envied those who can make a difficult job appear easy,' Lowri said quietly. She reckoned she might as well make a friend as an enemy, whatever Mrs Jenkins was up to.

'Thank you.' Mrs Jenkins seemed to have decided to take Lowri's words at face value. 'It comes in handy to be computer literate these days.'

'Well, I only work in the conveyancing side of things,' Lowri said, 'but I seem to be getting better the more I use a computer.'

She watched as Mrs Jenkins brought onto

the screen a list of clients' names and addresses and account numbers. The receptionist glanced up for a moment. 'If you'll excuse me, I have to get on.'

Lowri returned to her own office, making a rueful face at Sally. 'You were right, she's a dragon lady. Do you think she's for real?'

Sally looked up at her. 'I don't know what you mean.'

'Well, don't you think Mrs Jenkins seems an unlikely person for the job?'

'Not really,' Sally said. 'Receptionists aren't all glamorous. And young kids would be too frightened of some of the roughnecks we get wanting legal aid.'

'That's a bit sweeping, isn't it?' Lowri pulled a file towards her. 'I mean not everyone who needs legal aid is a villain. Look at it this way, would you or I have the money to take a big firm to court, for instance?'

'Well, no,' Sally said. 'But there's no need to get het up about it.' She gave Lowri a long look. 'What's got into you?'

'I don't know,' Lowri said. 'But just one thing, why would a receptionist want to look up clients' accounts on the computer?'

'I expect Mr Watson or one of the other solicitors asked her to,' Sally volunteered. 'I wouldn't waste time worrying about it if I were you.'

'Ah but then you are not under suspicion, are you? You are not a target for the police to shoot at any time they choose.'

'Time for a coffee, I think,' Sally said. 'You're getting snappy and just a wee bit paranoid.'

Lowri sighed. She probably *was* getting paranoid, suspicious of the most trivial event. 'A cup of coffee sounds just the job.'

As the morning wore on, Lowri found herself unable to concentrate on her work. She looked over at Sally, who seemed to have nothing better to do than repair her chipped nail polish.

'What about an early lunch?' Lowri said.

Sally agreed at once. 'That's just what I was thinking. I didn't have any breakfast so I'm starving.'

'What do you think?' Lowri asked. 'Shall we go to the deli and grab a sandwich?'

'Let's have a change.' Sally was enthusiastic. 'Let's try the Queens, they serve smashing grub and I've heard that the screws from the prison eat in there. We might see a bit of prime talent.'

Lowri smiled. 'Don't you ever think of anything else, Sal?'

'No, not really. Oh come on, Lowri, let's have something decent to eat for a change. You don't get a medal for wearing yourself to a frazzle in the office, remember.' She grimaced. 'Anyway, we can leave the dragon lady to look after things, can't we?'

In the Queens, the hubbub of voices rose and fell like some arcane chant. In the background Lowri heard the gentle hum of taped music, music that she and Jon had played together many times. Her vision suddenly blurred. She turned away, rubbing her eyes, not wanting Sally to see she was upset.

She tried to examine her feelings: she was disillusioned with Jon, wasn't she? Well, why let the sudden burst of nostalgia upset her? Lowri told herself to relax as she waited for Sally to study the board above the bar.

The pub was warm and smelled of smoke and food. Lowri looked around; the lounge bar was pretty crowded and as Sally had predicted there were several men in uniform, standing at the bar and sitting at tables eating lunch.

Lowri smiled. At least Sally would be happy; she blossomed in male company. It was a wonder she chose to work in a small office where she was unlikely to meet any fanciable men.

The sight of people laughing and joking together, smoking and enjoying a drink, made Lowri suddenly feel lonely. She wondered how long it was since she had felt carefree, had laughed and had fun. Certainly not since that night at the Swan when Jon had walked out on her. Why had he done it, why leave her to face the music? Whatever the music was . . .

'They've got steak and ale pie or fish and salad,' Sally reported back. 'Or you could just have a salad roll if you're thinking of your waistline.' She looked at Lowri. 'Not that you have to worry about that.' She stood with her hands resting on the table. Today her nails were bright blue.

'Oh and in case you're interested, your detective is by the bar with a gorgeous-looking policewoman. I've made a point of letting him know we're here.'

Lowri's heart did a flip. She swallowed hard. 'I think I'll just have a roll, I'm not very hungry,' she said.

'Suit yourself, I'm having the steak and ale pie.' Sally went to order the food and when she returned to the table Lainey was with her. Lowri was suddenly tense — she knew her colour had risen.

'Mind if I sit down for a minute?' he asked and without waiting for a reply he sat beside her. 'Mr Watson and your father were friends, I understand?' he said evenly. Lowri looked at him and frowned.

'Not to my knowledge,' she said. 'I don't

think Charles has any friends.'

'Didn't your father speak to Mr Watson about you, isn't that how you got the job in the solicitors' office?'

'I got the job on merit,' Lowri said edgily. 'And if you want to know anything about Charles you'd better ask him. I haven't communicated with my father properly in years.' She leaned forward, elbows on the table. 'He more or less disowned me when I opted out of college.'

A waitress brought the food and Sally immediately picked up her knife and fork and cut into the pie. Rich gravy spilled over the edges of the dish and suddenly Lowri felt sick.

'Do you think you could let us have our lunch in peace?' she said. 'I understand you are with someone. Isn't it rude and somewhat shortsighted to leave a beautiful colleague alone in a place like this?'

Lainey smiled. 'Maybe.' He rose and nodded politely. 'I'll be seeing you again soon.'

Lowri could have kicked herself. All she had done was to sound like a jealous wife. Lainey must think her a real fool.

'Go on, tuck in,' Sally said, 'the food is delicious, we should come here more often.'

Lowri ate a little of her salad roll. Her

head was aching and all she could think of was Lainey with a beautiful policewoman.

'Why don't you go to the loo?' Sally asked. Lowri looked at her, puzzled by the turn the conversation had taken.

'I don't particularly want to.'

'Well, I'm just suggesting it because Lainey and the woman are now sitting at a table near the door — if you go to the loo you can have a good look at her.'

Lowri hated herself for listening to Sally but curiosity got the better of her. She dabbed her mouth with the thick paper napkin and smoothed down her skirt. 'Aye, why not?' She smiled. 'I think I do want to go, after all.'

They were talking, heads close together. Funny, Lainey had always given the impression he was alone. He did not see her as she passed the table and Lowri was relieved. She had a feeling that DI Lainey would know exactly what she was up to.

In the ladies' room Lowri stared at her reflection, thinking how pale and uninteresting she looked. She was not a beautiful woman but she liked to think she had some degree of sex appeal. Now even that seemed to have gone. Was that because she had seen Lainey with another woman?

'You jealous cow!' she told her reflection.

When she returned to the lounge bar, the table where Lainey had been sitting was empty. Lowri hurried back across the room and flopped into her seat looking down at her watch.

'We should be getting back to work, you seem to have finished your lunch.'

Sally patted her flat stomach. 'Enjoyed every morsel. Good pie that, you should have tried it.' She picked up her bag and jacket. 'Right then, back to the grind.'

As they left the Queens and walked the short distance to the office, Lowri was silent. Sally kept glancing at her as though unsure what to say. 'Has that copper upset you?'

'Of course not!'

'Right.' Sally pushed open the door to the office and walked inside. 'It's colder in here than it is outside,' she remarked.

Mrs Jenkins was busy with clients — the small reception area seemed to strain at the seams whenever there were more than a couple of people in it. She glanced up as Lowri walked past the desk.

'There was a call for you,' she said. 'I wish you would not have private calls which I have to deal with.'

'I don't usually have private calls at all,' Lowri said. 'Perhaps it's an emergency. Was it my mother by any chance?'

'No it was not.' Mrs Jenkins's eyes narrowed. 'It was from a man, a Mr Brandon.'

Lowri stopped short. 'Say that again.'

Mrs Jenkins looked at her in surprise. 'I've got enough to do, can't you see that? It was a Mr Brandon.'

'Are you sure?'

'I'm not in the habit of taking the wrong information,' Mrs Jenkins said huffily.

'Did you take his number? It's urgent.'

'No, he didn't offer it and I didn't ask.'

Lowri picked up the phone. Mrs Jenkins took it back from her and replaced it, frowning disapprovingly. 'No good trying 1471, there have been at least six calls since then.'

Lowri went into her office and sat down. 'What do you think, Sally?' she said, feeling bemused. 'When we were out Jon phoned and that fool of a woman didn't take his number. I could cheerfully kill her!'

'Jon phoned?' Sally's eyes widened. 'Jon Brandon phoned?'

'That's right,' Lowri said, 'the inimitable vanishing man phoned and I don't know where I can get hold of him.' She sighed heavily. 'I could have cleared the whole thing up if I had been able to talk to him.'

'Well you could knock me down with a

feather!' Sally stared at her. 'Perhaps it's a hoax.'

'I'll talk to Mr Watson, see what he has to say.' Lowri took off her jacket and put it over the chair. 'I won't be long.'

Mr Watson was alone in his office. He looked up and smiled as Lowri opened his door. 'Can I talk to you for a minute, Mr Watson?' she asked.

'Come in. Of course you can talk to me any time, Lowri, you know that. Sit down and for goodness' sake relax, you look all wound up.'

'The receptionist, Mrs Jenkins, she said I'd had a phone call while I was out.' Lowri swallowed. 'She said it was from a Mr Brandon. Is there any way I can check that?'

'Possibly.' Mr Watson took off his glasses and leaned back in his chair. 'But I don't think it would help. After all, people call from mobile phones, from call-boxes, from hotels and public houses, don't they?'

He was right. Lowri shook her head. 'I just wish I'd been here! I could have found out what's going on once and for all.'

'It could be a coincidence,' Mr Watson said. 'There are possibly several hundred people called Brandon living hereabouts.'

'It would be a very strange coincidence, wouldn't it?' Lowri said. 'Even supposing you're right, why ask specially for me?'

'Look, my dear, put the whole thing out of your head,' Mr Watson said. 'I think you are worrying too much about all this. Let the police sort it out, it's their job after all.'

'But they suspect me of all sorts of things, colluding with Jon to move money about for one. I think they might believe I've done away with him so that I can have everything.' She rubbed her face. 'I just wish I'd been here to take the call.'

'Leave everything to me,' Mr Watson said. 'I'll get onto the phone company, see what I can find out.'

Lowri sighed with relief. 'Thank you, Mr Watson.' She moved to the door and paused, her hand on the knob. 'Mr Watson, were you and my stepfather ever friends?'

His white eyebrows rose to his receding hairline. 'Hardly,' he said. 'We both fell in love with the same woman.'

'Oh?'

'Go on, now, back to work.' Mr Watson waved his hand at her. 'All that is old history, water under the bridge.'

'But . . .'

'No buts, I don't want to talk about it.'

Lowri nodded. 'All right, but as soon as I get the chance I'm going to ask my mother all about you.'

'You'd better not do it in Charles's hearing. The man is extremely possessive of her, you must know that.'

'I do.' Lowri opened the door. 'Thanks for the chat, Mr Watson, it's been most illuminating.'

As she crossed the hall to her own office, Lowri heard Mrs Jenkins talking on the phone. 'Yes, Mrs Brandon, I'll pass your message on.'

Reception was empty and Lowri stood in the doorway staring at Mrs Jenkins. 'Another call for me?'

'No, not for you,' Mrs Jenkins said smugly. 'Actually, Mrs Sarah Brandon wanted me to give Mr Watson a message. Sorry, it's confidential.'

Lowri felt like slapping the woman. 'Thanks!' she said, her voice heavy with sarcasm.

Mrs Jenkins was equally sarcastic. 'You are more than welcome.'

Lowri went into the back office and closed the door sharply. Sally looked up at her.

'What's wrong?'

'Nothing new, just that Mrs Jenkins has been sent to try me, I'm convinced of it.' She sat at her desk and closed her eyes. 'Do you know something, Sally? This has been one hell of a day. Won't I be glad when it's over!'

12

Lainey stared at the piece of paper Sergeant Brown had just put on his desk. He picked it up and moved to the window where the light was better — he really should get himself a pair of glasses.

'Interesting.' He rubbed his hand over his chin; he needed a shave. 'Very interesting.' Someone had used Jon Brandon's credit card to take cash out of a bank in Bristol yesterday. It was a possible lead; it might mean that Brandon was still alive. It just might mean that someone else, his wife or possibly his girlfriend, knew Brandon's pin number and was not afraid to use it. Or perhaps it was one of those random attempts at theft that came up every day.

Still, Lainey felt a prickle of excitement. The bank, if large enough, would have a security camera; he must get someone to ring Bristol and have it checked out. He returned to his desk and opened the file on Brandon. Slipping the sheet of paper inside, Lainey felt he might be on the verge of a breakthrough.

So far, he had made one stride forward and two back. When he had felt he was unravelling the mystery, further evidence appeared that tangled everything up again. Now, just maybe, he would find something positive.

He tried to think the situation out logically. That was easier said than done when Lowri's face kept popping into his mind. Lainey made a determined effort to concentrate. Shortly before his disappearance, Brandon had been abroad on business, apparently importing and exporting goods — goods declared as computer software. Was that a cover for something more sinister?

The legitimate business Brandon owned was flourishing, the profit moderately good. And there was a stack of money in the Software International account, money that, in the event of Brandon's continued absence, presumably would go to Lowri Richards.

Lainey ran his hands through his hair. Jon Brandon was an enigma and so was his wife. Sarah Brandon had been left a fortune by one of her parents, so why did her husband find it necessary to get involved in crime? If indeed any crime had been committed.

Lainey sank into his chair and leaned over his desk. He was getting nowhere. It might be a good idea to start at the very beginning again and work his way chronologically towards the point of the man's disappearance, perhaps his demise.

He rested his head in his hands and closed his eyes, running the cast of characters in the drama through his mind. The list was limited, he had to recognize that. True, Mrs Brandon had a motive, she was the wronged wife, but then so did Lowri; if she had learned he was married she stood to gain everything, revenge and Brandon's money. The phone rang. Lainey answered it. It was Lowri.

'I wanted to talk to you, Inspector,' she said. He paused, staring at the receiver as if it could answer all his questions.

'About the case, was it?' He was aware he sounded like a pompous arse but Brown might come back into the office at any moment.

'Well, no, not really.' Lowri sounded wistful.

'Can I call you back?' he found himself saying. 'I've rather a lot on at the moment. Perhaps I could ring you later?'

The line went dead and he knew she had seen through him. He felt like a heel but he could not become emotionally involved with a material witness, however beautiful she was. It was some time before Lainey could force his thoughts back to the case in hand. The one glaring fact remained: Lowri had a lot to gain from Brandon's disappearance.

'Sod it!' It all came back to her. 'All roads lead to Rome.'

'First sign, sir.' Sergeant Brown was standing in the doorway. 'Of madness.'

He smiled. 'Just thinking out loud, Sergeant.'

'Don't do too much of it or men in white coats will be coming to cart you off!'

'Everything points to Lowri Richards,' he said. 'But it all seems too pat. What do you make of her, Sergeant?'

'I don't know, sir. She was definitely shocked when we showed her Brandon's clothes. My gut instinct is she doesn't know any more than we do.' He shrugged. 'Well, that's my opinion anyway.'

'Mine too but I haven't any other leads, have I?'

'My guess is that he's still alive, he's done a Lord Lucan,' the sergeant said. 'You know, run off, disappeared. Perhaps things were getting too hot for him here.'

'I get your drift,' Lainey said, his tone heavy with irony. 'He vanished, leaving behind a young woman who he must have known would be our main suspect in a serious fraud, if nothing else.'

'Do you think you're getting too personally involved in all this, guv?' Brown said mildly, echoing Lainey's own feelings.

Lainey looked up. 'Probably, but then I can't handle a case any other way.'

'Especially when there's a pretty woman involved?'

'It's not like you to be arch, Brown.'

'I'm not being arch, I'm being blunt. Whatever Lowri Richards has got, you fell for it hook, line and sinker, and I for one don't blame you.'

Lainey pushed aside the file and stood up. He would go and talk to Lowri again, go through the whole thing from beginning to end. There might just be something, somewhere, some vital clue that he'd missed. But first he would drive over to Bristol, see what he could learn at the bank. When he returned, he would see Lowri.

'Coming, Sergeant? We're going to Bristol ourselves. You can drive.'

The phone rang and Brown picked it up. 'Hang on, guv,' he said. 'Seems Jon Brandon has turned up at Heathrow! Just in from Jamaica, according to his passport. Good thing you asked major airports to look out for him, sir.'

'Right, let's go,' Lainey said.

'Where are we going, sir?'

'To Heathrow, where else?'

"What about Bristol?'

'If Jon Brandon has just arrived from Jamaica he could hardly have been in Bristol yesterday.' Lainey smiled. 'This could just be the breakthrough we've been looking for.'

When Terence Watson made his way into the back office he saw that Lowri was leafing through a pile of documents. He smiled — she really was a lovely girl.

'How are you getting on with the new receptionist?' he asked. 'She's efficient enough, don't you think?' He leaned over her desk, his glasses slipping down his nose and resting against his plump cheeks. He pushed them back; he needed new glasses. He also needed to lose weight.

'Oh, yes, she's very efficient, I'll give her that,' Lowri said. She smiled up at him and she was alarmingly like her mother, beautiful and yet without the arrogance that Rhian Richards carried with her like a cloak.

'I still think you are wasted in an office, you know,' he said, resisting the urge to touch her silky hair. 'I would very much like you to take up your studies again, my dear.'

'So would my mother.' She shrugged.

'But even if I wanted to go back, how could I find the money?' She thought of mentioning the sums put into her account, but Mr Watson spoke again.

'You could get a grant like everyone else, Lowri, and you know you'd have a place here when you qualified.'

'That's kind of you, Mr Watson, but haven't you heard, the Government has cut student grants to below a survival rate, let alone a living one. It's borrow now and pay back later. I couldn't afford it, Mr Watson. In any case, I'm not sure I'd want to go back to college, not full time.' She smiled. 'Though I might think of going to night classes and doing IT.'

'IT?'

'Information Technology. It's certainly something that really interests me, it's something I should have done long ago.'

He saw the enthusiasm in her green eyes and smiled involuntarily. 'Yes, this computer stuff does rather seem to be the way forward. I'm too old a dog to learn new tricks, I suppose, but you, my dear Lowri, have a lifetime before you.' He allowed himself to rest his hand on her shoulder. 'Ambition can be a good thing and I don't want you to waste your talents, but just remember this, Lowri, it's not possessions that make your life worthwhile, it's being with the one you love.'

She suddenly looked crestfallen and he cursed himself for blundering in so tactlessly. 'I'm sorry, my dear! I know your chap has vanished and it's all very upsetting.' He shook his head. 'But he wasn't right for you, he was a liar and worse. Anyway, I'd better be getting back to my office, we don't want Mrs Jenkins to think we're slacking, do we?' He smiled. 'Oh, yes, I know she's a bit on the difficult side but she seems to be on top of things.'

He returned to his office and sank into his chair. He was feeling tired lately, tired of the battle of life. Sally buzzed him.

'There's a call for you, sir, one of the clients.'

'Just say I'm in a meeting and don't put any calls through until I tell you.' He turned his chair so that he was looking out of the window. He was an old, dried-up specimen of a man; he had never become the great lawyer he had hoped to be. Instead he had settled for the humdrum and safe practice of conveyancing.

He would never set the world on fire, as he once thought. He smiled; but, and it was a big but, he had been happy once, a long time ago. He had fallen in love with a beautiful woman, a woman he loved still. That love affair had produced something very special and precious. His daughter, his little girl.

He reached for his pipe. Wasn't it better to have loved and lost than never to have loved at all? He supposed so but sometimes, just sometimes, he felt unbearably lonely.

Lowri walked along the High Street, her step brisk. She was spending the evening with Sally, and this time Timmy would not be tagging along.

'Hey, you're looking rather snazzy!' Sally said, greeting her as if she was a long-lost friend. 'What have you done to your hair? It's gorgeous!'

'You know why I didn't come into the office today? I went to Hair Kuts and had it styled. I needed some space.'

Sally ignored that. 'And that coat, wow! Turquoise is your colour all right, your skin looks lovely.' Sally took her arm. 'Come on, let's get into the pub, it's freezing out here, anyone would think it was winter already.'

They took a seat in an alcove a little way off from the bar and with a sigh Sally eased her high-heeled sandals away from her slender feet.

'How's Timmy?' Lowri sipped her wine. 'Still the ardent lover, is he?'

'I don't know about that.' Sally frowned. 'He's been acting very strange lately.'

'Strangely,' Lowri said. 'Your grammar is appalling!'

'Oh shut up!' Sally smiled good-naturedly. 'Whatever it is, he's been acting it. I'm beginning to wonder if he's up to something.'

'What?'

Sally examined her pristine nails. 'Another woman, perhaps?'

'Never!' Lowri said. 'He's crazy about you.'

'Still, it's not like Timmy to splash money about. I know his daddy's rich,' Sally said. 'But he's not giving him any more hand-outs.'

'What's he splashing out on?'

Sally frowned. 'He's only gone and bought a BMW hot off the stocks, brand spanking new it is! I don't know where he got the money.'

Lowri leaned back against the plush cushions. 'Well, he's probably getting it on the never-never. I'm sure he thinks it will impress you.'

'Normally, he's a mean bastard!' Sally's eyes sparkled. 'Anyway, let's talk about you. What else have you done today?'

'Not a lot. As I said I had my hair styled

and then I treated myself to some new make-up and a couple of blouses.'

'No more attackers looming up out of the night, then?'

Lowri shivered. 'How did you know about that?'

'You must have mentioned it.' Sally's tone was reasonable, 'Don't look so worried, it will probably all blow over soon, anyway. I mean, the police can't even prove if Jon Brandon is alive or dead, can they?'

Lowri sighed heavily. 'No, but that doesn't stop them treating me like they suspect me of robbing the Bank of England.'

'Are you trying to tell me that having a good-looking senior detective and the dishy young Sergeant Brown hanging around you is any hardship?'

Lowri thought of Lainey: he was no hardship. Given any other circumstances, they might have been lovers. The idea shocked her. Why on earth should she think that? Lainey was a man trying to solve a case, that was all.

'You've gone all dreamy. Thinking of Lainey are you?' Sally laughed. 'He must have something beside good looks, though I can't see it myself.'

'Look, Sally, I'm off men for the time being, perhaps for ever. Jon has shown me that no man can be trusted.'

'You'll change your mind, you just wait.' Sally took out a mirror and touched up her lipstick. 'This place should be livening up, soon,' she said casually.

Lowri would much rather have had a quiet meal in a nice restaurant, but that was far too tame for Sally. The door of the pub swung open and two men came in talking and laughing, making as much noise as if there was a crowd of them. Lowri frowned as she saw one of the men waving in her direction.

'Don't worry,' Sally said, 'it's me he's interested in.'

'What about Timmy?' Lowri asked and Sally shook her head.

'I don't know and I don't care. He's getting on my nerves lately. Do you know, he's no damned good in bed?' She smirked at Lowri. 'Yours looks nice.'

'Oh, Sally!' Lowri said. 'Are you trying to fix me up? I'm a big girl now, I can make my own friends.'

'Aye, and see where that gets you!' Sally retorted, 'with a pig like Jon Brandon!'

Lowri sighed. Sally was right, of course she was. 'OK, don't go on about it.' She looked up as the two men began to cross the room towards them.

'Sergeant Brown, hallo,' Lowri said. He nodded and sat close to Sally who fluttered her eyelashes at him. 'Are you planning to take down my particulars, Sarge?'

Lowri winced. Sally was so obvious.

'Talk to Matthew's friend,' Sally told Lowri.

'Ken Major.' The officer sat on a stool facing Lowri. He seemed as embarrassed as she was. He smelled of aftershave, a clean, fresh smell. He smiled, looking handsome and sporty in an open-necked shirt. He was doubtless a very nice man but Lowri was not interested.

'Lowri Richards.' She held out her hand and he took it.

Sally rushed into speech. 'How's the police force doing then, Ken, been solving any crimes lately have you?'

'Not a lot. I'm mainly a pen-pusher. Drink, anyone?'

'Yes please!' Sally said enthusiastically. 'Red wine for Lowri, white for me.'

Ken loped away to the bar, his step springy. Sally jabbed Lowri in the ribs.

'His sap is rising!' she whispered.

'Tough!' Lowri replied.

'Aw, go on, you could do with a bit of sex, it will ease the tension, don't you know what I mean?'

'Who says I'm tense?'

'Well, just look at the way you're gripping your hands together, your knuckles are dead white!'

'So suddenly you're a psychologist,' Lowri said sourly.

'Well, ease up, enjoy life, you're only young once, mind.' Sally rose to her feet. 'I'm going to the Ladies, coming?'

Lowri sighed. 'No, you go on, I'm fine.' Sally minced across the room on her high heels. She insisted on wearing stilettoes, whatever the fashion. To be fair, they suited her slim ankles and curving calf muscles. Sally was certainly a girl to make the most of her attributes.

Matthew Brown glanced at Lowri. 'Some girl, your friend,' he said cryptically.

'She sure is,' Lowri replied.

Ken returned and put a glass on the table in front of Lowri. 'Hope that's all right,' he said.

'It's fine, thank you.' She drank some of the wine. It was smooth and mellow — at least Ken was not a cheapskate. He took a mouthful of beer and the froth outlined his top lip. She was trying to think of something to say when he spoke again.

'I'm sorry if your friend sprang this on you.' He smiled. 'I didn't want to come here but now I'm glad I did.'

She returned his smile, liking him. 'Yes, me too,' she said. 'Still, perhaps I'd better tell you that I'm a police suspect. I wouldn't like you to get into trouble over meeting me.'

'Take no notice of that,' Ken said, 'half the population are police suspects.'

Sally came mincing back across the carpet. Her lipstick, reapplied, gleamed in the overhead lights, giving her a pronounced pout that was clearly appealing to her date. Matthew leapt to his feet, allowing her to slip into the seat beside him.

'You look lovely enough to eat,' he said and Sally winked up at him.

'We could talk about that later. Right now I don't want to shock my friend. Lowri is a stickler for modesty.'

The conversation became general and Lowri found that Ken had a quirky sense of humour. It was good to laugh again, to be carefree if only for a few hours. She liked Ken but she did not fancy him, and somehow that made laughing at his jokes much easier for her.

Sally was cuddling up to Matthew and Lowri hoped that Ken would not get the wrong impression.

'Married, engaged, going out with anyone?' she asked pleasantly and Ken shook his head.

'No, my last girlfriend dumped me. I kept letting her down all the time. Work, you know?'

'We're in the same boat then,' Lowri said. 'I was dumped too, in a way, and speaking for myself, I don't want to get involved in a serious relationship for a long time yet.'

'We're on the same wavelength then,' Ken said. 'Friends, right?'

Lowri felt relieved. 'I'll drink to that.'

'I'd like to take you home though,' Ken said. 'And it might lead to you learning something to your advantage, as they say.'

Lowri met his steady gaze. She wondered if he was bargaining with her, sex for information? Well, if he was, two could play at that game.

'OK,' she said and picked up her glass.

If Ken was surprised at her ready agreement, he concealed it very well. He probably thought she was a pushover. Many girls were these days, of course. In fact, some men expected a girl to be experienced, otherwise they thought there was something wrong with them.

'We could leave now,' Ken said. 'It's full of smoke in here, noisy as well. You can't hear yourself think.'

'Don't you want another drink?' Lowri asked.

He shook his head and a fall of dark hair covered his forehead. She noticed quite suddenly that Ken was a similar type to Jon Brandon: dark, well built, confident. Ken was younger, he was probably little more than mid-twenties, but he wore the same self-assured smile that Jon had worn.

She realized she was thinking of her lover, the man she had thought she would one day marry, in the past tense. And something else, she realized, she was no longer in love with him. Her spirits lifted at once; she was free, really free of her past.

'Hey you two, you love-birds there, there'll be plenty of time for drooling over each other later. Come on now, help me out here a little.' Sally was pouting, her newly lipsticked mouth full and inviting as she nestled closer to Matthew. He dropped a kiss on her cheek.

'Oh come on, Matthew! Such a peck is an insult to a red-blooded girl.'

'No offence intended, love,' Matthew said calmly. Sally flung back her hair, exposing the flesh of her white neck, and smiled.

'None taken then.'

Lowri looked at her watch — the evening seemed to be dragging. She wanted nothing so much as to get back home, have a quick shower and climb into bed to sleep the night away.

'Do you know, Ken, I think I'll take you up on your offer, let's get out of here.' She turned to Sally. 'I'm going home now.' Lowri smiled. 'Ken is going to take me. See you tomorrow.'

She was silent in the car, wondering what Ken had meant by saying she might 'learn something to her advantage'. He drove competently and Lowri felt relaxed by the wine she had drunk. 'It's been a very pleasant evening,' she said. 'Can you stop, just over there, look, that's my house.'

He drew the car to a halt right outside her door. She turned to him and touched his arm. 'Thanks for bringing me home, Ken, I've enjoyed your company.'

'Can't I come in for coffee, I've got something to tell you, have you forgotten?'

She stepped out of the car and Ken pulled on the handbrake and climbed out after her. 'I promise I won't bite!' he said. He bent to kiss her and Lowri twisted away.

'I told you, Ken, I don't want any involvement just now.'

'No but a little kiss wouldn't hurt anything, would it?' He pressed his mouth to hers and his kiss was childlike, he was clearly unpractised in the art of seduction.

'Come on, Lowri,' he put his arms one on either side of her, pinning her to the wall, 'let me come inside.'

'Thank you but no thank you!' Lowri pushed him away.

'What's wrong, don't you like me?' His tone was wistful and, immediately, Lowri felt sorry for him. Before she could think of a tactful reply, a voice rang out clearly in the night air. 'Miss Richards? Could I have a word?'

Lowri blinked in surprise. 'Detective Inspector Lainey!'

He loomed up out of the darkness, his shoulders hunched, his hands thrust into his pockets. 'How good of you to escort the young lady safely home, officer.' He turned his back on Ken and smiled down at Lowri. 'Can we talk? Inside?'

'Oh right. Thank you again, Ken.' He looked crestfallen and Lowri hid a smile. 'It was a lovely evening,' she added.

Lainey followed her into the sitting-room and she was surprised to see he was laughing. He was leaning against the door, his arms folded across his chest, watching her with obvious amusement.

'You saw, didn't you?' she said indignantly. 'And you didn't think to help me out of an embarrassing situation?'

'I did think of it but then I saw you were doing very nicely alone.' He perched on the edge of the table.

'Well, what have you come for, just to laugh at my antics?'

He sobered. 'No, I haven't. I've just come back from Heathrow. Sit down, Lowri, there's something I have to tell you.'

13

'What's going on between you and that policeman?' Timmy's voice held a familiar note of complaint and Sally pushed him away, moving to the other side of the bed with an impatient shake of her head.

'Nothing, you idiot!'

'I'm not an idiot! You're always talking about those cops, especially Matthew Brown, and then I catch you with the guy in Green's Wine Bar. What am I supposed to think?'

'You didn't catch me, I was having a lunch-break and happened to see Matthew. What's wrong with that?'

'It didn't appear to be an accidental meeting, not the way you were sitting up close to him.'

'For heaven's sake don't be so childish. Come on, get out of bed and get us a drink, will you?' She turned to punch the pillow, wishing it were Timmy's face.

'No, I won't get us a drink!' He grasped her arm. 'Tell me what's going on, Sally, you're driving me mad. Are you in love with the chap?'

She sat up, feeling a chill across her naked breasts. 'No I am not!' she said emphatically. 'If you want to know the truth I can't stand the guy.'

'Well, then, why were you talking to him like that, heads together as if you'd got secrets to share? I don't like to be made a fool of, Sally, especially by a yob of a copper.'

Sally fell back and stretched her arms above her head, knowing her breasts were pointing provocatively upwards. 'Don't be such a bore!' she said. 'I was just trying to pump him about Lowri and that man who disappeared. Don't tell me you're not curious about it all.' She ran her hand over his chest and down to his groin. 'Why should I want that big lumbering idiot of a cop when I've got you?'

Mollified, Timmy leaned over her and pinched her nipple between his thumb and forefinger. The pain excited her and she wondered if it would be worth giving it another shot with him? If he could prolong the session a little she might even get a thrill out of it.

He must have read her mind because he slipped out from under the sheets and made for the bathroom. Obviously he was not up to giving it another go.

Alone, she thought about Matt. They had

met earlier and he had been so sweet and contrite. He told her some man had turned up at Heathrow carrying a passport in the name of Jon Brandon. That was a surprise. She shivered. Could he have come back into the country, if indeed he had ever left it? Or was someone using his passport?

Her mouth curved into a smile: now *he* was what she called a lover. Jon was an expert, a real stayer. She could do with an hour or two with Jon right now.

She had asked Matthew what this man who called himself Jon Brandon looked like, but by the time the police got to the airport he had gone. The only description was one given by an air steward, and it was sketchy to say the least. The sharp-eyed security man who had spotted the name on the passport had gone off duty, and no-one else had taken any particular notice of Jon Brandon.

She heard the rush of the shower and the sound of the water made her realize she had a raging thirst. That was the way wine affected her — why, she wondered, did she drink it? She slipped out of bed, wishing Timmy would hurry up so that she could shower away the stink of him.

She crossed the room to the window and pulled aside the curtain. She could see students from the university next door standing in groups talking and smoking. They were all dressed the same, in jeans and old sweaters. They even carried books in the same way. And all of them with grey faces and bowed shoulders. They had so much time off from their studies, surely they should be happy? How she despised students!

Timmy returned to the bedroom, scented and clean. She had fancied him, once. Still, Timmy had money, privilege, and he could be very useful.

She brushed past him on her way to the shower. 'Won't be long, darling.' In the bathroom, she peered at the mirror. It was steamed up and she rubbed her arm across it. Her hair was a mess and the roots needed touching up. She thought of Lowri with her glossy, natural auburn hair and her fine skin. She might be older than Sally but she could still pull the men in spades.

Sally stepped into the shower and turned on the tap. The water gushed, warm and steamy, running sensuously between her breasts and down her belly. It was too bad when the shower gave her more of a thrill than the guy she was going to bed with.

Still, her face became dreamy, there were other pebbles on the beach. Take that DI Lainey, he was a man and a half. It would not do to let Lowri know she was attracted to him, though. Lowri seemed to think Lainey was her own private bodyguard.

Later, when she was dressed, Sally looked at her watch. It was too early to go home. Perhaps she should stop at one of the pubs on the way. It was about time she dropped Timmy and found someone more worthy of her.

'I think I'll have an early night.' She picked up her bag and her jacket and Timmy looked at her, agreeing at once.

'Yes, go on home, you look bushed.'

'Gee, thanks!' She moved to the door, immediately suspicious, wondering what Timmy was up to. 'Are you going out?'

He shook his head. 'I doubt it.' He kissed her cheek. 'Sorry I can't offer to drive you home but I don't want to risk a ban.' He picked up the empty bottle of wine and shook it as if to prove his point.

'No problem,' Sally said. 'Just ring for a taxi, will you, love?'

Timmy did so with alacrity and Sally looked at him sharply. 'Are you up to something, Timmy?'

He was the picture of innocence as he replaced the receiver. 'Me? What could I be up to? I can't drive anywhere, remember?'

She shrugged. 'I'll believe you, thousands wouldn't.'

As Sally sat in the taxi heading for the other side of town she put Timmy out of her mind. She had no trouble forgetting him — he was eminently forgettable. She might have thought differently if she had waited to see him slip out of the building, his car keys jangling in his hand.

It was crowded in the pub, the lounge filled with young people. The volume of the taped music, combined with the sounds of laughter and chatter, gave the room a party atmosphere.

She walked purposefully up to the bar. 'Any of the boys been in?' she asked the barmaid. The girl shook her head and her blonde pony-tail bobbed.

'I don't think they're coming here tonight. Sorry, got customers to serve.'

The girl disappeared and Sally ordered a drink from the eager-looking barman, who had eyes only for her cleavage. This was what she was used to, and she flashed him a smile and a glimpse of leg as she climbed onto the bar-stool.

She finished her drink and ordered another glass of wine, staring at the group of people coming through the door. A tall figure of a man detached himself from the crowd; the cow of a barmaid had lied. Sally began to smile.

'Well, Matthew, if you are taking me home tonight then I'm a very happy girl!'

Lowri sat at her desk and rubbed her temples. It was so stuffy in the office that she could feel a headache coming on. She thought of opening a window but she knew Sally would protest at the draught. It was either too cold or too hot in the office; there seemed no happy medium, and the air-conditioning had finally given out.

She rested her head in her hands and thought of Lainey's visit. He had raised her hopes, claiming he had something to tell her. He had sat in her little room and talked about Jon, about false passports, about the possibility of someone posing as Jon. It became clear that the police were no nearer to finding him than they had been before.

Lowri picked up her bag and rummaged in its untidy depths, hoping to find some painkillers. She was unlucky. 'Damn! No pills, just when I've got the mother of all headaches coming on.'

'I've got some,' Sally looked up from her computer screen, 'in my bag there. Hang on, I'll get them for you.'

Lowri took the tablets and thanked her. 'I'll just pop in the Ladies and get some water,' she said. It was cooler in the rest room, as it was euphemistically called. The windows were open and Lowri breathed in the cold air gratefully. She helped herself to water and swallowed the pills before sinking onto the one seat that had been provided for the comfort of women employees.

She would have to talk to Mr Watson again, ask his advice. He was wise and cool-headed and would offer an objective viewpoint on the whole sorry mess. He might even be able to get something out of the police. First Ken Major and then Lainey had raised her hopes, only to dash them again.

But she could not speak to Mr Watson today. He was away, in the country, a trip he did every few weeks or so. Sally claimed he had a girlfriend tucked away somewhere. Lowri's face softened. Even old Mr Watson had the right to his private life, his own secrets.

Sally looked up as Lowri returned to the office, her face grim. 'There's been a phone call for you, your mum I think. She wants you to ring her back as soon as poss.'

'Thanks, Sally.' Lowri picked up the phone and dialled the number of the house in Summer's Dean. It was Charles who answered. Lowri asked to speak to her mother.

'Your mother is out for the day, I haven't

seen her since breakfast-time.' The phone went dead.

'She's out,' Lowri said and Sally shrugged.

'Then she couldn't have been ringing from home, could she?' She paused and examined her nails. 'Want to go out tonight?'

'Why, have you fixed me up with Ken again?'

'Well, yes, but I'm sure you'll enjoy yourself.'

'All right, I'd love to come.' It would give her the opportunity to ask Ken what exactly he knew about Jon. 'Can you pick me up?'

'Sorry, my car's sick,' Sally said, 'I hoped you'd drive.'

'No problem,' Lowri said.

'That's settled then.'

Later, as Lowri drove home through the evening traffic, she wondered if she should tackle Sally as well as Ken. It was becoming increasingly clear that Sally knew more about Jon than she was letting on. It seemed quite possible that she had stayed at the Swan Hotel with him at some time. It was a mystery what Jon would see in Sally, though, she was hardly the big-business tycoon, she had little money and even less brainpower. Or was the dumb-blonde routine simply an act?

'Lowri my girl,' she said out loud, 'you are becoming a bitter and twisted woman!' She showered and put on her dressing-gown, made a cup of tea and some toast and sat in front of the gas fire.

It was colder now, with a bite of winter in the air, but the hot tea and the warmth of the fire cheered her. She was even looking forward to the challenge of a night out with Sally and the boys. Lowri wondered what to wear. Should she be the vamp with the hope of coaxing some information out of Ken or Matthew or should she simply be business-like and tough? She shrugged; it was a gamble either way.

The phone rang and Lowri rose in one supple movement, half expecting the call to be from Sally, but it was Timmy's voice that came over the wire.

'Hi, what can I do for you?' Lowri said. There was a long silence and then she heard Timmy clear his throat. It sounded as if he had been crying.

'It's Sally, I think she's had enough of me, we've had an awful row.' Lowri could almost feel his unhappiness.

'She's probably just in a mood. She'll come round.'

'I've tried to get hold of her but she's not answering her phone. And I know she's had her eye on another chap for some time.'

'She didn't say anything about you at work today,' Lowri said.

'She's probably keeping it for tonight, you know the sort of thing, women enjoy complaining about how awful we men are,' he said woefully.

'Maybe,' Lowri said, making a face at herself in the small mirror hanging in the hall. She looked pale, she noticed, and there were shadows under her eyes.

'What if I speak to her, see what she has to say about you. Is that any good?' Lowri felt the cold of the floor beneath her feet and winced, rubbing one foot against her leg in an attempt to bring life back into her toes. 'I'm picking her up later.'

'What time?'

'Oh, about seven thirty, eight o'clock, why?'

'Just wondering. Right then, you've got my number haven't you?'

'Better give it to me again. Hang on, I'll get a pen.' Lowri scribbled the number on the corner of the TV magazine. 'OK, I'll speak to you later.'

Back in the sitting-room she pulled a chair nearer the fire and put her make-up bag on it. She shivered, perhaps she was getting a cold. Or perhaps she was just becoming a nervous wreck.

As she outlined her eyebrows and padded shadow onto her lids she tried to rehearse what she would say to Sally. How could she begin?

Look, I know there's something you're hiding from me, Sally. No, that sounded like a jealous lover. How about: come clean, I know what's going on here and I want you to tell me about it or I'll go to the police. That sounded weak, pathetic, like a character in an old film. And if Matthew chanced to hear her, he would just laugh and remind her he *was* the police.

She dressed warmly and comfortably in black trousers and a black polo-neck sweater and brushed her hair until it shone. At last she could procrastinate no longer, it was time to go and pick up Sally.

It was cold in the Mazda. Lowri shivered as she settled herself in the driving seat and put the key into the ignition. She wondered why she felt such a reluctance to start the car, was she really so afraid of facing Sally? Or was she more afraid of what she might hear about Jon?

The roads were clear as she drove away from the house. A light rain had begun to fall and cursing her luck Lowri turned on the wipers; she hated driving in the rain.

The lights of the oncoming cars dazzled her and for a moment she panicked. She drew the car into the kerb and leaned on the wheel, wondering if she should simply turn around and go home.

A woman walking a dog came towards the car and knocked on the window. Lowri wound it down.

'Are you all right, dear?' The woman had a scarf tied tightly around her head. She was plump and homely, her eyes crinkled in concern.

'Yes, I'm fine.' Lowri forced a smile. 'I just don't like driving in the rain, stupid of me I know but there it is.'

'Oh well, my late husband was the same, dear, mind you he had bad eyes. You got bad eyes, have you?'

'No, no.' Lowri began to wind up the window and hesitated. 'Thank you for your concern but I'd better get on, I'm meeting my friend and I'm late already. Have you got the time by any chance?'

The woman consulted the watch on her plump wrist, holding up her arm to catch the light from the street lamp. 'Just past eight. You take care then and next time it rains, take a taxi.' The woman's face broke into a broad smile. 'You're so nice and there's me thinking all you modern young girls so brazen, frightened of nothing.'

'Ah but I'm past twenty-five, not really so young any more,' Lowri said, slipping the car into gear. The woman's smile widened.

'You're just a little chick compared to me, now go on out and enjoy yourself, make the most of it, that's my advice.'

Lowri felt more cheerful as she joined the broken line of traffic heading along the rain-swept street. She squared her shoulders. She had never been a moral coward and she did not intend to start being one now. She would tackle Sally first; she would be alone and perhaps more ready to talk. 'Nothing like hoping!'

The sound of her own voice made Lowri feel lonely and she turned on the radio. Music filled the car, loud, with no melody, only an insistent head-throbbing beat. She switched it off impatiently.

At last she drew up outside the end house in the terrace where Sally lived. Lowri switched off the engine and climbed out of the Mazda. As she walked up the path she saw light spilling out from the open front door.

Lowri knocked and waited. There was no sound from inside. Somewhere a dog barked; the noise was lonely, mournful on the still, misty air. She knocked again, louder this time. The door swung wider and she stepped inside.

'Sally, are you in?' There was no answer.

'It's me,' Lowri called. She moved further into the hallway. 'Are you there, Sal?' She hesitated and then went towards the living-room. It was empty, though the lights were on, and the images on the mute television screen mouthed unintelligible words. Sally must have become tired of waiting for her. But there was an eerie, empty feel about the place.

'Sally, where are you?' Her voice was shaky — she was suddenly very frightened. She should pull herself together — she was falling apart, imagining things.

She walked back into the hallway and looked around her, wondering what to do. Perhaps Sally had just slipped out for a moment, gone next door on some errand. Though even as she stood there, Lowri knew that was a remote possibility. Sally was always raring to go out — it was a wonder she had not been standing on the step waiting for Lowri to turn up.

She headed for the door at the end of the hallway. It was closed and from inside, Lowri heard the sound of the kettle coming to the boil. She sighed in relief. Sally was in the kitchen, no doubt making one of her endless cups of coffee while she waited.

'Sally, didn't you hear me calling?' Lowri pushed open the door just as the kettle clicked off. The room was empty, the back door swinging wide, letting in the cold. 'Sally?'

Lowri moved towards the back garden. 'Sally!' The garden was small, nowhere to hide, Sally was not out there.

'Sally, where are you?'

A dog began to bark in response to her voice and quickly, Lowri went inside and pulled the door shut. 'Sally?' She looked around, wondering what she should do next. Perhaps she should check upstairs.

The bedrooms were in darkness but Lowri switched on the lights, all of them, and looked in each of the three small rooms. Everything seemed normal, nothing was out of place. In spite of the open doors, nothing in the house had been smashed or vandalized.

Could Sally have gone out and forgotten to close the doors? It did not seem likely. She ran back downstairs into the living-room and noticed Sally's coat and bag were on the chair. Sally would never go anywhere without her stock of make-up and it was far too cold to leave her coat behind.

Back in the hall, Lowri picked up the

phone. She got through to Lainey right away. 'I think you should get over here,' she said. 'My friend Sally seems to have gone missing.'

His reassuring voice asked for the address and she told him, her voice shaking. 'Be as quick as you can,' she said, 'I've got a feeling something terrible has happened.'

14

'You've got to believe me, Jim, I've got nothing to do with Sally's disappearance.' Lowri sat in the interview room feeling as though she was in a recurring nightmare. She looked down at her hands without seeing the white of her knuckles.

'I'm not accusing you of anything, we don't even know where Sally's gone. She might just have gone round the pub or something like that.'

'And leave all the doors open? I don't think so.' Her eyes were burning and her headache had come back with a vengeance. 'I was going to pick Sally up to take her out.' She swallowed hard. 'I wanted to challenge her, ask her what she really knew about Jon Brandon. I was late, I —' Lowri only realized she was gabbling when Lainey held up his hand to stop her.

'Look, Lowri, calm down.' He touched her arm, smiling encouragingly. 'You might know more than you're letting on and there again, you might not.'

'So I am suspected of *something* then?'

'Perhaps. Even if it's only polluting the scene of the crime. If there was a crime.'

'What do you mean, polluting?'

'It's just a police expression. Witnesses, with the best intentions in the world, sometimes pollute the evidence. You know, fingerprints, fibres, that sort of thing.'

Lowri smiled. 'At least you are considering me as a witness, not a criminal.'

Lainey was silent for a moment and Lowri watched him doodling on a pad. 'What was the first thing you saw, Lowri? Think hard,' he said at last. 'Was there a car driving away or anyone walking away from the house?'

'Not that I noticed,' Lowri said honestly. 'First thing that struck me was that the front door was open. That wasn't like Sally, she moaned about the cold in the office often enough.' Lowri glanced quickly at Lainey, realizing she was speaking of Sally in the past tense. He did not seem to notice.

Laincy scratched his head and his hair lifted from his brow, giving him the look of a lost schoolboy. 'We've searched the house and the gardens round about, but there's no sign of any disturbance.' He leaned forward, his elbows on the desk, his hands supporting his jaw as if he was very tired.

'Is that significant?' Lowri asked.

'It could be if anyone tidied up the scene.'

'Is that a question, Jim?' Lowri asked.

He shook his head. 'The boys did a bit of a house-to-house in the vicinity. Major spoke to a woman who had seen you, the one who told you the time. She remembered you looked tired and she mentioned the colour of the car.' He smiled. 'She thought it was burgundy, the lamplight fooled her I expect.'

Lowri nodded. 'Does that prove anything, that I was seen coming towards Sally's house I mean?'

'No. As I said, we don't even know if Sally is really missing.' His eyes met hers. 'But I think you might have been right all along, you might have been set up by someone.'

'But how would anyone know I was going to her house? It was on impulse. I just made arrangements by phone.'

'Someone could have overheard the arrangements.'

Lowri regarded him steadily. 'Are you saying Sally's phone was tapped?' She paused. 'Or that *my* phone was tapped?'

'It's a possibility.'

'But why bother?'

'Come on, now, Lowri!' He sounded impatient. 'You are not stupid. You are at the centre of all this, whether knowingly or unknowingly. What's more,' he paused, 'you suspected Sally of being involved with Jon Brandon. Why?'

She rubbed her face. 'I don't know, intangibles, coincidences, it's like grasping at straws.'

'That's very often the way police work is done, believe it or not.'

'Look, all I know is that Sally stayed at the Swan Hotel some weeks ago with a good-looking man who answered Jon's description. The girl on the reception described Sally to a T.'

'Any other reason to think she knew Brandon?'

'Sarah — Mrs Brandon — suspected Sally of sleeping with Jon.' Lowri sighed. 'It's not much, is it? I just thought it funny that Sally denied knowing him. She wasn't always very clever, the things she said gave the impression she was hiding something from me.' She looked at him. 'I told you it was not much.'

'You're holding something back.'

She shook her head. 'No.'

'It's a uniform cop, isn't it? She was going out with one of the boys. Which one?' he said quietly. Lowri glanced out of the window.

'Matthew Brown, I think. From the little I've seen of him and Sally together I don't think they were an item as such, just friends.'

His eyes met hers and it was Lowri who looked away first, embarrassed and warmed by the way he was staring at her.

'Try to work with me, Lowri,' he said softly. 'Tell me every little detail of anything you turn up.' His eyes crinkled. 'It's trite but true to say big oaks from little acorns grow.' He looked down at the desk and picked up a piece of paper from the file.

'Someone used Brandon's credit card to withdraw cash a few days ago. Would Sally have had access to his pin number?'

Lowri shook her head, bewildered by the abrupt change of tack. 'It's possible, I suppose, but wouldn't it be more likely that Sarah Brandon withdrew cash from the account?'

'Hardly, there was just fifty pounds withdrawn.'

'Does that rule out Sarah?'

'Not rule out, it just makes it less likely. Mrs Brandon seems to be too well-heeled to bother with such a small amount.'

Lainey was silent for a long moment, tapping his pen on his desk, his eyes hooded by incredibly long lashes. 'So many questions,' he said, 'and never any answers.' He ran his fingers through his hair. 'I told you that a man calling himself Jon Brandon came into the country through Heathrow, didn't I?'

'You did.'

'What I didn't tell you was that he didn't answer to the description of anyone we know, at least, anyone I know. He was tall, well-built, balding, that's all we have. Any ideas?'

Lowri shook her head. 'If you're hoping to trap me into admitting something unlawful, forget it!' She did not wait for an answer. 'You should realize by now that it's no good asking me about Jon. He lied through his teeth all the time we were together.'

'All right, let's get back to Sally. Did she have any reason to disappear?'

Lowri felt as if cold water had been thrown over her. Lainey's tone had become formal, almost cold. She watched as he lit a cigarette.

'I don't know. I didn't know you smoked, either.'

'I'd given up,' Lainey said.

They sat in silence for a time and Lowri swallowed hard. 'Could Timmy have anything to do with this?' she asked. 'I think he was quite possessive with Sally.' She stopped speaking as a woman police constable came into the room and placed a cup of tea in front of her.

'Thank you,' Lowri said, her heart sinking. It seemed she was going to be questioned for some time.

'Possessiveness isn't unusual,' Lainey said smoothly. He was silent for a few moments and then he met her eye. 'Do you know Sally's father? She lived with him, I understand?'

'Of course, Mr White wasn't at the house either, that's odd.' She paused. 'I've met Sally's father once or twice but I can't say I know him. Why? Surely you don't suspect him?'

'No.' Lainey smiled. 'Mr White is away, visiting his sister in Birmingham, we've checked.' His smile vanished. 'The poor man is out of his mind with worry, he's coming back home on the first train.'

'I don't know what's happening lately — I seem to attract trouble.'

'Lowri, you were mixed up with a villain, what do you expect? Jon Brandon was a crook and you were a fool, get that fact into your head, once and for all.' Lainey sounded angry.

Lowri's voice was low. 'I thought I knew him, I was stupid enough to think I was going to marry him when all along I didn't know him at all. I feel enough of a fool without you rubbing it in.'

He rose to his feet. 'I'll get someone to take you home.' Lowri put down her tea and as Lainey walked past her, she resisted the temptation to catch his hand.

'I'm frightened, Jim,' she said quietly. 'I don't even know what I'm frightened of but the world seems to be going haywire.'

He rubbed his hand through his hair and paused. 'I can't authorize police protection. I don't think you are in any danger.'

'Because you think I'm hand in glove with Jon, is that it?'

Lainey shrugged. 'I'll drive by your place a few times through the night just to check.'

'Jim, why are you so good to me?' Lowri thought, for one magical moment, that he was going to say something kind, something thrilling about how attractive he found her. When he spoke, her hopes were dashed.

'Just doing my duty.' He left the room and Lowri felt like a schoolgirl who had received a lecture from the head teacher. She stood up, ignoring the quickly cooling tea.

'Come this way, Miss Richards.' It was Ken Major who led her out into the yard. 'What on earth can have happened to Sally?' he said when they were outside. 'I can see you don't know anything about it. Look, try not to take any of this personally,' he rested his hand on her arm, 'it's just that you were there at the house. It was inevitable you had to be questioned. Try not to worry.'

'Thanks, Ken.'

'I'd better get back.'

'Sure.' Lowri shivered as he strode back into the building. She suddenly felt lonely. She looked back once at the police building but only blank, empty windows stared down at her. Blank, like her life. She was jinxed and she was a failure. Once this business was over she would get her life by the scruff of the neck and change it. Perhaps she would even go back to college and complete her course.

Once in her house, Lowri curled up on her bed and brooded on the events of the night. What had happened to Sally? Poor Sally, so flighty, so vain. So involved?

She had a quick shower, enjoying the feel of the hot water on her skin. She was weary to the bone and worried sick. Something bad must have happened to Sally; the house had been deserted like the *Mary Celeste*, everything still in place but no-one there.

Lowri locked up carefully and was just about to go to bed when the phone rang. She picked it up, half fearful of what she would hear. She sighed in relief as Ken Major's voice echoed across the line.

'Lowri, can I come and see you?'

'What, now?'

'Yes, it's important.'

She glanced at the clock: it was after midnight. She wondered briefly if Lainey would be driving past just as Ken drew up outside, it would be just her luck. He thought her a tramp as it was.

'Please, Lowri, I need to see you.'

'All right. But for heaven's sake, be discreet, don't go flashing your car lights all over the road or my reputation will be well and truly in the gutter.'

She busied herself in the kitchen, filling the kettle, putting out clean mugs. As an afterthought, she brought out a packet of biscuits. Ken was probably still on duty, he would need something to sustain him through the long hours of the night.

He arrived a few minutes later. He sank down onto the sofa, his eyes closed. He was silent for so long that she thought he had fallen asleep. She waited, wondering what to say, but at last he looked up at her.

'It's about Matthew.' He took a packet of cigarettes from his pocket and held it out to her. Lowri shook her head and waited while he sparked a light and took a deep drag, blowing out smoke in a great gust.

'Well?'

'I think he knows something, about Sally I mean.' He looked at the glowing tip of the cigarette. 'He wasn't at the station when your call came in and he should have been. When I saw him later he seemed . . . well . . . strange.'

'Why strange, he could have been out on a call, couldn't he?'

'Yes, but there was nothing in the book about any call.' He bent his head, fiddling with his lighter.

Lowri frowned. 'Go on, what else?'

'Nothing, I wish there was more but there isn't. Should I mention it to Lainey, do you think?'

'I don't know what you should do, Ken.'

'Have you got a beer?'

'No but I can make a cup of tea if you like.'

He shook his head. 'No, don't go to any trouble.'

'It's no trouble, don't be silly.' She made the tea and put the cups on a tray. This was getting complicated. Matthew did not seem the sort of man who would get involved in anything underhand. But then, Sally could be very persuasive.

She brought the tea and Ken took a cup. Lowri noticed his hands were shaking. 'Ken, have you told me everything?'

'I don't know if I should say this, Lowri.'

'Go on, you might as well tell me what's on your mind.'

'I heard Matthew arguing with Sally on the phone, he sounded angry, vicious even.' He looked up. 'Would he harm her, do you think? Women are more sensitive about that sort of thing.'

'I don't know, I've only met the guy a few times.' Suddenly she felt uneasy. Did Ken have an ulterior motive in coming to visit at such a late hour? She no longer knew whom to trust, whom to believe. Men, they were enough to drive a woman mad.

'Drink up!' She heard the edginess in her tone, the sooner Ken left the better. 'Look, go on back to the station, we'll talk again tomorrow. I've got to get some sleep, I'm shattered.'

'I suppose I'd better be getting back.' Ken put down his cup and got to his feet. 'Thanks for listening, anyway.' He rested his hand on her shoulder. 'I expect I'm making a mountain out of a molehill.'

Lowri saw him to the door and watched as he walked away. Thankfully, he had parked his car out of sight. Lowri looked along the road: there was no sign of Lainey's car. She went inside and closed and bolted the door but she was restless now, sleep was out of the question. She walked about the house trying to sort out her thoughts. Jon had disappeared and so had Sally. Was there a connection? Maybe, then again, maybe not.

'The whole thing is one long nightmare, Lowri.' Her voice echoed loudly in the silence. She thought of Sally: she was silly and vain, she knew more than she ever let on about Jon Brandon but she had never meant anyone any harm, Lowri would stake her life on it.

She made herself a drink of hot milk and climbed into bed. She stared at the wall, reluctant to put out the light. She was overtired, she had been under stress and now the nightmares would come to haunt her, she just knew it. When she tried to sleep, the bed seemed full of lumps, the pillow made of concrete and she lay wide-eyed until the dawn light began to creep in through the window.

She slept then, but for only an hour. The nightmare did not materialize. Instead, her dreams were of Lainey, of him holding her, kissing her, making love to her. When she woke there were tears on her pillow. Lainey was a good man and she, well, she was nothing more to him than another foolish woman who had put her trust in the wrong man.

15

Lainey looked at the young man sitting before him in the interview room and decided he was extremely composed for someone who had just been told his girlfriend was missing. He was silent, wondering if Timothy Perkins was a violent man, a man on a short fuse. Was he capable of murder, even? Lainey knew that most murders were committed by someone close to the victim. In a case like this where there was a person missing in suspicious circumstances, every eventuality had to be covered.

Lainey tapped his pen on the desk. 'So you didn't see Miss White that night, then?'

The young man shook his head. 'No, I didn't. She had planned to go out with Lowri Richards, her friend from work.'

'But you admit that you quarrelled earlier that evening.' The man could not deny it; he had been overheard by a nosy neighbour, shouting abuse at Sally and slamming the door of her house behind him as he left.

'I asked her to come out with me but she said no. I was angry, I admit it. Haven't I said so half a dozen times?' Timothy's tone was patronizing; it was clear he saw Lainey as a stereotypical Mr Plod. 'I have agreed that we quarrelled but I never laid a finger on her.'

'So what were your movements yesterday? The police were alerted of a missing person at about 8.20: what were you doing then?'

'I was swotting for my exams.' Timothy looked up at the ceiling. 'Got a fag?'

Lainey ignored that. 'On your own?'

'Of course on my own! One can hardly study with a girl hanging around the place.'

The man was a pain in the arse, bigoted, conceited in the extreme, but looking at his long fingers and rather effete hands, Lainey doubted Timothy had the energy or even the strength to abduct Sally.

'All right, you can go.' Lainey rose to his feet. With deliberate slowness Timothy gathered his possessions, some books and a small plastic bottle containing spring water, and sauntered to the door.

'I hope you solve the crime, Inspector,' he glanced back at Lainey, 'but perhaps that's a distant hope, given the track record of our police.'

Lainey resisted the urge to swear. 'Who mentioned any crime? Don't get too cocky, Mr Perkins, otherwise you might find yourself cooling your heels in a cell.'

'In which case, you would be sued for wrongful arrest.' He smiled. 'I am studying law as well as IT, didn't you know?'

'Get out!'

Lainey watched as Timothy closed the door with a click that smacked of defiance. He would have liked to kick the young snob, jumped-up little bastard!

Lainey walked back from the interview room towards his office and thought about Lowri Richards. He seemed to be thinking about her a great deal these days. But then she was a suspect, though for what crime Lainey could not be sure. She also had beautiful eyes and splendid legs.

Lowri seemed to be the central cog of the complicated wheel that had been spinning ever since Brandon's disappearance. In his office Lainey drew a piece of paper towards him and picked up a pen. He stared down at his hands, his thoughts once again turning to Lowri. She was getting to him in a big way and it just would not do.

He doodled on a piece of paper, writing down the names of people who were associated with Brandon. Lowri, of course, Sarah the wife, Sally, just maybe, and, if Sally, Timothy Perkins as well. He stared at the paper. Some sort of pattern should be emerging but for the life of him, he could not see it.

It seemed that each and every one of them was good at playing games. Was Lowri really the innocent she appeared to be? Perhaps it was about time he began thinking with his brain instead of his groin.

Lainey lifted the phone and asked the switchboard to put him through to Watson Jones and Fry. When the line crackled into life, he spoke briskly, asking for Lowri Richards. The receptionist's voice bristled back at him.

'Is this a personal call?'

'No, it's a police matter,' he replied crisply. The line seemed to go dead but after a few minutes Lowri's voice reached out to touch him.

'Mr Lainey?'

'I have to speak to you again. Can you come down to the station?'

'What, now?'

'Yes. Right now.'

He replaced the receiver and wondered why, suddenly, the room seemed brighter, the sun through the windows sharper. He sat behind his desk and tried to concentrate on the questions he must ask Lowri but her face, the lift of her mouth, the soft fall of her hair, all of these things got in the way of logical thought. So he abandoned any pretence of work and indulged himself in a mental picture of Lowri Richards smiling up at him.

'It's very inconvenient, you know.' The new receptionist was no friendlier than she had been on her first day. 'I'm sorry your friend has gone missing but you are leaving me in a difficult situation.' Mrs Jenkins was bending over her computer, having stripped its innards. She seemed to know what she was doing as she slipped some chips into place. She glanced up and caught Lowri's look.

'I'm upgrading the RAM,' she said, 'Thirty-two megs just isn't enough. In any case, I like working with the guts of the thing, I think I should have been a technician.' She sighed. 'Now I'll just have to leave all this to do your work — it really is too bad.'

'Sorry about that.' Lowri was not sorry at all. She was happy to be getting out of the office, happy, if she was honest, that she would be seeing Laincy. She picked up her bag and shook her head. Her hair curled against her face, sleek and soft. It was rather a good feeling and Lowri wondered why she had ever thought that short hair suited her.

She was changing her looks and her life, determined to make a new start as soon as possible. Sally would have said 'new man new hairstyle' but Sally was no longer here.

She paused beside the receptionist, who was sliding the tower casing back into place. 'You are so good at operating the damn thing, it would be a pity if you confined yourself to just servicing the PC.' It was no idle compliment: the woman seemed to know more about the workings of a computer than anyone else Lowri knew. So why was she working in a solicitors' office, hidden away in a small place like Jersey Marine? Was she genuine?

'Flattery won't get you anywhere.' Mrs Jenkins really was a miserable sod, Lowri thought.

'I could hardly refuse to see the police, could I?' She knew she sounded defensive. The receptionist just shrugged, not even bothering to look up.

The telephone rang and Mrs Jenkins picked up the receiver at once. 'Yes, of course, sir,' she said. She still did not look in Lowri's direction.

'Mr Watson wants to see you.'

Lowri crossed the small reception area towards Mr Watson's office. She knocked on the door and he called to her to come in.

'I'm sorry I have to go out,' she said but Mr Watson waved her to a chair.

'No need to apologize, my dear. What's wrong now, why do the police want to see you again?'

She shook her head. 'I don't know, perhaps they think I'm mixed up in Sally's disappearance. It is very odd, Sally leaving the house open to all and sundry.' She glanced up. 'Don't you think it's odd?'

'Perhaps.' He was the typical cautious solicitor. 'What has this got to do with you?'

'I went to pick her up, we were going out for the evening.' She bit her lip. 'The house was deserted.'

'Lowri.' Mr Watson leaned forward and his leather chair creaked. 'If there's anything you want to tell me, if you are involved in anything — well — shady, I can help, you can trust me.'

'I know I can trust you.' Lowri made an effort to smile. 'You are one of the few people I do trust.' She sighed. 'I don't know anything, I promise you.' She shook her head tiredly. 'I think I'm beginning to get my life together and then something else goes wrong. Why am I always on the spot when it does?'

'Look, perhaps you should have a short holiday, my dear,' Mr Watson said. 'You could go home or if that doesn't appeal I've got a nice little cottage in the country.' He meant to be kind but Lowri shook her head.

'The police wouldn't like that one bit.' She regarded him steadily. 'Don't you mind about all this? Not just me having to take time off to see the police but all of it, the whole sorry mess I seem to have got myself into?'

'Lowri, my regard for you,' he paused, 'and for your family, is unconditional, of course I don't mind. I only wish I could do more to help.'

Lowri resisted the urge to hug him. He was much more fatherly than her own father had ever been. He smiled and his blue eyes shone behind the glasses perched on the end of his nose.

'Are you sure you don't want me to come with you?' He looked at her, his expression gentle. 'To the police station, I mean.'

Lowri returned his smile. 'How would that look, me turning up with a senior solic-itor? Lainey would think I had something to hide.'

'Lainey?'

'Detective Inspector Lainey, you know, I told you that he's the one in charge of the case.'

'And you trust him?'

'Yes.'

'Go along then, but take care what you say, these policemen can be very cunning when they want to be.'

Outside, the sun was shining but the air was chill. Lowri pulled her jacket closer around her body noticing that her clothes felt loose, she must have lost weight. She shivered; the wind was easterly, cold. She looked at the bare branches of the trees: autumn was well established.

Once in the Mazda, Lowri sighed and leaned back, enjoying a moment's peace before starting the engine. She seemed to be lurching from one mishap to another, she reflected. Her silly attempts at playing amateur detective down at the Swan had come to nothing, and now her suspicions about Sally seemed churlish, to say the least. Sally was a very attractive girl: why would she need to steal Lowri's boyfriend?

She turned the key in the ignition and as the engine burst into life she glanced over her shoulder, her eyes drawn towards a man standing in the shadow of the office doorway. Her stomach lurched; for a moment she thought she was looking at Jon Brandon. She turned to have a better view but the doorway was empty.

'I'm imagining things now!' She spoke aloud as she pushed the gear lever into first.

'I really must get a grip on myself.'

She drove carefully along the roadway and into the town, guiding the car through the one-way system with the ease of long practice. She had travelled this way to visit Jon so many times, so long ago, another lifetime it seemed. She swallowed hard. It did no good to dwell on the past, it was time she learned that.

She still felt cold so she turned on the heater. The air blew cold against her feet — the engine was not warm enough to generate a flow of heat. With a sigh, she turned it off again and concentrated on her driving.

Lainey looked grave as he led her into one of the interview rooms. There was no-one else present and Lainey, seating himself behind the desk, did not switch on the tape. That was reassuring; it meant the interview was informal.

He studied her face for a long moment. She smiled at him and he sat back in his seat as if she had slapped him.

'Have I got a spot on my nose? You were staring.'

He sighed. 'Lowri, what is going on here?'

She was puzzled — what did he mean? Could he be referring to them, to any feelings that might be growing between them? She was afraid to speak in case she said the wrong thing, so she just looked down at her hands.

'Lowri, you are involved in this business up to your neck, aren't you? Just talk to me, then we might get somewhere.'

Her heart plummeted. It was police matters he had in mind, nothing more. She had been a fool even to imagine it could be anything else. She felt like bursting into tears. The door opened and a woman PC carried in a tray and placed it on the desk. The aroma of coffee rose enticingly from the squat mugs.

'Thank you, Jen.' Lainey smiled at the girl and Lowri felt an absurd pang of jealousy. She watched the WPC walk away, noticing that she was very young and very slim with slender, black-clad legs. Lainey was surrounded by young intelligent girls; why would he even bother to look at her?

'Sugar, two wasn't it?' Lainey did not wait for her nod of approval. He spooned the brown crystals generously into her cup and pushed it across the polished desk towards her.

'Jim,' she said quietly, 'if you don't believe in me I'm lost.' She gulped her coffee and it burnt her mouth.

'How can I believe in you when all the evidence points to you being at least an accomplice in Brandon's illegal business matters? I'm asking you if you know anything — for heaven's sake tell me!'

She shook her head. 'I don't know anything. It sounds stupid, I know. All I'm guilty of is being in the wrong place at the wrong time.'

He sighed. 'Anything, even the slightest detail, might help me get somewhere in all this. It's like peeling an onion, skin after skin and no clue to what's underneath.'

Lowri drank more coffee, the hot sweet taste giving her courage. She looked directly into Lainey's eyes and he blinked.

'I swear to you, Jim, on my mother's life I am innocent of any crime,' she said earnestly. 'I am telling you the truth, I am baffled, and if you want to know I'm bloody scared, as well.'

'Why?' He sat up straighter. 'Has anyone threatened you?'

She shook her head. 'Not if I forget the brick thrown through my window and the intruder who broke into the house.' She forced a smile. 'But I take care to lock and bolt the doors and windows and I lay traps at night for anyone else who might try to break in.'

'What sort of traps?'

'You know, saucepans on the windowsills, plates ranged around the front door. All designed to make a row. Then I keep the phone by the bed, just in case all else fails.'

Lainey studied her for a long moment. 'Perhaps someone is protecting you.'

'Protecting me? Who and why?'

He tapped his pen on the desk, a habit he had when he was thinking. But what was he thinking? Lowri would have given anything to be able to read his mind.

'Jon Brandon guarding his investments perhaps?' He lifted his head. 'You know that your employer, Mr Watson, was once friendly with your family, don't you?'

'Yes,' Lowri said, surprised by the abrupt change of subject. 'Though I can't see what that's got to do with anything.'

'Humour me. Some years ago, Mr Watson and your father worked together in partnership.' He glanced up. 'Nothing illegal, I hasten to add, just the opposite, it was a very respectable business.'

'I knew they once were friends,' Lowri was puzzled, 'but I had the idea they fell out over something; at any rate, Mr Watson doesn't seem all that keen on my father. With reason, I'm sure,' she added dryly.

'Business partners often move on and forget about each other.'

Lowri looked at him, wondering if there

was a barb behind his words, but he did not meet her eyes.

'Watson and your father operated an advisory service for business people.'

'What about it?' Lowri said. 'I can't see where this is going, to be honest.'

Lainey began pen-tapping again. Lowri longed to reach out and cover his hand with her own. She waited for him to speak, sipping her quickly cooling coffee.

'I believe they had a serious quarrel. From what I have managed to find out there were legal implications. Your father, it seems, came out of the partnership the richer of the two men.' He put down his pen. 'I wondered if your father was putting pressure on Watson to look after you.'

'You must be joking!' Lowri wrapped her hands around her coffee-mug, clutching it as if for support. 'My father doesn't even know who I'm working for and if he did, he couldn't care less.' She leaned forward. 'In any case, protecting me from what, from whom? You want me to talk to you but you don't talk to me. Why should I need protecting? I haven't done anything.'

'Are you sure?'

'I'm sure.'

He leaned back in his chair, his voice casual. 'Lowri, tell me about your life. I want to know all about you.'

Was this personal now or business? Lowri could not tell. 'Why?'

'I just do.'

She smiled. 'OK, but prepare yourself for the most boring interview of your career.'

16

Matthew Brown stared out of the window at next door's dog running riot in the flower-beds. The weekends when he did not work were a drag. He hated to be alone. He banged the glass but, after a moment's hesitation, the dog began digging again. He pushed the window wide open, looking for something to throw.

'Get out of my garden, you mangy mongrel!' he shouted. Shortly after, he heard a whistle from next door and the dog scampered away. That little exercise had done nothing for any good-neighbour policy but so what, so bloody what? Matthew had other things to think about. She had wonderful legs, eyes to drown in and she was an enigma. He had lusted after Lowri Richards ever since he first set eyes on her. And was he ever tired of playing Mr Nice Guy!

On an impulse, he picked up the phone and dialled Lowri's number. The phone rang several times before he heard her voice come over the line.

'Lowri, I'm glad you're in,' he said. 'It's

Matthew Brown, I want to see you.' Before she had time to make excuses, he spoke again. 'It's a little bit of unofficial police business.'

'I've heard that somewhere before from Ken Major. I hope this is not just a pathetic attempt to get me into bed. Perhaps I should inform you police officers that I'm not an easy lay.'

She spoke edgily and who could blame her? 'It's nothing like that! I think we should talk. Come to my place, I'll leave all the doors and windows open if you'll feel safer.'

She was silent for a moment and he thought she was going to refuse. 'OK, Matthew, I'll be there in half an hour.'

Matthew gave Lowri his address, replaced the receiver and looked around him. The place was a bit of a mess; perhaps he should tidy up before she came. He was excited by the thought of having Lowri on his own. It had been some days since he had seen her and then she had been in company, Ken Major's company, while he had been stuck with Sally. But he would need to be careful, no point in scaring Lowri away by criticizing her friend.

In his bedroom he picked up several pairs of socks and some underpants and then flung the duvet over the bed, smoothing out the creases as best he could. It was a long shot that he could get her into the sack but there was nothing like hoping, and at least she was more of a challenge than silly little Sally White had ever been.

The kitchen was a bit of a disaster area so he took a bottle of white wine from the fridge and picked up some glasses. Then, with a last look at the chaos, he closed the kitchen door.

When Lowri arrived, she looked cool and sophisticated in a navy suit. Her hair hung to her shoulders, framing her face, giving it an almost elfin look. She was a beautiful woman, but unobtainable. What was it about her?

'So,' Lowri said, 'what's the unofficial business then?'

Matthew looked at her legs, slender, black-clad and tempting. A sense of almost unbearable lust filled him. He was a man who needed women, needed a lot of them and often.

She seemed composed, but her hands trembled as she folded them in her lap. 'What's happened, Matthew? Are the police any nearer to finding out anything about Sally?'

'Well . . .' Matthew wanted to prolong the meeting and instinct told him that once her curiosity was satisfied, Lowri would just get up and leave. In any case, it was not in his interests to reveal too much information; suspicions might be aroused if Lowri started asking questions in the wrong quarter. 'Well, it's difficult. Have a drink?'

'Tea?' she said helpfully.

'How about a glass of white wine? It's not going to knock you out, I promise.'

She looked at him and then at the glasses. He read her mind and decided to come clean.

'It's the kitchen, it's a mess.' He shrugged. 'I haven't washed the dishes or cleaned up or anything so I thought we would have some wine, less bother.'

'I'm driving.' Lowri took off her jacket and his gaze was riveted on her breasts as the soft material of her blouse clung to her. He coughed.

'Come on,' she said, rolling up her sleeves. 'I'll help you to clean up in exchange for a decent cuppa. The wine is out, as I said, I'm driving.'

He winced as he followed her into the kitchen; it looked worse than ever seen through Lowri's eyes. She pushed some empty milk bottles aside. 'Any washing-up liquid?' He picked the bottle out of the debris on the draining-board.

'I'm sorry, I shouldn't let you . . . I mean it's not fair.'

Lowri was already running the water, letting it get hot. She took the piled-up dishes from the sink and plonked them on the side.

'Didn't your mother ever tell you how to wash up properly?' she asked. 'You do the cleanest or, in this case, the least dirty things first. Glasses, cutlery and then the plates with the dried-on leftovers.'

She washed up efficiently and he stood watching her, wondering at the sense of peace the sight of her was giving him. Was he going soft in the head? She glanced over her shoulder.

'See if you can find a half decent tea towel and start drying.'

They worked together in silence, the scene needing only the morning news on the radio to complete the atmosphere of happy domesticity. He *was* going soft in the head, no doubt about it. All too soon, Lowri was finished.

'I'm not offering to put the dishes away for you.' She smiled. 'I'm afraid that I might see a piggy mess in your cupboards and I'm not starting on shelves, not on my day off.'

She returned to the lounge while he made some coffee. For the first time Matthew envied the married men in the service. Playing the field was all very well but there came a time when a man needed stability in his life, and there was no harm in having a bit on the side as well.

'Right, no more beating about the bush, what have you got to tell me?' She leaned forward expectantly. He saw the long white arch of her neck and the gleam of lipstick on her mouth and realized he had never wanted anyone as much as he wanted Lowri Richards. The fact that DI Lainey had an eye for her made the situation all the more intriguing.

'I'm waiting. Is this about Sally?'

He glanced up at her. 'It's not anything to do with Sally, I'm afraid, but I thought you would want to know anyway. It's about Jon Brandon.'

'Jon? Please, just get on with it, Matthew.'

'A small case he was planning to export has been discovered, down at the docks.' He sipped the coffee; it was so hot it burnt his tongue. 'Blast!' The cup jolted in the saucer, spilling hot liquid onto the table.

Lowri fetched a dishcloth from the kitchen and mopped up the mess. 'Were you born awkward, Matthew, or did it need training?' She was laughing at him and he did not like it. 'Do you want to hear this or don't you?' he said sharply.

She held up her hand; her nails were painted with some pink colour, very discreet, not like the garish polish Sally had favoured.

'OK, sorry, I am all attention.'

'Well, the customs declaration form says the case contains computer things, CDs and some other chips and stuff. It's all Greek to me.'

'So?'

'So it was due to be exported by Jon Brandon a couple of months ago, somehow it was overlooked.' He stared at her, waiting to gauge her expression. 'The stuff was meant for Canada and was addressed to one Justin Richards. Coincidence or what?'

Was it his imagination that she seemed suddenly to be alert? She lifted her cup, holding it with both hands, her slim fingers meeting around the china as if to comfort herself.

'Have the contents of the case been examined?' She held the cup to her mouth and the steam from the liquid seemed to cast a moistness on her parted lips. He wanted to leap on her, to carry her to his bed, to ravish her.

'Not yet. The customs and excise people are onto it and one of our lot, possibly Lainey, will be there at the great opening.'

Lowri put down her cup. She was frowning, she seemed genuinely puzzled. 'But what do they hope to find? Computer parts are not exactly contraband goods, are they?'

Matthew shrugged. 'I don't really know.' He could not reveal too much — Lowri was pretty friendly with Lainey. In any case, it was possible she knew more than he did and was acting the part of the innocent to perfection.

'Matthew, is that it? Is that what you've dragged me over here to tell me?' She rose to her feet. 'So some stuff of Jon's has been overlooked, left at the docks. What's that got to do with me?'

'Well,' Matthew said slowly, 'I thought you might know this Justin Richards, that's all, same name and all that. Inquiries are being made about him as we speak.' He wondered if he should reveal a little more.

'The thing is, the customs boys think there's something else hidden among the stuff. It's not drugs, the dogs would have sniffed them out. But it's something illegal, you can bet on it.'

'What?' Lowri seemed exasperated. 'What do you all think it is?' She turned to look at him. 'You're not being entirely honest with me, are you, Matthew?'

'I can't say too much, Lowri.' He was

aware he sounded smug but he did not expect the anger that flashed from her eyes.

'In other words you don't trust me, is that it?' She turned away from him, her shoulders hunched. 'You still think I might be a criminal; you've got me here not to tell me what *you* know but to find out what *I* know. Well, believe me, I don't know anything. Can't any of you get that through your thick heads? Did Lainey put you up to this?'

If she was acting then she was damn good at it, but, like most policemen, he had heard enough convincing liars in his career to be wary of righteous indignation. He sighed heavily.

'Lainey knows nothing at all about this meeting — my head would be on the block if he did, I'm telling you.'

'Well, what *is* going on, Matthew? Come on, speculate, you're a policeman, aren't you? Do a bit of brainwork, make guesses, anything.'

'All right,' Matthew said. 'I think that smuggling is going on here, not of heroin or arms or anything obvious like that, but it could be extortion involving money-laundering.'

He saw her sink back into her chair. She seemed to be digesting what he had just said, evaluating it. Then she shook her head.

'I don't even know what that means.' She picked up her cup again; it seemed she was prepared to stay and talk to him. 'Have you thought,' she paused, 'perhaps it's not modems or motherboards we should be looking at but disks or CDs containing some sort of information?'

She was bright, he gave her that. Perhaps too bright for her own good. 'What sort of information?'

'I don't know. Pictures of people in compromising situations, or information about porn rings, perhaps. If that is the case,' she added, 'the information would have to be protected in some way.'

'In what way?'

'Well, if, for instance, there were lists of leaders of vice mobs, they could be protected by a password. Either that or they could be loaded under some kind of code. Encryption it's called in computer jargon.'

She seemed to know an awful lot about computers suddenly. He stared at her. Perhaps she was just a dark horse and was more knowledgeable than he had suspected. She seemed to read his mind. She smiled.

'Nothing sinister, I assure you. I use a computer every day and we get magazines sent to the office. I take them home sometimes and read them. It's our receptionist

Mrs Jenkins who is the real expert. She can strip the things down as well as operate them.'

'Very impressive.' He heard the irony in his voice and Lowri did too. She rose to her feet and picked up her bag.

'I'd better go.'

'No, not yet, Lowri, stay just a little bit longer, I get fed up of being on my own.' He sighed. 'And I do miss little Sally, even though I cover it up very well.'

'I'm sorry, of course you must miss her, but haven't you got any friends you can talk to? You seem to be very popular down at the pub.'

'They are all workmates,' he said. 'It's not quite the same thing as having real friends.' He shrugged. Lowri's expression softened.

'Why not come for a spin with me in the car?'

She was taking pity on him and he knew it. 'Anything is better than sitting in here feeling sorry for myself,' he said.

Lowri smiled. 'Gee, thanks!'

'I didn't mean it like that. Let's start again: I'd love to go for a spin with you. You have beauty and brains, I couldn't ask for anything more, could I?'

'Don't go overboard.'

He followed her from the house and

watched as she unlocked the door of the small red car. She slipped into the driving seat and, nonplussed, he stood on the pavement.

'Get in.' She leaned across the passenger seat. 'I hope you weren't expecting to drive?'

'No, of course not.' He had been, actually, but he refrained from saying so and slid his tall frame into the car, fastening the seatbelt with a click as if to show that he was in charge of the situation and comfortable with it.

'Where shall we go?'

'How about driving down towards the coast, perhaps have a drink at one of the pubs there? Mine will have to be tea or juice, I'm afraid, but you are free to indulge in whatever you like.' Lowri was looking in the driving mirror and he hesitated, wondering if there was an ulterior motive in her suggestion. The Swan Hotel was situated right on the coast. Her next words confirmed his thoughts.

'I want to ask some questions down at the Swan,' she said.

His first instinct was to refuse, but she had already started the car and was manoeuvring it away from the kerb. She glanced at him, her green eyes fringed with golden lashes. 'There might be something I've missed.'

He sank back in his seat, suppressing a sigh. This was not going at all as he had anticipated. He wondered if she had remembered something about that night, something that might be significant. Perhaps Brandon had carried a briefcase with him, or a laptop or notepad, whatever the small computers were called. It bugged him that he could not find out exactly what Lowri knew about that night.

The drive was pleasant enough. The mists of early morning had been dispersed beneath a fitful sun. The roadway, almost a lane, curved and straightened, sometimes offering a tantalizing glimpse of sparkling sea.

The Swan Hotel was just the place for illicit meetings, and maybe not only of the romantic kind. He risked a look at Lowri; she was concentrating on her driving, her hands steady on the wheel. White graceful hands, innocent of any jewellery. He knew she had worn a diamond ring on the night she had been brought into the station. What had she done with it? Pawned it or sold it, probably. After all, it had no sentimental hold on her, not once she learned that Brandon was a married man.

'Know me next time?' Lowri was smiling.

'Sorry, I was far away, I didn't realize I was staring.'

280

'It's a bit unnerving, you know, being studied by a policeman. Do you suspect me of extortion, perhaps even murder, Matthew?'

'No.' He suspected her of many things, but murder was not one of them. He forced himself to look out of the window; he wished he had the power to read her mind. He might as well face it, Lowri Richards could represent a serious danger to his career and perhaps to him personally.

'That was pretty final,' Lowri said. 'Are there any other suspects then, beside me, I mean?'

Matthew needed to be careful and he knew it. 'I'm sorry, Lowri, I can't discuss the case. I suppose I shouldn't even be meeting you socially. You are still the only real link there is to Jon Brandon.'

That was not strictly true but he needed to keep up his guard, at least until he knew her a little better.

'Oh, come on, Matthew!' Lowri said. 'Surely you've got somewhere in your inquiries by now?'

'Well, a couple of things have come to light. Like I said, that suspiciously small case for a start. Strange really, it should have been shipped out long ago.'

'Why wasn't it?'

'I don't know, I haven't seen the paperwork. Some oversight. I think Lainey believes that the key to the mystery lies in the guts of a computer. Most people use one these days. Don't like them myself.'

'But you see the implications, don't you?' Lowri said. Matthew glanced at her; she was concentrating on turning the car into the grounds of the hotel. Her auburn hair swung over the sculptured curve of her cheekbone. She was so beautiful. Perhaps too beautiful.

'No, what implications?'

'Jon must have flown the coop, left the country, or else he's dead — otherwise he would have made sure that computer stuff was sent out at the proper time.'

'But he might just be lying low.'

'I suppose so.'

The foyer of the hotel was unoccupied except for the clerk behind the desk. It was only the lights and the piped music discreetly turned low that showed the place was inhabited at all.

'Can I help you? Oh, hi!' The receptionist's smile welcomed them both. He understood that she knew him, she had seen him on more than one occasion, but how come she recognized Lowri? As far as he was aware, Lowri had only been there once and that was on the night Brandon disappeared.

The girl leaned over the counter and smiled at Lowri. 'This your boyfriend then? If so, we'd better have a talk.' Matthew heard every word of the sibilant whisper but pretended to look behind him at the empty lounge.

'Hi, Trish. It's OK, Matthew and I are just friends.'

Trish smiled again. 'Tall, dark and handsome, very nice.'

Matthew forced a smile; damn the girl for recognizing him. 'As the lady said, she and I are just friends.' His tone was meant to be disapproving but the girl just raised her eyebrows.

'Oh, aye, well working here I've heard that before! What can I do for you, miss?' She looked at Lowri.

'I don't really know, Trish, I just wondered if anything had come to light, you know, about that matter we discussed last time I was here?'

The girl shook her head. 'No, not really. I did read about that "sister" of yours, Sally White. She went missing, didn't she? It was in all the papers.'

Matthew saw the colour rise in Lowri's cheeks. 'I'm sorry,' she said, 'I shouldn't have lied to you. Sally and I were workmates, not sisters.'

'Still a cat though, by the look of it,' Trish said. 'I recognized her at once from her photograph in the paper. She came here once or twice.' She glanced up at Matthew. 'But you know that. You were with her, weren't you, sir?'

Matthew cursed the girl — she was too clever by far. 'Not me.' He forced a smile. 'Must have been Ken Major, you said how alike we were.'

He decided it was time he took charge. He ordered a glass of wine for himself and a pot of tea for Lowri. He took Lowri's arm and led her across the wide expanse of carpet to a sofa near the window. He felt her glance at him but he waited until they were seated before he spoke.

'What's going on here, Lowri?' he asked, hearing the edge of hardness in his voice. She looked up at him, pushing back her hair.

'I don't know what you mean.'

'So,' he spread his hands wide, 'I liked Sally, I even slept with her sometimes but I assure you I know nothing about her disappearance.'

'It's really none of my business,' Lowri said, her eyes looking into his. 'I just wanted to make sure that Sally was never here with

Jon Brandon.' She smiled apologetically. 'The idea just popped into my head. The description Trish gave me of Sally's friend matched Jon — it also matched you, tall, dark, handsome. Ken too, as Trish so rightly pointed out.'

Was she trying to flatter him? He relaxed a little.

'You're a lot younger than Jon Brandon,' Lowri said. 'And a lot more honest.' Her eyes were innocent of any hostility. 'And I'm not blaming you for having an affair with Sally, she was a very attractive girl.'

'It wasn't an affair, as such. We liked each other and she had a vigorous libido. I wasn't the only one she had a casual relationship with.'

'Timmy, you mean?' Lowri leaned forward. 'What if he found out about you and Sally, what if he killed her?'

'Oh now, don't jump to conclusions!' Matthew said, making an effort to smile. 'Timmy's a bit of a wimp; from what I've seen of him he could never murder anyone. Anyway, we don't yet know if anyone has been murdered.'

'Don't you?'

'I don't know what you mean.'

'No,' Lowri said, 'neither do I.'

'Well, this little trip hasn't enlightened

you at all, then?' Matthew said. Lowri looked at him; he felt uncomfortable, as though she was trying to see inside him. Her next words rocked him back on his heels.

'Only in so far as you could be a suspect along with me, at least where Sally is concerned. You did come here with her, didn't you? Trish has a memory for faces, so why not admit it?'

He wanted to slap her and suddenly his mouth was dry. He sipped his wine and looked out of the window, anywhere but into her questioning eyes. He wished now that he had not let his lust for Lowri blind him to the danger she posed. He took a deep breath.

'If you feel like that,' he said, 'we might just as well go home.'

'That's all right by me.' The easy atmosphere between them had vanished. As they climbed into the car, he pressed Lowri back against the seat. 'You know I could do what I want with you and no-one would be any the wiser?'

'Ah, but they would. I rang my employer, Mr Watson, told him that I was going out with you. He's also my solicitor and he likes to be kept informed where the police are concerned.'

'Very clever!' He let her go and sank back

into his seat. 'I wouldn't harm you, Lowri, I was just fooling about. Can't you take a joke?'

She did not answer but gunned the engine into life and manoeuvred the car out of the car park. She drove in silence with her eyes on the road. She did not speak and though Matthew attempted to start a conversation a few times, he knew he was fighting a losing battle.

She dropped him at his door and immediately took off, the red car vanishing along the road in a shimmer of sudden sunlight.

Matthew watched for a time and then went into his house and picked up the phone.

17

'What the hell do you think you are up to?' Lainey looked at Matthew Brown with a feeling amounting to loathing. The officer's eyes were averted, like a schoolkid caught playing truant.

'You know Lowri Richards is a suspect in a serious crime.' Lainey thrust his hands into his pockets. 'I don't believe it — here am I making an all-out effort to have her followed and yet you take a drive with her.' Lainey paced around his office. 'You go with her to the very spot where a man went missing under suspicious circumstances. Are you soft in the head, or what?'

Matthew sighed. 'I suppose I didn't think, guv.' It was a poor excuse and Matthew stared down at his boots in a hangdog way that infuriated Lainey still further.

'You were too concerned with what's going on in your pants to think straight.' He took a deep breath, trying to control his anger. 'Did you sleep with her?' Lainey was possibly overstepping his right to know, but he persisted. 'I mean did you book into a room, sign a register, anything to prove who you were and who you were with?'

'No, guv.'

A sense of overwhelming relief washed over Lainey. Why he was so pleased that his sergeant had not had sex with Lowri was something he pushed to the back of his mind.

'Well, at least you didn't go completely overboard.' He walked over to the window and looked out at the rain-sodden sky.

'Look, I know she's an attractive woman,' Lainey said, 'I'd be a fool to pretend different, but we do have to try to be impartial in an inquiry such as this.' Pity he could not take his own advice.

A police car drew up outside and he saw Lowri stepping out into the rain. He had to question her about her trip to the hotel but, first, he needed to know Brown's version of the story.

She looked lovely, her hair swung over her face, a dark red curtain. She glanced up and her eyes met his briefly before she looked away. Her visit to the Swan with Matthew Brown, laughing with him, flirting with him, was something Lainey did not want to dwell on.

'Why did you go there, of all places, not for a bit of social chit-chat I take it?' He spun on his heel to face the other man, and saw a light of derision in his eyes. It was clear Matthew had his measure; he realized that Lainey was involved with Lowri over and above the call of duty.

'She, Lowri, wanted to find out if Brandon stayed there with Sally White. I didn't see any harm in it, guv, sorry.'

Lainey's eyes narrowed. He saw the connection at once and read the implications. Matthew and Jon Brandon were the same stamp, tall, dark-haired, handsome by some women's standards.

'Were you the one at the Swan with Sally White? Have you taken her there since the Jon Brandon affair began?'

Matthew looked down at his shoes. 'Yes, guv.'

'You stupid bastard! Out of all the hotels in the country you had to choose that one. Why?'

Matthew shrugged, unable or unwilling to answer the question. Lainey sat on the edge of his desk. 'Look, Matthew, you stayed at the very hotel where a man disappeared, perhaps died. You take Sally White there and then she vanishes.' He held up his hand when Matthew opened his lips to speak. 'Is there anything else you should be telling me?'

'No, guv, I just didn't think, that's all.'

'You were with Lowri Richards for some time on this foolish trip. I just hope you didn't discuss anything about this case with her, we are still not sure how deeply she is involved.'

Matthew shook his head. 'I wouldn't tell her anything important, guv, you know that.'

'Do I? Listen, I don't want to suspend you but you are pushing your luck a bit far. I suggest that you take your holiday as from today.'

'If you say so, guv.' Was it his imagination, or was Matthew relieved to be let off so lightly? When the sergeant left the office, Lainey returned to his chair and leaned back, his eyes closed. Matthew, Matthew and Sally White, Matthew and Lowri, Matthew and Jon Brandon? Lainey sat up straight. He could see some light at the end of the tunnel but he did not much like where it was leading.

Lowri sat in the interview room and looked across the desk at Lainey. 'What else can I tell you, Inspector?' She noticed how the sunlight touched his hair with red-gold and averted her eyes.

'I don't know. Go over it again, will you?'

Lowri sighed. 'I was talking to Matthew, he seemed a bit down. I suggested that we go for a run. It occurred to me it might be an idea to drive as far as the Swan. I knew Sally had been there with some man and Matthew answered the description.'

'I gathered that much,' Lainey said. 'So you were talking to Matthew. How and when did that come about?'

'He rang me. Asked me to come over and talk. I knew he and Sally were friends and as I said, I sensed he was feeling a bit low, so I went to his place.'

'And then?' They might not have booked a room in the hotel but they could have slept together at Brown's place before they left. 'And what, exactly, did you do to revive Brown's spirits?'

She gave him a hard look. 'We had a cup of coffee, I washed up some dishes for him and we drove to the hotel. Is that all right, Inspector?' Her tone was hostile.

'So you decided to do our work for us, did you?'

'It was a whim. I felt that Matthew knew more than he was letting on.' She paused. 'In any case, you are not quite up to Inspector Morse standards, are you?'

Lainey almost smiled. He watched Lowri covertly: she seemed genuine enough but was that his heart talking, or his head? He still felt that she was hiding something. 'So you wanted to check things out at the hotel?'

'That's right. I caught Matthew out in a lie. He said he was never there with Sally but he was, and on more than one occasion I'm sure. In which case, Sally was never with Jon.'

'I wouldn't rule out that possibility if I were you.' Lainey rubbed at his chin. He was aware of Lowri watching him, doubtless wondering what was behind his insistent questioning. 'So, what do you make of that, Brown and Sally White as lovers? Jealous, are you?'

Lowri shrugged. 'No. Why should I be jealous?' Her chin was tilted upwards; her expression was challenging. 'And what *can* I make of it except that Matthew and Sally were having an affair behind Timmy's back?'

'And what about Sally and Jon Brandon? Mrs Brandon might be correct in suspecting them of having an affair, don't you think?'

Lowri bit her lip for a moment. Her green eyes were very dark. 'I suppose so. Look, how the hell do I know what they did? I don't seem to know anything very much about men, do I? I seem to have been a dope as far as my love life was concerned.'

'But an affair between them is a possibility, don't you agree?'

'Yes, of course it's a possibility. Jon was not the faithful kind, that much has become abundantly clear to me.'

She sounded hurt rather than angry. This Jon Brandon must have been one hell of a con man. He noticed that he had been thinking in the past tense. The possibility that Brandon was dead was a good one. Maybe he had fallen foul of his accomplices, because it was a certainty that the man had been mixed up in something dangerous.

If he was alive, he had probably gone into hiding, though whether from the police or his own colleagues, it was difficult to decide. It was a rare puzzle, a very unusual case, and Lainey felt a rush of adrenalin. He would get to the bottom of it if it killed him.

'Anything else?' Lowri's voice interrupted his thoughts. He looked across the desk at her and saw the shadows under her eyes and the lack of colour in her face. He felt sorry for her; as she said, she was not very good at choosing her men. One by one they seemed to let her down.

There was more than pity in his feelings, if he was honest. There was the strong desire to kiss her soft lips, to take her to bed. He caught himself up sharply.

'I can't think of anything, not right now.'

'You sound unsure. I haven't been able to tell you very much, have I?'

'What's new?' Lainey said. 'All right, you can go.'

Lowri rose quickly to her feet. She was still very pale but the light was back in her eyes. She had guts, this one. Guts enough to kill someone?

'Are you having me watched, Mr Lainey?'

He spun his chair so that he was looking away from her and out of the window. 'No.' He hated lying to her.

She hesitated. She moved closer and he smelt her perfume. He closed his eyes, willing her to go.

'I think you are.'

He sighed. 'I'm afraid I can't discuss police procedure with you, Miss Richards.' He sounded like a pompous arse. That was becoming a habit where Lowri was concerned. He heard the rustle of her clothes as she walked to the door but he did not look at her.

When she left his office, he stood at the window and watched as she walked towards the police car. He saw Brown open the door for her and anger tore at his guts. Lowri, with a last look towards the building, climbed into the back seat.

Lainey waited until the car drove out of the yard and then returned to his desk. He looked down at the file before him. None of it made much sense. But Lowri was up to her neck in it all, that was certain. Well, he could not wait around doing nothing; it was time he made a move.

'I hope you realize that I'm left with all the work when you go jaunting off all the time.' Mrs Jenkins's tone was icy and Lowri sighed.

'I've apologized, what else can I do? And seeing the police isn't exactly "jaunting off", is it?'

The receptionist did not answer. She resumed her work, her hands flying over the keyboard with the speed of a trained typist. She was a clever woman, far too skilled to be wasting herself in a small office. Lowri stared at her back, wondering why she did not aim for a job in London where the wages were three times higher than those in Jersey Marine.

She watched as Mrs Jenkins slipped a disk into the slot in the computer and called up a block of text on the screen. Lowri envied her, her easy confidence with all things technical. Lowri herself was becoming more proficient on the computer, but it would take years for her to come anywhere near Mrs Jenkins's standards.

The intercom buzzed and the receptionist pressed a button. The voice of Mr Watson came over the line and she looked up, a frown of disapproval on her face.

'You're wanted.' She jerked her head in the direction of Mr Watson's office. 'Don't be all day, will you? I'm trying to be receptionist, clerk and general dogsbody round here as it is.'

Lowri made a face behind Mrs Jenkins's stiff shoulders and immediately felt ashamed of the childish response.

She knocked on the door of Mr Watson's office and entered the room, her notebook in her hand. There was a man with Mr Watson; he was standing in front of the desk. He was thickset, his hair longish and streaked with white. Lowri's stomach lurched as he turned to face her.

'Charles! What are you doing here?'

He looked at her with his usual disapproving stare. 'I came up to London to see your mother.' He half smiled. 'Don't you know she's moved out, left me?'

Lowri shook her head. 'You could have told me this before! No wonder I haven't been able to get any answer on the phone in the evenings. I expect you're too busy with your latest woman to answer phone calls!'

'Don't get shirty with me, Lowri! I have business up in London and I thought I'd call in on an old friend. Isn't that right, Terence?'

Mr Watson glanced at her and shook his head. 'Don't worry, Lowri, everything is going to be all right.'

'Is Mother OK?' She glared at Charles. 'Where is she staying?'

The two men looked at each other. 'That's her business,' Charles said. 'Your mother will talk to you when she is good and ready.' He spoke indifferently, but why should she be surprised? There had been very little love and affection between her parents for as long as Lowri could remember.

'Still making pots of money, Father?'

Mr Watson looked up, his expression grave. 'Sit down, Lowri,' he said, 'we have to talk.'

'Why, what's wrong?'

'Your father — that is, Charles — is trying to blackmail me.'

Lowri looked from one to the other. Charles was composed, his hands thrust into the pockets of his greatcoat, his collar crisp and clean. He smelled of aftershave and he looked every inch the successful businessman.

Lowri sat. 'How, why?'

Charles gestured to Mr Watson. 'Go on, Terence, tell her, if you dare.'

Mr Watson shook his head again before opening a drawer and taking out a faded photograph, pushing it towards Lowri. She picked it up and saw her mother, young, vibrant, full of life, with a baby held tenderly in her arms. Beside her was a man, but it was not Charles. She stared at it for a long time.

'So?' She glared at Charles. 'Mr Watson knew Mother, what's the big deal?'

His laugh was heavy with irony. 'He knew her all right, in the carnal sense!'

'Charles!' Mr Watson sounded agitated. 'Do you have to be so damn crude?'

'So, what are you saying?' Lowri did not look at Charles. She sensed what was coming and was not sure she wanted to hear it.

'You are my daughter, Lowri,' Mr Watson said quietly. 'Your stepfather has been silent about this for years but now, for reasons of his own, he is choosing to speak.'

Lowri was silent, digesting the facts. Was she shocked? She just did not know how she felt. She looked at the photograph and saw something in her mother's face that she had rarely seen before. Happiness.

So her mother and Mr Watson were lovers once and she was the result. She looked up at the man who had always made her life hell and all she felt was relief that she knew who her real father was at last.

'How much does he want?' she asked Mr Watson. 'Whatever it is, don't give it to him, he's not worth it.'

'It's not money, Lowri.' Mr Watson sighed. 'He wants me to help him with what he calls his business dealings.'

Charles leaned forward, a pugnacious expression on his face. 'And if you hadn't been poking around into what doesn't concern you, Terence, none of this would have been necessary.'

Lowri stared at them both. The implications of what had been said were striking home. She was the daughter of a humble urban solicitor. And all she felt was a sense of release.

'I don't know what you're talking about.' She turned away from him and smiled at Mr Watson. 'Tell him to go to hell!' she said firmly. 'You don't owe him a thing and neither do I.'

'It's not that simple.' Mr Watson sank back in his chair. 'As Charles indicated, I have been snooping around, more to protect you and your mother than to land him in trouble.' He dismissed Charles with a flick of the wrist.

'What's going on? Mr Watson, just tell me!'

'Charles is still working the same old scams he always enjoyed, blackmail being the least of it.' He looked at Charles. 'When I split up the partnership years ago it was because you were too stupid to handle things properly. Who is pulling your strings now, Charles, because you haven't got the brains to manage alone?'

'Just don't worry about him,' Lowri said forcefully. 'Let him go to hell his own way.' The venom with which Charles stared at her, his eyes narrow, the cold blueness glittering at her, made her shiver, despite her brave façade.

'I can't do that,' Mr Watson said. 'He intends to hurt your mother if I don't help him.'

Lowri felt a frisson of fear. 'Haven't you hurt Mother enough? I always knew you were no good but I didn't realize you were such a sick bastard!' She paused, staring at his set features, the nose large with deep lines on either side, the mouth narrow, cruel beneath a thin moustache. 'What if I tell the police about all this?'

Charles smiled. 'The police? Oh, I know you've bedded half the force. You are a trollop just like your mother. But it won't do you any good — the police have been well paid. In any case, where's your proof?' He smiled thinly. 'They might listen to you but then they will do absolutely nothing.'

He looked triumphantly from Lowri to Mr Watson. 'And don't bother about any rough stuff, my personal security boys are watching out for me.'

Lowri faced her stepfather, her gaze unwavering. She was trying to understand how this man, whom her mother must have loved once, could be so cold-blooded. 'So what are you mixed up in, I would like to know?' A thought struck her. 'It wasn't you who sent some thug to break into my house, was it?'

He laughed without humour. 'You are so stupid, Lowri, and your mother thinks you will benefit most from her money, money that I have a right to and my son too. My advice to you is marry money because you won't have any of mine.'

'It's you who are the stupid one,' Lowri said calmly. 'You underestimate Mother and you underestimate me. How do you know what I can achieve? You don't even know me properly.'

She put her head on one side. 'You're the one behind Jon Brandon, aren't you? You set me up.'

He moved closer, his face pushed towards hers. 'Your mother has kept her eyes shut all these years and it would pay you to follow her lead.'

Lowri was suddenly very angry. 'You've knocked the spirit out of my mother with your temper tantrums and your constant string of women friends. Well, I'm not Mother and I'm not afraid of you.'

'Perhaps I'd better explain my methods.' Charles sat on the edge of the desk. 'I'm not above having those who cross me rubbed out. Killed. Is that clear enough for you?'

'Oh, yes, very clear.'

'As for your mother, I put up with her and her little peccadillo with this loser.' He looked meaningfully at Mr Watson. 'She provided a good front for me, you see, beautiful, apparently respectable. She would never protest whatever I did.'

He jabbed his finger towards Mr Watson. 'She always was spineless, she must have been, to sleep with him. So, what you do is shut your mouth and your precious father there does a little bit of work for me.'

'What sort of work?'

'That's between me and him.'

'What if I go to the police in spite of what you say?'

'Just remember, my arms are long, they

reach everywhere. Your acquaintance with your newfound father won't last long if you go to the police.'

Lowri stared at him long and hard. 'Now I know why I've always disliked you. You are a cold-hearted, crooked, no-good bastard!' There was a wealth of scorn in her voice. Charles appeared unaffected.

'It's you who are the bastard,' he said calmly. He addressed Terence Watson. 'I'll be in touch and you'll be ready to do what I want, do you get that?' He smiled. 'It's time I paid you back for the wrong you did me all those years ago. My best friend had an affair with the woman I loved. You're such a loser. I never did understand it.'

With a last scathing look in Lowri's direction, he walked out leaving the door open. Lowri watched through the window as he left the building and then turned to look at Mr Watson. If she had been expecting him to be distressed, she was wrong.

'Your mother is all right, I'm taking care of her. I'm sorry about this, Lowri.' He took her hands. 'Not because you are my daughter but because I didn't want you to learn the truth in such a brutal way.'

'It's difficult to take it all in,' Lowri said, 'but be careful, Charles will do all he can to spite us, the three of us.'

'No, no. Don't let Charles worry you, Lowri. I'm not the idiot he thinks I am and he isn't as clever as he would like us to believe.'

Lowri's fingers closed around his. 'Look, he's made you tell me the truth. He's a spiteful man, aren't you at all concerned he might . . . ?'

Mr Watson shook his head and his wispy hair stood up on end. 'You don't know him like I do, he's all bluster. I repeat, you are not to worry, I have everything under control.'

Lowri doubted it. Mr Watson seemed like an innocent abroad compared to Charles Richards. 'What does he want you to do?'

'He wants me to be a front man for him. To travel abroad to Europe, the Caribbean. He has ordered me to extort money from some very rich men. If they call my bluff and bring the police in, I'll be the one to carry the can.' He smiled without humour. 'Charles always was such a fool.'

He took off his glasses and rubbed them against his waistcoat. 'I thought I had got away from his bumbling methods long ago but I was wrong. He keeps meddling in my life, trying to pay me back for what happened in the past. I don't blame him, I suppose, but he could be a little more intelligent in his dealings.'

'He kept silent about you and Mother all these years,' Lowri said. 'He was biding his time until he was ready to punish you. And me. I hate him!' She leaned against the desk.

'How has he got away with it for so long?' she asked. 'All his dirty little schemes, why has no-one caught him out?'

'So far he's only dealt in petty crime, now he hopes to enter the big league. As I said, he's a fool.'

'But he must have aroused suspicion over the years? Hasn't anyone ever checked him out? He doesn't exactly live like a poor man and his wealth can't have gone unnoticed, can it? Surely the pose of respectable businessman hasn't fooled everyone?'

'It fooled your mother, once.' Mr Watson held up his hand. 'Since then he's made use of whatever of her money he can lay his hands on. Now, don't ask any more, Lowri, it's much better that you don't know too much.'

'You are going to do what he wants, then?'

Mr Watson smiled at her. 'Forget all that. What's more important now is what you think of me. I hope I'm not too much of a disappointment to you, my dear, as a father I mean.'

Lowri saw a mist of tears behind his spectacles and, after a moment's hesitation, she put her hand on his arm. 'I'm glad he's not

306

my real father!' She resisted the urge to smooth Mr Watson's hair into place. 'I knew he was my stepfather and that I'd been conceived before the marriage but I didn't know Charles was a crook.'

Unable to speak, Mr Watson squeezed her hand. He took out a spotless handkerchief and mopped his eyes.

'Look,' Lowri said, 'why not talk to me, tell me everything, perhaps between us we can sort it all out.'

Mr Watson shook his head. 'No.' He looked up at her. 'I said I don't want you to worry, Lowri. I might appear weak but I have everything under control, I promise you.' He seemed to have grown in stature; there was a new light in his eyes. He returned to his desk and smiled at her.

'You go back to work, my dear, and we'll keep all this to ourselves for now, shall we?'

Lowri nodded but as she left the room, she knew she could not let the matter rest there. She would see Charles Richards, have it all out with him, tell him to back off or she would expose him, threaten to go to the press as well as the police. Then she thought of her mother, tearful, begging her not to expose the family to ridicule, and she knew that Charles had them all, herself included, in his power.

The warehouse smelled of damp and decay and Lainey thrust his hands into the pockets of his coat as he followed the customs men to the back of the building. There, a door opened into a small room, well ventilated. Here the case addressed to Justin Richards had been stored out of sight.

'So, George, what do you think is here, then?' He stood beside the excise man and watched as the case was prised open.

'Says computer parts here,' George said. 'Can't be perishables or it would be stinking to high heaven by now and it's not drugs, the dogs would have sniffed them out.'

Lainey heard the crunch of the crowbar against wood and then the tearing sound of the timber splitting. The lid was forced open and George stepped forward, pushing aside the packing material. He fished out a shrink-wrapped black box and looked at it doubtfully.

"What is this?'

'It's a fax modem, sir,' one of his men said quietly.

'Right. Empty the lot, let the dog see the rabbit.'

The contents of the case were tipped onto the concrete floor; packages spilled everywhere. It all appeared innocent enough.

'The business this is addressed to, Justin Richards, is a firm that deals in wines and spirits.' George opened a Jiffy bag containing slim plastic envelopes. 'This is just a pack of CDs,' he said. 'I suppose the company needs to run a network of computers so there's nothing of any significance here.'

Lainey picked up a CD and studied it. He took out another one, turning it over.

'Kids' games, by the look,' George said. 'All harmless rubbish if you ask me. I suppose this stuff just got overlooked when your man disappeared.' He grinned. 'No-one to make a fuss, see?'

'Do you mind if I look through these?' Lainey asked. There was something wrong here, he could smell it.

'Aye, I'll leave one of my boys with you to pack it all back up.' George rested his hand on Lainey's shoulder.

'Don't go doing anything I wouldn't do, now.' He winked and Lainey winked back; he and George understood each other.

He took off his coat and rolled up his sleeves. At his side Ken Major was waiting for instructions.

'Could you do with a bit of overtime, Ken?' he asked. 'You know something about computers, don't you?'

Ken nodded. 'Aye, guv, I know how to

play games on one anyway.'

'We're going to find something here, if it takes all night to do it,' Lainey said. He caught the look the remaining customs man threw at him and grinned. 'It's overtime, lad. You win some, you lose some.'

He began to search through the plastic envelopes. What exactly he was expecting to find he had no idea. But if there was something, anything, hidden among the computer parts, he was going to find it.

18

Lowri sat at the table in the coffee-shop, fiddling with her spoon. Opposite her, Timmy was white-faced, his hands trembling as he picked up his cup.

'Are you all right?' Lowri said. He nodded. His eyes were shadowed and he needed a shave; he did not look at her. He was so unlike the Timmy Lowri knew that she scarcely recognized him. Sally's disappearance had hit him hard, but was it more than that?

'You wanted to talk, Timmy?' she prompted gently. She picked up her cup and sipped the rapidly cooling drink, spilling a little on the table. She was not in the best of spirits herself. She was worried about Mr Watson . . . her father, he was planning to go to Germany as arranged by Charles. He refused to discuss what he would do when he got there. All things considered, Lowri could have done without the complication of the phone call from Timmy.

She studied him. He was worried, no, frightened might be a more apt description of the way he was acting. He rubbed his hands through his hair, glancing every now and again over his shoulder. He seemed edgy, scared of shadows, and Lowri wondered if he was on the verge of a breakdown.

'I think I know what happened to Sally.' He spoke almost in a whisper. 'I know she was mixed up in something shady.'

'How do you mean?'

'That night we had a row I went round to see her later, and she told me to get out of her life.' He rubbed his eyes. 'She told me she now had enough money to keep her in comfort and she didn't need me any more.'

'That's odd,' Lowri said. 'Where would Sally get money from?'

'That's the problem — I just don't know. After all a clerk in an office doesn't get paid a fortune.'

'Was it her way of fobbing you off, do you think?' Lowri asked. 'Or was she just hitting out at you because you'd quarrelled?'

Timmy shook his head. 'I walked around for a bit trying to cool down. I was wondering if I should go back and try to make it up. I was near the house when I heard footsteps coming behind me. I wondered if Sally was cheating on me and so I thought I'd ask her outright, then maybe we could get back together.'

'What happened?'

'I saw her getting into a flash car.' He hesitated. 'I don't think she was keen on going, she was trying to pull away from a man who was holding her arm.'

'What did this man look like?'

'It all happened so suddenly.' Timmy shook his head. 'I didn't get a good look at him but he was tall, I saw that much.'

'If you were suspicious why didn't you call the police, Timmy?' She spoke challengingly.

He frowned. 'I stepped out into the road waved my hand at the driver and he almost mowed me down! I was so scared I didn't know what to do so I went home.'

'Timmy!'

'I know, I know I should have done something. The police took me in for questioning of course, but by then I was so mixed up I acted like I didn't care. Lord knows what that detective made of me.'

'Did you tell Jim Lainey about the man you saw?'

Timmy shook his head. 'As I said, I was mixed up. I think I'd decided she was doing a moonlight by then. And I was frightened. I thought if I opened my mouth too wide someone would come looking for me. That's the honest truth, Lowri.'

'Can't you remember anything about the man's appearance?'

Timmy swallowed hard. 'Perhaps a bit like Matthew Brown, but could have been older.'

'I wonder if it was Jon Brandon,' Lowri said softly. 'Or maybe it *was* Matthew, but why would he want to abduct Sally?'

'When we had the row she taunted me about Matthew, how good he was in bed and how he could pull any woman.' He paused. 'Even you seemed to like him, I thought you had more sense.'

Lowri felt her colour rise but she remained silent. It was not worth trying to explain that she was only nice to Matthew to find out about Jon and Sally. Nothing she could say would make any difference to the way Timmy was feeling now.

'I'm telling you the truth, Lowri,' he said. 'I know it looks bad for me, I should have tried to help Sally.' He looked down at his hands. 'I'm the wimp Sally said I was, I know.'

With his hair tangled across his forehead, Timmy looked even younger than he was. She could not believe him capable of abduction, but then neither could she imagine Matthew, a responsible sergeant, capable of acting like a criminal.

'Perhaps it would be a good idea to tell DI Lainey everything, Timmy.'

'I can't. I've burnt my boats there, the man thinks I'm a prig.' He shrugged. 'He's right.'

'Lainey is very shrewd, he won't take things at face value, he'll use every little bit of information he can get his hands on.'

Timmy shook his head. 'No, I can't. I don't know what's going on but I've a feeling it's something big. I might be in danger myself if I went to the police of my own accord.'

'How would you?'

'The man who took Sally might come back, find me and beat me up, even kill me.'

Timmy seemed past rational thought but Lowri tried to reason with him anyway.

'You could always give the information over the phone, you needn't even give your name.'

'It's too risky. I think I'm better off keeping out of it.'

Lowri leaned forward. 'Look, if this man thought you saw him clearly and was worried, wouldn't he have come back right away?'

Timmy shook his head. 'I don't care what you say, Lowri, I'm not going to the police and that's flat. I have some of Sally's things

— will you come back to my room with me? It's near the college, not far away.'

'What for?'

'To take Sally's stuff. I can't bear to have anything of hers in my place now.'

'Well, yes, I suppose so.' Lowri was surprised by the abrupt turn in the conversation. Timmy was behaving so strangely; perhaps she would be a fool to go with him. He looked at her pitifully, as if reading her thoughts.

'I wouldn't hurt you, Lowri, you've nothing to fear from me.' He rose to his feet and swung his bag of books over his shoulder. Lowri hesitated for a moment and then picked up her handbag.

'OK, Timmy, but if you have anything illegal that you want to palm off on me, the answer is no!'

As Timmy did not seem inclined to pay for the coffee, Lowri took some coins out of her purse and left them on the table. She followed him out into the unexpected sunlight, wondering if she was putting her head in the lion's mouth.

Timmy was glad when Lowri had gone, taking Sally's things with her. He showered and as he tied his bathrobe round his waist there was a loud knocking on the door.

Timmy stepped back a pace, looking round him, but there was no way of escape. He was on the third floor and never had been good at heights. The knocking was repeated and a voice called out harshly.

'Police! Open the door or I'll break it down.'

Timmy felt a sense of relief; the police he could deal with. Nevertheless he opened the door on the chain and peered out.

'Identification please.'

The man held out his card and, taking it, Timmy examined it. 'OK,' he said, 'you can come in.'

'I have a warrant to search the premises.' Matthew Brown stood in the doorway, large and somehow menacing.

'Well, this is a surprise!' Timmy said. 'On your own, isn't that unusual?'

'Not on a busy day, no.' Matthew looked round. 'In any case, it won't take long to search two rooms, will it?'

'Go ahead,' Timmy said. 'You won't find anything here that's illegal, I assure you. I'm not one of those fools who take smack so if it's drugs you're after you're wasting your time.'

He sat in the armchair and watched as the sergeant made a systematic search of the sitting-room. 'Hey, careful with those books, they cost money!'

Matthew ignored him and shook out the pages of each book. He was frowning. 'Where's your CD player?'

Timmy pointed to the corner. 'Over there. I haven't got much of a collection — it's here mainly for Sally's entertainment,' he said, but the jibe had no effect on Matthew who walked into the bedroom.

At last, the sergeant gave up. He returned to the sitting-room and stood in front of Timmy. 'You're clean this time but I'll be back, don't you worry about that.'

'Come back any time you like,' Timmy said dully. 'I've got nothing to hide.'

Matthew left the door open as he departed and Timmy closed it with a bang.

Lainey was not in a good mood. So far Ken Major's efforts to find out what was in the pile of CDs had come to naught. There had been several bundles of CDs in the case: to try them out on a computer would take days, weeks. Ken Major knew it and Lainey knew it. Still, Major had stuck at it and was searching diligently through the packages.

'Any idea what we're looking for, guv?' Major said at last. Lainey shook his head.

'No idea. Just something that doesn't fit, I suppose. A CD that appears different to the

318

others. I'm hoping if we can narrow the search down to only a few of the discs we will find a code, a program you can't access.' He shrugged. 'I have to admit I don't bloody know what I'm expecting but there's something fishy going on, I can feel it in my gut!'

He glanced at his watch. 'Look, I'll have to push off. Do your best to sort this lot out and then come back to the station.'

Ken Major did not seem too happy but he made no protest.

Lainey drove back to the station and parked his car in the space reserved for the superintendent and got out, slamming the door behind him.

The corridors were quiet. It was getting late and there would only be a skeleton staff working.

In his office, Lainey turned his attention to the paperwork on his desk and opened the file on Jon Brandon; his researcher had traced the man back over the years to his college days. He had, predictably, been into electrical circuits and microchips even then. These days, progress in information technology had not so much as marched as sprinted forward out of all recognition. How had Brandon kept up to date? Easily, Lainey supposed, if it was bringing him in a fortune.

Something was teasing his mind. The name of Justin Richards had come up in a list of Brandon's associates. Lowri's brother, perhaps? The case of computer stuff had been addressed to Justin Richards: it was a coincidence.

Lainey stared at the file. He did not believe that Justin Richards ran a wines and spirits business. It would be easy to launder money through the legitimate books. There was a tingling feeling at the back of his neck, a sure sign that something was not right.

The duty sergeant peered into the room. 'Someone to see you, sir, Timothy Perkins. I've put him in interview room three.'

'Right.' He closed the file and slipped it into his desk. He might be getting paranoid but he had the feeling his work was being checked. As Lainey left his office, he reflected that life was never simple. He had at last found a girl whom he could fall in love with, and she would probably turn out to be a liar or worse.

As he walked into the interview room, Timmy Perkins looked up at him. He seemed terrified. His hand, holding a cigarette, was trembling.

'What can I do for you, Mr Perkins?' Lainey asked and the boy looked up at him with haunted eyes.

'I think I'm in danger,' he said. 'My rooms were broken into when I went for a drink in the student bar. Books were torn, my papers thrown all over the floor.'

'Anything stolen?' Lainey asked easily.

'Just my laptop computer and some CDs.'

Sounds like some kid looking for something to sell, probably to fund a quick fix.'

'I suppose you could be right. That sergeant called Brown had gone by then so the coast was clear for any petty thief.'

'Brown?' Lainey asked. Brown was supposed to be taking his holiday — what the hell was he doing going to see Perkins?

'What did the sergeant say he wanted?' Lainey asked. Perkins looked surprised.

'Is this a case of the left hand not knowing what the right is doing, DI Lainey? Brown had a search warrant, he went through my place like a dose of salts!'

'Did you actually read the search warrant, Mr Perkins?'

'Well . . . no, I didn't but it looked official enough.'

'Tut tut, and you studying law.' Lainey switched on the recording machine. 'We'd better go through this step by step. Just take it easy and start from the beginning.'

Lowri looked at the large handbag containing make-up and other odds and ends that Timmy had put into her hands with as much reverence as if it was the Holy Grail. There were a few CDs which she looked through idly. They were mostly pop music, some of Sally's favourite groups. One of the CDs was different from the rest. The plastic case was blank and when Lowri lifted the flap and drew out the disc she saw that the title of the music was in some foreign language. But nothing that Lowri could recognize. Strange, she shrugged, but then Sally could sometimes be a little strange.

Lowri pushed the handbag into the shoe cupboard along with a pile of discarded bags bearing the names of the various shops she frequented. Why Timmy had been so fanatical about giving her Sally's few belongings she couldn't fathom. There was nothing of importance among any of this stuff.

The phone rang and she picked it up.

'Lowri, it's Ken Major. Can I come over for a drink? I've had one hell of a day. Lainey's had me searching through boxes of rubbish, CDs, that sort of thing. He doesn't even know what he's looking for.'

'Ken, is this a joke? No, you can't come over and don't ring again because I've got company.'

She put the phone down and looked

round her empty sitting-room. Company, she should be so lucky. So Lainey was interested in CDs all of a sudden. Why? She went to the shoe cupboard and rummaged in Sally's bag, pulling out the small pile of discs. Perhaps it would be just as well to look them over again.

If only she had a computer at home she could try out the one with the foreign title. She turned it over in her hands but could see nothing suspicious. Still, there could be something on there that Sally did not want anyone else to see, then she had better keep it safe.

Lowri looked around the room, wondering where was the safest place to hide it, then she made herself a cup of coffee and sat down to watch her favourite soap.

19

'Look, guv, if anyone had wanted to flash any sort of information around the world, wouldn't they have used the Internet? I mean, why handle CDs when a telephone line can take the message for you?'

Lainey looked out at the early morning sky through the one small window in the back room of the warehouse. He had wanted to take another look at the case. He glanced at Ken Major. 'Apparently, as soon as anyone goes online, the address of their computer is logged. It wouldn't be too difficult to trace it.'

'Oh, I know that!' Ken's tone was disparaging and Lainey concealed a smile. 'But it would take an awful lot of time, wouldn't it, especially if the user had a code name or had encrypted the information? All the same, surely it would be easier than exporting all this stuff.'

Lainey looked down at the neatly packed case. It had been late when the search was abandoned the night before, and though he had taken a second look he had found nothing out of the ordinary. It seemed that he had been barking up the wrong tree.

'Nothing but kids' computer games,' he said. 'Though there could be just one CD hidden among the rest that's different.'

'That's possible.' Ken flipped the last of the CDs into the case. 'But if so, it's not here. I've done my best but I can't find anything remotely interesting.'

'You're sure?'

'I'm sure, guv.'

Lainey wondered if he had been wrong all along. When the case of goods Jon Brandon was sending to Justin Richards had been found, he had high hopes that it would yield some answers, but a thorough search had proved him wrong. But no, his gut instinct told him he was on the right track. Some time ago, he had begun to suspect what the scam was all about, and this episode had reinforced that suspicion. The CDs were part of the scam and, maybe, Matthew Brown had guessed it. Or was Brown somehow involved in it all? It was not a pleasant thought.

'I still think information is being smuggled out of the country,' Lainey said. 'Something of import. It's either financial or political, could even be Secret Service stuff.'

Ken glanced at him. 'You been watching

too many police soaps, guv.' There was a smile on the officer's face and Lainey grimaced.

'I know it sounds far-fetched but we need to consider all possibilities. Could anything from the case have gone missing? I mean, could anyone have pocketed one of the CDs?'

'I don't know, guv.' Ken smiled. 'But it's not likely, not with your eagle eye overseeing things.'

It was true he had been present at all times when the boxes inside the case were opened. But then, there had been a lot of boxes, all but one containing computer parts. Only one box had contained software. It was just possible that one CD could have been slipped in with the hardware. Alternatively, perhaps the relevant disc had never reached the case, and that was why the case had been abandoned at the warehouse.

It was like trying to unravel a ball of string and never coming to the end. He hated being beaten by a puzzle, and this was a cracker. He had been on the investigation for months and as yet had made very little progress. At least, that was how it would appear to his superior officers. Lainey knew otherwise.

'We might as well get back to the station,'

he said. He turned to the customs and excise man and nodded. 'Thanks for your help.'

Lainey had scarcely sat at his desk in the office when the door opened. 'Guv, the Perkins boy's come in again. Are you going to interview him or what? To be fair, I think he's been cooling his heels long enough.'

'Oh do you!' Lainey said sharply. 'Well, I'll decide that without any help from you.'

Ken Major grinned. 'Sorry, guv. What about Perkins?'

'What about him?'

'He looks as if he's about to have a nervous breakdown, he's shaking like a leaf.'

'All right.' Lainey sighed. 'I'll see him now — come with me.' On an impulse, he glanced at Major. 'Got any CDs in the station, by any chance?'

'No, guv, but I've got one or two in the car.'

'Get one for me.'

'All right, guv, but I don't think heavy rock is your kind of thing, is it?'

'Doesn't matter, just get any CD. I'm not going to play it.'

'Right.'

Ken Major returned within minutes and dropped a disc on the desk. Lainey slipped it into his pocket.

In the interview room, Timmy Perkins was sitting head down, smoking a cigarette; from the look of the ashtray, he had been smoking for some time. Do the boy good to sit in a cold police room for a while.

Lainey took a seat opposite him. Perkins knew more than he was letting on about the whole sorry mess, and perhaps now he was prepared to talk.

'Sorry to keep you waiting.' Lainey leaned back in the chair, waiting for Ken to switch on the recorder. 'What can I do for you?'

'I think I'm being followed.' The boy seemed definitely agitated. 'Don't look at me as if I'm stupid, I was straight with you the last time we talked and I don't know anything I haven't told you already.'

Lainey took the CD from his pocket and put it on the table, label down, and covertly watched for the boy's reaction. There was none.

'Know anything about this?' Lainey said at last. Perkins stared at the gleaming reverse of the CD and shook his head.

'No, should I?'

'It's from a warehouse on the docks,' Lainey said. 'It might contain valuable information.'

'What's that got to do with me?'

'You use a computer. I know that because

328

you reported it stolen.'

Timmy turned the CD over. 'Games! I think I'm a little past childish pursuits. Why don't you play the damn thing and leave me alone?'

'I can't.' Lainey took a wild guess. 'It's in a strange language I've never seen before.'

Timmy shook his head. 'I doubt if it's in a foreign language, it's probably encrypted.'

'Explain it to me.'

'If you want to hide information you can encrypt it. You can even buy a cheap package to protect any e-mails you want to send.'

He paused; he seemed to be in a better mood now. He was the sort of lad who liked to show off his knowledge.

'You could put masses of stuff on one CD. You can hide a message in what appears to be the music in a game. Didn't you know that?'

'No, I didn't.' Lainey looked at Perkins thoughtfully; the boy was no fool. Whether he would be helpful was another matter. He tried a different tack.

'I'm sure you want to know what has happened to your girlfriend, don't you? So if you have any information that would help . . .' Lainey stopped speaking as Perkins leaned forward in his chair.

'All I'm concerned about now is my own

safety,' he said. 'Why are you so curious about computer stuff suddenly?'

Lainey smiled dryly. 'Leave me to ask the questions, there's a good lad. Just talk to me some more about this encryption business.'

'What do you want to know?'

Lainey shrugged. 'I'm not sure, just humour me. The sooner we get this over, the sooner you can leave.'

'Anyone got a cigarette?'

'No.' Lainey smiled. 'I don't smoke.' He switched off the tape. 'Ken, see if you can cadge a cigarette from one of the boys.'

Ken left the room and Lainey stared at Timmy Perkins. 'Carry on.'

'I don't really know anything more about it. I've never actually used encryption myself, I don't have the facilities or the need.'

'What about Sally White?'

Timmy shook his head. 'Sally was no computer buff, she used the one at work for basic accounts, that sort of thing.'

Lainey pointed to the CD on the table. 'If someone was sending information to certain parties across the Continent, why wouldn't they use the net?'

'Too risky,' Perkins said. 'Any fool can tap into information on the net, if they know what they are doing.'

'Do you? Know what you are doing?'

'I don't like that implication.'

'Too bad. Are you a computer expert or not?' Lainey persisted.

'I'm taking IT at college, but I wouldn't call that being an expert.'

'Right, but you'd know enough to work out the most profitable way to send information to other countries? What could be sent on a CD?'

Perkins frowned. 'I don't know! I suppose it could be lists of debtors, people whose business is going down.'

Lainey looked at him in surprise. 'To what end?'

Perkins shook his head. 'You don't know much about making money, do you?'

'Tell me, then.'

'Some people, sometimes the bailiffs themselves, buy up the assets of firms going bust at a knockdown price,' Perkins said. 'Buildings, equipment, rolling stock, lorries, anything that's there for the taking.'

'Are there enough people in Britain going bust to fund such a scheme?'

Perkins laughed. 'Probably, but you wouldn't limit yourself to this country, would you?' He spoke as if Lainey was an ignorant child. 'People go bust everywhere, the Continent, America, all over. With the right connections, you'd be laughing.'

'Is this what you were doing?'

'I'm just surmising, Inspector, as you wanted me to.'

'What about extortion?' Lainey threw the question into the conversation casually. Perkins sat up straighter.

'Hackers can get in anywhere, banks' records, defence systems, anywhere. Extortion is possible, of course.'

Lainey's neck was tingling again. Perkins's face gave nothing away but he was definitely rattled. 'Go on.'

'Take this scenario, you get some dirt on a few rich people, insider dealing, porno films, anything, then you blackmail them with the threat that the info will be sold to competitors or fellow politicians, anyone.'

Lainey thought about it. The boy was right. The fact that he was right probably meant he was not involved in any scam. Or the scam was not quite what he was making it out to be.

'Well thank you, Perkins, you've been very helpful. How would I find someone who could translate encrypted information?'

He stared at Lainey; he was looking smug now, damn him! 'I've no idea. Heaven help us if this is the best our police force can do. Why haven't you brought in the metropolitan police?'

'Because I like to solve my own puzzles. Two people have disappeared in suspicious circumstances on my patch. I will solve this crime if it's the last thing I do.'

'And it could well be.' Timmy pointed to the CD. 'No-one would think twice about getting rid of anyone planning to spoil their little game.'

He rose to his feet just as Ken Major returned to the room, holding out a cigarette. Timmy Perkins took it and immediately lit it, dragging smoke into his lungs like a desperate man.

'Can I go, then?'

'Yes, you can go.' Lainey watched him walk to the door. 'And thanks for your help.'

'Get anything out of him, guv?' asked Major.

'Just a lesson in computing,' Lainey said, throwing the CD down on the desk. 'It looks as if I've been barking up the wrong bloody tree thinking Perkins was involved.'

'Bad luck, guv.'

'It's not back luck, it's just that sometimes the criminals are cleverer than me, but I'll get there in the end.' He sank back in his chair and closed his eyes. It had been a long day.

Lowri felt the late autumn sun on her back as she sat in her office, the computer whining its way into life.

She looked at the CD that had been in Sally's bag of possessions and after a moment slipped it into the drive. Immediately weird symbols appeared on the screen. Lowri went to the door and looked into reception.

'Mrs Jenkins, I wonder if you could help me out here? My computer's having a funny turn.' Mrs Jenkins frowned, but got to her feet and followed Lowri into her office.

'Look at all this stuff,' Lowri said. 'Has some sort of virus got in there, do you think?'

'I'll just have a look.' Mrs Jenkins sat down at the desk and began clicking away on the mouse. After a few minutes she ejected the CD from the drive and brought up Lowri's normal desktop icons.

Lowri smiled. 'Thank goodness I haven't ruined it.'

'No harm done but you should be careful what you put on the computer, some give-away discs have been tampered with and are designed to cause problems.'

She still held the CD in her hand and Lowri took it from her. 'Thanks, I appreciate your help.'

'If I were you I should bin that right away,' Mrs Jenkins said. 'It could be faulty. Just bin it!'

Why was she so insistent? 'Thanks,' Lowri said, 'but I can't do that, it's not mine, it belongs to Sally.'

Mrs Jenkins shrugged. 'Please yourself.' The phone in reception rang stridently and she went out, leaving the door wide open. She could really be a pain, Lowri thought, as she moved to close the door.

Mrs Jenkins was answering the call. 'You wish to rent one of the cottages in Plunch Lane? Right, I'll inform Mr Watson at once.'

Lowri stood by the open door as Mrs Jenkins knocked on Mr Watson's door. Lowri heard him call for her to come in, then the two of them talked in subdued tones.

She returned to her desk and sat in her chair, remembering vividly how she used to visit Jon at Plunch Lane. She remembered the log fire, remembered her feelings as she and Jon had made love there. Now it was nothing but a burned-out ruin, like her love life really.

She heard Mr Watson leave and bit her lip. Something very odd was going on, and she just wished someone would see fit to put her in the picture.

She sighed heavily, thinking how much her life had changed over the past months. Her mother and Mr Watson had been lovers: the idea was really strange. She opened her bag and took out her mother's letter. It had only arrived that morning and she had been in too much of a hurry to read it.

Her mother's first words were to say sorry for deceiving her all these years. Rhian was begging for understanding, if not forgiveness. Tears blurred Lowri's eyes as she leaned back in her chair to give the letter her full attention.

20

Timmy Perkins sat staring out of the window into the college quad next door to his rooms. His head ached and he felt sick to his stomach. He had received a phone call that threatened to push him over the edge. He had been a fool to get involved in the scam in the first place, but the biggest mistake of his life was getting rid of that damned CD.

Timmy sat, his head bowed, his hands clasped together. Perhaps he should go to the police, tell them everything. But tell them what? That he had been involved, however unintentionally, in a gigantic fraud?

DI Lainey was bright: he was well on the way to working it all out, even though Timmy had done his best to put him off the scent. By talking about the sort of profit that could be made out of repossessions, buying up bankrupt stock and suchlike, he had, he hoped, given Lainey the impression that he was innocent. At least it bought him some time. Maybe.

Timmy rose to his feet, his hands thrust

into his pockets. He glanced at his reflection in the mirror — he looked pale and sick. He would look a damn sight sicker if anyone hunting for the CD caught up with him, that much was obvious. He was trembling and he tried to pull himself together. A weak link did not last long in any organization.

Timmy fetched a can from the fridge and pulled the ring. The beer tasted flat and unappetizing, it was probably past its sell-by date. He put it on the table with a grimace of disgust.

He moved to the window and looked down into the quad where a girl was sitting on one of the benches, her hair blowing in the breeze, her skirt riding above her thighs. She reminded him of Sally.

Timmy sighed. He had tried so hard to please Sally and look where it had got him. He was right in the shit!

Sally had lured Timmy with her fabulous body, and it had made him feel good to have a lovely girl on his arm. She had finally betrayed him and vanished from his life, leaving him with a time bomb waiting to go off.

Timmy had handed the stuff over to Lowri because he was scared to hold onto it. By now, Lowri might well have damaged the disc, or destroyed it altogether. The thought made him shudder.

It was possible that she might have found a way through the encryption. Lowri was a bright woman and she had just the sort of enquiring mind that would make sense of what appeared to be nonsensical. But even if she did crack it, the information would mean little to her.

If Lowri did work it all out, there was no question in his mind that she would go to the police. He would be dragged in for questioning again, and this time he might not be able to keep his mouth shut.

'Oh God, what am I going to do?' Timmy paced around his room like a trapped animal. On an impulse, he threw some clothes into a bag and searched in the drawer for his passport and the envelope of money that was his reward for services rendered. He would get right away until the fuss blew over.

Outside, he felt the cool of the wind against his face. His car keys jangled in his hand and he looked at the BMW, gleaming in the cold sunlight. It was a great car, a status symbol, but it could cost him his freedom, even his life.

He climbed into the driving seat and stared for a moment up at the blank window of his room, then he turned the key in the ignition. He drove away from the town and joined the motorway at the nearest slip-road.

Once in the flow of traffic, he felt safer. He put his foot down and wondered which was the best route out of the country. Perhaps the docks at Bristol would be a good place to start. He would have to dump the car, of course, just leave it in a car park. It would take a long time for anyone to realize it had been abandoned.

He heard the drone of a heavy vehicle behind him and indicated that he intended to move into the middle lane to allow the lorry to pass. It was a mistake. The driver was not prepared to wait. The lorry pulled out and caught the car with a solid crunch, jerking Timmy forward.

He grasped the wheel in an effort to regain control, but it was useless. He felt the car spin crazily. He saw the central reservation loom up in front of him. He made another attempt to correct the car but the momentum carried him relentlessly towards the steel barrier.

He felt the crunch, saw sparks leap from the impact of metal against metal. The car veered back across the three lanes and he could do nothing but sit staring helplessly at the back of another vehicle as he powered towards it. There was a blinding flash, flames rose like the fires of hell around him and then there was nothing but a merciful darkness.

Lainey stood in the cold sunshine of the afternoon and looked at the ruins of number 4 Plunch Lane. The chimney stood out like a blackened tooth against the sky. Watson stood beside him, shaking his head.

'Arson, you say?'

'Afraid so.' Lainey looked at the older man. 'The boys take their time working these things out, but they get there in the end.'

'Dreadful,' Mr Watson said. 'Thank God the fire didn't spread to the rest of the row, someone might have been killed.'

Lainey nodded. 'What could be the motive for burning a small holiday cottage? There seems no sense to it.'

Mr Watson shook his head. 'I really don't know. It could be someone had a grudge against me of course, but in that case why not burn down the whole damned lot?'

'We might never find out,' Lainey said. 'That's the trouble with fires, they make a good job of concealing the motive for the crime. If there was one.'

'You mean this might be random, the

work of a pyromaniac?' Mr Watson asked. 'I suppose you're right — there are some idiots about.'

He moved slowly back towards his car. 'If that's all, Detective Inspector Lainey, I'll get off.'

'Thank you for coming down, Mr Watson,' Lainey said. 'I would have come over to the office under normal circumstances, but there just wasn't time.'

He watched as the solicitor drove away and then stood in the cold sunlight, pondering his real reason for bringing Mr Watson to Plunch Lane. He had to admit that he did not relish the thought of running into Lowri at her office, not when the case was getting so complicated.

He climbed into the waiting police car. 'Good thing the man's a solicitor, I bet he had the best insurance money can buy.' Lainey fastened his seat-belt.

'Right, Ken, we've got work to do, let's get back to the station.'

Terence Watson was deep in thought as he drove to the office. He pulled in around the back and found that the car park was almost empty. Nearly everyone had finished work for the day. Except, that was, for Mrs Jenkins.

'Still here?' he said.

She nodded but did not look up from her computer. She might have an excellent flair for business but she was the most dour of women, with no social graces. But then he had not employed her because of her charm. He had employed her because she seemed the type to get on with her work and keep her nose out of anyone else's business.

'Right then, you'd better get off home.' He forced a smile. 'You don't get medals in this life for working yourself to a standstill, you know.' He opened the door of his room and went inside. The smell of old books and lavender furniture polish enfolded him.

He sank down into his chair and looked at his watch. Seven minutes past five, hardly worth the effort of coming to the office. He waited patiently until he heard Mrs Jenkins leave the building and then he went into the reception area and locked the front door.

Systematically, he began to go through the files, looking for anything out of the ordinary. He searched Mrs Jenkins's desk. It smelt of her deodorant, and half hidden beneath a pile of papers was a packet of cigarettes. So she was not as flawless as he had thought.

He could find nothing. He stared at the blank screen of the computer; no doubt anything Mrs Jenkins wanted to conceal would be on there. He shrugged. He had no chance of finding it, he knew very little about computers.

On an impulse, he played back the tape on the answerphone. The first message was from a customer with a complaint. The man was anxious about the time it was taking to complete on a house purchase. There was a silence after that, and Terence reached out to switch the machine off.

Then a masculine voice came over the line, the words softly spoken.

'Report to me ASAP. I'll be waiting in the usual place.'

The machine clicked off and Terence replayed the message several times. It told him very little. Mrs Jenkins might have a husband somewhere or even a lover, unlikely though that seemed, but then the word 're-port' sounded more like an instruction than an invitation.

He admitted defeat and sat down on the upright chair. Perhaps there was nothing to find. Perhaps Mrs Jenkins was playing a straight bat. He looked at the pile of letters waiting to be signed, and when he picked them up a small scrap of paper fluttered to the floor.

He retrieved it and saw some scribbled

digits, presumably a phone number, in what looked like Mrs Jenkins's handwriting. Terence picked up the telephone and pressed out the numbers and, to his satisfaction, a phone began to ring.

Lowri climbed into the taxi and glanced at her watch. She would have been at the office by now but for the fact that Lainey was having her watched. She had not failed to notice the figures outside her house and the intermittent glow of a cigarette. It had been simple enough to leave her car parked at the front of the house and let herself out of the back door. She had walked around to the main road and picked up a taxi almost straight away.

She gave the address of the office to the driver and sank back in the cold leather seat with a sigh of relief. Soon she would be safely there, and then Mr Watson would explain everything to her. She slipped her hand inside her bag and felt the edge of the CD. Whatever was on it must be very important for Mr Watson to ask her to bring it round so late at night.

She looked out of the window and frowned. 'Driver, aren't we going the wrong way?'

'I've been paid to carry out instructions

and that's what I'm doing,' he said, without turning round.

The road narrowed down to a small lane and Lowri leaned forward in her seat, rapping on the window.

'Where are you taking me?' But she knew where: the taxi was heading coastward in the direction of the Swan Hotel.

'I want to get out, stop the cab!' she shouted, but the driver took no notice. He manoeuvred through the lanes at breakneck speed and Lowri held her breath. She felt a sense of relief when the cab drew up a short distance from the Swan's main entrance.

Lowri climbed out of the taxi and before she could open her bag to pay him, he had pressed the accelerator and roared away into the night.

She looked towards the lights of the hotel and her heart rate slowed a little. Mr Watson must have changed his mind about the meeting-place. No doubt he had his reasons.

She swung her bag over her shoulder and began to walk towards the foyer. She shivered a little, the breeze from the sea cutting through her coat.

What on earth did Mr Watson want with Sally's CD?

So suddenly that she had no time to react,

someone cannoned into her from behind. Lowri fell, hitting the gravel of the drive with a thud that knocked the breath from her body. As she lay gasping, her bag was dragged from her shoulder. She tried to struggle but a fist caught her at the side of her head. Slowly, Lowri sank against the ground, her senses reeling.

She blacked out for a moment and when consciousness returned, she tried to sit up. She could feel blood trickling down her cheek and it took her a few minutes to rise to her feet. Her head was still spinning as she limped into the foyer of the Swan. With a sense of relief she saw Trish was on reception.

The girl noticed her at once and came rushing from behind the counter. 'Oh my lord what's happened, have you been mugged?'

Lowri nodded. 'Get the police, Trish, will you?' She staggered, the darkness pressed down on her and she slumped to the floor.

21

Lowri sat still as the police doctor cleaned up the scratches on her cheek. She was trembling and Lainey could see through her efforts to appear unruffled.

'There, no harm done,' the doctor said. 'You won't have any scars, Miss Richards, so don't worry about that.'

'Thank you, doctor, you've been very kind.'

'No problem.' The doctor snapped shut his bag. 'If that's all, Mr Lainey, I'll get back to my dinner party.'

Lainey nodded. Ken Major opened the door and the doctor departed. 'Are you up to answering questions, Lowri?' Lainey's voice was gentle and Lowri felt tears come to her eyes. She shook them away impatiently.

'Yes, of course I am,' she said. 'Though there's not a lot I can tell you, I'm afraid.'

He leaned forward. 'If you hadn't given my man the slip none of this would have happened. Lowri, you do realize you could have been seriously injured, even killed?'

'I know, it wasn't very clever of me to pick a taxi up in the street and get into it. I should have realized that seeing a taxi around my place at that time of night was one hell of a coincidence.'

'What did the driver look like?'

Lowri sighed. 'I don't know, I just saw the back of his head and it was dark. I heard his voice though, he sounded more like a Londoner than a local man.'

Lainey got to his feet. 'I don't suppose you noticed what taxi company the cab was from? Was there a leaflet stuck up inside, a card with a number on, anything?'

'No, I'm sorry,' Lowri said. 'Once I realized we were going the wrong way I think I panicked.'

'And why the Swan?' Lainey said. 'Why would the driver take you to the Swan — it's rather far out, isn't it?'

'I know,' Lowri said. 'I intended to go to the office, I needed to see Mr Watson but the driver had other ideas.'

Lainey sat down again and leaned back in his chair. 'Right, Lowri, what was in your bag?'

'The usual stuff, make-up, purse, that sort of thing.'

'Come on, Lowri, don't treat me like a fool! What else did you have in your bag?'

'A disc, that's all.'

'What sort of a disc?'

'The sort you put in a CD-ROM drive in a computer.'

'You know what I mean.' He sounded impatient. 'Was there anything different about it, anything that was out of the ordinary?'

'Well yes, there was funny writing on it, foreign but not like any language I've ever seen.'

'And where were you taking it?'

'I told you, to my boss, Mr Watson.'

'What you said was that you needed to see Mr Watson. Now, why would Mr Watson want this disc?' His eyes narrowed and he looked as if he could see inside her skull.

Lowri shrugged. 'I really don't know. Mr Watson just asked did I have it and if so would I take it over to the office.'

Lainey nodded. 'Right, we'd better talk to Mr Watson then. Now, Lowri, where did you get the disc? It's most important that I know.'

'Timmy Perkins, you know, Sally's boyfriend. He asked me to take care of Sal's belongings, make-up and stuff, and the disc was in the bag with the rest.'

'Ah!' Lainey sighed heavily. 'That's the one part of your story we can't corroborate.'

'Why, what do you mean?'

Lainey sat forward. 'I mean that Mr Perkins has met with an unfortunate traffic accident. He's in Morriston Hospital with burns and serious head injuries.'

'Oh, I'm sorry, I didn't know.' Lowri suddenly felt ill. It was as if the world was closing in on her. 'Poor Timmy, how did it happen?'

Lainey shrugged. 'Just one of those things, I suppose. Wrong place at the wrong time.'

'Are you saying it *wasn't* an accident?'

'I'm not saying anything until the matter has been investigated further.' He looked up at Ken Major. 'Sergeant, you had better get on the phone to Mr Watson and ask him to come over.'

Ken glanced at his watch. 'It's getting a bit late isn't it, guv?'

Lainey shook his head. 'Too bad. In any case, I'm sure Mr Watson is wondering where Miss Richards has got to by now.'

Ken left the room and Lainey gently touched the grazes on Lowri's face. 'You should be more careful of the company you keep.'

Lowri drew away from him, a hard knot of anger inside her. Lainey clearly thought she knew more than she had told him. He probably imagined her being involved in some complicated plot to rob the Bank of England. She wanted a hot bath and a comfortable bed. She was tired and her bones ached from the fall.

'I want to go home,' she said. 'I haven't done anything wrong, I've just been attacked by some lunatic who probably wanted my credit cards. I don't know why you're making an issue of all this.'

Lainey looked up as the door opened and Ken Major came back into the room. He stood beside the desk and looked down at Lowri.

'Sorry, Miss Richards, your Mr Watson had no idea what you were talking about.' He shook his head at Lainey. 'I got him out of bed, guv, he wasn't even in his office, he was at home.'

'Well?' Lainey looked at Lowri and she stared back, with a feeling of hostility.

'Well, he probably gave up waiting for me and decided to call it a day. He can't think the damned disc very important if he didn't wait for me, can he?' She shook back her hair. 'What on earth is on the CD anyway? I can't see it can be of much importance if it's been hanging around in Sally's bag all this time.'

'I'm not at liberty to discuss police matters,' Lainey said, rubbing his hands wearily through his hair.

Lowri wanted to tell him how pompous he sounded but instead she got up from her chair. 'If that's all, Mr Lainey, I'm going home. Could you please get me a taxi?'

'I would have thought you'd had a bellyful of taxis. The sergeant will run you home.'

Lowri moved to the door and Lainey's voice seemed to reach out to her. 'I will want to interview you again in the morning, along with Mr Watson.'

'Fine.' Lowri did not turn round. 'I want to talk to Mr Watson too.'

She was silent on the drive home; she felt tired and dispirited. It was clear Lainey thought she was lying about the disc, lying about everything. Well, to hell with Lainey. He was the cop, let him work it all out. As for her, she would have a large whisky and climb into bed and hopefully get a good night's sleep.

Sarah Brandon sat on the balcony of the Jamaican Royal, staring out at the Caribbean. It shimmered against the shoreline clear as crystal, sparkling in the sun. The palm trees waved fingers at the soft, warm breeze and Sarah sighed in contentment. She had eaten a delicious meal, been serviced by a vigorous young waiter and now all she had to do was sit in the sun and get richer by the minute.

She had been glad to leave the cold damp climate of Britain behind. But first, she had ransacked the cottage; searched number 4 Plunch Lane from top to bottom but found nothing. It was a pity it had been necessary to burn the place down but she might have missed some piece of evidence that could fall into the wrong hands. That was all over now. All she needed to do was manipulate her underlings from afar and relax in luxury.

Not that she had ever known poverty, of course. Her mother came from an affluent background, while her father had made his way in the world of finance, cutting many corners as he went. They were both dead now and Sarah had inherited their joint fortunes, as well as her father's financial knowledge.

She glanced at the diamond on her finger. It was clearer than the sea, a dazzling four carats of near-perfect stone. She enjoyed being rich and soon she would be in possession of more wealth than even her father had envisaged.

She glanced up at the discreet knock. 'Come in,' she said lazily. The door opened and the waiter stood there, a tray of drinks in his hand. She sat up straight.

'Where's Errol?'

'He's off sick, mam. Will I do?' He put down the tray and stretched to his full height. His chest muscles bulged beneath the pristine linen of his shirt. He smiled, his teeth very white against his dark skin. 'I'm Paul if it pleases you, mam.'

'Yes, I think it pleases me very much.'

She slipped out of her robe and took off her glasses. 'How much time have you got, Paul?'

'All the time in the world for you, mam.' He began to disrobe, laying his shirt carefully over the back of the chair. She was pleased to see how neat he was.

When they both lay on the bed naked Sarah touched his bronzed chest and felt the boy shudder. He was very grateful and so he should be, she would pay him well.

'I'm surprised at you Caribbean boys,' she said, 'I understood you were all very religious.'

'Oh we are, mam, I go to church every Sunday and axe for forgiveness of my sins.' He smiled a slow smile and touched her breast. 'But first I have to commit them sins.'

'I think we understand each other perfectly, Paul.' She lay back and allowed herself to enjoy his attentions. Funny, when she had been with Jon, she had never climaxed, not once. It was not his fault, he was an ardent lover and he had staying power, but he always wanted to manipulate her and Sarah never enjoyed that.

'Come on board, Paul.' She stretched her long legs, her skin startlingly white against his darkness. He obeyed and she smiled. She was the one to do all the manipulating now and she meant to enjoy every minute of it.

Lowri could not sleep. The whisky she had drunk, far from relaxing her, had made her feel anxious. What on earth was going on? Why did Mr Watson, her own father, deny he knew anything about the disc? She could scarcely wait for the morning to confront him about it. And what could be so important about the disc anyway?

She gave up trying to sleep and climbed from the bed. Perhaps a cup of tea would help. Downstairs, she took Sally's bag out of the closet and carried it into the kitchen.

She tipped the contents of the bag onto the table. They smelt of Sally's perfume, and she sorted through them. As well as the pop-music CDs, there was a comb, lipstick, nail polish, even spare pants, nothing out of the ordinary for a girl who stayed over at her boyfriend's at regular intervals.

Lowri felt the bottom of the bag and her fingers touched the plastic-lined card that held it in shape. She prised it up and underneath felt the hard edges of a book. She tipped up the bag and the book fell onto the table with a slap. It was a thin leather-bound diary and between its pages was a credit card. Jon Brandon's credit card.

Lowri made tea and sat at the table staring at the black cover of the diary, wondering if she had the right to look inside. But Sally was gone, goodness knew where, and might never come back. What harm could a little prying do her now?

There seemed to be nothing of significance written in the pages. Appointments with the hairdresser were noted along with brief comments about Timmy and his performance, or lack of it.

Lowri drank some tea to wash the stale taste of whisky from her mouth. The taste would always remind her of Jon and the last evening they had spent together. Then her dreams had been intact. She had believed in Jon, believed he loved her. She gave a short laugh. The only one Jon Brandon had ever loved was himself.

Sally, who denied ever knowing Jon, carried his credit card with her and had used it on at least one occasion, according to Lainey.

As if conjured up by her thoughts, Lowri came across Jon's name pencilled lightly into one of the dates in May. There was no other information. The entry was at the beginning of May, before Jon disappeared.

Sally did know him, then, probably had slept with him as Sarah had claimed all along. According to his wife, Sally was more Jon's type than Lowri could ever be. So why had he spent so much time, energy and money convincing Lowri that he was in love with her?

She looked through the pages more carefully and to her disappointment found no further references to Jon. Had his name been pencilled in for September or October that would mean that he could still be alive after he disappeared so mysteriously from the Swan Hotel.

Lowri sighed and glanced at the phone; perhaps she should call Lainey. To hell with Lainey, he did not believe a word she said so he could just wait until morning.

Lowri put Sally's make-up and other belongings, with the exception of the diary and credit card, back into the bag.

The diary she slipped under the carpet and then went back to her bedroom, having left lights on in the kitchen and sitting-room, and climbed into bed. Hoping that the house was still being watched, she fell asleep.

22

'So,' Lainey said, 'we searched through that damned case for nothing. It was a complete waste of time. Someone had taken the trouble to remove the CD, and who does it end up with? Lowri Richards — a coincidence, do you think?'

'I don't know, guv,' Ken Major said tiredly. 'Look, when are you going to get Matthew Brown back into work? We could do with him now, don't you think?'

'Why now?' Lainey asked.

'Well, he's been on holiday for long enough. Anyway, he knows more about computer stuff than I do.'

Lainey nodded. 'You're right. I'll try and get hold of him first thing in the morning.'

'Brown's a really good officer, guv. He was a fool to go prancing around with a suspect but then Miss Richards is a very attractive lady, isn't she?'

'Aye, if you say so.' Lainey rose to his feet. 'I'm off, I don't feel as if I've been to bed for weeks. See you in the morning.'

Lainey left the station and unlocked his

car. It was a cold night and the sky was studded with stars. He could see the Plough quite plainly — why had it seemed much more impressive when he was a boy?

Summers were hotter, winters full of snowmen and Christmas gifts when he was a boy. Memories distorted by time, no doubt. He drove out of the station yard and along the road towards Jersey Marine.

'You're as bad as Matthew Brown, Jim Lainey,' he said out loud. Here he was, a responsible detective inspector, and he could not keep away from Lowri however hard he tried. But then she was the main suspect. 'That is a rationalization, Lainey, and you know it,' he told himself.

Lowri's downstairs lights were on, and he parked the car and walked round the side to the back door. He rapped on it lightly. 'It's me,' he called, 'Jim Lainey.'

After a moment, the door was opened and Lowri stood there, her dressing-gown tied loosely around her slim figure, her hair tangled over her shoulders. It was quite clear he had woken her up.

'Can I come in?' he asked.

'If you must.' She left the door open and walked away from him. As he followed, she picked up a handbag and held it out to him.

'Whose is that?' he asked, seating himself

on one of the upright kitchen chairs.

'It's Sally's. I suppose you can look through it, I've been prying into her possessions so you might as well do the same.'

Carefully, Lainey took each item out of the bag and examined it minutely. A half-empty, sticky nail-polish bottle held a puce-coloured polish and he grimaced before putting it down. He took out a pair of knickers, lace-edged and minute, and wondered what on earth women wore them for — certainly not to keep out the cold, or anything else for that matter.

'These weren't designed for warmth,' he said dryly, putting the pants next to the nail polish.

'Jim,' she said. 'Why did Mr Watson deny asking me to bring the disc over to him? Are you sure there was no mistake, a breakdown in communication perhaps?'

'I'm sure.' Lainey felt sorry for her. Nothing Lowri touched seemed to work for her.

'I see.' She paused. 'There's a diary,' she said. 'I think you might find that more useful than poking through Sally's knickers!' She took it from the hiding-place under the carpet and Lainey smiled.

'First place a burglar would look,' he commented dryly.

He took the diary and began to flick

through the pages, finding the credit card immediately. He saw Jon Brandon's name written into one of the dates and sighed. 'So our Sally kept a great deal of her private life private,' he said. 'I suppose you didn't know for sure if he was running Sally White as well as you and that wife of his.'

Lowri switched on the kettle and took two mugs out of the cupboard, along with a packet of tea bags. He watched as she made the tea, knowing just how he liked it. They were getting to know each other's foibles like a married couple but without the intimacy, worse luck.

'Did you notice this?' He pointed to a date in November. 'See what it says here?'

'Not Jon's name again,' Lowri said, 'I looked very carefully.' She put the mugs down on the table and drew her chair alongside Lainey's. She smelt faintly of soap and whisky. He took a deep breath, resisting the urge to take her into his arms.

'No, not Brandon's. It's a meeting arranged with someone called Chas, short for Charles I would imagine.'

'So what's the significance in that?'

'Summer's Dean,' Lainey said. 'Look, it's written very faintly, but it's there. Isn't that where your parents live?'

'Yes it is.' Lowri leaned closer and the

softness of her breast against his arm was almost too much to bear. He was falling in love with this girl and he knew it. But it would not do, it would not do at all.

'Charles, your stepfather?'

'Possibly. But why? What would Sally have in common with my stepfather? Sally liked them young.'

'I don't know,' Lainey said truthfully. 'Was he the type to enjoy being a sugar daddy, perhaps?'

'Very likely!' Lowri's tone was bitter. 'But even Charles would see through Sally, surely?'

'You mean she was a gold-digger?'

'Well no, not exactly. But like any girl she enjoyed beautiful things. A decent car, a good wardrobe, gold jewellery.' She hesitated. 'Why are we talking about her in the past tense? Do you think she's dead?'

He shrugged. 'I just don't know. People seem to go missing all around you, Lowri. Or have road-traffic accidents.'

'Is it my fault if Timmy Perkins crashed his car?' Lowri's voice was edged with anger. 'All Timmy ever meant to me was that he was a boyfriend of Sally's.' She paused. 'How is Timmy?'

'He's recovered consciousness but he can't remember anything about the incident. A temporary loss of memory is quite common in cases of head injury. At least, that's what the doctor at the hospital said.'

'Look, was this just an unfortunate accident?' Lowri asked. She leaned back in her chair and for a moment her lips trembled. 'Come on, Jim, tell me.'

'The CD he gave you, it must be very important. Someone wanted it very badly. His rooms were ransacked, and various things were stolen. I think Timmy was driven off the road on purpose. The car was searched before it had time to become a fireball while Timmy lay there unconscious.'

Lainey paused. 'Would Timmy be able to access the information on the CD, do you think?'

Lowri shrugged. 'I suppose so, he was studying IT among other things.' He could see she was thinking the matter over. She closed her eyes for a moment and curving eyelashes rested against her pale cheeks. The graze from her fall looked red and sore, and a feeling of protectiveness engulfed Lainey. He took a deep breath, about to speak, when Lowri beat him to it.

'Yes, I'm sure Timmy would be able to do most things he put his mind to. He certainly came into money before the accident. At least that's what Sally said.'

'Weren't his parents rich?'

'Yes, but not so rich they'd give him a brand-new car like that. Anyway I think Timmy was the sort of man who would see himself applying to take silk.' She smiled. 'But then he always was a bit on the pompous side.'

'I can't believe the car smash was an accident,' Lainey said.

'Jim!' Lowri sounded exasperated. 'Can't you stop thinking like a policeman for once? Accidents do happen to innocent people all the time and opportunists rifle cars and houses. Isn't that how thieves make a living?'

She was right, of course. It was just his gut feeling that told him that the crash was no ordinary accident. He leaned forward. 'Lowri, why would Jon Brandon be sending software to your brother in Canada?'

She looked at him as if he had grown two heads. 'Don't ask me! I haven't spoken to my brother in years. We don't get on.' She smiled wryly. 'Justin deals in wines and spirits but I suppose he'd need to run a network of computers, wouldn't he?'

'So you had no idea that Brandon was involved in dealings with your brother, then?'

'Got it in one.' Her sarcasm was evident. He smiled ruefully.

'I'd like to believe you, Lowri, but it's inconceivable you didn't know anything about Jon Brandon and his business.'

'Like I didn't know he was married. Why don't you go and question his wife? She's bound to know more than I do about the man.' She rubbed her eyes wearily. Lainey got to his feet.

'I'd better go.'

'To ask silly questions of Mrs Brandon, I take it?'

'I've made inquiries and Mrs Brandon is out of the country,' Lainey said, cursing his bad luck. He had no reason to order Sarah Brandon to return to England; so far as he knew she had committed no crime. Still she needed watching. He could send one of the men out there. Matthew Brown would jump at the chance and at least he would be out of Lainey's hair. And at a safe distance from Lowri Richards, but that was his jealous streak talking.

'Right, I'm off.' He walked towards the door and Lowri followed him, tying her dressing-gown more securely around her. He stopped abruptly and Lowri cannoned into him.

He caught her arms, felt the thinness of them under the robe and, before he could stop himself, he had drawn her to him and was kissing her with a passion that surprised him.

He felt her lips soft against his. The blood pounded in his head. He felt himself harden. Suddenly embarrassed, he released her.

'Sorry!' he said. 'That was out of order.'

Lowri caught hold of his lapels and drew him back into her embrace. 'Jim,' her voice was thick, 'I've told you, you must stop thinking like a policeman all the time.'

He kissed her, he just could not resist the lure of her mouth. Her ragged breathing matched his own. Lowri drew away and taking his hand led him upstairs to her bedroom. He could not be rational any longer; his desire to possess this beautiful, challenging woman was too much for him.

He watched her slip her robe from her shoulders and his mouth was dry as he took in the alabaster skin of her breasts tipped with pink, the nipples standing proud. Her hips were gently curved and at the base of her belly her pubic hair shone golden in the soft light from her bedside lamp.

Emotions he had subdued for so long rose to the surface. He lay with Lowri on the bed and touched her tenderly. Her mouth curved into a smile. 'It's all right,' she whispered. 'I won't break.'

She drew his head onto her breast and he took her nipple into his mouth, tasting her, wanting to absorb her into himself.

She cried out as he slid inside her and her legs wrapped round him, holding him close. He lost himself then, hearing her cries of delight with a surge of such love and power that he felt he could move mountains.

They lay together in the darkness of early morning and, wrapped in each other's arms, they slept.

Lowri stepped out of the shower and studied her reflection in the long bathroom mirror. A flush of happiness illuminated her features. She was in love, really in love, madly, crazily. No man had ever moved her the way Lainey did.

She heard the phone ring. She pulled on a fresh robe and hurried downstairs. Her hair hung damply on her shoulders and she smiled, feeling reborn.

Before Lainey had left he had held her close and though he had spoken no words of love, she knew deep in her being that he felt the same way as she did.

She picked up the phone. 'Hello?' After a short pause, a voice came over the line.

'Hi, Lowri! It's Justin, your long-lost brother. I'm in London.' His voice betrayed the Canadian accent that he had acquired during his time abroad. 'I'm catching the next train down to your little backwater — can you give me a room for a couple of nights?'

'Justin!' She frowned. Why had he come back now, of all times? 'Yes, sure, what time is your train due in? I'll meet you.'

When she put the phone down, Lowri stared at it for some time. Her joy of the morning seemed to vanish as she thought of her childhood. Being with Justin had always meant trouble. She squared her shoulders. Surely things were different now they were both adults?

She phoned the office and was answered by the impersonal voice of Mrs Jenkins.

'Will you let Mr Watson know I can't come in today?' Lowri said. 'Something's come up.'

'Not again!' Mrs Jenkins was exasperated. 'I shall really have to insist on other staff in the office.' She spoke in her usual manner, as though she hated the entire world and all its inhabitants. 'I cannot continue to man the office alone.' With that she put down the phone.

Lowri shrugged. Mrs Jenkins could do as she liked because Lowri was not sure she wanted to work for Mr Watson any longer.

He had let her down when she most needed him. He had lied to the police about her, and the thought hurt. Fathers? A girl was better off without one.

She picked Justin up three and a half hours later. As he came towards her he looked tanned and healthy. His hair, blond where hers was red, gleamed in the pale sunlight. He was smiling and his teeth were white and perfect. Canadian dentists must be a superior breed; Lowri remembered that her brother had once had protruding front teeth.

'You're looking good, Lowri.' Justin hugged her. 'Quite the little beauty instead of the bespectacled, pimply sister I remember.'

She slid her arm through his. 'Same horrid brother then, no change there.' She smiled up at him. 'Come on, you can treat me to lunch, we'll go somewhere posh seeing as you are the wealthy businessman these days.'

Justin grinned. 'Yes, I am wealthy and successful, aren't I? I always said I would be, remember?'

'I remember, you smug bastard!'

As they walked out of the station arm in arm a police car drew up at the side of the kerb. The doors swung open and several uniformed police stepped out. Lowri watched in disbelief as Lainey emerged from the back seat and gave her a withering look that seemed to shrivel her heart.

'Mr Justin Richards,' Lainey said, 'I want you to come with me.' He did not look at Lowri again. 'I have reason to believe you are in possession of certain information that could help me with my inquiries.'

'Get me a lawyer, sis,' Justin said as he was bundled into the car. Lowri stood in open-mouthed astonishment as it drew speedily away from the kerb, leaving her standing on the pavement feeling as if the world had just crashed around her ears.

23

Lainey sat at his desk and stared at the flickering images on the computer screen with little interest. So far, Justin Richards had given him nothing of value. Lainey closed his eyes. One thing he could be grateful for, immigration had passed on the information that Richards was back in the country. It made up in part for the fact that they had let him down over Jon Brandon.

Lainey had been surprised when the solicitor who came to the station to act for Richards turned out to be Terence Watson. He had been led to believe that there was no love lost between Watson and Charles Richards, so why would Justin retain him? Still, he probably had no choice, Watson might be the only solicitor Lowri could get.

He thought of Lowri with a sinking heart. He had made love to her. Fallen in love with her. She was the woman he wanted to spend the rest of his life with. And she had lied to him. He had seen her come out of the station, arm in arm with her brother, smiling up at him, no doubt part of all that had been going on.

The door to his office opened. 'Shall we interview Richards again, guv?' Matthew Brown stood in the doorway. 'I know his solicitor got him out pretty sharp but I would like to see the cocky little bastard on his own, if only for ten minutes.'

Lainey shook his head. 'There's no point. We lost him through lack of hard evidence. The tip-off we received was that Justin Richards was entering the country carrying a case full of contraband.' He sighed. 'By then he could have deposited it somewhere near the airport.'

'I thought security there had him watched. Surely they would have searched his stuff?'

'Maybe, but he could have had an accomplice or even got some unsuspecting fellow-traveller to carry a case through for him. Perhaps I should learn a lesson from this, never trust a caller who wants to remain anonymous.'

He glanced at his watch. 'Anyway, it's getting late, better get off home.'

Brown nodded. 'I expect you're right, sir, but what about putting a tail on Richards? He might try to contact someone a bit iffy.'

'Are you volunteering, Sergeant Brown?'

Lainey rose to his feet and shuffled the papers on his desk. 'If so, go ahead with my blessing. I assume his sister has taken him back to her place at Jersey Marine?'

'Yes, guv, and I don't mind a bit of extra work. I had enough of time off when I was on holiday.' He grinned. 'It was a case of nothing to do and no-one to do it with.'

Lainey looked at him. 'No girlfriend, Brown?'

'No sir, not at the moment. I'm playing the field until I meet the right one.'

Lainey moved to the door, wondering if Brown considered Lowri a candidate for the 'right one' spot. 'Grab what you can when you can, Sergeant,' he said. 'Life has a nasty habit of sneaking up on you and before you know it you're a lonely old man.'

'You're not old, guv.'

'I was speaking hypothetically,' Lainey said, 'but by God, at times like this I feel a hundred and one!'

Lainey left the office and climbed into his own small car. The Golf was past her best but she was a reliable old thing and, in any case, Lainey did not have the sort of money to splash out on new cars, his ex-wife saw to that.

'Women!' he muttered as he turned on the ignition. 'Why do they always let you down?'

'What on earth do the police suspect you of?' Lowri and her brother were sitting in her living-room, drinking coffee. Justin shook his head and his bright hair fell across his forehead. It was hard to believe he was the same person who used to torment her when they were children.

'I'm not sure.' He smiled. 'Perhaps I look the criminal type.'

Lowri wondered what had made Lainey suspicious of Justin in the first place. The police usually had a good reason for picking someone up and carting them off to the station. At least Mr Watson had turned up trumps and come at once when she telephoned him.

Lowri had been tempted to ask him why he had lied to the police about her, denying he had asked her to bring the CD to him. He had forestalled her.

'Let's get this little matter sorted out, Lowri, and then we can have a talk.' But would he ever find the time to talk to her?

'Ah well, let's forget all about the damned cops.' Justin smiled and his teeth gleamed whitely against his tan. 'Have you got any good-looking girlfriends you can fix me up with?'

'Sorry, you'll have to sort out your love

life yourself. Anyway, I thought you were living with someone in Canada.'

'So? A man likes a bit of variety in his life. Didn't you learn that from Dad?' For a moment Justin looked serious. 'I often felt sorry for Mother, but then she should never have put up with it in the first place.' He looked carefully at Lowri.

'Mother took the blame for having me,' Lowri said. 'But a premarital fling isn't the end of the world, is it?'

'It is when there's a child involved, I suppose,' Justin said. 'I don't think I'd like to take on another man's baby.'

'Mother had a great deal to offer, mind,' Lowri said. 'In return for a wedding ring Charles was able to live in luxury. He never had to worry about money because Mother had enough for all of us for the rest of our lives.'

'Still, you've got to admit that in their day illegitimacy was a stigma, and Dad saved her from that.'

Lowri changed the subject. 'When are you going down to Summer's Dean?' She looked at Justin, wondering how much he knew about the split between their parents.

'I'll stay here with you for a few days,' he said. 'That's if you'll have me. Then I'll pop over to see Dad. My car is being sent directly to the old homestead, so once I'm mobile I can drive up to see you any time.'

'Your car is being sent over? Wouldn't it have been cheaper and easier to hire one when you arrived?'

'Maybe I like to show off my swish American job,' Justin said. 'She moves like a dream — wait till you see her.'

'You always were a show-off,' Lowri said. 'Anyway, if you want to see the hot spots of Jersey Marine for yourself I'd better shower and change. You'll have to put up with a ride in my little red Mazda and be glad I've got a car at all on the money I earn.'

'Surely the old girl makes you an allowance?' Justin said. 'You always were her favourite.'

'No, I get nothing from Mother, I am young, free and independent.'

'And working in a crummy office for a worn-out solicitor! I thought you had more ambition than that.'

'We're not all like you, Justin. I'm no high-flyer.' Lowri got to her feet. 'Read the paper or something while I get ready.' She walked to the door and Justin's voice stopped her.

'So where is Mother? I'd like to see her.'

He knew they were separated, then; that meant he had been in touch with Charles.

Lowri glanced back over her shoulder.

'It's some little cottage somewhere. I'll have to look it up, you know what a memory I've got for addresses and numbers.'

She turned the shower setting to hot and stood under the spray of water, feeling the heat wash the tension from her shoulders. It was only natural Justin would want to see Rhian, it was years since he had last been in the country.

Her brother had changed, Lowri conceded that. He had brought generous gifts for both Rhian and for her, and he seemed far more open and honest than he had ever been as a child.

She remembered the times Justin would lock her in her room and dangle the key at her from a ladder outside the window. Once he had shut her in the walk-in pantry at Summer's Dean and she had only been let out when Rhian returned home from a shopping trip.

Still, that was all a long time ago. Justin had been a normal healthy teasing boy. Most sisters hated their brothers when they were children. Lowri soaped her body, enjoying the feel of the hot shower on her skin. Her hair clung wetly to her cheeks and shoulders and she thought of Lainey touching her hair, making love to her.

She turned off the shower and stepped out into the bathroom, pulling on a towelling robe. The last slant of sun shone through the window and, for a moment, Lowri was reminded of the night when Jon had disappeared.

Where had he gone? Was he even still alive? She supposed those questions might never be answered. She realized now that she had never really loved him. The feelings she had for Jon faded into insignificance whenever she thought of Lainey. She was in love with him — more fool her. He simply saw her as an accomplice in a crime.

'About time too!' Justin said when she returned to the living-room, her face carefully made up, her hair dried into soft curls. 'But I must say the wait was worth it! You look a million dollars, sister mine.'

'Well, compliments from my brother! Things are looking up.' She picked up her jacket and handbag. 'Right then, are you ready to paint this town red?'

'Sure am, sis.' He took her hand and slipped it through his arm. 'Raring to go, as they say.'

She smiled up at him. 'You're not half bad, you know,' she said.

He winked at her. 'I'm a perfect specimen

of manhood. Now come on, let's get out of this poky little place, it's making me claustrophobic.'

'Hey, you're talking about the home I love.' Lowri slapped her brother's arm. 'Now get into the car and shut up or I won't take you out.'

She started the car and drove away from the kerb and, glancing in the rear-view mirror, she saw a dark car pull out from behind them and follow them up the road. The police, no doubt. Well, that was no surprise. Indeed, Lowri found the thought comforting. Even if it was in just a professional way, Lainey cared.

'I should see Lowri, explain everything to her,' Rhian Richards said softly. 'I know Justin is my son but I'm not looking forward to meeting him again. What is it that the police suspect him of, Terence?'

'It's probably nothing to worry yourself over.' Terence pushed his glasses back into place and Rhian smiled.

'You should get yourself a pair of glasses that fit, at least,' she said fondly. 'I know you are a small-town solicitor and I know you won't let me help you, but surely you can afford essentials now and then?'

'I'm just too lazy to go for an eye test, my

dear. Anyway, how are you feeling today?' He put his head on one side. 'As far as I can see the roses are not back in your cheeks yet, so worry about yourself, not about my glasses.'

'I'm all right. Now, getting back to Justin, what do the police think he's done? I hope to heaven he isn't following Charles and indulging in dubious, hare-brained schemes.'

'No no, nothing like that.' Terence sat down in the chair on the opposite side of the fire, and Rhian thought how cosy it was in his little house. She loved Summer's Dean, but home was where the heart was, and her heart had always been with Terence Watson.

If only she had not been too proud to go to him when she learned she was pregnant with Lowri, how different her life might have been.

'What then? Tell me.'

'The police had a tip-off that Justin was carrying contraband goods. Probably a malicious joke, I should think. Has the boy got any enemies in this country?'

Rhian shrugged. 'I shouldn't think so, but then you never know your children, I suppose. Justin might well have stepped on a competitor's toes in some business deal or other.'

'That's most likely it, then,' Terence said.

'At any rate, nothing suspicious was found among the boy's possessions.'

'That's a relief.'

The phone rang shrilly from the hall and Terence went to answer it. He returned in a few moments, looking grave. 'Talk of the devil,' he said, 'that was your son.'

'Justin?'

Terence smiled. 'Justin, that's unless you've got some other son you have omitted to tell me about.'

'No no, he's the only one. What does he want?'

'He thinks the police are having him followed.' Terence sank into his chair. 'He wanted to know if I could call them off.'

'And can you?'

'Not at this time of night,' Terence said, shaking his head. 'In any case, he could easily be mistaken. A dark car followed him and Lowri from her house to the restaurant where they were having dinner, and waited outside until they came out. It could be nothing at all. I can't see the police wasting money on observation duties when there is no concrete evidence of any wrongdoing.'

Rhian felt a qualm of fear. 'Could it be a malicious competitor then?' She knew in her heart it was Lowri she was concerned for. Justin led his own life, he always had. He seemed to have become very wealthy and Rhian often wondered if his splendid house with the vast swimming-pool had been bought with the proceeds of illicit deals.

'Don't worry about it or I'll be sorry I told you. Look, phone Lowri if you like. She's at home now, both of them are, they're quite safe.'

Rhian sighed. 'No no, you're right, no harm will come to them tonight, not if they are back at home.'

Terence heaved himself to his feet. 'I've got a splendid idea — let's have a stiff drink and then go to bed.'

'You randy devil!' Rhian said. 'I thought you were telling me to rest, that I looked pale.'

Terence smiled mischievously. 'Well, I can do all the work, can't I? All you need to do is lie back and enjoy it.'

'You conceited man!' Rhian said but she took the drink he poured her and the blood sang in her veins. She was with the man she had always loved, and that was worth more to her than all the riches in the world.

Lainey walked past Lowri's house, seeing the lights on in the window. The curtains were closed but he could hear the distant sound of music coming from inside. At least

Lowri was with her brother and not with another man. The thought should not have been a comfort to him, but somehow it was.

How deeply was she involved in the net that was drawing in her brother, her stepfather and Jon Brandon, always supposing he could be found? Lainey had at last come up with some answers to his questions and they did not put his mind to rest, not one little bit.

His counterparts in Canada had e-mailed him some information which revealed that Justin Richards was worth a great deal of money. Money that could not possibly be accounted for by the proceeds from the wines and spirits business that Justin owned. Somehow, somewhere, something else was being peddled and the most likely item was information. It was easy to transport, especially by CD.

Blackmail was always an option. Digging into other people's lives and learning something best kept secret meant ready cash. Careers could be ruined, marriages jeopardized; even lives could be put at risk.

If only that damned disc could be found, the one that had been given to Lowri by Timmy Perkins. The boy had not recovered his memory as yet and even when he did, he might not know if there was anything of significance on the disc left at his house by his flighty girlfriend.

The music stopped abruptly and the lights in the downstairs room went out. Lainey glanced at his watch and the luminous dial showed him it was after one a.m. He was a fool, standing in the road watching Lowri's house. What would he learn wandering the streets at this time of night, when the suspects would soon be tucked up safely in bed?

He took out a cigarette, watching as lights went on upstairs, first the landing, then the front bedroom. He lit the cigarette, shading the flame with his hand, and puffed as though he could find inspiration in the curls of smoke arising from the tip.

One by one the lights were switched off. He sighed; he might just as well go home. He walked back to his car parked a little way along the road and unlocked it. A light rain had begun to fall and he felt the dampness penetrating his jacket. He huddled in his seat and fastened his safety-belt. He was cold and hungry and painfully lonely for the one woman he loved but could not have.

'Damn you, Lowri!' he muttered. He was just about to turn on the ignition when he saw a figure emerge from Lowri's gateway. It was Justin Richards, he could be seen clearly in the light from the street lamp.

He climbed into the Mazda and started it up and Lainey sighed in satisfaction. He had known in his gut that something was going to happen tonight and when it did, he meant to be right there.

24

Lowri sat at her desk, her hands idly resting on her lap. The computer screen seemed to stare blankly at her and she sighed. She was never going to be able to concentrate on work until she had seen Mr Watson and demanded an explanation from him.

She glanced impatiently at her watch: the hands seemed to be creeping from minute to minute. It was ten past eleven, late even for Mr Watson.

Restlessly, Lowri got up and walked towards the reception area. Mrs Jenkins was working on a document, her hands flying across the keyboard.

'Have you heard from Mr Watson?' Lowri asked. She stood in front of the desk, leaning forward so that Mrs Jenkins was forced to look up at her. The woman frowned.

'Why?'

'Because I need to speak to him.' Lowri's tone was curt. It was a mistake. Mrs Jenkins returned to her task, ignoring Lowri.

'Mrs Jenkins, does being rude come naturally or have you had training?' Lowri asked. The woman did not show even by a flicker of an eyelash that she had heard. Lowri tried again.

'If you don't answer me I shall be forced to ring Mr Watson, and you know he doesn't like to be disturbed at home.'

Mrs Jenkins shook her head. 'Do what you please.'

Lowri was seething as she returned to her office. She sank down onto her chair and glowered at the phone as if it was not an inanimate object but had a life of its own. Mr Watson might be on his way to work. She had better wait at least another hour before taking steps to contact him.

Following Sally's custom, she made some coffee. She looked at the other empty cups and, with a sigh, spooned coffee into one for Mrs Jenkins. She could hardly be so petty as to leave the woman without a drink.

She overfilled the cup and, suspecting that Mrs Jenkins would not approve of coffee in the saucer, held it away from her and made her way slowly to the door. Fortunately she had left it ajar and opened it easily with her foot.

Mrs Jenkins did not hear her coming. Lowri stood behind her, her eyes drawn to the computer screen which was filled with indecipherable cybertext. Lowri narrowed her eyes, trying to see more clearly without moving any closer.

Mrs Jenkins sensed her presence and immediately exited the program. The screen returned to the desk top as, carefully, Lowri put the coffee on the desk.

'Sorry I was rude earlier on,' she said. 'I'm just a bit fraught this morning, that's all.'

'Thank you for the coffee,' Mrs Jenkins said. 'But I never drink the stuff, hadn't you noticed?'

The woman had no social graces to speak of, but Lowri bit her lip against a flurry of angry words.

'You might as well pour it away, I can't abide even the smell of it,' Mrs Jenkins said. She took an herbal tea bag from her drawer. 'A cup of hot water would be acceptable, however.'

Lowri took the coffee away and grudgingly poured hot water from the kettle. When she returned to reception Mrs Jenkins simply nodded as Lowri put the cup beside her.

'What on earth was all that stuff on the computer just now?' Lowri asked casually. 'Some sort of bug, was it?'

'I don't know what you mean.' Mrs Jenkins dipped the tea bag into the hot water, squeezed it thoroughly and then dropped it neatly into the bin.

She sipped the tea, not meeting Lowri's eyes, her head bent over some documents on the desk beside her.

'What made you come here to work?' Lowri changed tack. 'I mean, aren't you a little overqualified for the job of receptionist?'

Mrs Jenkins put down her cup with great deliberation. 'I am doing two jobs now that Miss White has taken off so whatever my reasons for being here, just be glad I am. Now if you will excuse me I have work to do.'

Lowri shook her head and returned to her office. She picked up her handbag and took her jacket from the hanger and slipped it over her shoulders. On her way out she paused for a moment, her eyes on Mrs Jenkins's bent head.

'You will have three jobs to do today because I'm taking the rest of the day off.' Lowri did not wait for a reply. She sailed through reception and out of the door, stepping into the unexpected sunshine with a sigh of relief.

'Well, Mr Watson, if the mountain won't come to Mohammed then Mohammed will have to go to the mountain.'

Lainey knocked again on the door of Lowri's house but it was becoming increasingly clear that no-one was going to answer him. He had phoned her office only to be told that she had taken the day off.

'No joy then, guv?' Ken Major was leaning against the car, his arms folded across his chest.

'Doesn't look like it, does it, Sergeant?' Last night Lainey had followed Justin Richards as far as the main road out of town and then had promptly lost him. He was still seething with rage that he had been outwitted.

Lainey watched as Ken Major climbed into the car and listened to the crackling message on the radio. He leaned out of the driving seat and waved.

'Guv, just had word that Perkins has got his memory back. Shall we go to the hospital and speak to him?'

'Might as well.' Lainey looked up at the blank windows. He resisted the urge to kick in the firmly closed door. Turning away, he glanced along the street, but it was empty except for the milk float grinding its way up the incline.

'I wonder if we'll get anything useful out of Perkins, guv?' Ken Major started the car and slipped it into gear. 'He's a bit of a wimp but I suppose being a student he's quite intelligent.'

'False assumption, Major,' Lainey said. 'Some kids just have good memories.' He sounded as surly as he felt and leaned back in his seat, closing his eyes. Lowri Richards, she was the pivot in all this confusion. She was the one woman he could readily spend his life with; yet how could he trust her when she had lied to him so convincingly?

Lowri must know what was going on. She was linked to all the parties involved. Jon Brandon, Justin Richards and his father, Sally White and Timmy Perkins. And, of course, she had more than a nodding acquaintance with Sarah Brandon.

'I wonder if Sarah Brandon knows more than she's been telling us,' he said, sitting upright. 'Strange that she should swan off abroad with her husband missing.'

'Well, can you blame her, guv? Looks like her old man was not exactly the faithful kind.'

'Still, I think it's about time we took a little trip, Major. You're not tied up over the next week or two, are you?'

'No, I'm not. And I wouldn't mind a couple of weeks in the sun.'

'Don't get carried away. It would be more

like a couple of days in the sun, if we can get the go-ahead at all, that is.'

'Well, I'm all for it. I've always thought the Brandon wife a bit of a dark horse. The jealous type certainly but the kind to look after number one whatever happened.'

'It could be that she is out in Jamaica waiting for her husband to join her,' Lainey said. 'He might even be there with her already. Anyway, first things first, let's talk to Perkins, see what he can remember.'

Lainey had never liked hospitals. The smells, the sounds, the very paint on the wall turned his stomach. Whenever he was required to attend a post-mortem he did his best not to look too closely at the corpse. It made him only too aware of his own mortality.

'Go and find out which ward the boy is in,' he said as he stepped through the swing doors into the reception area. Ken Major obeyed with alacrity and Lainey half smiled. The receptionist was a very pretty young woman.

Ken took a little longer over his enquiry than necessary and Lainey moved impatiently towards the double doors leading to the corridor.

'Ward H, guv.' Ken Major caught him up. 'Seems the boy's had other visitors already.'

Lainey stopped walking. 'What other visitors?'

'Mr Watson and some bloke who didn't give his name. Popular fellow, isn't he?'

Timmy Perkins's bed was near the door of the small ward. Lainey went towards him, observing the boy's swollen eyes and bandaged head. His hands were wrapped in gauze and covered with plastic bags. He looked absurdly young, with all the cockiness knocked out of him.

'How are you feeling?' Lainey asked, seating himself on a plastic chair. 'Had a rough time of it, by the look.'

'I don't remember a great deal about it,' Timmy said. 'But why are the police sending a detective inspector to make inquiries about a road accident?' His voice was thin, as though he was very tired.

'It's not about the accident,' Lainey said. 'Someone else has probably taken all the details of that from you already, haven't they?'

'Yes, but knowing the police they need someone to blame for it. Well it wasn't my fault, I can tell you that much.'

'Remarkable for a man who can't remember much about it, wouldn't you say, Sergeant?'

'Remarkable,' Ken affirmed. He had positioned himself at the foot of the bed, arms folded across his chest, almost as if he expected Perkins to make a run for it.

'It's about the possessions Sally White left in your care,' Lainey said. 'I believe there was a CD amongst her things?'

'Well yes, there might have been several CDs come to that, I didn't really look.'

'So what did you do with her things?'

'I thought I'd told you.' Perkins rubbed his forehead. 'Didn't I tell you I gave them all to Lowri Richards?'

Lainey leaned forward. 'Try to think, try to remember, what did you find among her belongings, nail polish and make-up and what else?'

'Nothing else as far as I know. Make-up for sure, Sally wouldn't move without a load of cosmetics about her person.'

'So how come she left them with you?'

Timmy Perkins looked confused. 'Why shouldn't she leave things at my place? We were sleeping together, you knew that already.'

'When you called over to Miss White's house the night she disappeared why didn't you take her things back to her then?'

'Why should I? Is it important?'

Lainey rubbed his chin, he needed a shave. 'This CD — it was no ordinary CD, was it?'

'Wasn't it?' Timmy closed his eyes. 'Look, I'm tired, I don't know what you're getting at and I just want to sleep.'

'This CD, it was written in some sort of code, wasn't it?'

Timmy sighed and opened his eyes. He leaned over and rang the bell for the nurse. She appeared almost at once.

'I've a headache, nurse. Could I have a painkiller please?' He was like a small boy asking for sweets. The nurse plumped his pillows and Lainey watched her with interest. In his experience nurses had little time for motherly duties these days.

'I think you'd better go, sir.' She tucked the sheet in at the sides with fierce efficiency. 'Mr Perkins has had quite enough visitors for one day.'

'So I understand.' Lainey got to his feet. 'I believe Mr Watson called? Now why did you need the services of a solicitor?'

'I'll need to claim compensation for my injuries, don't you think?'

'All according to who caused the accident. If it was an accident,' Lainey said. 'Come along Sergeant, we've taken up quite enough of Mr Perkins's time.'

Out in the street Lainey sighed heavily. 'He's hiding something. Did you know his car was ransacked after the crash?'

'Heard something about it, guv.'

'Strange sort of vandals breaking into a car involved in such a bad crash, don't you think?'

'It happens.' Ken opened the door of the car and climbed in. 'No doubt given a little time the thieves would have nicked the wheels and the chassis too, if they thought they could get away with it.'

He drove for a time in silence and Lainey tried to sort out the complex tangle of events surrounding the case. Two missing persons, another almost killed. A CD containing a weird code, and Lowri Richards. It all came back to her. There was no getting away from it. Lowri must be involved up to her pretty little neck.

'So, Lowri, now you can understand why I chose to leave Summer's Dean now, after all these years. When I became ill, I realized I wanted to live with Terence more than anything in the world.' Rhian lay against the pillows in the pretty bedroom and looked up at her daughter.

'Mother! What exactly is wrong with you? And why didn't you tell me about your illness before this? I could have come home and looked after you!' Seeing how pale and thin Rhian had become made Lowri feel guilty. 'I really should have spent more time with you, Mummy.' The childish word slipped out without her noticing. Rhian smiled.

'No, not you and Charles in the same house,' she said. 'In any case, I didn't want to upset you with all this sickness business, you have enough on your plate as it is.'

The door opened and Terence came in. Rhian held out her hand and he took it, his expression soft with love. He raised her hand to his lips and kissed it. Rhian smiled at him and then turned back to Lowri.

'You are not to worry about me, these few weeks with Terence have been the happiest ones of my life. I should have left Charles years ago.'

Lowri sighed. 'Have you seen Justin? He's popped up to London for a day or two but he'll be back soon.'

'He never came near,' Rhian said sadly. 'I suppose it's only to be expected. After all I left his father for another man.'

'Still, you are Justin's mother, he should try to understand,' Lowri insisted. But then Justin had always been selfish, just like Charles. Suddenly she was very glad that she was Terence's daughter, not Charles's.

'I'm sorry, Lowri.' It was as if he read her thoughts. 'I know you think I let you down with the police but I never made any call asking you to meet me. It was some cruel trick to get you out of the house.'

Lowri remained silent, not sure if he was telling the truth. The voice on the line had certainly sounded like Mr Watson's. And the attacker at the hotel had been familiar somehow. She recalled a certain scent, it reminded her of someone. Still, she might just be confused. She had blacked out, after all.

She looked at Mr Watson carefully, he was so sweet, so innocent. She must have been fooled by a very clever con man. Jon perhaps?

Her father bent over Rhian and Lowri saw the glint of tears in his eyes. 'I know the treatment isn't very pleasant, darling, but you'll be better for it, I know you will.' Alarmed, she looked at her mother.

'What treatment, what does the doctor say is wrong?'

'The doctors are doing all they can, Lowri, and don't worry, I intend to be around for a long time yet.'

Lowri felt chilled. Her mother was too cheerful; her illness must be serious. Lowri took a deep breath. 'But Mother —'

'No buts,' Rhian said. 'Now you two are supposed to be cheering me up, not looking at me as if I was dead already.'

'I'm sorry, Mother.' Lowri forced a smile, her mind numb with fear.

'We think Charles is up to his old tricks again,' Rhian said, her voice deliberately bright. 'He's definitely engaged in something crooked and it would be nice for once to be able to prove it.' She touched Terence's hand. 'He's tried often enough to put you out of business, hasn't he, love?'

He shrugged noncommittally. 'But he hasn't succeeded yet, and he won't.'

'Mr Watson,' Lowri said, 'do you trust Mrs Jenkins? I went into reception today and saw her computer screen had a load of funny writing on it. She's not spying on us for someone, is she?'

Mr Watson shook his head. 'I don't think so, Lowri, and I don't expect you to call me Father but how about Terence? Why don't I go and get us a coffee?' He left the room and Rhian smiled up at Lowri.

'He's being tactful, in case we want to talk privately together.'

'Oh, right. And do we?' Lowri frowned, fearing her mother would talk about death or wills, say things Lowri did not want to hear. Rhian shook her head.

'No, of course not. There's nothing I can't say with Terence present, I trust him absolutely.'

Lowri heaved a sigh of relief. 'Coming back to Mrs Jenkins, I wonder if she had some sort of secret code on the computer,' she said. 'Perhaps a formula for some chemical that no-one's thought of inventing before?'

Rhian smiled. 'Now you're being over-imaginative again. You always were, even as a child. The nightmares you used to have.' Rhian reached out and touched her hand. 'The nightmares have gone away, haven't they?'

'Yes, Mother, of course they have,' Lowri lied. 'I'm a big girl now, remember. Still, I think Mrs Jenkins must have been up to something. Arms deals maybe, she looks big enough and ugly enough to be involved in anything!'

The door was pushed open and Mr Watson came in with a cup of coffee in each hand. 'Nothing as dramatic, Lowri. Though it's possible our Mrs Jenkins is working with the police.' The idea seemed to worry him.

'Surely not!' Lowri said. 'She could have been working for Justin, of course.'

'Justin?' Rhian said, 'What's he got to do with anything crooked?'

'I don't really know if he is,' Lowri said cautiously, 'it's just that Jon Brandon, my one-time fiancé, was sending a case of software to Canada, to Justin's business address.'

Terence was silent, his fingers gently smoothing the skin of Rhian's arm. He was frowning worriedly and Lowri understood his concern.

'I'm sorry, Justin's probably got nothing to do with Charles or with anything crooked. No doubt he just wanted some innocent software, games or something, sent out to him.'

'That's likely,' Terence said. 'Canada hasn't got the expertise in computer technology that we have here.'

Rhian smiled. 'That's rather a sweeping statement for a solicitor to make, Terence!'

'It's true, darling.'

Lowri stared at him. It was so strange to think that he was her father, and had been her mother's lover for years. Her boss, the angelic-faced respectable solicitor, and her mother had shared a passion and she was the result.

'Why are you staring at us as if we've grown two heads?' Rhian asked, a smile turning her mouth up at the corners.

'Just thinking,' Lowri said. 'Well look, I'd better go.' She stood up. 'I came here to see my sick mother and I find I've barged into a love-nest!'

'Why shouldn't we be in love?' Mr Watson asked. 'Is it because you think we're a pair of old fogies?'

'Of course not! I'm very happy for you both.' Lowri kissed her mother. She felt the thinness of her shoulders and knew that Rhian was much more ill than she was willing to admit.

25

'It's true, Dad, I've had a phone call from Lowri and apparently Mother is really sick. I'll go to see her tomorrow and perhaps this might be a good time for you two to kiss and make up.' Justin sat in the lounge of the exclusive London hotel and looked at his father's bent head. A knot of anger and resentment began to tighten inside him.

'I know it's been hard to take all these years, Mother parading her love-child in front of you.' He shook his head. 'A lesser man would not have put up with the situation for one minute.'

Charles looked up. 'All I want now, Justin, is to protect your inheritance. You deserve to have everything, the money, the house at Summer's Dean and all that's in it. You are the true heir, Justin, and I won't let that sly bitch take it away from you.'

Justin tried to read the expression in his father's eyes. Whom was he calling a sly bitch, his wife or Lowri? 'Anyway, Dad, I think you should see Mother, talk to her.'

'Perhaps. Now, let's talk about the

business, we must do all we can to salvage it, get everything under control again. Rhian's estate is all well and good but we deserve jam on our bread, something our business *was* providing.' He lit an expensive cigar. 'If only some bastard had not run away with that CD everything would be all right.' There was venom in Charles's voice. 'I blame Jon Brandon, he always did want a bigger cut of the action and he was careless into the bargain. Where the hell *is* the vital disc? It's got to be found or our business is down the pan.'

'Well at least Brandon got all he deserved didn't he, Dad? After that going-over he got from your friend with the white hair he won't trouble you any more, will he?'

'No, but he's been working for someone else, it's obvious. He kept some details of the accounts to himself, didn't he? He could still sink us.'

'You tried asking his blonde bimbo?'

Charles nodded. 'Sally White had nothing in the house, we made sure of that.'

'Are you really sure? A CD is easily hidden, you know.'

'Of course I'm sure, do you think I'm an idiot? I also arranged for an accident to happen to that sucker of a boyfriend of hers, he'd outlived his usefulness, but there was nothing on him, or in his rooms.'

'Lowri!' Justin said. 'Maybe Perkins gave the CD to Lowri. After all, his girlfriend worked in the same office as my dear half-sister.'

Charles's eyes narrowed. 'You know, you might just have hit the nail on the head, boy!' He smiled. 'So it's back to you. Go and stay with Lowri again — you've done it before so she won't be suspicious. Do you think she's in on it? She was sleeping with Brandon, wasn't she?'

'Well, she knows all the parties concerned. She's the pivot that Brandon, Sally White and Perkins revolved around.' Justin drank some of his brandy. 'And she's number one suspect with the police. Our Lowri could just be smarter than we've given her credit for.'

But she would not get the better of him. Justin rose to his feet and stared out of the hotel window. The street below was thronged with traffic but he was thinking about Summer's Dean. He loved the house, the good paintings, the heavy antique furniture and one day it would be his, whatever he had to do to possess it.

'I have to go to Jamaica on police business, Lowri,' Lainey said and she looked up at him.

'So why are you telling me? I thought I was your main suspect.'

'Your involvement can't be ruled out,' Lainey said. Lowri heard the sharp tone in his voice and felt her spirits plummet. When he had arrived at her door she hoped he had learned something, found whatever it was he was looking for.

'Why are you here, Jim?'

He sank down on the sofa and put his head in his hands. 'I don't know why the hell I'm here!' He looked up abruptly. 'Yes I do, it's because I've fallen in love with you, dammit!'

'But you can't trust me?'

He shook his head. 'I only wish I could, Lowri, believe me.' He moved towards her and took her hands, pulling her to her feet. 'When I look into your eyes my gut instinct tells me you are innocent.'

She thought he would kiss her but he dropped her hands and walked towards the door. 'Sadly, all the evidence points to your involvement. You might even be the brains behind this whole scam.'

Lowri swallowed hard; how could he think even for a minute that she would be involved in anything crooked? He stopped and looked back at her.

'Timmy Perkins gave you Sally's belongings and among them was a CD, a very important CD. Now I don't know how or why it's so important, I can only guess that it holds incriminating data of some kind.'

'Right, I'm with you so far,' Lowri said, clasping her hands together. She waited for him to go on but he sighed and put his hand on the door-handle. 'Come on, tell me the rest, you can't just leave me with everything up in the air.'

He turned to face her. 'And you still claim that the CD was stolen from you by someone you didn't recognize in the car park of the Swan Hotel?'

'Yes I do!' Lowri said. 'It's the truth. Why else would I be attacked? I'd got no money in my bag, I've got a credit card but anyone trying to use it would get short shrift because my credit is out of date. I'm waiting for a replacement.' Her tone was suddenly hard. 'The only thing that could be of value was that blasted disc and I had nothing to do with any of it!' Anger began to build up inside her. She had been badgered and hurt and put in the most invidious position and she did not need any of it, particularly now with her mother so ill. Lowri moved towards Lainey.

'This is all your fault! My life has been turned upside down by men! My stepfather hates me, Jon Brandon dumps me and vanishes, and you sleep with me and then when you've had what you want you turn against me. I hate you, Jim Lainey!'

She thumped his chest. She wanted to hurt him — she wanted to make love to him. 'Oh, Jim, hold me,' she said.

He took her in his arms and smoothed back her hair. She cried against his shoulder, wanting his love, his trust, so much. She looked up at him and he wiped the tears away with his fingers.

'Make love to me, Jim,' she said. 'Please, let's forget everything for now and just be lovers one more time.'

He undressed her carefully, almost reverently, and together they lay on her bed. Lowri arched her neck as his lips touched her shoulder and then her breast. She cried out when he took her nipple into his warm mouth.

'I love you, Jim,' she murmured against his skin. He silenced her words with a kiss and she clung to him. He touched her breasts, the flat of her stomach and his hand moved to stroke her thighs. He teased her until she was almost screaming for release.

He came into her then, their bodies fitting together perfectly. He gasped, as desperate as she was for release. His powerful body seemed to dominate her, her mind became a gleaming white crystal as she shuddered with the almost painful sensations of love and lust. She cried out, her back arched upwards, wanting him to reach every part of her being.

They lay together then in silence, wrapped in each other's arms. At last Lainey sighed. 'I have to go. Can I use your shower?'

She nodded, the sweet languor of their loving stealing her voice. She heard the shower being turned on, the hiss of the water, and imagined Lainey standing there naked, his skin gleaming with soap, his hair flattened against his face. His dear face.

Lowri began to cry. Life was so cruel, it gave with one hand and took away with the other. She sat up in bed as Lainey returned to the room and began to dress. She watched him, the silk of his back turned towards her now, the arch of his strong neck where his hair curled wetly against his skin. She longed to hold him again, just hold him.

'I haven't done anything wrong, Jim,' she said softly. 'I'll swear to that on anything you like.'

He turned to face her, tucking his shirt into his trousers and pulling up the zip. It was such an intimate moment, more intimate in a strange way than their lovemaking had been.

'I wish I had a pound for every time I've heard that.' He knotted his tie and pushed it into place beneath his collar. 'I want to believe you, Lowri, I want with all my heart to believe you.'

She fell back against the pillows and put her hands over her eyes. 'Just go, Jim, and when you finish this case and find I am innocent don't try to come crawling back.'

She heard the door close behind him and turned her face into the pillows and sobbed as if her heart was going to break.

It was almost an hour later when Justin let himself into the house with the key she had given him. Lowri had showered, washed her hair and remade her bed. She knew she had to put Lainey out of her mind and out of her life for good.

'Just driven back from the bright lights, I called in to see Mother. She's set herself up nicely but it's a shame she walked out on Dad,' Justin said. 'Got anything to eat?' He flopped down onto the sofa.

'How about some steak and chips?' She was glad he was back, his presence gave her something other to think about than lying in bed with Lainey.

'Lord, you parochials are still stuffing

yourselves with bad food, aren't you? Got any pasta?'

'Sure I've got pasta and I take it you don't want normal mince to go with it?' She saw him shake his head. 'I've got borlotti beans and some pesto, any good?'

'Sounds great.' He followed her into the kitchen. 'Tell me about your love affair then.' He was leaning against the door-frame, his arms folded across his chest. Lowri looked up at her brother, startled. For one minute she thought he knew about Lainey.

'This geezer you were seeing, what happened?'

'Oh, you've heard about that from Charles, I suppose?' Lowri said, taking a pan from its hook. 'I expect he thought it one big laugh.'

'No not at all, he was angry with the man.'

Lowri sighed. 'Same old story,' she said, 'foolish woman taken in by an older, not to mention good-looking man.'

'And to make it worse the man was married. You are a fool sis.'

'You are well informed.'

'What happened to him, this chap? Where is he now?'

Lowri looked at him suspiciously; he was very interested in her life all of a sudden.

413

She tried to recall the attraction Jon had had for her, and failed. 'He was a good-looking man, great fun, generous and good in bed,' she said. 'But why he vanished suddenly I can't imagine.'

'Didn't he talk to you much, then?' Justin asked. 'Obviously he wouldn't talk about his wife but did he ever *talk* to you? All the experts say that's the way to succeed with women.'

'He talked a little about his business, but never at a serious level. Why are you so interested suddenly?'

'Bored, I guess. I'm so used to a high-powered life that I find Jersey Marine a little dull. Come on, talk to me, what did this married man do for a living?'

'He was selling computer software if you must know.' She turned and looked at him. 'But then you must know that because the last consignment was addressed to you.'

'So I believe, but I don't recall doing business with the man. Maybe one of the others on my team dealt with it. If I'd known what a shit he was I would have given him and his software the big heave-ho!'

'Go and set the table,' Lowri said some time later, as she tipped the pasta into a colander and ran it under the tap.

'Why are you washing the pasta?' Justin

took some cutlery out of the drawer. 'I thought you'd have done that before you cooked it.'

Lowri smiled. 'It's just to remove the residue of starch,' she said. 'It's clear you never do any cooking.'

'True.'

Justin went into the sitting-room and Lowri heard the rattle of the cutlery against the polished table and winced. She tipped the pasta into a bowl and mixed in the beans and the sauce.

They ate in silence for a time and Lowri fell to dreaming about Lainey, how he had loved her, how he had made love to her. Anything she had ever experienced before paled into insignificance beside the way she felt for Jim Lainey.

'You look like a woman who's just been well shagged,' Justin said. He leaned across the table. 'Come on, sis, if you've found a new boyfriend you can tell me.'

'Mind your own business.' Lowri's tone was sharper than she intended and Justin's eyebrows shot up.

'Touchy!'

'Sorry. Eat your dinner and stop making personal remarks.'

He ate his pasta and dabbed at his lips with one of Lowri's best napkins. Her mother had given the set to her when Lowri moved into the house, and she sighed inwardly. She would never get the tomato stains out.

'Has your married man come back to you, then?' Justin probed. 'This food is delicious, you'll make some man an excellent wife.'

Lowri shook her head and without answering pushed away her plate. She had no appetite. She was in love, really in love for the first time in her life, with a man she could never have.

'Come on, Lowri, talk to me. I'm your brother and if there's anything going on in your life I should know about then tell me?'

She took the plates into the kitchen and dumped them into the sink. She turned on the tap and the water swirled and gurgled, effectively shutting out the sound of Justin's voice.

Was he trying to make up for all the time they had been apart? He had been to see their mother and had taken her gifts. He even apparently accepted the fact that Rhian was living with another man. Perhaps she should be more charitable and not judge him by his past behaviour.

She made a pot of coffee and called to Justin to come into the lounge. She poured the coffee and sat opposite her brother, smiling at him.

'To answer your question, no, my married man has not come back and even if he had, I wouldn't want anything to do with him, not now, not ever.'

'So you don't think that your snatched handbag was anything to do with Brandon, then? I mean it wasn't that he'd given you anything to keep for him and wanted it back urgently?'

'How did you know about that?' She had not mentioned the attack, not to her mother and certainly not to Charles. She never said much at all to Charles.

'That solicitor, Watson, he said something about it. He wondered if there was some sinister motive behind it.'

It seemed unlikely that Mr Watson would say anything at all to Justin. She shrugged. 'I have never had anything remotely valuable,' she said. 'I thought I was merely returning a funny old CD to its rightful owner.'

'What CD and how was it funny? A game or something, you mean?'

Lowri shook her head. 'No, not a game. It had odd writing on it, the sort of writing that might be a code of some kind.'

'Sounds fascinating. Who was the rightful owner?'

'I'm not sure. I was supposed to take it to the hotel and meet him there.' She shrugged. 'Before I could get into the lobby I was knocked flying and my bag stolen.' Why was she lying to her brother? She just was not sure she wanted to talk about the CD, or anything to do with it. Anyway, what good did talking do? The thing was gone now, probably in the hands of some petty thief who would just toss it away as a useless bit of junk.

'There has to be a copy somewhere,' Justin said. 'If this CD is so much in demand then whatever is on it must be valuable.'

'It's probably on some hard disc, I expect,' Lowri said frowning. 'I did wonder about Mrs Jenkins in the office.' Immediately she had spoken she regretted it. Justin jumped on her words.

'What do you mean, wondering? Has this Mrs Jenkins got two heads or something?'

'No, she's just odd. It's probably my fault, clash of personalities I expect.'

'No but why did you think she might have something to do with the CD? Come on, Lowri, half a story is just no good.'

So what harm would it do if she told him? Lowri looked at her brother. He was leaning forward earnestly, a frown of concern on his face. She warmed to him. Justin had changed. He was no longer the spiteful little boy or the surly teenager of the past. He had grown up.

'I came up behind her recently very quietly. Not on purpose, it was just one of those things, anyway she didn't hear me coming. She had some weird writing on the computer screen.' Lowri smiled. 'I suppose there's a simple explanation for it, some downloaded bug or other. But Mrs Jenkins would never admit to being caught at a disadvantage. She got rid of what was on the screen very quickly.'

'She must be clever. She's not some sort of spy, is she?' Justin's eyes were alight, like a boy being told a fairy story.

'I've no idea. She just exited the program. I expect she lost some of her work but she's very efficient, is our Mrs Jenkins.'

'What would a woman of such expertise be doing in a small office?' Justin asked.

'I've wondered that myself,' Lowri said. 'Anyway, enough of cloak-and-dagger stuff, you can take me out for a drink.'

'My carriage awaits,' Justin said, rising to his feet and bowing with a sweeping motion of his arm. 'Or rather your carriage awaits in the shape of a little red Mazda. Come on, get your glad rags on and let's get going.'

When Lowri was ready to go out, she stood looking round her bedroom. Her hour with Lainey had been memorable. Just as well: it was probably the last chance she would ever have of being with the man she truly loved.

26

'Bloody hell, it's hot!' Ken Major descended the steps of the plane ahead of Lainey and stood on the tarmac of the airport at Montego Bay, blinking up at the sun.

'Put your sun-glasses on,' Lainey said dourly. 'And stop complaining.'

The sergeant smiled. 'I'm not complaining, guv, I'm loving every minute of it.'

Lainey was not so happy; he did not cope with the heat very well. Still, a few days by the Caribbean should be long enough for an interview with Sarah Brandon. Clearly, Jamaica was a favourite spot with the Brandons. The one postcard from Jon Brandon that Lowri had in her possession was sent from there.

'Once we get through customs find a taxi, Sergeant.' That was one of the perks of being a DI — he usually had someone to run around for him. Irritably he joined the queue to be checked through customs. Standing behind a line waiting to be beckoned forward to show his passport went against the grain.

He followed Ken Major out of the baggage reclaim, glad that he had only taken a small bag which had passed as hand luggage. Then they were out in the hot sunshine again.

There were small buses everywhere waiting to take holiday-makers to their destinations. Ken managed to get a taxi and the driver, with a wide, white-toothed smile, took the luggage and bundled it into the back.

'Know any place suitable for two police officers to stay in?' Lainey asked, showing his warrant card. The man nodded.

'Sure do, sir. I know some places nice and clean and not too pricey.' He drove through the streets of Montego Bay and out along a pitted roadway.

Lainey looked at the address of the hotel where Sarah Brandon was staying. Fortunately she had booked in using her correct name, which had made it easy to trace her.

'How far is it to Negril?' he asked the driver.

'Far, sir? Two, three hours' drive.'

Lainey sighed. 'Nice there, is it?'

'Very nice hotels, luxury places with a long beach stretching for seven miles, sir. But not cheap. Want to go there?'

'That would be a good idea.' Lainey slid

open the window and felt the breeze blow pleasantly into his face. Beside him Ken Major was slipping out of his jacket and already his shirt was stained with sweat.

Lainey had never seen the joy in lying around baking in the sun. Still, the place was certainly beautiful with the azure sea occasionally visible from the window of the taxi.

'Look over there, guv.' Ken leaned forward, pointing to a little cluster of huts at the side of the road. 'Shacks with TV aerials, I don't believe it!'

Lainey nodded. He caught sight of a group of children and they appeared well fed and well dressed. 'I suppose that sort of hut affair is practical in a place where there are typhoons and such,' he remarked.

'I suppose so, still I'm very glad to share my parents' terraced house. At least I can always have a bath in hot water and a decent shave.'

Lainey did not reply. He leaned back against the seat, his eyes closed. The nine-and-a-half-hour flight from Gatwick had been tedious. He had been unable to sleep because of the constant activity of the cabin crew pushing trolleys of drinks and duty-free goods, not to mention cartons of plastic food.

Well, the first thing he would do when he reached the hotel would be to strip and shower, and then flake out on the bed.

'I don't want you here, do you understand?' Sarah Brandon looked at her husband with loathing. 'And to bring that, that tart with you is an outrage!' She was trembling with fury. None of her well-laid plans included Jon. She had thought he was out of her life for good. In any case, her lover, her gorgeous man with the shock of white hair, would be joining her soon. Everyone thought Snowy was a small cog in the wheel, especially Charles Richards, but now with her help Snowy had all the information needed to take over the business.

'I have as much right to the money as you do,' Jon said. 'Sit down, Sally, you must be exhausted.'

Sarah watched as the painted hussy sank gratefully into one of the armchairs, making herself quite at home in Sarah's suite of rooms.

'What money are we talking about here?' Sarah said. 'If you mean the money left to me by my parents, forget it! You are not having a penny of it.'

'You know quite well what I'm talking about.' Jon moved closer, his manner threatening. Sarah stepped back a pace.

'If you are referring to your prospective ill-gotten gains then I think you are out of luck. A vital list of your, shall we call them clients, went missing, didn't you know?'

'And now you have it.' Jon moved closer still, his fist raised. 'Now tell me where the disc is before I kill you.'

'Don't be so foolish!' Sarah said icily. 'How do you think you'd get away with killing me?' She moved to open the doors leading to the narrow balcony.

'You have proved to be so inept in the past that you would bungle anything, let alone a murder.' She looked scathingly at Sally. The girl was wearing a skimpy dress that looked as if it could do with a good wash. Her nail polish was chipped and the bleach was growing out of her hair, revealing ugly dark roots.

'Not much fun being with Jon, is it?' Sarah said. 'He never could cope without me, only he was too much of a fool to realize it. Well, you are welcome to him, he's nothing but a loser in and out of bed.'

'You cow!' Sally said. 'Jon is worth two of you.'

'Well,' Sarah looked her up and down, 'if you are all he can pull these days then he's really getting past it.'

The girl leapt up from her chair and launched herself across the room at Sarah, who, attempting to defend herself, felt a stinging blow across her cheek.

'You skinny horrible bitch!' Sally screamed. 'I hate you, all you want to do is make more money. No wonder Jon doesn't want to sleep with you! You're nothing but an old harridan!'

Sally lashed out again and, incensed, Sarah struggled with her. She felt the hot breeze from the balcony as she wrestled with the girl, finally pushing her away. Sarah felt blood running along her cheek.

'You no-good tart!' she said in disbelief. 'You've marked me!'

Sarah was taller than Sally but she was not able to keep her at bay as the girl lunged forward, her fists beating into Sarah's face.

'I'll kill you!' Sally was spitting in her fury. 'I'll bloody kill you!'

'Jon!' Sarah called. 'Get this tart off me!' Jon did not move. There was a strange look on his face as he watched the women fight. Sarah would get no help from him. She was on her own against a madwoman.

Sarah leaned away from Sally and picked up the pot of flowers from the balcony table. 'Get away from me!' she said fiercely, 'or you will be the one lying dead.'

She raised her hand and Sally cowered away, suddenly frightened. Jon came to life, rushing at Sarah, his fists raised. Sarah screamed — she knew she had little chance of defending herself against him. He was a big man, a strong man, and right now he was more angry than she had ever seen him.

As he came towards her Sarah instinctively moved away from the balcony. Unable to stop himself, Jon collided with the table. The momentum carried him over the balcony rail as if taking a dive into a swimming-pool. Sarah watched in disbelief as he plummeted to the ground four storeys below.

For a moment there was silence and Sarah slumped against the wall, her heart beating so fast she felt she would choke.

'You've killed him,' Sally whispered in disbelief. She began to cry. 'What am I going to do without him, I loved him!'

Sarah made an effort to pull herself together. She looked over the balcony and saw a group of people gathering around Jon's prostrate body. She must get her story in first. She hurried across the room and picked up the phone. It was Errol who answered.

'Sorry, mam, the manager is attending an accident to one of the guests.'

'Then you must come. The guest you are

talking about fell from my balcony.' She replaced the phone. Errol answered her call swiftly, knowing there would be a generous tip on offer.

'Come in, please.' Sarah opened the door and leaned weakly against him. 'Something terrible has happened,' she gasped. She pointed to Sally. 'This woman is my husband's mistress.' She dabbed at her eyes. 'She came here with my husband trying to get money from me. When I refused this woman attacked me.' She pointed to the blood running down her face. 'My husband was going to join in, he raised his fists to me, he wanted to kill me.' She paused for effect.

'I have to be fair to this woman,' she said shakily. 'She saw my husband's fury and tried to stop him hitting me. In the fray she accidentally pushed Jon over the balcony. I'm sure she didn't mean it.'

'You liar!' Sally was white-faced. 'He just fell, Jon just fell.' She appealed to Errol. 'This woman is lying, can't you see that?'

Errol took Sarah's arm and guided her to a chair. 'Don't worry, Mrs Brandon,' he said softly, 'anyone can see this woman is no good and I for one believe everything you've said.'

'It's a lie!' Sally protested. 'I didn't push Jon over, it was an accident.' She began to sob. Errol shook his head.

'I know that you came here with Mrs Brandon's husband. I can see from the scratches on Mrs Brandon's cheek that you have attacked her. It's pointless trying to cover up. When the police come you'd best tell them the truth.'

'Police?' Sally said.

Errol ignored her and turned to Sarah. 'Two English policemen have come from your country to see you. They are outside with the security guard looking at the, excuse me, the body of your husband.'

'Oh dear, this is all so awful!' Sarah said. 'Will you pour me a brandy, Errol, I need something to give me strength to deal with all this.'

She covered her face with her hands and tried to clear her mind. The police had come a long way to talk to her; they were clearly suspicious of her. It seemed that Jon's arrival had been timed just right, after all. Now Sarah could claim that she knew nothing at all about his business or his associates and reiterate her story that he had come to Jamaica to demand money from her.

She took her hands away from her face as the police came into the room. She looked up and recognized DI Lainey. She dabbed at her eyes and fingered the drying blood on her cheek.

'Thank God you are here!' she said. 'My husband and this woman have just tried to kill me.' She was aware of Sally's shocked face, and a feeling of triumph welled up inside her. Revenge, she found, was very sweet indeed.

Lowri looked at Mrs Jenkins with narrowed eyes. 'You've been in there with Mr Watson for an awfully long time. You've kept him well after the normal closing time — what's going on?'

'I'm leaving.' Mrs Jenkins began clearing her desk. 'I've been offered a better position. You said it yourself, I'm overqualified for this job.' She paused and for once looked almost human. 'I tried to talk to Mr Watson, I waited a long time while he was on the phone but he seemed very upset and didn't even look at me.'

'Oh? Who was he speaking to?' Lowri asked.

Mrs Jenkins did not reply. She picked up her belongings and without saying another word left the office. Lowri watched her with a frown. She really was an odd woman. She strode along the street flat-footed. Like a policeman. Was she working for Lainey?

Was he having Lowri spied on even when she was at work?

Lowri switched on the computer on Mrs Jenkins's desk but when she attempted to locate documents, unless the correct password was used, access was denied.

She looked through the drawers of the desk: they were bare. Nothing remained to show that Mrs Jenkins had ever been there, not even a paper-clip. Lowri picked up the waste-paper bin. It was empty.

The intercom buzzed, startling her, and she heard Mr Watson's voice coming over the line.

'Come in here please, Lowri.'

She knocked on the door of his office and went in without waiting for a reply. Mr Watson was sitting with his head in his hands.

'What is it?' Lowri said at once. 'Aren't you feeling well?'

He looked up and his face was grey. 'I'm all right. It's your mother, I'm afraid. She's been taken into hospital. I have to go. Close the office, Lowri, and follow me over to Singleton in your car, will you?'

Lowri bit her lip. 'What's wrong with Mother?'

Mr Watson got awkwardly to his feet. 'There's no other way to put this, Lowri, my dear. Your mother is dying.'

'No!' Lowri watched as the solicitor picked up his glasses and pushed them onto his nose. 'Who has said so?'

Mr Watson shook his head. 'Just get over to the hospital as quickly as you can, Lowri, there's a good girl.'

'Should I phone Justin . . . and Charles?'

Mr Watson shrugged. 'That's up to you, but I'm sure your mother wouldn't want Charles there.'

He left the office, his shoulders slumped. He looked like a beaten man. Lowri hesitated for a moment and then dialled her home number. To her relief, Justin answered.

Lowri told him quickly what the situation was. 'I'll be there as quickly as I can, Lowri,' he said. 'In the meantime try not to worry too much.'

'Right, I'll see you at the hospital then.' She hurriedly picked up her bag and the keys and let herself out of the door, locking it behind her.

The drive to the hospital did not take long. Lowri parked her car and walked briskly towards the main entrance. She rang for the lift and it seemed an interminably long time coming.

Her mother was in a side room and Mr

Watson was already sitting next to the bed, holding her hand.

'Mummy, are you worse?' Lowri asked, closing her mind to the prospect of her mother dying. She bent to kiss her cheek, noticing the drip which was feeding liquid into Rhian's arm.

Rhian tried to smile. 'I'm ready, Lowri, I've had enough now and I want to go.' She held out a thin hand. 'But I'm happy to have the people I love most in all the world with me right now.'

Lowri fought back her tears. 'Don't talk like that, Mum, you'll get better, you'll see.'

Rhian shook her head without replying. Mr Watson moved his chair so that Lowri could sit near her.

'Rhian is being transferred to the hospice at Morriston,' he said in a subdued voice, and Lowri felt her spirits plummet. Everyone knew that the hospice, wonderful though it was, was the end of the road for most patients.

Rhian had closed her eyes and seemed to be drifting into a peaceful sleep. Mr Watson rested his hand on Lowri's shoulder. 'Try to be brave, Lowri.' He sighed heavily. 'Rhian has suffered enough. Death will be a release from her pain.'

Lowri began to cry. Silent tears rolled

down her cheeks, running saltily into her mouth.

'You're bound to be distressed, Lowri.' He put his arm around her shoulders. 'But you'll feel better for a good cry.'

He was talking platitudes but in his own pain he was doing his best to help her deal with hers, and she was grateful. 'I'm glad my mother had you with her at last,' she said quietly. 'These last months she's been happier than I've ever seen her before.'

'Thank you for that, Lowri.'

The door opened and Justin entered the small room. He looked at his mother and his face creased into lines of despair. He bent over and kissed her lightly on her forehead and Rhian's eyes flickered and opened.

She smiled when she saw her son, and touched his hand. 'You've been taken care of in my will,' she said, her voice a breathless whisper. 'But Charles has a great deal he can leave to you, and so I've given Lowri the bulk of my estate.'

'That's all right, Mother,' Justin said. 'None of us want to talk about things like that, not now when you are so ill.'

'I knew you'd understand,' Rhian said, 'you're a good boy.' She closed her eyes and drifted off to sleep again. Her face became even paler, her lips were turning blue. Lowri knew then that her mother would never see the inside of the hospice. She would never see anything again. She had said her good-byes and now she was going to die. Lowri began to sob and Justin came to her, taking her in his arms, smoothing her hair, holding her close against his shoulder. 'There, don't cry, Lowri, it's for the best, you know it is.'

She nodded and moved away from him, with a feeling of unreality. This could not be happening.

'Oh God!' She ran from the room, down the stairs and out across the broad Mumbles Road to the beach beyond. The sea was calm, the beach deserted. Lowri sat down and hunched up her knees, wrapping her arms around herself.

She wept large gulping sobs; she cried as she had never cried before. Everyone was deserting her, even her mother had left her.

After a while she pulled herself to her feet and began to walk down to the water's edge, her bout of self-pity over. She looked out to sea and made a silent farewell to her dying mother, the mother who even at the last had made sure that Lowri would never want for anything ever again.

27

Lainey sat in his office staring out of the window. It was good to be home.

It had taken a great deal of discussion with the Jamaican police to convince them that Jon Brandon's death was a tragic accident. He had urged Sarah to take back her story that Jon was pushed to his death by Sally. Sarah saw sense when Lainey pointed out that perjury was a crime, and Jamaican jails were not the most salubrious of places.

Finally he had been allowed to bring Sarah Brandon and Sally White back into the country where the courts could sort out who was to blame for what. At least it was progress of some sort.

His mouth creased into a smile. On the plane, the two women had quarrelled constantly. Sarah denied knowing anything about her husband's business enterprises while Sally claimed that Sarah was the brains of the operation and was waiting for her accomplice — a man called Snowy — to join her in Jamaica.

The police had apprehended Snowy and

found he had in his possession a disc containing all the evidence needed to convict Sarah of taking part in, if not masterminding, a gigantic fraud.

The door opened and Lainey looked up at Mrs Jenkins and smiled, congratulating himself on bringing her into the case. The woman was a specialist, an undercover officer with computer qualifications a yard long. She sat opposite him without waiting for an invitation and placed a thick file on the desk.

'So, Mrs Jenkins, what have you got?'

She began to talk in computer jargon and Lainey held up his hand.

'Quite frankly, Mrs Jenkins, I haven't a clue what you are talking about. Can't you put it all into plain English?'

She eased off her shoes and settled herself more comfortably into the chair. 'Very well. To put it simply, a sophisticated form of encryption was used to facilitate the transference of sensitive information. The data was then saved on a CD to be accessed only by one who had the key to the encryption.'

'Can you explain a little further?' Lainey asked. Mrs Jenkins was very worthy but she was more than a little pedantic.

She stared at him as if he was a moron. 'Right then, Justin Richards as well as his father were into the scam up to their necks.' She heaved a sigh and her large bosom struggled against the buttons on her jacket. 'They used a computer hacker to access the required data, one Timmy Perkins. You know of him?'

He nodded, feeling all sorts of a fool. Timmy Perkins had been almost killed in a road accident; only now was it becoming clear that someone had wanted him out of the way. 'What sort of information was being transferred?'

'Personal bank records of the rich and famous, mainly. There is a dossier on the targets' private lives, little "mistakes" that had never been disclosed before.'

'So it was extortion?'

'Yes, and I must congratulate you on picking up Sarah Brandon, she expected a massive amount from the scam.'

'How was the money laundered?'

'Simple. Justin Richards's business was a wholesale outlet for wines and spirits. He did a fair bit of legitimate trade and cooked the books to tell a story of far greater sales than he actually made.'

'So the money was cleaned through Richards's legitimate business, is that what you are saying?'

'Precisely.'

Lainey looked up as Ken Major entered the room. 'I've asked one of the girls to make us some coffee.' He looked down at Mrs Jenkins. 'You don't drink coffee, do you, Mrs Jenkins?'

'Just fetch me hot water and I'll use one of my own tea bags.'

'Thank you, Ken.' Lainey felt a little sorry for the sergeant. The woman had spoken to him as though he was the floor-sweeper, not an experienced police officer.

Ken grimaced and left the room. Lainey leaned forward, his elbows on the desk. The question trembled on his lips, a question he did not really want to ask.

'And Lowri Richards, was she involved in all this?' He looked up impatiently as the door opened and Ken returned carrying a tray. He put it down and gave Mrs Jenkins her cup of hot water. By his expression he might well have added arsenic to it.

'Shall I sit in, guv?' Ken asked, and Lainey really had no reason to refuse him, although he would have preferred to hear Mrs Jenkins's answer in private. Instead, he gestured for Ken to take a seat.

Mrs Jenkins was carefully squeezing the tea bag against the side of her cup, determined to extract every bit of goodness from it. Lainey watched, fuming with impatience.

'Lowri Richards?' he prompted. She looked up and at last dropped the tea bag into the bin.

'She is not involved at all,' Mrs Jenkins said. 'The foolish girl was set up by her brother, Jon Brandon being the bait.' She sniffed. 'Some of these modern girls have no discrimination when it comes to men. Look at Sally, she dropped everything to go away with Brandon.'

Lainey felt an overwhelming sense of relief. Lowri was innocent. 'You are sure Miss Richards was not involved? She was with Brandon the night he disappeared.'

Mrs Jenkins's look was frosty. 'Are you questioning my ability, Mr Lainey? I told you, the girl has no taste in men, she's simply a fool. As for her brother, he's a very nasty piece of work.'

'Apart from the extortion, you mean?' Lainey wished the woman would just tell him everything. Talking to her was like trying to pull teeth.

'Well, he and his father intend to get their hands on Rhian Richards's very considerable wealth.'

'Why, if they were both making money at the extortion game?'

'I should have thought that was obvious. Charles Richards hates his stepdaughter.

He tried to discredit her by having large sums of money put into her account. You see he's determined that his son will inherit everything.' She stared at Lainey for a long moment. 'All the money in the world won't satisfy the greed of some crooks.'

He sank back in his chair, his thoughts racing. Mrs Richards was in hospital in a serious condition. In the event of her death almost all her money would go to her daughter, he had learned that much for himself. Did that mean Lowri was in danger?

He got to his feet. 'I'd better get over to the hospital, speak to Mrs Richards. I'll bet my bottom dollar that's where the not-so-loving son is at the moment. Thank you for your help, Mrs Jenkins, you've been a real asset to the case.'

He got as far as the door before Mrs Jenkins spoke again. She was on her feet, her handbag clutched close to her ample chest. 'You're too late for fond farewells. Rhian Richards died a short while ago.'

'Are you sure?'

'Of course. Furthermore, wouldn't you like to know who was Mr Big in all this?'

Lainey froze, the door half-open. 'You mean someone else was pulling all the strings?'

'If you'll stop your headlong flight for a moment I'll finish what I came here to tell you.' Mrs Jenkins actually smiled. 'And when I do, I think you are going to have the surprise of your life.'

Lowri sat on the beach, staring out to the lights of a ship on the horizon. Her mother was dead and it was as if she had lost her best friend, her only friend.

A mist came down suddenly over the sea and Lowri shivered, feeling damp and clammy. She got up and brushed the sand from her skirt. Some instinct made her look round and she saw a figure coming up behind her. He was hooded and she felt a sudden sense of impending danger.

She realized there was no-one she could turn to for help. She began to run towards the promenade, her feet sinking into the sand. She heard heavy breathing behind her and knew it was her worst nightmare coming true.

She tried to scream as someone caught her hair and forced her down onto her knees. Hands were around her throat and she was being dragged to the shoreline, kicking uselessly, trying to find purchase in the softness of the sand.

She felt the shock as the coldness of the

sea enveloped her. She caught the rough wool covering her assailant's head and tugged with all her might. In her nightmare the face of her attacker was never revealed. Now it was.

'Justin!' Lowri screamed. 'What are you doing?' The moon shone through a break in the clouds and she saw her brother's expression clearly. It was twisted with anger.

'I'm going to kill you!' he shouted. He pushed her, his hand covering her face, and she felt the water close over her. She thrashed about and managed to rise to the surface.

'Why?' she gasped.

'For money, what else?' He stared down at her with no hint of compassion in his eyes. 'Oh, you persuaded Mother to leave you all her money, didn't you? Sorry, Lowri, but you leave me no choice.'

'Justin! Listen to sense. If you want the money so badly I'll give it to you, all of it.' Her words were lost as she was plunged into the water again. The sea swept around her — she could feel the bottom and thrust against the sand, pushing upwards through the silent coldness.

'Justin, don't do this!' She hardly had any breath left. Justin looked down at her for a long moment. He smiled, demonlike in the moonlight. 'Goodbye, Lowri.'

She was beneath the water again, and she felt her strength ebb away. She could not fight any more. She opened her eyes once and saw the blurred shape above her. And then she lost consciousness.

Lowri opened her eyes slowly and became aware that she was lying on the cold ground of the promenade. Lainey was kneeling at her side, and with him was a paramedic. Lowri could see the flashing blue lights of an ambulance and struggled to sit up. She began to cough and Lainey held her upright, brushing her hair from her face.

'Jim, thank God you came!' She put her arms around him and he held her close. 'My brother was going to kill me!' She began to cry.

'It's all right, you're safe now.' He kissed her forehead and her cheek and then lifted her in his arms. 'Come on, you have to go to the hospital for a doctor to look at you.' He smiled down at her, and she saw in the light from the open doors of the ambulance that he was as wet as she was.

'You were the one who rescued me!' she said, burying her face against his wet shoulder. 'I always did feel safe with you.'

Lainey helped her into the ambulance and

sat beside her, holding her hand. The paramedic hovered near by but he ignored him.

'You've had some shocks tonight, Lowri, but you're going to have to be brave because there are a few more coming. I'm afraid Justin has been arrested — he tried to kill you, you know.' He rested his hand on her wet hair. 'When this is all over, we have some serious talking to do.'

As the ambulance jerked into movement, her heart sank. Lainey still thought she was involved in the mess left by Jon's disappearance.

The hospital doors shed a bright light onto the forecourt and Lainey guided her down the steps of the ambulance. She shivered in the cool of the night air as she lowered herself into the waiting wheelchair. A blanket was tucked round her and she was hurried towards the entrance of the hospital.

Mr Watson was there in the corridor, his head bent. Lowri looked up at Lainey. He shook his head. As she was wheeled forward, she saw that Mr Watson was handcuffed. A policeman appeared to be in charge of him. 'What on earth is going on?'

'I never meant you should get hurt, Lowri, believe me,' Mr Watson said. 'And now I see the futility of allowing this feud

445

between Charles and me to become personal. I hated him for the way he treated your mother so I took over his crooked businesses one by one.' He sighed. 'I wanted to ruin Charles and all he stood for.'

'I don't understand,' Lowri said.

'I know, I know.' Mr Watson shook his head. 'This is a terrible shock coming so soon after you've lost your mother, but the truth is, Lowri, I'm just as much a crook as the rest of them.'

'Mr Watson, no!' Lowri said. 'It's all a mistake, surely?'

'I'm afraid not, my dear.'

The police officer urged him forward and he glanced over his shoulder with difficulty. 'Try to forgive me, Lowri, for everything.'

'I'll come and see you, Mr Watson.' Her voice trembled. 'I'll come and see you wherever you are.'

Lowri put her hands over her face. The events of the night had all been too much for her; she felt as though she would crack wide apart at any moment.

Lainey his arms around her. 'Lowri come on, let the doctor take a look at you.'

He wheeled her into a side room and a doctor appeared almost at once, possibly due to Lainey's presence.

The doctor looked into Lowri's mouth,

listened to her breathing and took her pulse. 'I'll just check your blood pressure while I'm here,' he said easily.

Lowri sat quite still, trying to absorb all that had happened in the past hours. Within the space of one evening she had lost her mother, learned that her brother had planned to kill her, and seen her natural father taken into custody.

'You seem to have survived your impromptu swim, Miss Richards,' the doctor said. 'You're in remarkably good shape considering you were dunked in the cold sea at this time of night.'

'Can I go home, then?'

'Yes, you can go home. I take it you have transport?'

'I'll be taking Miss Richards home,' Lainey said. 'Come on, Lowri, the sooner we get you out of those wet things the better. Thank you for your time, doctor.'

'You're welcome.' The doctor left the room and Lainey drew Lowri to her feet. He held her for a moment.

'You look like a drowned rat!' he said, kissing her nose.

'Do I?'

'Yes, but I still love you.' Lainey tipped her face up and looked into her eyes. 'And I am going to tell you what happens next. I'm taking you home, undressing you and to-gether we'll have a hot shower. Then we'll hold each other until morning comes.' He kissed her mouth. 'Then we'll make all the arrangements.'

'What arrangements?'

'For our wedding, silly. It'll have to be the registry office, I'm afraid!'

She looked up and saw the love in his eyes, and suddenly the nightmare receded and the world became a brighter place. 'You're taking a lot for granted — who said I'd marry you?'

'You'll marry me or I'll take you into po-lice custody and you'll be my prisoner for ever and ever.'

She smiled wanly up at him, pushing back her wet hair self-consciously. 'Do you really love me, Jim?'

'I really love you. Now don't ask again.' He led her out of the hospital and the doors swished shut behind them. Softly the trees were coming into focus; the sky was light-ening from indigo to rose. Lowri slipped her arm through Lainey's and drew a deep breath. A new day was beginning and she would share this dawn and all the other dawns for the rest of her life with the man she loved.